Wycaan Master: Book Six

CALHEI
NO MORE

A Novel

ALON SHALEV

Tourmaline Books
Berkeley, California

CALHEI
NO MORE

Calhei No More
Wycaan Master, Book 6

Copyright © 2016 Alon Shalev

Tourmaline Books, Berkeley, California
http://www.tourmalinebooks.com

ISBN: 978-0-9884428-3-2
LCCN: 2016909023

First Edition: October 2016

Published in the United States of America

Dedication

This series began six years ago when I read the first draft of *At the Walls of Galbrieth* to my sons, then eight and eleven years old, around the campfire under the ancient redwood trees of Northern California.

Every summer, the tradition continued, one book at a time. Today, my sons are no longer boys, but young men, preparing to go out and create their own imprints on the world.

This book is dedicated to their children. Maybe one day, their fathers will tell them how every summer their grandpa donned his mountain hat and led them to the world of Odessiya.

Then again, maybe they will have their own stories to tell.

The Wycaan Master Series:

ACKNOWLEDGEMENTS

- To Monica Buntin, my editor, for once again making sense of an awful lot of words.

- To William Kenney, my book cover artist, for your amazing ability to continually transform my jumbled ideas into such beautiful pieces of art.

- To Jeny Lyn Ruelo and her team at The Fast Fingers, for the interior design and formatting, and always being willing to deal with my tech-challenged questions.

- To my good friend, Janet Frankel, who gave the manuscript one final polish and saved me a few blushes.

PROLOGUE

In every race, stories abound about a youngster who grew up with apes or ran with wolves. The dwarves tell of a young dwarf who lived deep underground with a dragon and eventually grew scales and breathed fire. The pictorians speak of a pictorye who died young in battle but was so brave that the gods allowed him to fly with the eagles.

Such tales have sent the young of all races to sleep over the ages, their heads filled with rich fodder for dreams. What would it be like to communicate with and really understand another animal? What potential power could it offer?

In the land of Odessiya, the legends tell of the Age of Mist and Shadows, when the land was new and its magic young and powerful. Some of the most mysterious talismans came from this age — the anwars, the charred staffs, and the dwarf stones.

The stories describe how the gods created four creatures to rule the lands. The great dragons, masters of fire, were fierce, but their vision was not always true, and the gods feared their unbridled strength and rage. The wolves were admired for their intelligence and unwavering loyalty to the pack. But they were independent of spirit and did not care for anything beyond their own collective needs. The majestic eagles were wisest and fastest. Their deadly talons and incredible accuracy earned them the respect of all the beasts in the lands. But they sought solitude in the skies and rarely came down among the other animals. They lived on the high peaks and kept council to themselves.

Then, there were the bears: strong, ferocious in battle, deliberate in council, loyal to their families. The bears were not as powerful as the dragons, as intelligent as the wolves, or as fast as the eagles, but the qualities they did share with each brought balance to the lands.

It is curious that there are no legends of a young one growing up with a bear pack, for perhaps bears best suited this role. What wisdom could they have imparted? What strength and tenacity could they have taught? Rumors abound of a Wycaan Master—still alive, some swear—who can transform into a bear and run with the pack. A few lost souls even swear they saw him with their own eyes.

But there is no story of a young human, elf, dwarf, or pictorian who grew up with bears. That is a shame, for if the bears are the stewards of the earth, maintaining balance in the land, what role might such a youth play in the destiny of Odessiya?

What role, indeed?

> From *Musings of a Humble Monk,*
> The Most Venerable Shingzi

CHAPTER 1

The scream tore through the stone castle. The smooth, stoic rocks carried the desperate cry along corridors and filled halls with painful echoes. It was not the first time such a harrowing sound woke the castle's inhabitants; it had, in fact, become a nightly occurrence. Nobody in the castle remained asleep when the young elfe had nightmares; all shared in her suffering.

Mharina lay curled in a ball, her hands clutching her stomach as sweat dripped from her brow onto a pillow that her mother or siblings changed at least once a night. Her white hair splayed, knotted and wet. Rivulets of tears stained her cheeks. Though she carried herself with reserved dignity by day, her guard dropped when exhaustion lured her into restless sleep, and she was always interrupted by the same violent dream.

The elfe saw her teacher, the woman she loved—small but powerful—standing before her. She saw Sa'gola's black and purple hair, her beautiful face staring back, and then, slowly, the sorceress's head sliding from her body, falling to the ground and bouncing away, before her body slumped, lifeless. Even in death, Sa'gola was so graceful.

"Shhhhh," Sellia whispered, mopping her brow. "I'm with you, my *calhei*. It'll all be alright."

Mharina's eyes shot open, and she glared at her mother. "Can you bring her back? Can you attach Sa'gola's head back onto her shoulders?"

"No," Sellia sighed. "I can't. I can only be with you and offer you the love of a mother."

Mharina curled into an even tighter ball and screwed her eyes closed. "That's not what I need."

She felt her mother stiffen. Mharina knew she deserved more, that she had repeatedly risked her own life for her *calhei*. Sellia was not to blame for Sa'gola's death. But she was no help, either, refusing to recognize the bond between student and mentor. Her mother could not understand Mharina's love for her teacher…or perhaps refused to.

Mharina didn't blame anyone for Sa'gola's death except Ithea… and herself. She had sworn to defend her teacher from the abusive sorcerer. Ithea was dead, his neck snapped by her father, Seanchai, as he transformed into the Great Grizzly. Her *ahdahr*, the great Wycaan Master, had come to his daughter's aid, summoned by Denalion, the Dreamwalker of the West. In summoning Seanchai, Denalion sacrificed his own life but ignited an instinctual spark buried deep in the broken Wycaan, prompting Seanchai to kill the most powerful sorcerer ever.

But neither of Mharina's parents could help her now, though at least Sellia tried. Her *ahdahr* barely spoke to anyone, preferring solitude and meditation as he clung to his exercises, a tenuous anchor to his shaky sanity. He had no memory of his past, his family, or his powers. All he claimed to know was that he hated the magic he possessed. Seanchai was convinced he was responsible for the deaths of thousands of elves, humans, and dwarves.

Mharina tried to be sympathetic, but had little inside to offer. All that remained was a great, searing pain that ignited every time she thought of Sa'gola. She rose stiffly from her bed, and her mother leaned back, giving her room. She stared at Sellia, the once-fearsome warrior-mate of her *ahdahr*. Sellia's ferocity was gone, replaced with apprehension, hurt, maybe a sense of failure.

It was ironic. Her mother had never thought of herself as a competent parent, and yet Mharina treasured the times they spent together riding, shooting the bow, tracking, and hunting. But that was in a different age, a distant past, far longer ago than her sixteen cycles justified.

She tugged on her boots and pulled her cloak around herself.

"Where are you going?" Sellia called after her.

Mharina shrugged. "To get some air."

"I'll come—"

"No."

"I'll wake Senzia or Maugwen."

"Don't."

Mharina left her room and descended the stone stairs. She shuddered as she passed the hall where the final confrontation had transpired. Outside, the air was cold and refreshing. She closed her eyes to better feel it and almost bumped into Montclair.

"Why are you prowling about?" she snapped.

The handsome fortune-sword shrugged, his blond, crinkly hair bouncing once with his shoulders.

"Habit," he replied, and she noticed his hand on his hilt and his roving eyes seeking anything untoward.

He was lying. Once Ithea died, the taragusii continued to guard the outer walls, but Montclair had divided up guard duty for the inner keep among their party, with the exception of Mharina.

"Do you want me to replace you?" she asked, knowing his answer.

"That's very nice of you," Montclair replied. "But I enjoy the night. Perhaps you can join me as I stroll."

"Perhaps not," Mharina replied. "You may be a formidable swordsman, Montclair, but you're a rotten liar."

She turned and walked into the garden. He called after her. "I'll take that as a compliment."

She shrugged. She was fond of Montclair. He was straightforward, untainted by magic. He possessed no powers, and she found this refreshing. It reminded her of...of him.

She sighed. Her Mushroom Man had fled when he saw her unleash her magic. He was Ithea's brother and had apparently lived in fear of Shadona, their mother; of Ithea; of Sa'gola; and now, of her.

She approached the small pond. The moon was three-quarters full, reflected in a shimmering ball in the water. Her father stood in a meditation pose, his hands held up. Mharina moved two steps to her left so that it appeared her father's outstretched hands held it. Even entrenched in her sorrow, Mharina appreciated the beauty.

She sat on the bench to his left, watching him. His face, usually wrinkled and haunted, was smooth and relaxed. She otherwise only ever saw this when he listened to the twins or moved in his slow sword exercise. Otherwise, his face was hard and hollow. It was how she herself felt inside.

"Join me," he said suddenly, and she jolted as the silence was broken.

"I don't want to."

"Then seek your own anchor, Mharina."

"Is that the best you have to offer?" She winced at her sharp tone but could not stop. "You taught at a Wycaan Academy, learned from great teachers."

"They can't teach you how to embrace sorrow—not the deep sorrow you're feeling."

"You don't know what I'm feeling. You could go to mother's bed and seek solace if you wanted. You might be estranged, but there is a lifeline." She cringed again and took a deep breath. "I'm sorry."

"It's okay. I initiated the conversation. Don't hold back with me. I have little to offer you beyond shared experiences and pain. Remember, I, too, lost another...forever."

"Ilana. You remember?"

"No. But Pyre has told me. I cannot see her face in my mind, but I feel the pain of her loss every time I look at you."

He stretched out of his pose and walked to the bench. He sat next to her but made no attempt to hug or console her. Somehow, he understood that it would be perceived more as suffocation than consolation.

"What do I do?" she whispered, hearing the meekness in her voice. "What did you do when Ilana died?"

He frowned. "I can't remember. Apparently, after a period of mourning and wandering, I was forced to confront my responsibilities. I found solace with your mother. I didn't love her, not at first. I was way too intimidated by her. But love grew between us, a love based upon a sense of shared mission and respect.

"Your teacher is gone, but your love still lives. Go after him, Mharina. That's what I would suggest. Go forage for your Mushroom Man."

"He ran from me. He was terrified. I saw his expression. He won't be with me."

"If he loves you—"

"He does."

"Then he will listen to you and, if he is smart, he'll seek counsel with one who shares his fear."

"What?"

Seanchai smiled. "I'd like to come with you, just the two of us."

Mharina snorted. "You want to leave the family already? Your friends?"

"Sellia will take the twins to the Elves of the West. They must be trained. It's best I don't join them. I wouldn't be accepted there as I am. Rhoddan and Pyre will follow their sense of duty and go north to serve the prince."

"His name is Shayth," Mharina snapped, instantly regretting it. "He's your friend, too."

"I cannot serve him as I once did. So that just leaves you."

"Oh, you'll accompany me because I'm your only choice? I'm touched."

To her surprise, her father laughed. "Perhaps I should have chosen my words more carefully. No. I don't go with you for lack of choice. I go with you because I want to, because I both abhor and am drawn to your dilemma, and, I must admit, to Ithea's brother."

"What do you hope to achieve by coming with me?"

"To help you find your anchor. In doing so, I might find mine."

"We make quite a pair," Mharina said, and put a hand in his. "Two of the most powerful people in the land of Odessiya, and the two most broken."

Her father nodded. "But maybe in that, we'll find a glimmer of hope. At least we have each other."

They sat together in silence, watching the moon move across the pond. Occasionally, the slightest of breezes made it shimmer in the water.

"The moon is vulnerable in the water," Seanchai said. "That's because it can't be true to itself there. It is only complete when in the sky."

"I'm drowning," Mharina whispered. "Can you pull me from the water? My sorrow drags me under."

Slowly, Seanchai moved his arm and tentatively put it around her. She moved closer. "I don't know," he whispered into her ear. "I don't know. But I can try."

CHAPTER 2

"He said what?" Senzia asked.

"He said he'll come with me," Mharina hooked her white hair behind a pointed ear.

"And will you go?"

"I think so."

"You can't…either of you."

"We can, and I think we will."

Ilan entered the room and stared at his two sisters, who immediately went silent. He was growing, Mharina thought, glancing at his trousers, which now dangled quite far above his ankles.

"What are you two talking about?" he asked, his eyes darting from one sister to the other.

They were sitting on Senzia's bed. Senzia and Ilan no longer shared a room due to their emerging puberty, but they were still very close, even for twins.

"Mharina thinks our *ahdahr* will go off with her to search for her beloved."

"The Mushroom Man?"

"Does she have other males besotted with her?"

"I don't know. Is that even allowed?" Ilan paused, and then, perhaps realizing what was at stake if Mharina and their father left, added, "She can't go!"

"I told her. Do you think she listened to me?"

"I am in the room, you know," Mharina said, simultaneously laughing at their double-team and being annoyed with their presumptuousness.

"You can't go," Ilan declared. "Are those bananas?"

He walked over to the table; took a curved, purple fruit; and began to peel it. Mharina knew he would bite off a chunk and then continue speaking with his mouth full. He chewed, and his cheeks expanded.

"We must stay together," he said. "We were forced to separate, and all of us nearly got killed. Many of our friends died. We almost lost *Ahdahr*—perhaps we actually have, in a way. Sa'gola barely saved mother, Pyre, and the others. You can't leave."

"She must leave," Senzia said. "But not to chase lovers."

"Then she should come with us to the Elves of the West. She is Wycaan, too, now. She can study with us."

"She must go north and help Prince Shayth. *Ahdahr*, too. Our armies are in retreat, and more clans and tribes pour out of the north to join the Gray Elves all the time." She turned to her big sister. "It's your duty."

Mharina rose and walked to the window. Her sister's bedroom overlooked the valley, and her eyes followed the path that Sa'gola had brought her along, the path that led back to where she thought her Mushroom Man had fled.

"Haven't I faced enough?" she erupted, rounding on her siblings. "I lost Sa'gola, Abel, and my father, too. I can never bring Sa'gola back, but maybe there's a way to heal—"

"How do you think you can help *Ahdahr*?" Senzia's eyes flashed. "You use him as an excuse."

"No!" Mharina felt her own anger rise. She took a deep breath. "There is a connection between Abel and father."

"How do you know? They barely met. Did they even speak?"

Mharina shook her head. "But they are linked," she persisted. "They share a hatred for a magic they cannot ignore."

"They can," Senzia snapped, "and it seems to me they are. One runs away, and the other mopes around."

"Can't you feel any compassion?" Mharina loomed over her sister, but Senzia didn't flinch.

"If I've learned one thing since we were kidnapped from Wycaan Island, it's that if we ignore our duty, others die. Ilan is right. There are many we were close to who are dead now. Perhaps they wouldn't be if—"

"Shut up!" Mharina shouted. "You're so cold, so arrogant. How do you presume to know so much when you're just a stupid little *calhei*?"

She whirled around to leave, but Ilan stood in the doorway, blocking her exit. She stopped, shocked. Usually, he buried his head under a pillow or ran away when they fought. But now, he stood, meeting her gaze.

"Please sit down," he said, his voice soft but strong. "This is too important."

Unbelievably, she found herself turning, walking to the table, and slumping in a chair. Out of the corner of her eye, she saw Ilan look at his twin and hold her gaze. Where had he found this composure? Senzia rose from the bed and slunk over to the table, sitting opposite Mharina.

"I'm sorry," she said, taking a deep breath. "You're right. I'm young and impulsive, but I'm also afraid. We saw the Emperor's and Ithea's power. We hear tales of the Ashen Elves and the magic they wield. Pyre will go north; Rhoddan, as well, I think. But neither can offer what Prince Shayth needs."

"Pyre's Wycaan," Mharina said.

Her sister stared back, wordlessly reminding her that Pyre was not a complete Wycaan. "If they go without you or our *ahdahr*, we send them to their death."

If Sa'gola was here—" Mharina started.

"But she isn't, and I'm sorry for you that she isn't. You're the key. Father will follow you."

"What makes you so sure?" Ilan asked, pulling up a chair.

Senzia hesitated, then shook her head. "I don't know."

"Senzia. We must go to the Markwin Forest. You and I must train and—"

"There's no time!" his twin snapped back. "The Elves of the West are flawed. They should have come to the defense of Odessiya. It's their arrogance—our ancestors' arrogance—that created this conflict in the first place. I have nothing to learn from them."

"I need to go there," Ilan said, his voice still measured. "I'm not like you two. I'm no warrior. I need wise teachers. I…I don't want us to separate, Senzia. You know that."

Mharina expected her sister to ridicule him, but she didn't. Instead, she leaned over and took his hand. "I know," she said, her voice as soft as Mharina had ever heard it. "But if you and I are so different, no matter how close we're connected, we have different paths to walk."

Ilan sprung to his feet. "We will stay together as long as we can. You promised."

Senzia just stared at him.

"Senzia," he started, his voice wavering. "I can't. Not yet. You promised. You did."

Senzia stood and went to her brother. He was a head taller than her but seemed to shrink in her presence and his own distress. She took both his hands.

"Yes, I promised. But things change, and I don't know—"

"What are you talking about?" Sellia stood in the doorway, her strong voice reverberating through the room.

It was as if the three instantly reverted to being the *calhei* they were. No one spoke. Their mother huffed.

"There is a meeting in the small hall. Take some food and join us. A messenger has arrived from Shindellia. We need to make some decisions."

CHAPTER 3

The small hall was cramped for such a meeting, but Mharina would not enter the Great Hall, where the confrontation with Ithea and Sa'gola's death took place. A dozen austere chairs sat around a gray stone table.

Mharina watched her brother sit with their mother and Senzia move next to Pyre, their heads bent together in a private conversation. Troja sat at one end of the table with her arms folded, thin and pensive, while Rhoddan stood behind her with one hand on her shoulder, talking earnestly with Montclair, who was shaking his head, his straw-colored bangs swishing. Opposite Mharina's mother sat a man, his face shadowed from a week of not shaving. He looked stern and uncomfortable, staring at the table as an involuntary yawn escaped him. He shook his head, peering around to see if anyone had noticed.

Riona entered and took a place by herself. Mharina poured two cups of water, took one to the messenger, and then sat next to Riona. She felt a strange connection with the woman, who was an outsider now that Seanchai no longer offered patronage. He greatly admired the healer when she sought to study with him at Wycaan Island. She had displayed an extensive understanding and commitment to the healing arts even before studying with him.

"What are we waiting for?" Mharina mumbled.

"Your father."

Mharina nodded and leaned forward to address Sellia. "Mother. Does *Ahdahr* know of this meeting?"

Sellia shrugged. "I told him. He's in the garden by the pond."

"I'll go," Rhoddan said, a bit too quickly, and left the room.

Mharina wondered why he had been so eager to go. She watched Troja's haunted eyes follow him out. What had happened to her? They had barely exchanged words, and Mharina knew nothing of Rhoddan's new mate.

Mharina leaned closer to Riona. "So, what's your next move?"

"I'll go to my brother," she replied, her eyes also on the door. "I promised."

"Your brother? Who—"

She stopped as Riona glared at her, but the healer's expression quickly relaxed.

"You're not up-to-date," Riona said. "You've had enough to deal with these past few weeks. Prince Shayth of Odessiya has a sister. It's a long story, and now is neither the time nor place."

Mharina sat back in her chair, too stunned to respond. She knew nothing of Riona's past—only that the woman had always been secretive and aloof, even during her days on Wycaan Island. At first, the twins and she had been scared of Riona, thinking her a ghost or spirit because of her pale complexion.

Rhoddan and Seanchai entered, the former moving back to stand behind Troja, the latter taking a glass of water and sitting next to Mharina. Mharina realized this meant that her father was now opposite Sellia—not a good arrangement.

"Where is Ahad?" Pyre asked.

"Our Master Assassin left," Montclair said. "He has some pressing matter."

"When?" The messenger glared at him.

"A short while ago. We should begin."

The room went silent, and those still standing sat down. The messenger glanced at Seanchai but then looked to Sellia to begin. Sellia seemed perplexed by this, and Rhoddan spoke up.

"What is your name?" he asked the messenger.

"Jaziah."

"When you are ready, please share your message."

Jaziah cleared his throat and finished his cup of water. Mharina, to bury her own impatience, rose and refilled it.

"Thank you," he said, and straightened. "I come with the authority of Prince Shayth Shindell, crown prince of Odessiya, and the individual messages I have are from him. However, he has charged me to give you an update of the campaign, and any inaccuracies or interpretations in it are my own."

He paused, waiting to see if anyone had questions. When there was none, he continued. "We have lost the north. All lands above the snow line are now in the hands of the Ashen Elves. Prince Shayth has only been able to halt their advance with the aid of his fine cavalry. As the first snows fell, he was forced to withdraw further south.

"The pictorians have suffered great losses. They are, physically, the best match for the enemy, and have therefore been in the forefront of battle. There are many times more Ashen Elves, and when one falls, a dozen take his place.

"The prince has tried to draw them out to the marshlands in the west and toward the Cliftean Path, but we fear they have enough soldiers to press on two fronts, and Shindellia could soon come under threat."

"Why does he not concentrate his forces and defend the capital?" Montclair asked.

"He looks to the Elves of the West for help," Sellia surmised.

"He will get none," Senzia said. "Only a Wycaan can hope to persuade them."

Everyone stared at her. She stared at her father. She was the youngest person in the room, and yet so assertive and confident. Mharina felt both awe and apprehension at her sister.

"They won't listen to me," her father muttered. "They wouldn't listen to me then, right?" He looked at Sellia for confirmation. She nodded.

"What about you, Pyre?" Montclair asked. "Could you—"

"I'm not welcome back, either. Neither do I have any credibility. I chose to follow Seanchai and disobey the wishes of the Elven Council. I am blamed for the deaths of Cheriuk—the Weapons Master—and all who fell at the Battle of the Cliftean Pass." She looked at Seanchai. "And I am not you."

"Neither am I," he replied, and the room went silent.

The messenger cleared his throat again. "The prince requests that you, Sellia, take the twins to the Elves of the West so they will be safe and trained. He requests that Rhoddan and Riona ride to Shindellia to help prepare the defenses of the capital.

"He requests that Pyre, Mharina, and Montclair head north to join forces with him." He looked over at Troja. "My lady, I do not have orders for you. I—"

"I go where Rhoddan goes," she replied, her eyes flashing a challenge to him.

"I will convey that to the prince," he said, bowing his head.

"What about my husband?" Sellia asked, and the way she said husband—a human term—rather than the more intimate mate as elves use, sent a shiver through Mharina. Her eyes met her sister's and then Ilan's. They had all felt it.

"My message to the Wycaan is not meant for all ears," Jaziah replied.

"Leave us, please, everyone," Sellia announced. "We'll meet again at dinner."

Troja, Riona, Montclair, and the twins all rose and exited.

"You, too, Mharina," her mother said.

Mharina just shook her head. She was furious that her mother wanted her to leave but did not question Rhoddan's presence.

"She stays," Seanchai said. There was no room for argument left in his tone, and he turned to Jaziah. "Finish your message."

"You're to come with me, sire. I'm instructed to bring you before the prince. He will hear your defense and decide upon your destiny. Any sentence you receive will be postponed until after you've helped repel the enemy."

A brief smile of comprehension crossed Seanchai's face. "I'm under arrest?"

The man flinched, but nodded.

CHAPTER 4

"The prince has ordered me to be discreet," the messenger continued after a pause. "I'm not to bind you or embarrass you in any way. Your presence will fill the people with hope, and this must be encouraged. Still, you disobeyed his orders to come to his aid when he first encountered the enemy, and many died as a result. The prince wants you to know that among those who sacrificed their lives was Ballendir, the dwarf general."

"Ballendir!" Sellia exclaimed. "Oh, no." She cupped her face in her hands.

"Who?" Seanchai asked.

Sellia looked up, grief stretched across her face. "He was a close friend of yours. He defied the First Decree and helped you form your first alliance with the dwarves. You owe him…owed him so much."

"I'm so sorry," Seanchai said, to console his mate more than anything.

Mharina wanted him to stand and go to her mother. But he did not move—just stared at the table—and she found herself rising to hug Sellia from behind. Rhoddan turned to the messenger.

"Jaziah, please go and eat. Pyre will find you a room where you can rest and show you where to wash."

The older man hesitated, toying with his cup.

"I'll take responsibility for Seanchai this evening," Rhoddan said evenly.

"What do you plan to do with him?" Jaziah asked.

"Just talk," Rhoddan said. "Somewhere quiet. Seanchai and I were together from the beginning. Shayth would accept his word and my integrity."

The man sighed. "Very well. But do not leave the walls of Grogin."

He rose and left them, his boots clicking on the stone floor in a slow, deliberate rhythm. Once the door was closed, Seanchai rose and poured himself some more water. Then he walked to the opening that looked out on the outer walls and the mountains beyond.

"Tell me about Ballendir," he said.

Sellia let out a sound that Mharina thought was exasperation. Rhoddan also noted it and quickly jumped in.

"I'm not sure now is the time to discuss him," he replied. "It wouldn't do him justice and, to be frank, we have more pressing matters."

"I need to know," Seanchai replied, still gazing out the window.

"Why?" Sellia snapped, and Seanchai turned.

"My past is an ever-thickening fog," he said. "I need to understand whom my past decisions have influenced before I make any in the future."

"Yes," Rhoddan replied. "But first, I need to know that you plan to go to Shayth as he requests."

"Requests? I heard no request. I'm under arrest, which I assume means that man must drag me back, if necessary."

Rhoddan laughed. "He looks smart. I doubt he's under any illusion that he can force you to do anything."

"Is Prince Shayth smart? Does he know me well?"

"Yes."

"Then that man is no simple messenger. He's an assassin."

"An assassin?" Mharina stared at him. "What makes you think that?"

"Because Ahad left rather abruptly," Seanchai said. "Pyre told me the other day that he's an outcast, a death price held over his head by the other assassins. If this man confronted him, one of them would have to die."

"Will you go to Shayth?" Rhoddan repeated.

"It's Mharina's choice. I'll follow my daughter."

"*Our* daughter!" Sellia's voice burst out.

Seanchai turned to Sellia, an undeniable pained expression on his face. "*Our* daughter," he repeated. "I'm sorry. I hurt you at every turn, but never intentionally."

"That's what cuts even deeper. A mate who deserts me is bad, but at least I can blame him. You are just there, right in front of my eyes, utterly helpless."

Rhoddan cleared his throat. "Mharina is present, as am I. And again, I think we should focus. If Mharina is going to answer Shayth's call, then—"

"I, too, am in the room, Rhoddan, thank you, and you presume upon my decision." Mharina inwardly winced at her tone. She was not angry with Rhoddan but sad at the interaction between her parents.

"Mharina," Sellia began. "Your *ahdahr* and I should have a say—"

"I am a *calhei* no more, mother!" She sprung to her feet. "Please do not treat me as one. I'm apparently the most powerful weapon Odessiya possesses."

"It is your decision to make," Seanchai said softly. "But a wise leader heeds good counsel even when the decision is hers alone."

"Please sit down," Rhoddan said, and both Seanchai and Mharina did so.

"I'm sorry, mother," Mharina sighed. "What do you suggest?"

"I will take the twins to the Elves of the West. I'm one of them now that I have family there. Perhaps I can influence them. I would like your *ahdahr* to stay with you, to teach and counsel you. He was once a wise elf, a noble Wycaan, and a just leader." She looked over at her mate. "It's why I fell in love with him."

Seanchai lowered his eyes, unable to meet Sellia's gaze. The silence was thick, and this time, even Rhoddan was at a loss as to how to take up the conversation. As dusk settled, the room became even gloomier.

At length, Mharina turned to her *ahdahr*. "My plan remains as we discussed, but in light of what we have heard, we must make it a short detour."

"What is your plan?" Sellia asked, bristling at being kept outside the conversation.

Seanchai put his hand on Mharina's before she could answer and turned to Rhoddan.

"Though I don't remember, I understand that you have been a true and worthy friend. Sellia tells me you hold loyalty and honesty above all. If you serve the prince—and I think you do—then you should leave the room. When he asks why you come without me, it's best you're not put in a position where you need to lie or betray me.

"Tell the prince that we will come, though I do not promise I can provide the aid he requires. Tell him not to send his assassins after me and that if anyone harms my daughter or the others of my family, I will hold him responsible."

There was another long silence. Rhoddan rose. "I'm hungry," he said. "I'll join the others for dinner and expect to see you there." He paused and winced. "Take care, old friend."

When Rhoddan was out of the room, Sellia stared first at her mate and then at her daughter. Neither offered to expound upon their plans, and she pursed her lips. She rose slowly and then leaned on the table toward Seanchai. Her voice became a hiss, and Mharina barely recognized her own mother.

"And I'll hold *you* responsible if anything happens to any of *my* calhei. It's tragic that you don't remember our past. Know that I was once a great fighter, that I protected you, and that I taught you how to use the bow. I became your mate out of an oath to Ilana, but I learned to love you more than I ever loved anyone…until *my calhei* were born.

"Whatever was between us is history. I live only for *my calhei* and grieve the mate I once loved."

Through tear-blurred vision, Mharina watched her mother leave. She glanced at her father and saw a lone tear wind its way down his face.

Chapter 5

Prince Shayth Shindell bit down on a piece of leather as the healer realigned his shoulder joint. He shuddered as the healer realigned his shoulder joint and would have cried out with pain, but there were too many men around. His strength was all they had to hang on to in these dark times. So, he put a thick piece of leather in his mouth and bit hard.

He had dislocated his shoulder when an Ashen Elf smashed his shield with a huge axe. Shayth had only just begun to use a shield, previously preferring the double-handed broadsword, but his weapons master had been adamant that the enemy would quickly identify his technique and devise a way to defeat him. He was vulnerable against multiple trained warriors or in close battle quarters. After four Gray Elves cornered and almost killed him, he conceded to the experienced man's advice. Now he was not so sure about his decision. If he was being honest, though, it wasn't clear whether the blow to his shield damaged his shoulder or if it was the rage with which he drove the serrated shards of the shield into his opponent's neck, severing most of the gray elf's head.

"Lay down and get some rest," the wrinkled healer said.

Shayth started to rise, instead, and the old man rested a firm hand on his shoulder. "You may be the future king of Odessiya, but in this tent, I rule. You could faint or throw up, and that wouldn't do in front of the men."

Shayth managed something between a grimace and smile. "You know how to get your way," he conceded.

"I've been doing this for too many years, my prince. Now, sip this and rest."

The sweet drink took its intended toll, and Shayth slept more deeply than he had for some time. When he woke, he felt strangely relaxed and reinvigorated. He opened his eyes and saw a familiar face.

"Maugwen!" He began to rise and immediately regretted it as his shoulder protested.

She gently pushed him down again and took his hand in both of hers. "I leave you for a short time, and you go play rough with the big boys? I can't trust you to be out of my sight."

"I wish you wouldn't," he replied, squeezing her hand. "And it's been a considerably long time, as I remember. Tell me everything."

A young healer—an apprentice, judging from the lack of hair on his smooth face—approached them. He wore an apprehensive expression, presumably from serving his prince. "M-master Tolrin requests you drink this. It will h-help reinvigorate you."

Maugwen relieved the young man of the shaking cup before any spilled. "Did Master Tolrin *request* he drink this or order him to? The old fox rules his roost, no?"

The poor youth looked perplexed as he glanced from Maugwen to Shayth. "Um," was all he could manage, which made them both laugh.

"What is your name?" Shayth asked.

"Cyrin, milord."

"Thank you, Cyrin. As long as your intentions are good, you have nothing to fear in my presence. I require loyalty and respect, but no cowering. Understand?"

"Yes, milord." The boy straightened and cleared his throat. "Master Tolrin told me to watch and make sure you drink it all."

Shayth couldn't help grinning at the young man's expression. "Did he use those words?"

"No, milord. He said that if you argued, I was to shove it down your royal throat."

Again, Shayth and Maugwen laughed. This time, the boy joined in.

"Master Tolrin is a great healer, sire. I have learned so much from him."

"And I probably owe him my life a half dozen times," Shayth replied. "As do many of my men. Study well with him, Cyrin. The best way to honor him and serve me is to become as great a healer as he is. Now, look." Shayth gulped the elixir down. "Finished. You have fulfilled your task admirably and not lost your head in the process. Go report that your mission was accomplished. I must speak with my friend. Thank you."

Cyrin beamed as he took the cup and left. Maugwen watched him leave and then turned back. "Every time I come back from being separated from you, I'm impressed anew at how much more you embrace your role. I remember the cruel, angry boy in the dungeons at Galbrieth."

"He's still here, Maugwen. I call him up more with each day this fruitless campaign continues. He kept me alive a few times, too."

"Is it as bad as I hear?"

Shayth winced again, but this time it was not from the pain in his shoulder. "The pictorians can stand their ground with the Ashen Elves, but they are few in number and getting fewer with each encounter. Otherwise, I have precious few men who are skillful enough to compensate for the enemy's superior strength.

"The Ashen Elves follow me and have yet to seriously test my cavalry that defends the plains near Shindellia. Meanwhile, we attack and retreat, leading them away from the populated areas. Without the Elves of the West, I'm at a loss about how to win this."

"Have you heard from them?"

Shayth went into a brooding silent. Then he shook his head. "We sent them one of the red stones the Ashen Elves wear and received no response. I sent a delegation of respected elves through the Cliftean Pass. They were never even allowed past the barrier to present my message. Is Pyre with you? I would counsel with her about going."

"She says she is unwelcome since she rejected their ways and dedicated herself to Sean…"

Her voice trailed off as Shayth felt his scowl tighten.

"He did not come?"

Maugwen shook her head. "He is…he's changed, Shayth. The Seanchai we knew is, at best, locked away somewhere inside of him. At worst, he is lost. The only trait remaining is his love for his *calhei*. He follows Mharina, and she says they will come soon."

"Soon? Where is she?"

Maugwen offered a short smile. "I can only guess. She has lost those dear to her, but she'll come soon and bring Seanchai."

"*Then* what will I do?" Shayth spat out. "Sentence my dear friend, the hope of our nation, and behead him for treason?"

"In truth, he needs to go to the Elves of the West. Not as your representative, but to heal himself. If anyone can help him, apart from Mharina, it's them. But…"

"But what?"

"I don't know if they'll let him enter in his current state. And you need Mharina with you. She has grown powerful and strong— perhaps so strong that you don't need Seanchai. But she is also young and mourns her mentor."

"We have seen that story played out by her father. I hate him, Maugwen, more with every day that passes, with every brave soldier that falls defending me and our land. But more than that, I just miss him so much. He was my anchor, keeping the angry boy in place and letting the prince shine."

Maugwen took his hand again. "And he will serve you in that role again."

"How can you be so sure?"

Maugwen grimaced. "I can't. I just refuse to believe there's another option."

"That's the problem," Shayth replied. "There isn't."

CHAPTER 6

Shayth and Maugwen climbed up onto a ridge above the army camp. Cooking fires were being lit, and, to their left, men went through drills or sparred, learning techniques to compensate for the Ashen Elves' superior strength and agility. Before Shayth and Maugwen had even gone twenty paces, there was a yip from behind them, and a big puppy, its paws splaying out awkwardly, bounded after them.

"Who is this?" Maugwen asked. "Your new bodyguard?"

"Azura," Shayth replied, bending to scratch the dog behind her ear with his good arm.

Maugwen bent, too, and the puppy gave her a sniff, then a long lick. The healer managed to both laugh and cringe.

"Nice eyes," she said. "I guess you took steps not to miss me. Where did he come from?"

"*She* was a gift from the mage of the Ashen Elves." They both stood, and Shayth continued as his friend stared at him. "I went to her under the protection of parley, offered them land, and asked them to join Odessiya as free elves. But they are crazed for revenge. Their stories tell how the fair elves defeated and incarcerated them and took their land, using magic to condemn them to exile under the mountains in the north."

"So, why the gift?"

"Her eyes," Shayth replied, staring down at his companion. "They are the same deep blue as the Ashen Elves'. Every time I look at her, I'm to remember their threat."

"Great," Maugwen harrumphed. "Why keep her?"

Shayth shrugged. "I've always wanted a dog. Samoyeds are smart, loyal, and strong. She's grown on me, literally and figuratively. She's actually doubled in size in little over a year."

They walked for a while, Shayth's guard near but unseen, giving them the space they needed.

"There are rumors," Maugwen began, lowering her voice. "Are they true? Did Ballendir name you king with his last breath?"

"He did," Shayth confirmed, "and the courts and regional governments cry out for my coronation."

"Why? It seems the least important thing, given that we're at war. Survival seems a bit more pressing."

"I agree," Shayth said, "but it is connected. I need an heir. It silences the predators at court and offers the people a sense of future."

"Azura isn't acceptable?"

Shayth laughed. "It wouldn't work. Azura!" the dog looked up expectantly, tongue out, ears straining. "This wench makes fun of the crown. Wag once if I should cut off her head and twice if I should have her flayed!"

Azura cocked her head to one side and then stared at Maugwen, who put her small fists on her hips and challenged the dog with her stare. Azura responded by wagging her tail furiously and letting out a yip.

"Not guilty," Maugwen declared, and leaned down. Azura bounded forward, and Maugwen hugged the dog, scratching under her chin and behind her ears.

"I see a conspiracy," Shayth declared, an eyebrow raised. "Dangerous." But then he turned serious and pulled Maugwen to her feet, putting a hand on each of her shoulders. "Maugwen," he began.

"Don't," she interrupted. "We both know it can never be. You've always been very dear to me, Shayth—except when you bullied me in the dungeons of Galbrieth. For a long time, I compared all suitors to you, and, as you know, there has been no one. Maybe there never will be."

"And if I wasn't the prince?" He raked a hand through his spiky, black hair.

She ruffled her own. "Then our children would have the unruliest hair ever. Anyway, you *are* the prince, so there's no point saying things that might force us apart. When your bride sees us together and asks if there has ever been anything between us, what will you say?"

"The truth," Shayth said. "That you are, and will always be, a true and dear friend, a confidant, and one of my special companions."

"And so it must remain. I won't give you cause to lie to her. Neither should she ever feel insecure on my account. That would be so unfair."

Shayth frowned. "We could have been, though."

"No," Maugwen replied. "You were always destined to be king, Shayth. Any thoughts or feelings we harbored for each other were never more than dreams and fantasies."

"So you've had such thoughts, yourself?" he asked, but did not wait for a response. "There were nights we laid together, hugging each other for warmth, reassurance, or security. I often wondered if the bonds of friendship were growing, if..."

Maugwen pulled away from him and stood upright. Her voice hardened, though it strained to do so. "Only dreams and fantasies, Shayth." She turned and looked out into the valley below. When she spoke, her voice was soft again. "Has someone been chosen?"

He moved alongside her but did not touch her. "Yes. In a month's time, we plan for me to slip back to the capital. We'll hold the coronation and marry the following day. I shall stay with her a few days before I rejoin my troops."

Maugwen laughed. "Let me guess. Men devised this grand plan? Do not think it will be so easy to leave your young bride pregnant after only a few tries. Poor woman. Isn't it hard enough for her that she has to marry you? You practically have her with child before she can even get used to her predicament."

Shayth only sighed. "It is nothing to make fun of," he said.

"Humor is how I deal with things that are hard for me," she replied, her voice quieter now.

Shayth put his arm around her and moved closer. She bristled.

"Just hugging a friend," he said. "A good friend, who is dealing with something hard."

"Is she pretty?" Maugwen asked.

"I don't know. I've never met her."

"I'm sure she is."

They stood together and watched the sun slowly set over the peaks across the valley.

Chapter 7

Shayth's troops attacked two days later, at dawn. The Ashen Elves had established several camps, attempting to prevent Shayth from returning to the capital to join his two armies together. Shayth was happy the mage thought this was his plan. He needed to keep them away from the capital while the magical red stones were studied.

The mage was using her stone-bearing elves sparingly now, perhaps fearful that he would capture more. Shayth's revelation that it took the elves wearing the stones a few moments to be able to move once they appeared had also blunted some of their effectiveness.

Since no man could touch the stones, a ranger had taken Azura back to the capital with them strung around her neck. Shayth received confirmation they were being examined, but that had been several moon cycles ago. One of the stones had been taken to the Forest of Markwin, but it was unknown if the Elves of the West, who had knowledge of ancient magic the elves in the capital didn't, were seriously studying it or not.

Now, Shayth led a small band to attack the westernmost elf camp—the one closest to Shindellia. His primary intent was to strengthen the mage's belief that he wanted to reach the capital. But he also wanted Pyre, who arrived with Maugwen, to experience fighting this enemy.

He led one band, which included both Pyre and Montclair, while a second force of mainly pictorians wreaked havoc from the other side. Pyre and two soldiers silently dispensed with the Ashen

Elf guards, who were tired at the end of their guard duty. However, the surprise was short-lived as barking dogs woke the camp.

They fought for a while, and Shayth was impressed with the fluency of Pyre's swordplay. Her muscular body and gray-white hair was often a blur, and her Win Dao swords cut through the Ashen Elves with shocking efficiency. Three Ashen Elves wearing red stones momentarily matched her, but she swiftly adapted. When Shayth heard the pictorians charge, he instructed his force to retreat.

Shayth saw Montclair in front of him, following a scout. The fortune-sword had done well, struggling at first against stronger adversaries but adapting well to his opponents. Shayth was pleased and needed to remember to tell him. He wondered how Montclair felt about being separated from Shayth's sister, even though Riona needed to be safe in the capital. Only a few knew she was Shayth's sister, but a clear line of succession was imperative.

They passed two archers who had held back from the attack to take out the fastest pursuers. One of them raised a second bow belonging to Pyre. She grabbed it and crouched with them.

"What are you doing?" Shayth demanded.

"If you're going to stay, then get down," Pyre snapped back. "I won't be blamed for losing the prince on my first foray." The other two archers gaped at her, but Shayth did as she said.

"Why are you doing this?" he said again. "I have excellent archers."

"My skills with the bow are as important as they are with my swords. I need practice with all weapons." Then she nocked an arrow and shot toward the Ashen Elves as they came into view.

The two archers managed to each kill one elf, while Pyre shot four. All three men stared at her.

"Not too shabby," she said, when the rest of the pursuers retreated.

They waited a few moments before going to retrieve their arrows from the fallen Ashen Elves. Pyre pulled back the hair from one, gazed at his pointed ears, and then looked at Shayth. It was the first opportunity for her to really examine the enemy close up. "These are my people. It's hard to believe."

"Your people are good," one of the archers—a human—said. "These are vicious brutes. You share pointed ears, nothing more. DON'T TOUCH!" Pyre had reached out to the red stone that one of the elves wore. "I saw my friend turn into dust from touching one," the man continued. "Leave it alone."

Pyre looked at Shayth. "Have you had an elf touch a stone?"

"No. And I won't risk it with you. Perhaps we shall give Seanchai that privilege, should he ever show up." She bristled at this, but just watched as a soldier carefully cut the chain and allowed the stone to fall into a burlap sack, which he carefully tied.

"Pull back," Shayth called, ruffling his spiky hair. "We're finished for today."

They began moving—all except Pyre, who grabbed Shayth's arm. He glared at her, but her hold was iron and her expression just as hard. When she spoke, it was in a low hiss meant only for his ears.

"With the exception of Sellia and the *calhei*, there are none who mourn him more than me. You have every right to be angry, but he is still the Wycaan Master, still the elf who saved you and made you who you are today.

"Do not insult him in front of your soldiers and especially not in front of me, or we *will* be finished this day."

Shayth could feel his rage rising, but when he spoke, his tone was icy. "I am still your prince. Unhand me now. There are six elite guards surrounding us. You are outnumbered."

"My hair is yet to become pure white, but do not doubt my skill with the Win Dao swords, nor my loyalty. You are my prince, but I serve Odessiya, as my teacher did before me, as he will again, I hope. I—"

"Stop," Shayth said, his voice now conciliatory. "I apologize. You're right to call me out, to remind me of the respect I hold for you as I once held for your teacher. I'm sorry." She removed her hand, and he saw tears welling in her eyes. "It is tragic, what has befallen Seanchai. I hurt so much, because I deeply admired and loved him."

"You haven't seen him." Her voice lost its harshness. "It's so painful to see his constantly lost expression, his guilt when he looks upon the *calhei* and Sellia. Poor Sellia."

They had started walking.

"Tell me how she fares," Shayth requested.

"She is so cut up inside. She thought she had lost him, lost Mharina, and she mourned them both. Then they come back—but so changed. Mharina is young but transformed. Sellia was not part of her daughter's change and cannot comprehend it. I don't understand all Mharina has gone through and I'm not her mother. Somehow, Mharina carries the memories of older teachers inside her, which seemingly gives her limitless experience. She's an old, wise elfe inside the body of a confused *calhei*.

"She offers her mother support, especially regarding Seanchai. And yet, the bond she has with her father is strong. I believe...I *hope* she might become his lifeline. It's why, even though they have not come here, I hold desperately to a glimmer of hope from them at least traveling together."

She went silent for a while, and Shayth waited before urging her on. "And what is happening between Sellia and Seanchai?"

"He has closed her out. It seems he feels nothing for her, remembers nothing of their relationship, and is barely aware that she's his mate. He offers respect and deference but nothing more. The pain is clear on her face. She has always been so strong, so fierce, but now she's barely holding herself together. If it were not for the presence of their *calhei*, I fear she would snap."

Shayth nodded. "Her love for him is deep. They may have come together through oaths each swore to Ilana, but her love grew for him as they bonded. It must be very painful."

"What will happen when he comes? Will you judge him as king or as a friend?"

"That's a good question, Pyre." Shayth stopped and looked back toward the camp of the Ashen Elves. "Let's hope we are all still alive to find out."

CHAPTER 8

Senzia stopped abruptly as she entered the eating hall for breakfast. Her mother was standing near another doorway, flanked by two soldiers and confronted by the prince's messenger, who now looked like anything but a simple soldier. His cheeks were flushed, and, more worryingly, his hand was on the hilt of his sword.

"What's happening?" Ilan whispered from next to her, his stomach rumbling.

Senzia shook her head, walked in silently, and stood on tiptoes next to Jaziah. "Remove your hand from your sword," she said, her voice quiet, but firm.

He looked down and saw the blade the slightly built, white-haired elfe held at his wrist.

Then he smiled. "Just habit," he said, and slowly removed his hand.

"Mother. Will you help Ilan with breakfast? He's about to faint from hunger."

Sellia turned to Jaziah. "I shall walk with my children to take food and then sit at the table over there. I suggest you post sentries all around us. When my *calhei* and I have finished eating, we'll talk further, though I can't think of anything I haven't already said."

With that, she stepped past and led the twins to food with one arm around each. When they were seated, Ilan leaned forward. "What happened?"

"Your sister and *ahdahr* have left."

"Have they gone to the prince?"

"I don't think so," Sellia replied. "The prince's guard came to arrest him, and I'm not sure a Wycaan Master—even in your father's current state—takes too kindly to such things."

Ilan and Senzia laughed, and Senzia glanced over at the irate soldier. "The prince didn't really expect *Ahdahr* to go, did he?"

"I'm not sure," Sellia replied, "but it has forced our family to separate again."

"Does that make you sad?" Senzia asked. "You've suffered so since he joined us."

Sellia looked at her daughter and sighed. "I love your father, Senzia; never doubt it. When I thought him dead, I mourned him. But somehow, I realized I had always prepared for such a moment, and I was ready to compensate by channeling my energy into the three of you.

"At first, seeing him alive was exhilarating. But the higher you go, the greater you fall, and yes, I plummeted. I'm sad he's gone from me again, but yes, there's a sense of relief. Knowing that he's with Mharina is comforting."

Her daughter nodded. "I'm sorry, mother. We both are." And with that, they resumed eating in silence. Suddenly, there were guards surrounding them.

"Ilan," Jaziah said, his voice quiet but commanding. "Please join me over at that table. Alone."

"I am his mother, and—"

"You may sit here and supervise. I won't harm or intimidate him in any way."

"I will not!" She made to rise, but a soldier appeared behind her. She turned her head. "Pyre! Montclair!"

"They left at dawn, heading toward where the prince requested. Rhoddan has left, too. All very convenient, no? Do you take me for a fool?"

"If you thought you could arrest a Wycaan Master, then you're a fool following a fool's instruction," Sellia snapped back.

"Be careful, madam."

"Or what?" Sellia rose, uncurling her taut body, muscles tensing.

Jaziah turned again to Ilan. "It is best you come with us and allow your mother to calm down. Please take more food first if you're still hungry."

Ilan shook his head and rose. Senzia did the same.

"Only your brother, my dear," Jaziah said. "He'll be fine and isn't in need of anyone's protection."

Senzia offered a cynical laugh. "Oh, my poor man. They really didn't prepare you, did they? I'm not coming to protect Ilan. He is a natural-born Wycaan and has a fiendish temper. I'm coming to protect you and your men. Even an assassin like you is no match for a Wycaan, as my father and sister have clearly proven. Now, you are not frightened of two young *calhei*, are you? What would that say about the Assassin's Order? Come, Ilan, and please do not intimidate these poor men. They are humble servants of Prince Shayth, our father and mother's good friend. We'll join you soon, mother."

It was a speechless set of soldiers, assassin included, who followed the twins to another table. Senzia glanced back and winked at Sellia. Her mother was grinning. It was a lovely sight.

"Thank you both for coming," Jaziah said, offering a congenial smile. "This is very serious. Prince Shayth required your father to come with me, and your father has disobeyed. Now, if I can find him quickly, I can put everything right and, hopefully, get your father to the prince so that they can have an important conversation and then, together, drive the enemy from our lands."

"Did the prince *ask* my father to go, or order him?" Senzia asked.

"That is a question of nuance, my dear."

"How do you think my father and sister, possibly the two most powerful weapons the prince has, interpreted these…nuances?"

Jaziah smiled. "Apparently not too well." For his efforts, he received a laugh. "I need to find your father. He digs himself a deeper hole with each move. I want to help him. I want us all to fight alongside the prince for the sake of Odessiya."

Ilan leaned forward. "He did not consult with us. I'm not sure I would tell you where he went, even if I did know. Honestly, I also think he should join the prince, unless he has gone somewhere to regain his memory and strength. If that is the case, he is best left alone."

Senzia looked at her brother. He was sitting taller, and she was impressed. "I don't know anything, either," she said. "I offered to help the prince with the limited training I have received. Apparently, he thinks it better that Ilan and I finish our training, and we'll do as he requests."

The man went to speak again, but Ilan raised his palm, and the experienced assassin immediately deferred.

"The prince should also consider the risk of bringing my father to the frontline in his current state. If I were the enemy, I would prioritize his capture. Think what they could extract from him."

"I think you might overestimate the Ashen Elves, young elf," the assassin grunted back.

"Really?" Ilan replied. "That makes our inability to outthink and outmaneuver them all the more worrying."

The man nodded. "You have a point. I should not brush aside your comments. You have both experienced more than you should as childr—"

"*Calhei*," Ilan said, and flashed a smile.

"You see, Ilan and I are nice and amiable." Senzia also smiled and leaned forward. When she spoke again, her voice was harsh. "But when you return empty-handed to the prince, please pass on a message from the amiable Wycaan twins.

"Time passes, and the players change. Soon, Ilan and I may well be the most powerful people in the land. We'll be two fully trained natural-born Wycaans, and the bond we share potentially makes us even more powerful than any two Wycaans in our lifetime. There have never been natural-born Wycaan twins, and the masters who taught us saw huge differences in our growth and power.

"So please, tell our prince that, just as our *ahdahr* served him faithfully, so will we to the best of our ability. Tell him we share many of our father's attributes. So neither he, nor any of his minions, shall ever threaten a member of our family...ever. Safe travels, sir."

The conversation was over.

CHAPTER 9

"Senzia," Ilan asked. "Do you really believe what you said to the assassin back at Grogin?"

They were resting near a stream, Sellia and the twins, accompanied by four taragusii sent to protect them. Senzia found it interesting that the taragusii, who had first kidnapped them from Wycaan Island and brought them to Grogin, and then captured them when they left after the death of the Emperor, were now actually escorting them.

Senzia glanced around. The taragusii had each taken a position looking out, as if on guard, but she wondered whether they were guarding them from escaping or protecting them.

"No. I think Mharina and *Ahdahr* are wrong not to go to the prince's aid. Good men and elves are dying in combat. It's not the time to go looking for your lost lover or yourself."

"So why say what you said?" Ilan asked.

"Because my first loyalty is to my family…for now, at least."

"What does that mean?"

"I'm not sure we're doing the right thing, Ilan. So we go off to safety and train with the Elves of the West. But what happens if, in the meantime, Shayth loses? What if the Ashen Elves win and kill all the elves—all our friends—and destroy everything *Ahdahr* and Shayth fought for?"

Sellia had been filling her water skins and now returned. She stared at the twins, who had stopped talking. "Your silence is deafening. Might I ask what you were discussing?"

The twins exchanged a look. "We were wondering about Mharina and *Ahdahr*," Senzia replied. "Where have they gone? What part will they play in supporting the prince? Have they really made the correct decision? That kind of thing."

"I have no answers," Sellia replied, shaking her head. "I wish I knew where they went or why. But I think we need to trust them, that they are doing what they believe is the right thing. Come, we have a long way to travel before we settle down for the night."

Sellia rose and went to the horses, calling the taragusii to saddle up. Ilan scuttled over to his sister.

"I know what you're thinking, sis. Don't do it. If you go, I'll have to follow. We cannot be separated. The idea terrifies me, the silence if our bond is cut. If we go, mother will be devastated and come after us. You'll put the entire family in danger. I need to find out who I am, what my abilities are. I need to prepare for the roles that await us. It's too soon."

Senzia looked at him and put a hand on his shoulder. "I must make my own decision and you, yours. If I go and you decide to continue to the Markwin Forest, I will support you. But please, consider this: *Ahdahr* never had the opportunity to train properly with one teacher. Circumstances always spurred him to act for the general good before he could finish.

"I am angry—very angry—with Mharina, and even with *Ahdahr*, helpless though he is. I agree with the prince. Their actions have likely signed death warrants for thousands of soldiers, among them possibly Rhoddan and Pyre. I can't stop thinking about Pyre. You know how much I look up to her.

"I will never forgive *Ahdahr* or Mharina if she dies and they weren't there trying to prevent it. But, more importantly, I'll never forgive myself. Do you understand?"

Ilan pursed his lips but nodded. Then he rose and went to his horse. Senzia followed, but noticed her mother watching, a foreboding look on her face.

"We're being followed," Senzia called out, and the lead taragus stopped his strange steed. Their creatures resembled black horses, but they were scaled, and their necks stretched out like lizards'.

All four taragusii raised their reptilian heads, sniffing the air and licking their noses with their forked tongues. The lead taragus uncurled his two antennae, and they flickered in the air. They all shook their heads.

"It's nothing, Senzia," Sellia said.

"It *is*," Senzia snapped.

"Wolfheids," Ilan confirmed. "They're downwind."

Wolfheids, the mutated beasts from the Age of Mist and Shadow, had once been more man-like and moved freely among the races. But dark magic turned them into beasts, destined to prowl in packs around the deserts and mountains.

"How—"

"It doesn't matter right now," Senzia snapped again. "We need to move fast and find defensible shelter."

No one questioned them, not even the taragusii. They spurred their horses forward, all the time looking for shelter. The mountains ahead of them were still a way away, and they already doubted whether they would reach them before nightfall. Entering the mountain pass would offer a hiding place or at least somewhere to defend themselves. They soon heard the pounding of paws as the wolfheid pack closed on them.

"Ride through that grove," Ilan yelled.

"It'sss not the way," the lead taragus shouted back.

"Do it," Senzia screamed, not knowing what her brother planned.

They swerved toward the grove, allowing the wolfheid to close the gap. Snarling, wolf-like creatures, heads low, teeth bared, saliva dripping from powerful jaws rapidly replaced what had been a column of dust.

The taragusii were reforming behind the elves, ready to protect them, but Ilan shouted for them to ride ahead of him. "Do it!" he tried to command, but his voice squeaked.

They galloped through the spindly trees, following the one lone path. The wolfheids were closing on them. Hearing the beasts' growls made Senzia question her brother's judgment, but just then, her lungs filled with the smell of burning brush. She heard the crackle of flames and felt an intense heat on her back.

The air filled with smoke, forcing them to cough and their eyes to water. Now she could hear the wolfheids screaming in pain and terror. When they broke from the grove, they were no longer being followed. Sellia was at the front and began to slow.

"Keep going," Ilan called. "I have stopped them for only a short while. They will circle around the fire when they start to think again. But now we can reach the mountains. Go. We'll find a place like last time."

Senzia grinned to herself. Last time had not been a success. They had gone into caves to escape the taragusii and ended up walking right into the middle of their camp. But at least this time they made the beginning of the mountain range. It was beginning to get dark.

"First cave," Sellia cried. "We need to gather wood to keep them at bay."

It seemed to take forever to find a cave, and they could already hear the wolfheids' baying getting closer. They coaxed their horses and the taragusiis' mounts into the darkness. The taragusii and the twins scrambled to gather wood, and Sellia stood guard, her bow nocked and ready.

They did not light the fire, but waited. It was not long before they saw a growing number of pairs of bright yellow orbs. They could hear the growls now and sense the impatience and excitement the beasts felt.

"I should have a bow," Senzia said to her mother. "I've been practicing."

Sellia had nocked an arrow but did not draw the bowstring. She nodded. "It would be a big help," she replied. "And Ilan's plan was great. At least we can keep them in front of us."

As her mother said this, Senzia felt a chill go through her. She turned and saw her own look of dread on her brother's face. From inside the cave came a deep growl, and two big, red eyes appeared before them in the blackness.

Chapter 10

Senzia's heart leapt. Her father had come in his bear form to save them and would ferociously cut down the wolfheids.

"*Ahdahr?*" she called into the darkness.

The bear growled and lumbered cautiously forward. The taragusii moved to protect Senzia, but she signaled them back.

"*Ahdahr?*" she said again.

The bear, a brown grizzly, bared its teeth and shook its massive head vigorously. It began to rise on its hind legs but thought better of it, as the cave was not tall. Then it stared at the small elfe and, at that moment, Senzia knew it was not her father. She reached out with her mind.

Whoever you are, mighty bear, you must know the Great Grizzly. He is my ahdahr in two-legged form. Please, show him honor and fight for us. Feast on the wolfheids that trap us in this gorge.

The bear stared at her, grunted, and bared its teeth. Now Ilan's voice joined her. *We are part of your world, great bear—the cubs of the Great Grizzly. We, too, will one day claim our animal form and forge another chain in the ancient link.*

The bear looked from Senzia to Ilan and then back again. Then it raised its mighty muzzle and roared, shaking the rock walls and leaving their ears ringing. The *calhei* stepped aside, and the huge bear charged out of the cave.

Another roar was followed by snarls and yelps.

"Help him!" Ilan roared, and this time, no squeak betrayed his command.

The taragusii, axes and swords in hand, charged out of the cave. Senzia watched Sellia glide out and raise her bow, entranced as her mother's face transformed. The pain, the hurt, the anger all disappeared, and a smooth, focused expression took over as the beautiful, black-haired warrior-elfe that Senzia worshiped unleashed arrow after arrow in a fluid and deadly rhythm.

Ilan drew his thin, curved sword and raced at a wolfheid. Senzia held her breath, knowing that her brother had trained extensively with Master Sythen at Grogin. His first strike was somewhat erratic and wayward, but he nimbly skipped out of the path of his lunging adversary, flicking his blade in a deft arc that cut through the creature's neck.

He held the sword with two hands, and his footwork was fluent. She was admiring him when a second wolfheid jumped at him from above the cave. It was met by a crashing taragus that lunged in front of Ilan, and they rolled together to the ground. Ilan froze momentarily before he sprung at the two fighters, aimed, and pierced his sword into the wolfheid. He stood there, panting and protecting the taragus until it rose to stand by his side.

Around them, the battle raged. At its center, the bear leapt and bit and continually swatted with huge, clawed paws, roaring and raging. When its jaws closed around a wolfheid, the crunch was deafening, even above melee. Senzia saw its mouth frothing as it ducked and rolled, sending any wolfheid who successfully mounted its back flying into the throng.

One beast found itself flung in front of Senzia. It sprung to its feet and, even though it bared its teeth, it looked as surprised as she felt. She pulled her elven knife from its sheath. Though she had no discernable defense, she felt strangely calm—even detached from the confrontation.

The wolfheid rose on its hindquarters, towering over her, and lifted its front paws. Two rows of sharp claws extended, and it threw its head back and roared. Senzia flung her knife straight into its throat and then, without realizing what she was doing, stepped forward and pushed the air with both palms, sending her weight deep into the ground. The knife pushed further into the wolfheid. Fascinated, Senzia twisted her hands and pushed again. The knife followed her movement, twisting and burying deeper. She felt it slice through a cord, and the wolfheid, eyes bulging, collapsed in front of her. She put one foot on its huge muzzle and it took three attempts to yank the knife out. She felt blood trickling from her nose—or was it her mouth? She wiped it away and stared at the creature.

Neat! She heard her brother's voice in her head and smiled, rather proud of herself.

It was soon over, and Senzia left the cave entrance, her mouth open as she counted twenty, thirty, forty wolfheid carcasses. The bear limped past her back into his cave.

Thank you, she said, wordlessly.

You were so brave, noble friend, Ilan added.

Then Senzia saw that her mother was leaning over a still taragus, checking his pulse. Another taragus rose from his knees, his sword dripping with blood from another friend who needed to be put out of his misery. The fourth taragus lay a way off, lifeless and torn apart.

The surviving taragus joined Sellia. She looked up and shook her head. He said something that Senzia could not hear, and Sellia rose to join her children. Behind her mother's muscular form, Senzia saw the blade of the taragus rise, dripping with blood. Sellia reached out, and the two of them hugged.

Ilan had gone to the taragus. "I am sorry for your friends. They fought bravely and sacrificed their lives for my sister and me. It was a tragic but noble end."

Still hugging her mother, Senzia watched her brother. It occurred to her that perhaps seeing *Ahdahr* in his broken state provided Ilan with the subconscious impetus to grow up. A primitive instinct pushed him to become the dominant male of the family. Whatever it was, she was witnessing it for the first time—she who was so close to him, so connected.

She realized her mother was staring down at her. "What are you thinking?" Sellia asked. "Does the carnage upset you?"

Senzia considered sharing her thoughts about Ilan with her mother but decided against it. Sellia would just feel like another *calhei* was growing away from her. Senzia sighed.

"You were beautiful when you were focused on the fight," she said. "I can see why so many elves were in awe of you."

Sellia laughed and actually blushed a bit. "Your father couldn't look me in the eye when we met. Rhoddan reddened, even if I just asked him to pass a water skin." Then her smile faded. "We have all changed, all grown older."

"But it's inside you still. I saw it," Senzia heard herself say. She couldn't stop. "It's inside him, as well. I know it is. Give him time."

Her mother forced a smile and stroked Senzia's cheek. "I would disagree with you, Senzia, but I also doubted you when you were convinced he wasn't dead. Do you remember that discussion? I would be so happy for you to be right again, so very happy."

Chapter 11

s Sellia, Senzia, Ilan, and the one surviving taragus rode in tense silence, Ilan regarded the huge guard. He held himself erect, but his forked tongue licked his nose too often. Ilan realized he was a young taragusii soldier. The *calhei* had spent the best part of the last two years in the company of taragusii, primarily as their captives.

At first, Ilan had been terrified of them—especially Third Scale, who led the attack on Wycaan Island and kidnapped Ilan and his sisters. But time had brought him close to Third Scale, who was now dead, and he had sparred with some of the taragusii in Grogin.

"What is your name?" Ilan asked.

"Ssseventh."

"Seventh Scale?"

"I have yet to earn the title. But when I do, yessss, that will be my name."

"How do you earn the title?"

"Bravery, excccelenccce on a mission."

"You were very brave when we fought the wolfheids. Does that count?"

"No one sssaw."

"I did."

"You are *banta.*"

"I would actually be considered a young elf. I'm also a natural-born Wycaan, and so I deem you Seventh Scale."

The taragus licked his nose. "Thank you, but that'sss not enough."

"No problem. Senzia?"

Senzia turned her horse and sat erect. She offered a stern expression of one conveying judgment. "By the power vested in me as a natural-born Wycaan, I hereby decree that, within our company, you shall be known as Seventh Scale. When your mission is successfully completed, you shall thus be recommended as such to your commanders."

The taragus looked from one *calhei* to the other and shrugged. "Thank you…I think."

"I'm sorry about your friends, Seventh Scale," Ilan said. "It's hard to lose those we care about."

Seventh Scale nodded, his tongue flicking in and out. "One wasss my father."

Both *calhei* stopped their horses, forcing Sellia to do likewise. But the taragus shook his head. "We do not mourn thossse who fall fighting. It wasss a fine ending for him. I am sssure he isss proud."

"And you?" Senzia asked.

"I will proudly tell of hisss bravery." His tongue moved faster as he struggled with his next line. "But for now, I misss him. Even though it isss not taragusssii way."

"Maybe," Ilan said. "But we understand. We thought our father died and mourned him. It's very hard, no matter how well you hide it."

"Thanksss. Now let'sss ride ssso we can finisssh our mission and you can commend me to be Ssseventh Sssscale."

That night, they sat around a campfire, their bellies full from a doe that Sellia hunted. She cooked half of it over a fire gave the rest to Seventh Scale to eat raw. He finished most of it and now slept, snoring lightly, while Ilan stood guard.

"What is it, Senzia?" he asked, his back to the fire and his sister.

"Nothing," she replied.

"I can't turn around, or I'll lose my night vision, but if I could, I'd be glaring at you."

"I know."

"What is it, then?" he repeated.

"Pyre. She is fighting."

"Is she okay?"

"I think so."

"How do you know?" Sellia asked. "Are there others there?"

"I can only sense Wycaans, I think," Senzia replied. "I could sometimes sense Mharina before, which was weird at the time, but now we know why."

There was silence, and then Senzia sighed. "She's been fighting for a long time."

"Pyre is an excellent fighter. There are very few in Odessiya who could last against her." Sellia said. "Try not to worry for her."

"But I do worry for her. Pyre and I were—are—very close. She used to teach me things in secret."

"I know she did."

"How? Secret means…"

"She sought your father's permission when you persistently begged her to teach you."

"She did it because he told her to?" Senzia sounded so disappointed; Ilan was tempted to turn around. He could feel her emotions and knew how much she treasured her relationship with the elfe.

"No. I'm quite sure that's not how it happened," their mother replied. "She pushed for it and enjoyed being with you as much as you did her."

"Thank you," Senzia replied. "Still, I worry. She has not tested herself against the Ashen Elves. They must have some kind of magic, themselves. Otherwise, Prince Shayth would have driven them back with sheer numbers and the ferocity of the pictorians."

There was another long silence, broken only by the crackle of the last burning logs.

Ilan paced to keep alert while on guard. He knew his sister, knew what she was contemplating—or rather, what she was struggling with. He jumped when he turned to pace back. Senzia stood right beside him.

"We mustn't be apart," he snapped.

"It'll be very hard," she replied.

"I will follow you. You know that. I can always find you."

"You mustn't. One of us should train to full Wycaan potential."

"We *both* should, Senzia. Don't go."

She did not reply, and they began pacing together. Ilan glanced over to see if his mother was awake. She was lying down, but he couldn't be sure she wasn't listening. He lowered his voice.

"When?"

"I haven't decided. I was actually planning to go to the Markwin Forest. But if Pyre is fighting—if Mharina and our *ahdahr* are not helping her…" She trailed off and sighed again. "I can't leave her. If *he* taught us anything, it's that we don't leave our friends behind. That's why I'm so angry with them."

"Mharina and *Ahdahr*?" Ilan asked.

"Yes. We've talked about this. She has no right to—"

"But what if she is doing it for the greater good? What if her plan is to help *Ahdahr*? Together, they could surely repel the Ashen Elves."

"At what price? Pyre? Maugwen? Montclair? The prince? They're his friends, our family. Pyre, especially."

"I don't want to be separated from you, Senzia. It scares me so."

"You're stronger than you think or let on. Go to sleep, Ilan. It's my turn to guard."

"Will I see you in the morning?"

"Good night, Ilan."

CHAPTER 12

Marina did not ask her father how he knew of the secret passage the people around Grogin used to visit their families working in the castle, and he did not volunteer the information. Even now, with Grogin far behind, they did not speak. A chilly breeze cut through the darkness, and they both seemed content to focus on watching their step as Mharina set a brisk pace. The only sound penetrating the night was the click of her staff on the ground as it sang her rhythm.

Mharina's hand fit so comfortably between two of the carved runes that wound their way up the entire length of the staff. She had taken the staff from the spirit of Shadona, the founder of the sorceress's order, against her will, and she still felt the intensity and guilt from doing so. But she was convinced the staff was meant for her and held a crucial part of her destiny. Certainly, it had elicited fear when Ithea saw it, but she was still unable to defeat him with it.

She glanced back at her father. He had defeated the powerful sorcerer, heeding the last sacrificial words of Denalion, the ancient Dreamwalker of the West, by transforming into his grizzly form. He had reached into this magic, driven by the desire to save his daughter's life, when Ithea had threatened to decapitate Mharina just as he had her teacher.

She pushed Sa'gola from her mind. The pain was still so raw, and she forced herself to think about her *ahdahr*. Seanchai had been such a lively and warm father, constantly hugging his *calhei* and telling them stories about how he, their mother, and friends had freed Odessiya. Often, he led them on adventures around Wycaan Island acting out these tales.

He had been particularly lavish with his attention to Mharina, and she treasured every moment together. The demand for his presence in the newly emancipated land, however, meant this was somewhat of a rarity.

She turned and glanced at him. He followed her, but his eyes revealed that he was in a different place and time. Was it one he shared with her? Or her mother? There was nothing in his expression, and, even when she turned to look forward again, it haunted her.

She sighed and wrapped her cloak tighter, though it was not cold. Why was she doing this? She and her *ahdahr* should have gone to confront the Ashen Elves. It was the patriotic and responsible thing to do. Searching for Abel, her Mushroom Man, was not a good enough reason to disobey the prince, even if she loved him.

Abel, fearful of the magic his mother and brother wielded, had fled when he saw Mharina fuse her Wycaan and sorceress' magic. He hated what had become of Ithea and how the magic controlled him. In his mind, it was the magic that compelled Ithea to kill their mother. Abel had made it clear from the start that he would brook no contact with magic, even as he was drawn to Sa'gola, and now Mharina.

Hers was a fool's errand—the desperate wishes of a spurned lover—and her timing was atrocious. She felt wretched, but then she wondered what would have happened if they had gone straight to Shayth. Her father would, most likely, have been arrested and possibly executed. The prince was famous for his harsh, unforgiving temper. And she would discover that possessing great potential power was not the same as wielding it.

She learned this lesson from Ithea, and Sa'gola paid for it with her life. Mharina felt a sob erupt and escape her lips. Her father's arm pulled her around, and she stared at his concerned frown.

"I'm fine," she muttered. "We've no time to talk now."

She was right. Though they walked at a Wycaan's pace, and with enduring stamina, there was an angry assassin probably leaving Grogin just about now on horseback. They climbed up through a mountain pass and stopped around midday. In the silence they heard the sound of galloping horses.

"There is a tunnel through folded time near here," she said. "I—I should be able to see it."

The horses were getting louder, and Seanchai and Mharina could hear the rattle of armor and weapons. But the portal was…where was it? Sa'gola had weaved several and showed her apprentice how to summon and collapse them. Had they disappeared with Sa'gola's demise? Was she simply a pale shadow of her teacher?

"Why can't I see it?" She heard the panic in her voice.

"Ground yourself, Mharina." Her father was calm. "It's here if you say so. Focus on your breathing."

She tried as an arrow flew by, missing them by several feet. She couldn't complete her deep breathing. She was panicking. What if the tunnels had collapsed with her teacher's death? They would have to fight, and she feared how her father would react to killing more people.

"It's over here," Seanchai said, and offered a hand. She took it and almost instantly felt herself calm down as his smile bathed her and the shimmering tunnel appeared.

They stepped inside, feeling the cold shiver and hearing only muffled curses as the tunnel collapsed behind them.

CHAPTER 13

Everything felt different when they stepped out of the tunnel. They were far from Grogin now and had only to pass through the mountain range they were currently in and then enter the valley that led to the mining town where her Mushroom Man lived. They would sleep in a cave nearby and reach the town late the next day or the day after.

They walked for quite a while as Mharina sought out a cave with a mineral pool. She learned well from her teacher to take advantage of the calm and relaxation gleaned from such a natural treasure.

With no horses to tether and groom, they entered into the cave and followed a rocky path downward. The heat was quickly upon them, and not long after, they smelled the mineral vapor wafting up from the pools.

Seanchai seemed pleased with her choice and threw his bag down, casting off his clothes. Mharina stared. She had gone swimming naked in Lake Mhari countless times with her father, but that had been a long time ago. She was relieved that he left his underclothes on. He seemed to sense her unease and blushed.

He made a clumsy entry into the water indicating with comical exaggeration that his eyes were closed. She nonetheless removed her own clothes quickly and with her back to him. Like him, Mharina wore her undergarments and submerged quickly into the water.

"You can open your eyes," she said, laughing.

He smiled. "It's better this way, for you're no longer a *calhei*. I'm sorry if I embarrass you."

"It's more the sudden realization that I'm no longer who I once was," she replied, and he nodded.

"For me, too. You are still the little terror who comes to me in glimpses of memory. Almost every flashback is of you or the twins."

"And mother?"

He grimaced. "No. I only see the pain I inflict upon her. There is another elfe whose memory fills me only with guilt, and then resentment that I cannot keep such memories preserved as they should be." Seanchai's eyes sprung open. "I'm sorry. I forget to whom I speak. I—"

"You speak to your daughter, an elfe!"

"True. And you don't deserve to hear of the chasm that exists between your parents. Please, if you are ready, tell me about your relationship with Sa'gola."

"Maybe I shouldn't talk to a dead elf about his murderer."

It was a poor joke. Seanchai dutifully smiled, and Mharina grimaced. She submerged under the water and, though she could breathe if she wanted to, she held her breath. She needed to be normal—a grieving daughter talking to her father.

When she broke the surface, the words tumbled out. She spoke of how wise and learned Sa'gola was. She told of her strengths and insecurities, her love and loyalty, her fears, and the barriers she had built around her. She told of Sa'gola's abuse at the hands of Ithea and how only her love for Mharina had driven her back to confront him.

Mharina's words mixed with tears, and sometimes she paused to gain control of herself. When she finished, she stared up at him.

"She was sorry she tried to kill you. She hated the pain it brought me, and, as she got to know you through Ilan, Senzia, Maugwen, and me, she wished she had the opportunity to know you, herself."

"I wish I could have gotten to know her, too," Seanchai replied. "If only because she made my daughter so happy."

Mharina stared at him, seeking duplicity, irony, or smugness. But all she saw was the sadness he felt for her. Suddenly, she found herself wrapped in his strong arms. He held her tightly, pulling her head and body to him. She shuddered and sobbed. His huge, muscular frame offered shelter, and she clung to him. Their near-nakedness meant nothing now. She sought only the safety of her *ahdahr*, of the Wycaan Master—no, the elf—who truly knew her and loved her and her siblings unconditionally. Wave after wave of tears and sorrow poured out of her. He lifted her out of the water, wrapped her in her sleeping blanket, and held her again as he sat against a rock. She burrowed into his security.

After a long while, she sat up, wiping her puffy eyes and sniffling. "I'm so sorry. I thought I had…"

"It takes a long time," her father replied, "sometimes it never fades. But you don't need to apologize. Ever."

She looked up at him. There was a slight smile on his face. "What are you thinking? Be honest."

"This will sound selfish," he said, "but for a few moments, I found profound solace in your pain. Apparently, there is something I can be good at—being a father. I felt strangely content. I'm sorry for the self-indulgence. It caught me unaware."

"You don't need to apologize. Ever." Mharina grinned as she repeated his words back to him.

Seanchai smiled back. "I'm glad we shared this."

They sat together in comfortable silence, chewing absently on dried meat and other goods they had pilfered from the kitchen at Grogin. Mharina watched her father as he gazed into the pool.

"What are you thinking now?" she asked.

"Do you see the bottom of the pool?"

Mharina shook her head.

"It's there. We both know it is, but we cannot see it. Occasionally, there is a shimmer in the water, and we see a shadow, a darker hue, and a hint at its depths. The bottom is there but out of reach. We want to see it because it contains and defines the pool.

"I need to know the depths of my memory so I can use them as a foundation for raising myself above the water. Yet, they remain elusive and disconcerting. It prevents me from enjoying the present and deciding what I should be doing.

"Worst of all, I know my inability to stand upon my memories means others flounder in the water and could drown because of me."

Mharina stared into the pool. "I'm so sorry," she said. "When you do glimpse the bottom of your pool, I'll be there to help you claim it."

She wondered if that was a promise she would be able to keep.

Chapter 14

People avoided the two hooded, heavily armed travelers. Those who could moved their horses or oxen pulled wagons to the side of the road. Those who could not murmured their apologies and watched tentatively, no doubt sighing with relief once the travelers passed.

Compared to the farmers and traders, Seanchai was huge, and he led the way. Mharina, following in his wake, saw that her father's head faced straight ahead at all times. He never acknowledged those who tried to communicate, which projected a sinister and uncompromising aura that proved most effective.

As a young *calhei*, she was obsessed with stories of the Wycaan Master. She would beg her mother, Pyre, Denalion, or any outside visitor to regale her with tales of his courage and prowess. Sellia would caution the enthusiasm, stressing that Seanchai was kind, forgiving, and always seeking peace. It was hard for a young *calhei*, deprived of her father's presence and grasping at strands of stories, to imagine both sides of his character. When they were together, he encapsulated everything her mother had described, and he lavished love and affection on his three *calhei*.

Now, though, she had glimpsed his Wycaan side. His transformation into the Great Grizzly had been so abnormal that it was hard to comprehend, even though it happened right in front of her. But she felt the way he dealt with her panic when she could not find the portal Sa'gola built to be even more insightful.

She had no idea what Wycaan powers her father had intuitively used, but she knew they worked only because he had kept a calm and focused mind. She recalled how, when others had praised him for defeating the former Emperor a number of times, Seanchai had been quick to point out that it was due to outthinking his adversary, who was more powerful and experienced than he was.

Mharina was so caught up in her thoughts that she almost bumped into her father. He had stopped, and she could sense his tension. Confronting them was a hastily erected barricade where armed men inspected goods. Apparently, these men seemed happy to take a share of the goods they inspected, as a large pile of wares was heaped at the side. The men all wore purple sashes or ribbons, though their clothes were otherwise scruffy.

An argument broke out, and two of the men pushed an old man into his cart and pulled off three crates of chickens. When a younger man stepped forward in defense of the old man, a sentry drew a long knife and held it to his throat.

"Stop this," Mharina called out, and stepped around her father. "What is the meaning of this?"

"We serve the Order of the Purple Lady, girl," a soldier replied. "We check all who enter the town to prevent vagabonds and other undesirables from entering."

"Very noble," Seanchai said, his voice grim. "And do you steal from poor farmers by the same authority?"

"Watch yeh mouth, peasant. Mind we don't take your pretty girl as tax for you entering the—"

His sentence finished in a gurgle as Mharina grabbed him by the throat. She had moved forward in a blink, and her hood had fallen back. "What Purple Lady?" she hissed. "The Purple Lady died in Grogin fighting the evil sorcerer Ithea. On whose authority do you dare foul her memory?"

The man managed little more than a squeal. His brave colleagues had their swords out but were not closing in. Perhaps the huge, wild-eyed elf, crouched with two gleaming swords at the ready, held them in place as they looked from one to the other.

"Mharina," Seanchai said quietly. "Loosen your grip on the man. He can't answer your question."

She did, and the man staggered backwards, clutching his throat. "Y-you c-can't do—"

"Oh, I can; believe me. And I can do much worse. I was the Purple Lady's apprentice, and I have surpassed even her considerable power."

Mharina was immediately ashamed of such a brash statement. It might be true, but she lacked her teacher's experience and wisdom… and maturity. And besides, it felt just plain disrespectful.

The man looked to his friends, but there was no help there.

"Well," he gulped. "If you're her apprentice, I guess you should pass." He glanced up at Seanchai. "Your bodyguard, too."

"There will be no more tax collecting until I have spoken with whoever is in charge," Mharina said, and walked through. "Come, bodyguard," she said without looking back. "Be quick about it."

The soldier scrambled aside and again stared at his friends. Seanchai moved forward, lifted the barricade that three men might struggle to move, and threw it beyond the side of the road. Then he followed the Purple Lady's apprentice.

The town looked run down during Mharina's first visit, but now it had considerably deteriorated. The bustling market was half empty—many stalls were bare, and there were very few shoppers. She glanced back at her father's bland expression. He had not seen this place before and had nothing to compare it to. The miners congregated further into the center where the bars and hostels were, and this area had felt like the center for the locals.

Mharina stopped, momentarily disorientated. She was looking for the old couple who had adopted her Mushroom Man. When she was no longer sure if she had passed their stall, she tried to stop someone for directions. No one responded. With eyes cast down, they scurried past her. When she grabbed a woman's arm, the poor woman screamed in panic, and Mharina let go, shocked.

"Abel?" an old man's voice asked from the shadows.

Mharina turned.

"No. But I am Mharina. Is Abel not here?"

The old man was bent, and he wore a threadbare blanket over his head. He looked each way before shuffling past her. "No, praise the Goddess. Follow me, but keep your distance."

He moved so slowly that Mharina had trouble maintaining distance between them. She found reasons to stop—to tie her boots or exchange a quiet word with her bodyguard—and all the time, she sought out who might be watching them.

They were there, three of them, in the shadows. When the old man made his way between two stalls into a sunken hut made of clay and straw, she hesitated about following him.

He disappeared inside and came back out when he saw she had not followed him. He held a jar full of yellow mushroom powder. "You won't buy this? Such a price! You won't find anyone else with the chanterelle powder. It keeps your skin smooth and young, milady.

"No? Come, come. I have other goods for a beautiful young woman." He took her arm in his spindly hand and led her inside.

"Stay in the entrance," Mharina said to her bodyguard, and Seanchai took up position just outside the doorway.

"You must go, my dear. Abel would not want you here. Why did you return?"

"To find him. He ran from me. I—I love him. We need to talk."

"He's in the mountains and forests, I pray—far from this madness. This imposter knows he served the real Purple Lady and already tried to kill him. They killed my dear wife, you know. Spirits. The only reason I don't join her is in case he returns. I promised her, see, that I'd wait, and, if he came, tell him that she loved him like a son. The brightest moment of her day was when he called her *mother*."

"I'm so sorry for your loss."

"Yes. Yes. She had the bone eater. It was painful and getting worse. Even his mushrooms were no longer helping. I hope she rests in comfort with her ancestors." He tried to smile. "Let us talk of you. How can I help?"

"Tell me where he went," Mharina requested.

The old man shook his head. "I don't know. I begged him not to tell me. If they wanted to, it wouldn't be hard to torture it from an old man. But if you find him, tell him what my wife said. Ask him to remember her as his mother and me as his father. Good luck. Follow the mushrooms, my dear."

"I will," Mharina said, and turned. Then she turned back and asked, "Who is this imposter?"

"She has powers like the Purple Lady did. The miners don't dare come into town, and everyone suffers for it. Her soldiers beat us and take what they want. We never had much, but now people starve."

"Where is she?"

"The mayor's residence, I guess. He…he isn't there."

"I will pay her a visit."

"Keep your staff close," the old man said. "She has one, too, and she's very good with it."

Chapter 15

"Buy something from him," Seanchai whispered as Mharina stepped outside.

"I don't need your charity," the old man said.

"No. But you need our business. We are being watched," Seanchai whispered. "What's this?" He asked in a normal voice, as he picked up a burlap pouch with broken gray mushrooms inside.

"That is the trumpet mushroom. Drink a tea of it, and you will feel restored. A man might rediscover his appetite, and I don't mean for food. It is not for women, though. The lady should not take it."

"How much?"

"The whole sack? I would sell that for three draktans, but you don't... Thank you." The old man opened his hands, which Seanchai had enclosed around coins. There were at least a dozen draktans. Mharina picked up the bag and stopped where the shadows could see.

"You carry this," she said in a loud voice as they passed a watching shadow, and handed it to Seanchai. "I need a bath. Let's go to the inn."

They walked out of the market into a wider street, and Seanchai caught up to her.

"Why stay? If the man you seek isn't here, let's leave," he said.

Mharina turned and put a hand on his arm. "I'm my father's daughter. Do you really think I'd walk away from such injustice?"

"Very noble." The Wycaan smiled at her. "I'd like to get to know your father."

"I would like you to, as well," Mharina sighed.

They made their way to the main square, absent of the usual crowds of boisterous miners enjoying a few days off. There were still foot traffic and wagons, but everyone seemed subdued and anxious to reach their destinations quickly and unnoticed.

Mharina led them into the main guesthouse and immediately felt the change in atmosphere. The bar area was packed with men wearing the purple sash, all of them well armed and enjoying their libations. A young man leaned over the counter and openly leered at her, his eyes roving down her body and back up.

"Ain't seen you before," he said. "Whatcha want?"

"A room," Mharina answered. "Two beds. We will eat dinner up there, and I'll require hot water for a bath."

"I 'ave a room, I think, but ain't gonna be no room service, see. None o' the girls work here 'cept in the morning, when they come t' clean an' cook fer the day, see. You can take your meal down 'ere."

Mharina looked around again, remembering how Sa'gola had dealt with being told there were no rooms when last they had come. "Call the owner," she said. "I will speak with him."

"Ain't gonna happen either, see. 'e's kinda indisposed right now."

"Where is he?"

"In 'is bed, I fink. 'e don't come out much, not since a few o' them soldiers beat 'im up, see. Got real ugly, 'cause old Healy stopped 'em playing wiv one of the girls, see. Knocked 'im 'ard an' only stopped when the Purple Lady 'erself come in, see. Now 'e don't leave 'is room once them come in to eat and drink away the evening. Drinks 'ard 'imself, see. Ain't good, but at least 'e's alive. Now. You want that room?"

Mharina nodded. He gave her the key and directions. It was near the room they had stayed in last time. Seanchai leaned over the counter.

"When does this Purple Lady come here?"

"Whenever she wants." The boy leaned away. "Ain't no need. She 'as the 'ouse of the Mayor, see."

Seanchai leaned over even more. He took the boy's hand and put a gold coin in it. "There is a second one if we leave tomorrow undisturbed. I won't ask you not to tell our room number, because if they torture you, you'll squeal. So be clear with what else you tell: anyone who opens our door will be skewered…if they're lucky.

"How do you plan to handle this?" Seanchai asked quietly, leaning over the small table.

It was hard to hear anything in the boisterous atmosphere. A juggler—quite a good one, Mharina thought—was being heckled. It was not clear why he was incurring the wrath of the soldiers until, as one voice, they broke into cheers and whistles.

A young black skinned woman with beautiful brown eyes, took the stage. She wore flowing purple robes, sheer and layered to reveal skin at different angles. Her hair was long and black, curly and shining.

Two men sat at the side of the stage and drummed a beat. One drum was long and sat between one man's legs. Its sound was deep and rich, which contrasted with the lighter sound of the smaller, round drum the second man held in his arm.

The woman began to dance in intricate movements, and Mharina saw she wore bells on her wrists and ankles. Every pair of eyes in the crowded room followed her, and the elfe began to wonder how a drunken mob might react when she stopped.

But the dancer did not stop. She kept a steady rhythm with a smile etched upon her face that Mharina began to realize was fixed and forced. She turned to tell her father and gasped when she saw his expression.

Seanchai seemed transfixed by the dancer; his eyes were wide, and his mouth hung open. Mharina was shocked and infuriated. Surely he saw that the elfe was not here freely. Every few moments, she looked over behind the drummers to a large man with cold, blue eyes and a flowing white mustache. He stood with his arms folded across his chest and a scowl on his face as he watched her. Behind him were two huge, heavily armed guards who periodically scanned the crowd.

When the dancer caught his gaze, the blue-eyed man just nodded curtly. One time, he looked from the stage to Mharina, and their eyes met. She forced herself not to look away, though her eyes watered with the intensity.

Mharina finally broke off. The dancer had stopped and was sipping water and wiping herself with a towel. The spell that held the room was broken. Men jumped about, ordering more drinks, and young servers ran to fill orders.

The elfe turned to her father and leaned closer. "Did you enjoy that?" she snapped. "A young girl forced to dance for her master's wealth. She's terrified. Can't you sense that?"

Seanchai's eyes were watery, and tears trickled down his cheek.

"What is it?" she asked.

"That's how your mother looked when I first saw her. So graceful. She could hold the whole camp under a spell."

"You remember?"

"Yes. Bits and pieces. It feels as if I could reach out and touch or smell her. I wish I could tell her."

Mharina's anger faded, and she took his hands in hers. "It's not too late—not when you're in love."

He forced a smile. "Before I left, she told me that she does not want me to return. I cause her too much pain, and I know she is right. If I live through whatever is happening, I'm not to seek her out, even if she is with the twins."

"She didn't mean—"

"She needs to start anew with an elf who is not damaged. I understand and will honor her request."

"Why? Go back and tell her you remember. Tell her that you want her. I don't underst—"

"I can't." He shook his head. "I swore an oath. I said the binding word—*Ashbar.*"

CHAPTER 16

The light that surrounded them disappeared. The two men guarding the dancer and her owner now towered over the table. They grabbed Seanchai and swept him out of his chair. The man with the moustache sat down in the vacant seat and leaned on the table. He smiled and it sent chills through her.

"Are you bound to that man?" he asked.

Mharina, still shocked by her father's revelation, just nodded, and the man waved a hand without looking behind him. His guards dragged Seanchai—who didn't struggle—outside. They would get a shock soon, Mharina thought while the man held her attention with his stare.

"You won't have to worry about him, the brute. Elves don't know how to treat a fine woman. Did you see my princess on the stage? Isn't she beautiful? I give her good food, clothes, and riches. No man touches her without regretting it. I protect her.

"Every couple of nights, she dances and delights the customers in one tavern or another. She loves to dance, and they gladly shower her with money. It is a wonderful life. You have a good body—one too delicate for weapons—and I bet you can dance, too. Imagine, her black hair and your white, entwining to the rhythm of the drums. I can make you very comfortable, put money aside for when you grow old. It would be far more comfortable than following a scraggly elf."

"I'll think about it," Mharina said, considering this to be the most diplomatic response. "Thank you."

"I never take no for an answer," he said, and laughed, a sound as cold as his eyes.

"Tell me." Mharina leaned in close. "If she decided to leave you and go her own way, would you let her?"

"Why would she do that? She loves to dance, to be worshipped by every man in the room. It's a kind of magic. Do you believe in magic?" Thankfully, he did not wait for an answer. "I bet you do. She would never—"

"Of course she wouldn't," Mharina persisted. "But if she did, would you let her go?"

The man's cold, blue eyes provided a clear answer. Mharina leaned back in her chair and glanced at the door. She suddenly worried for her father, but he reappeared at the entrance, only slightly more bedraggled than usual. She almost grinned but stopped herself and leaned in.

"Have you ever heard of the Purple Lady?"

"Of course." The man's smile vanished.

"I'm in town because I have business with her. Now, if you'll excuse me, my bodyguard awaits."

The man turned around, a look of surprise on his face. When he looked back at Mharina, she thrust the point of her staff under his chin. She could feel the runes stir, and a brief flash of orange power flared. The man's eyes bulged. Mharina leaned in.

"Don't get up on my account and certainly not before I walk outside. I will meet your dancer here tomorrow morning for breakfast…without you. If she does not turn up, I will come looking for you, and my bodyguard will be the least of your problems. He just took out your two bears without breaking a sweat, and I can do the same to him. Thank you for the business offer. Pray I do not come with a counter offer."

She rose, looked over at the dancer, who had been watching, and nodded slowly. Then she walked past Seanchai, who followed her outside. The two bodyguards were just helping each other to their feet, swaying unsteadily. Mharina walked up to them, hooked her staff around one's neck and grabbed the other in the same spot. Then she cracked their heads together.

"Don't mess with my father," she said, and continued walking down the street. "Me, a dancer?" she laughed to herself, and tried a jig.

Chapter 17

Mharina felt comfortable in the darkness. The streets were empty, and anyone staggering along at the end of a night of drinking was still sober enough to give this tall lady with the staff and her heavily armed bodyguard plenty of space.

She led Seanchai past the well where she first heard her Mushroom Man tell a story to children and into the square at the center of town. The boy at the hotel desk told them the mayor's house was just off the square. Two guards sat outside the main building, and when they saw Mharina and Seanchai, they stood up. One turned and called something up the stairs to the entrance of the building.

The two guards approached and stood a few feet away from each other. They wore old chainmail and the purple sash. Each held a pike and had swords strapped to their belts. Hilts of other blades protruded from their boots and belts.

Mharina stopped and waited for them to speak, but neither did. She glanced back at her father, who showed no emotion. Then she looked around the square and saw an opulent house just off to their right. It had a low wall and elegant brass gates.

"Good evening, gentlemen," she said, and nodded. Then she turned and began walking toward the house.

A dozen more men appeared and fanned out, blocking their way to the house. Evidently, this was the right abode, Mharina mused.

"State your business," one man demanded, his chest puffed out with inflated authority.

"Do people need a reason for a stroll before bed?" Mharina asked.

"In this part of town, they do, young lady. This is a peaceful city. We don't like heavily armed strangers walking the streets late at night. They're rarely out for a stroll."

Mharina turned to Seanchai. She had not asked whether he thought they should come here now. She had just wanted to escape the tavern. Perhaps this was a mistake.

"Then we shall return to our room," she said, facing the officer. "We mean you no harm. Good night."

She turned and began to walk back the way they had come.

"I think it's too late for that," the officer said. "Stand where you are."

"We have broken no law," Mharina replied, turning back. "We'll be on our way, and you may continue to bravely guard the deserted streets."

She turned again and began to walk. The man drew his sword, which produced a long rasping sound as it left its scabbard. She stopped.

"You'll come with us," the officer said.

"Says who?"

"The authority of the purple sash," he replied. "I think we need to have a chat."

"And if I refuse?" Mharina replied, injecting some steel into her tone. "We don't wish to harm you. You are simple minions following your lady's orders."

"Mharina," Seanchai whispered, "do not provoke him."

"We'll be on our way now," she said, mustering more respect. "Good night, sir."

She turned and began to walk. The officer harrumphed. "I said wait," he yelled, and charged at her. Mharina swung around and thrust the end of her staff forward. It connected with his chest. His feet continued their momentum and rose in front of him, and he grunted and fell to the ground, gasping for breath. The other men shuffled closer, unsure of who should lead the attack.

"You are not soldiers," Seanchai called out as he drew his Win Dao swords. "You're no match for either of us alone and especially not the two of us together. Think carefully about your next move. It might be your last."

The men just stood there. Without leadership, they were confused about what to do.

"There'll be no bloodshed," a woman's voice said from behind the men. "Sheathe your weapons."

The men did so and parted to allow a medium-sized woman through to face Mharina. The woman's straight black hair was streaked with what Mharina thought was purple, but she couldn't see well in the darkness. There was something chillingly familiar about this woman. She looked like Sa'gola, but different.

"Are you the one they call the Purple Lady?" Mharina asked.

The woman crossed her arms across her ample chest. There were tattoos along her thick, firm forearms.

"I *am* the Purple Lady. Who might you be?"

"My name is Mharina. I served as apprentice to the real Purple Lady."

"The *real* Purple Lady? You refer to my sister, Sa'gola? Your visit is in vain, my dear. I'm so sorry to inform you that she fell. Sa'gola is dead."

"How do you know?" Seanchai asked before Mharina could respond.

"In ways you can't understand, young man." The woman smiled at him but immediately looked back at Mharina. "You may stay the night, but then you must leave. Do not try and enter her domain. I did not succeed, and, if I know my sister, there are plenty of traps in place to keep us out."

"When you say sister, what exactly do you mean?" Mharina asked.

"If you were truly close to her, you would know the answer to that question. Good night."

The woman turned to go.

"By what right do you hold this town in fear?" Mharina called out.

"Be gone, child," the woman replied over her shoulder. "Out of respect for my sister, I'm allowing you to leave in peace."

Mharina took a step forward, but Seanchai held her arm.

"No," he said. "Let's talk first. I have no desire to kill these men. They're no less victims than the townsfolk."

Mharina nodded and began to walk away from the square. Two men followed at a distance, making no attempt to hide themselves. Mharina was not happy that this purple imposter would discover where they were sleeping.

Apparently, her father was having the same thoughts, as he called for her to join him and enter another tavern. The place was the opposite from where they were staying. It was dark and had a low-beamed roof. A thin layer of straw was strewn on the floor.

They settled at a small table in the corner and hunched together. There were only five other patrons, each in his own space. The two men following them entered.

"I'm not sure how to throw them off our scent," Seanchai said. "There are hardly many places to stay in this town. Perhaps we should leave tonight."

"What?" Mharina was surprised. "I have an account to settle with this imposter and breakfast with that poor dancer."

Seanchai smiled. When Mharina questioned why, he laughed. It was apparently a strange sound in this tavern, judging by the stares from the other men. He leaned forward. "We are so alike. I feel I was exactly the same, unable to walk away from an injustice. Still." He glanced around and lowered his voice. "We need a plan. Could this woman really be your teacher's sister?"

"I don't think so. Sa'gola was found starving and alone as a child and rescued by her teacher, Dina."

Two more men with purple sashes entered the tavern and took up positions by the back door and at a table near the Wycaans. Another four entered and stood by the door. The barkeep stared at them, a look of fear on his face. The other patrons all decided it was time for bed and staggered out.

Then the woman who called herself the Purple Lady entered and walked over to their table. The barman raced over and placed a shiny goblet in front of her.

"My compliments, milady. I'm honored you come here to drink. Can I get—"

The woman dismissed him with a wave of her hand and turned to Mharina. "Perhaps your bodyguard might find another table?"

"He stays," Mharina said. "But as long as you're only here to talk, I guarantee your safety."

The woman let out a throaty laugh. Her chest heaved, causing the purple beads and red stone strung around her neck to jiggle.

"I have another half-dozen men outside. I don't feel threatened."

"That might prove a costly mistake," Mharina said, her voice cold. "Now, tell me: Who are you, really?"

The woman smiled, glanced around the dark room, and then subtly brushed her hair back to reveal pointed ears. "I am one of you," she whispered. "Like I said, I don't feel threatened."

ChApter 18

" I also wear heavy makeup, my dear, to hide my ashen face. No sense in scaring these puny humans. So, you see, I have more than just a bunch of brawny men to do my bidding."

"You're an Ashen Elf?" Seanchai asked.

"And you're a bodyguard?" The elfe arched her eyebrows. "It is late, and we all want a good night's sleep. Let us be honest with each other. My name is Synwyn, and I left my people to be the mistress of the Master."

"The Emperor consorted with an elfe?" Seanchai asked, knowing his adversary's racist values.

Synwyn chuckled. "Most males are attracted to the exotic and unattainable. Only, when you're in his position, everyone is attainable. At first, he showered me with love and romance. As I grew older and he didn't, I fell from favor and was all but forgotten.

"When your teacher came into his life, I hated her, seeing her as a younger competitor. But, with time, she fascinated me, and I eventually loved her. I shadowed her, tried to enter her home, and begged her to apprentice me.

"She scorned me and never allowed me to get close. But I'm an Ashen Elfe and used my own tricks and tools to learn what I could without her knowing. Eventually, she discovered and banished me from these parts. I returned when I heard of her demise. I thought that, if I took her place, I would continue to learn about her. That's the truth. What is your connection to her?"

Mharina spoke of her time with Sa'gola, detailing the rescue at the Tutan ambush, their life at Grogin, how she killed Mharina's father and took the young elfe as an apprentice in return for rescuing her mother and friends, her apprenticeship, and the final confrontation with the Emperor.

Tears fell down Mharina's cheeks, and she stopped frequently to sip her wine. When that was finished, she sipped from Synwyn's cup. It felt good to talk about her teacher, the woman she had so loved and idolized. Her father sat in silence, listening intently and occasionally resting a hand on her arm.

They sat in silence for a while, and then Synwyn spoke. "So, what now?"

"Why do you oppress the people here?" Seanchai asked. "Mharina talks of this place as a tough but functioning town. It's hard for us to walk away from people living in fear."

"I have a good life here with people who fear me," Synwyn said. What can I say? It works. Besides, if I was to leave, where would I go?"

"Back to your people?"

Synwyn smiled and shook her head. "I broke every sacred law when I left that captive world. I consorted with others—humans and pale elves, as we call them. Going back has not been an option for me for a long time, and, in truth, I find the option…claustrophobic. I've been away too long—been free for so long—that I could not return even if I was accepted."

"They are no longer trapped," Mharina said. "Either the Emperor or Ithea released them. They wage war on the armies of Odessiya. We will go north soon and assist the prince."

Synwyn did not hide her surprise at this turn of events. She frowned. "Still, I cannot return. I won't wage war on my kin *or* help them. They are driven by a desire for revenge on the pale elves, on your people. A terrible injustice centuries ago has eaten away at my people's souls, instilled itself in our bones and blood. It is frightening and tragic."

"Come with us, then," Seanchai said, ignoring his daughter's glare. "Perhaps we can find a way not to defeat them, but to absorb them into an alliance."

"Alliance!" Synwyn harrumphed. "I hope you make a better bodyguard than you do a strategist, dreamer."

Seanchai smiled. Mharina was bursting to tell Synwyn with whom she spoke, but something held her back. She sensed her father would not want his secret known.

"Perhaps," he said. "But I reserve the right to keep trying to persuade you. Leave this place and return go to Grogin. There are taragusii there, but no one commands. Wait for our call and consider it well when it comes. There are always options to fighting."

Synwyn stared at him. "Who are you?" she said.

"That is a good question," he replied, rising to leave. "I ask myself the same thing."

Mharina glanced at her father as they ate breakfast the following morning. She had woken a couple of times during the night when a floorboard creaked outside their door or an altercation erupted in the street below. Each time, she found her father awake.

Now, they sat opposite each other with a steaming pot of oat gruel between them. Seanchai had filled his bowl, but she was not aware that he had eaten more than a mouthful or two. The distant expression on his face as he stared out the greasy window suggested he was far away. She looked around for the dancer from the night before. Neither she, nor the ice-eyed man, was present.

"What's wrong?" she finally asked. "What triggered this…this mood?"

Seanchai looked at her and forced a smile. Then he played with his spoon. "Alliance," he said. "Using that word triggered something."

"Your memory returns?"

"Only fleeting moments that disappear before I can understand them. I created alliances?"

Mharina was about to answer when the dancer appeared at their table. She stood awkwardly, her head bowed.

"Thank you for...for tryin' to 'elp me, but I'm dead if I don't go back to 'im."

Mharina sprung to her feet and grabbed the woman's chin. Her face was swollen, her cheeks were puffy, and one of her eyes was purple and black.

"Did he do this to you? I'll kill him. I'll—"

The dancer was shaking her head. "'e 'as my little sister. Ain't an option to lea—"

"Where?"

The dark, curly-haired girl shrank from Mharina's ferocity. "'e 'as many men."

"Where?"

"West of 'ere. Two days' walk. There's another town. Rinstone. 'e 'as a compound just outside."

"When will you return there?"

"I perform again 'ere tonight. Then we leave. 'e mustn't know I told you anythin'." She was looking around frantically.

"How will you dance looking like this?"

"I 'ave a lot of makeup. Ain't the first time. I'm used to it."

Mharina opened her arms and embraced the girl. "Say nothing, then," she whispered into the dancer's round ear. "We have something else to deal with, and then we will come for you and your sister."

"'e's vicious," the girl whispered back. "'e'll show you no mercy."

Mharina disengaged from the embrace and looked the girl in the eyes.

"I hope not," she said.

CHAPTER 19

Mharina exited the tavern to find about thirty men, all wearing the purple sash and wielding swords, cudgels, spears, and axes. She was relieved to see there were no archers. Seanchai followed her, stared, and just shook his head as though this was an inconvenience.

The blue-eyed man stood in the center near the Ashen Elfe with four burly men surrounding him. Mharina moved slowly to join her father, standing far enough apart to allow them to each swing their weapons. She could feel her rising anger channeling into the staff. Synwyn leaned lightly on her own staff.

"Such a guard of honor to mark our departure," Seanchai said. "We're honored, but you really shouldn't have gone to all this trouble."

"You ain't leaving," the blue-eyed man growled.

"What do you want?" Mharina asked. "That we come quietly? To where?"

"Ain't interested in taking you prisoner. You're too dangerous. Your kind don't just walk away when they've stuck their—"

"*Your kind,*" Seanchai interrupted, an edge in his voice. "What does that mean?"

Mharina saw one of the men at the back fall silently to the ground. A second fell, and then a third. She wondered whether her father was doing this and knew she had to keep the conversation going.

"What do you want, then? Our considerable wealth? Our weapons?"

She saw a shadow moving quickly through the alley behind their adversaries. A man at the other end of the line fell, and another.

"We ain't come to negotiate," the leader said.

Mharina nodded, as if giving his words consideration. Something was happening, and the men were looking around uneasily at those who had collapsed. When one tried to speak, Synwyn held up her hand, and he went silent. Two more fell. A third let out a cry as his legs buckled, and all turned. But there was nothing to see. When they turned back, Seanchai had his bow in hand and Mharina swirled her staff, its runes glowing orange in the gray morning.

"Charge!" the Ashen Elfe cried, the desperation in her voice suggesting she realized she had lost the initiative.

But of a dozen men, only two reached the elves, and Mharina's blazing staff felled them. The others lay writhing in the dust, pierced by arrows with green fletching through thigh or calf. Seanchai had managed to incapacitate them without taking a life.

The blue-eyed man was furious. He had only eight fighters with him now, none of whom seemed overly anxious to enter the fray. As he drew his own sword—a wicked curved blade—Synwyn put a hand up to restrain him.

"How is your quiver still full?" she asked Seanchai, a tone of awe in her voice.

"Very useful," Seanchai replied with an almost cheerful tone. "I could do this all day. How many more men do you have?"

"We're finished here," the Ashen Elfe said. "You may leave town."

"I'm not finished," Mharina said, whirling her staff as she walked slowly forward. Its whooshing sound seemed to fill the air around them. "I want to chat with him."

She pointed her staff at the blue-eyed man, who was still holding his sword. "If the rest of you want to live, move aside."

The eight remaining men slowly backed away. The wounded tried to drag themselves to the side. Mharina was aware that her father, bow still nocked and taut, had moved so her advance wouldn't block his range of fire. She was impressed this instinct was still intact.

As she neared the blue-eyed man and Ashen Elfe, Synwyn shimmered and disappeared. Mharina had to force herself not to react.

"Drop your sword or die," Mharina threatened.

But the man, towering over her, held up his blade. "Perhaps you ain't so impressive if your bodyguard is not protecting you, little she-elf."

"*She-elf!*" Mharina spat, then took a breath, feeling her nostrils flare. "You die, you racist bigot. Bodyguard! This scum is mine. You will not interfere. Do you understand?"

"You don't want me to stop you from killing him?" Seanchai called out.

"Right. It'll be an interesting exercise in self-control. Can I vent my fury on this despicable piece of human waste and leave him alive? What do you think?"

"I think he might regret not meeting a quick death," Seanchai replied, and Mharina noted a few men smile.

The blue-eyed man snapped. He roared and sprung at Mharina, his sword held aloft. She began to move to his sword side, but then sidestepped to his left, crouching and springing forward so that her staff thudded into his stomach. He grunted and staggered a little from the momentum but turned quickly.

Mharina took a side stance, her left foot and hand forward, fingers pointing to the man. She anchored her weight on her bent right leg. The staff swirled behind her, hissing with anticipation. The man crouched and flicked his sword through the air, trying to instill an air of menace.

When he attacked again, she swirled and struck him again in his stomach. Her follow-through struck him with the other staff tip in the backs of his knees. He fell, and she jumped in the air, kicking the back of his head into the dust.

He groaned, slowly turned over, and rose.

"Do you feel so powerful now?" Mharina taunted, her voice loud enough for all to hear. "Your little dancer must make you feel very tough when you beat her. Maybe you and I should dance some? You were interested last night. Show us all what a nimble-footed man you are."

He stepped forward, wielding his sword with caution this time. She deflected his parry and sent him staggering off balance. Again, she sprung into the air, and this time jabbed him hard in the ribs with her staff tip. There was an ominous snapping sound.

The man went down on one knee and grunted but did not cry out. Mharina landed and twisted again. One end of her staff hit him behind the head, and, with unbelievable speed, she continued her circle and smashed the other end of her staff into his falling face. Another crack echoed in the morning air, and blood spurted from his nose.

He took his time rising again, and his white mustache was now stained a rich red.

"I will kill you," he screamed.

"No, no. We are merely dancing. Only this time, you don't get to make the rules."

"I will…" he began again, straightening with considerable effort. But then he froze mid-sentence, his sword aloft. His eyes bulged, and his sword clattered to the ground. Then he keeled forward and slowly fell on his face, this time lying still.

Behind him stood the dancer, her curly black hair wild and her eyes ablaze as her chest heaved with exertion. In her hand was a knife, blood dripping from its tip onto the dusty ground.

"I believe 'e owed me the last dance," she said.

Chapter 20

The future king of Odessiya stood at the mouth of the Cliftean Pass, staring into an empty canyon. Behind him, his exhausted and increasingly ragged army camped and gathered their breath. He had considered bringing his cavalry here and placing them in the pass. There were only three ways into this narrow flatland. One would see the advance of his enemy, a second would serve as a means of escape into the Ruskin Mountains if the battle fared badly, and the third was through the pass.

He had employed his cavalry only in brief skirmishes as they retreated from the ice lands, but he knew their place was on the plains outside Shindellia. His troops only held their ground because of the fierce pictorians, who though as ragged as anyone else, seemed to regenerate on the energy of battle. Each night they sat around campfires together with the remaining dwarves and sang into the dark.

But he had not chosen this place to fight just because it offered a chance to win, nor because it offered a good means of escape. He chose it because he hoped the Elves of the West were watching the pass.

He had considered taking his troops through the pass and across the desert, meeting the Ashen Elves at the magical boundary the Elves of the West had erected. But the walk would weaken his men and leave all of Odessiya exposed. The Ashen Elves could block the pass and then turn on Shindellia. No, he would make a stand here and hope the Elves of the West saw.

A whimper from his left made him turn and smile. Azura bounded up, a stick in her mouth, tail and rump wagging. Shayth bent down to take the stick, his mind on other things. He tossed it and watched Azura race after it. She was a smart dog and now good at retrieving. She offered Shayth a few precious moments each day to escape the pressing responsibilities and just play.

Someone walking toward him from the canyon grabbed his attention. Was this a messenger? His heart leapt and then sunk as he recognized not a messenger, but Pyre, a silhouette of her two Win Dao swords sheathed on her back and bow in hand.

"Where are you coming from?" he asked.

"Hunting," she replied, holding up a brace of brown rabbits.

"Good. That should satiate my hungry hordes. I wonder if we can stretch your catch through lunch and dinner?" It was an attempt at a joke, and Pyre gave a loyal smile. "You needed your own space as well, no?"

She nodded. "I've spent my entire adult life in exile, following one who is now adrift. It's hard being here so close to what had once been home."

"Can you really not go back?"

Pyre shrugged and gazed back the way she had come. "I probably could, but what would await me? I would never be trusted with any leadership responsibility, never offered a chance to teach. It's not only that I chose the Wycaan over my people, but I have not yet become a true Wycaan, myself."

"Why is that?"

"If only I knew. I had hope when Denalion was alive. He seemed convinced I would experience my own transformation, different from the recognized ways. Seanchai, too, never doubted it would happen. But now I have no teachers left."

"I'm sorry," Shayth said, tossing the stick again. "I wish I could suggest you go home, complete your training, and decide your destiny. But I need you. I think Mharina will need you, too. And who knows? One of you might just tip the balance to keep Odessiya free."

"Us? What about Seanchai?"

Shayth shrugged. "Best we don't broach that subject again."

Azura returned with the stick, and Shayth bent down to take it. He stood and pulled his arm back to throw it.

"Stop!" Pyre cried. "Give that to me."

He looked at her, puzzled, and then at the stick. Now he saw that it was not a random piece of wood. Its reddish hue was carved with three symbols etched in either end.

"Where did you get that?" Pyre demanded, taking it from his hand and turning it in wonder.

"Azura must have picked it up somewhere. What is it, Pyre?"

"When two elves have argued and are not speaking, one will carve a stick and send it to the other as an invitation to communicate. It carries a respectful connotation."

"Do you think…?"

"I don't know," Pyre said. "Maybe they're watching the pass. Maybe they're reaching out to you."

Shayth stared into the pass and then turned back to the camp. "Come with me," he called back to Pyre as he strode purposefully away. "We will meet them mounted."

"Are you sure you want me along?" Pyre asked, jogging to catch up.

"Absolutely."

They took the first saddled horses they came across, bewildering two cavalrymen. Six well-armed men ran quickly into formation, but Shayth called out to his guard. "I have Pyre with me. No one else follows. My orders."

Then he dug his heels into his horse and galloped out. Pyre was behind him and shouted after a minute for him to slow. He turned. Azura was racing along behind, her ears pinned back and her tongue hanging, determined to stay with her master.

"You don't know where they are," Pyre called. "Slow to a trot. They shouldn't see how eager you are."

Shayth obeyed, appreciating that she said eager instead of desperate. When Pyre brought her stallion alongside his, he grinned at her. "See why I need you?"

Pyre grimaced. "Hope you don't regret it."

They trotted through the pass for only a short while before a figure caught their eye and disappeared into a narrow canyon. They followed, glancing around to see if there were others.

They spotted the elf, who was waiting to make sure they were coming. He stopped and looked up to the surrounding peaks, producing a shiny stone that he flashed in the sunlight, the glare of which momentarily blinded Shayth. He followed the elf's gaze to another flash. A similar communication took place from another angle with a different sentry. Satisfied, the messenger stepped forward.

"Welcome, Prince of Odessiya," he said, and then bowed to Pyre. "I have no official welcome for you, Pyre the Outlander, but for my own part, you are welcome, too. The *calhei* who stood up to the High Council. Though you are of course no longer a *calhei*."

He stood aside and signaled for them to proceed into a small canyon. At the end, an overhanging ledge offered shade. Under it sat four elves, their hair white and their skin dark. They rose together as Shayth and Pyre dismounted and surrendered their horses for care.

One elfe stood taller than the rest. She was lean and well defined, suggesting that she was fit and knew how to use the Win Dao swords that hung on her back.

"I am Shathea, Prince Shayth. My hair was black when we last met, and we fought together at the Battle of the Cliftean Pass alongside Seanchai the Wycaan Master. I remember him warmly as a friend to the Elves of the West and, in his honor, volunteered to meet with you."

Shayth bowed his head. "I remember you and your bravery in battle. You fought alongside the Weapons Master and Cheriuk.

Seanchai spoke of their courage and guidance and of your friendship and warmth while he studied in the Forest of Markwin."

He turned and addressed all four elves. "I come in similar dire circumstances. Thank you for meeting with me. We have much to discuss."

CHAPTER 21

"I do not understand," one old elf said, a frown stretched across his lined face. "These creatures may have pointed ears, but I suspect that is the extent of their connection to us."

"Tell me about the ancient stories of the Elves of the West," Shayth requested. "How do your legends describe the land they found?"

"There is no mention of any civilized creatures, let alone elves," he replied. "The land was rich with beast and herds, with mighty forests and clean rivers. We found a paradise; otherwise, I suspect we would not have chosen to settle so far from our homeland."

"Could it be that your legends were edited? That those who perpetrated such acts omitted some less endearing details?" Shayth asked.

The old elf's frown hardened, and the others stiffened. Shayth remembered too late that, while he was the ruler in Odessiya, these elves held no loyalty or commitment to him. He refilled his goblet of water. It was refreshing and sweetened with orange flowers.

A bark from behind made him turn. Azura had reached the canyon and bounded toward him. The elf who had taken their horses drew his bow, but Pyre called out quickly, and he lowered it.

Azura stopped by the elf and cocked an ear, smelling carefully. The elf spoke to her quietly. Shayth could not hear his words, but the dog sniffed his hand and let him stroke her head before approaching at a more regal pace.

"A beautiful dog, my prince," Shathea said.

"A gift from the mage of the Ashen Elves. My dog's eyes are the same ice blue as theirs. She is a reminder of what waits for me—for us."

Azura came to Shayth and put her head on his lap. He stroked her and scratched her ears but kept his eyes on the elves before him.

"Why did you not offer them safe passage through your land and let them reach our boundary?" Shathea asked. "Do they even know of our existence?"

"Know of you? Oh, they know of you, though not from me," Shayth replied. "They live by the breath of the revenge they feel they need to inflict on you in order to be set free."

"Then why lead them to the Cliftean Pass?" the old elf asked.

"For you to take notice. You have ignored my emissaries, though you took the red stone I sent. Have you discovered anything?"

"No," Shathea replied, rather too quickly. A look passed between the elves, and Shayth bristled.

"You would tell me?" he asked and heard the uncertainty in his own voice.

"As you are aware," an older elfe said in a high, crackling tone, "no non-elf is allowed to pass through the barrier. Why do you think we do this? It is not for our physical protection; we have Wycaan warriors, all brave and well armed. It is to protect the magic. It is the magic that holds this world together. When a person with, shall we say, questionable motives—such as your uncle—gains too much magic, our entire civilization becomes endangered."

"Our entire civilization *is* endangered," Shayth snapped. "Have you not been listening to what I told you of the Gray Elves?"

"Oh, I have listened carefully, young man. But I am not sure *you* have."

Shayth looked at Pyre, a puzzled frown on his face. The young elfe stared back, eyes grim and her tone cold.

"When she refers to civilization, she means those who live in the Markwin Forest and beyond our shores. She speaks only of the elves."

"You came to our aid against my uncle," Shayth said to the old elfe. "What is the difference?"

"We came to the aid of the Wycaan Master—an elf, I might add. Had he been human or dwarf, I doubt we would have."

"But you weren't going to come to Seanchai's aid," Pyre snapped. "You all cowered in your bloodwood chairs until the Weapons Master challenged you."

"As I remember it," Shathea said, smiling, "it was a hotheaded *calhei* who challenged the council. The Weapons Master simply announced her intentions to go with Seanchai."

"And the Weapons Master paid for her choice with her life," the old elfe said. "In addition, we lost a future leader in Chamack," she leaned forward, "my youngest son."

Shayth put a hand on Pyre's arm before she could respond. "I'm sorry for your loss. My parents were murdered when I was a boy and, though I have not yet become a father, I cannot imagine anything worse than losing a child.

"However, you, like me, are responsible for the welfare and freedom of Odessiya. You know our destinies are entwined, that we can only survive if we stand united. The mage offered to leave the people of Odessiya—humans, dwarves, and pictorians—unharmed if I stood aside and let them wreak their revenge upon the elves. Do you think their thirst will stop with the elves of Odessiya? Do you think they'll not discover the Markwin Forest and your boundary once they have conquered my people?

The old elfe leaned forward. "Do you think they don't already know?"

Shayth stopped in stunned silence. He glanced at Pyre, who wore the same expression he imagined he did. "You've been in contact with them?"

"Not us, but the one we spurned. Your uncle is the one who set them free. What do you imagine the Emperor's interest was in cultivating the Ashen Elves, driving their thirst for revenge?"

"I suspect they had reason to hate you long before my uncle intervened," Shayth replied.

"Apparently, but what was his motivation in setting them free, in giving them magic that might one day be turned against him?"

"To attack and conquer the Elves of the West?" Shayth swallowed hard. He realized that he still remained several steps behind his uncle in this intricate game. He could imagine the man mocking him from whatever hell he was in. "So, what have you done to prepare for this? Why not align with us if they're coming for you anyway?"

"We have faith in our barrier and that the Markwin Forest will protect us as it always has." The old elfe stretched and sipped from a red goblet.

Shayth ran his hand through his rebellious hair. "You have tested the stone we gave you and decided the magic of the Ashen Elves offers no threat?"

"Correct," the old elfe said.

"How did Seanchai force his way in?"

"The forest allowed him in. It saw he was of pure heart and intention," the wizened elf said. "What is your point?"

Shayth rose and walked away from the table, pushing his hands through his spiky hair. He turned slowly. "Your whole plan rests upon the will of the forest that is the foundation of your magic. But the forest has its own moral parameters. It overruled you once when Seanchai passed through the barrier."

"And it supported him when he challenged the council," Pyre added. "The whole forest vibrated with his power. It chose him over you."

Shayth walked back and leaned over the table, pressing his weight on his fists. "How can you be so sure that the forest won't choose the

Ashen Elves over you? The forest is more ancient than the Elves of the West. It has seen other races, including the Ashen Elves. Perhaps it has a better grasp on the moral landscape than you do. That is why it chose Seanchai over you. Do you think it is impressed that you condemn thousands of innocent elves in Odessiya—and tens of thousands elsewhere—to die by the swords of the Ashen Elves because you are as arrogant and racist today as you were when you first stepped foot in Odessiya?"

Chapter 22

The meeting was over; Shayth straightened and turned to walk away.

"That is not the way to show respect for the Council of Markwin," the old elf called after him. "No man or elf should turn his back on the elven council."

Shayth stopped in his tracks, breathing hard to control his mounting rage. He turned and once again walked slowly back, the crunch of gravel under his boots the only sound in the canyon. He leaned again on the table.

"I am Prince Shayth Shindell, and, in a few days, I will be crowned king of Odessiya. I never sought the crown, nor do I crave it today. I desire only to keep my people safe—all my people, including elves, humans, dwarves, and pictorians. I grieve when any one of them dies if I think I could possibly have prevented it.

"This is no game, whatever you think. You can't sit at the end of a board and move pieces around. You are archaic, clinging to a magic that just might disdain you as much as I do. You turn your back on your own people, on the elves and all the innocent populations of Odessiya.

"That is why Seanchai never returned to you. It is why Pyre was so comfortable leaving, even if it meant exile. Your Weapons Master knew it. Chamack recognized it as he sparred with Seanchai." He glared at Shathea. "You fought alongside the Wycaan Master and befriended Seanchai. How do you not understand this?

"Your purist theologies subjugated an indigenous people when your ancestors first came to Odessiya and though the indigenous people they met had pointed ears, yet they were deemed beneath you because they lacked magic. So you cast them aside—out of your eyesight and, regrettably, out of your conscience. Then you continued to ignore the needs of others, even when my uncle enslaved the elves of Odessiya. How is it that, even now, you cannot see past your bigotry?

"Why do I turn my back to you? I am the future king of Odessiya. I also have a terrible blemish from the past upon my character, but I have learned to put the past behind me and serve my people."

He paused a moment and met each elf's stare.

"Consider well whether my uncle told the Ashen Elves of your arrogance. They know of your existence. I have met them and believe they will glean little pleasure from killing the noble and innocent elves of my kingdom. It is you they want and I could let them pass through without harming those who look to the crown for protection. When they mass upon your borders, when the forest withdraws its support from you and allows them through the barrier to wreak their revenge, to whom will you look for help?

"As the crown prince of Odessiya, I show respect only to those who deserve it. I will not reveal your presence because I have a responsibility to protect all people. But don't assume that makes you deserving of my royal respect."

He wheeled around and strode to the horses, his boots grinding on the gravel and echoing eerily on the rock walls. He grabbed his stallion's reins and led it out of the canyon.

Azura trotted at his heels as the future king of Odessiya turned his back on the Elves of the West.

Pyre remained seated in her chair. She stared across the table at Shathea who met her gaze but did not speak.

It was the old elfe who broke the silence. "Are you still convinced of your choice, *calhei*?".

Pyre ignored her and continued to lock eyes with the younger council member.

"What kind of a king will he make?" The old elf who sat to Shathea's right asked.

Still, Shathea alone held Pyre's attention.

"Go on," Shathea said. "Get it off your chest."

"Without them," Pyre hissed.

"They are council members of—"

"They don't recognize me, even though I grew up as one of them. They do not respect my decision to support the Wycaan Master and bring aid to the people of Odessiya. So I, in turn, do not recognize them. They are the past. The king who deigned to share his presence with you is the future. I am the future. What of you?"

"What makes you think I support your decision?" Shathea asked. "I may have left with the Wycaan, but I came back to serve my people."

"Because I always believed in you. Because I worshipped you, wobbling after you as soon as I could walk, following you around the forest. I drank in your beauty, your wisdom, and your skill. But more than anything else, because I loved my big sister." She paused as she heard her own voice crack then whispered: "Because blood binds."

Shathea swallowed. "Come," she said, rising to her feet. She turned to the council. "Excuse us."

"She's in exile," the old elf said. "Remember who she is."

"I remember," Shathea replied, her voice firm and steady. "She is my sister."

Pyre led her sister up a path to a peak that overlooked the vast desert expanse. Below them, Shayth and his horse were becoming an increasingly smaller dot, and Azura, who ran after him, was barely visible.

"Will you bend your knee to him at the coronation?" Shathea asked.

"I haven't decided. I swore to serve Seanchai, though he doesn't recall my oath, and—"

"What of Seanchai?"

"He remembers nothing of his past. His skills are instinctive, yet the magic eludes him. But it will return."

"How do you know this?"

"Because I know him so well." Pyre's voice had become a whisper, her tone revealing far more than her words. "There is still hope."

"Hope or desperate dreams?" Shathea put an arm around her little sister, and it felt so familiar, so safe.

"Hope. His core remains, and his essence is Wycaan, but it is guided by love. He has the *Iyzun*, Shathea. I am convinced of it, and it is the female magic that is escaping. He locked his Wycaan identity away to protect himself, but he was unaware of the other side of him. It survived because it was hidden."

"Your hope sounds fragile, Pyre. I'm sorry, but such damage can often be permanent. And you only guess that he possesses the *Iyzun*. We have not seen it in any but one for centuries."

"Yes, but there is more."

Pyre paused. Her older sister moved her head closer and put her free hand on the younger elfe's arm. "I am a council member of the Elves of Markwin and seen by many as the future leader. I cannot keep in confidence what I hear, even if it is from your lips. Consider well your next words, but if it might change the game, perhaps you should share."

Pyre picked up a stone and threw it down the slope. It created a small rockslide. They listened to the clatter of the rolling stones into the canyon. When it stopped, the contrasting silence was deafening. Pyre threw a second stone and the same sequence happened. When she picked up a third, Shathea grasped her forearm.

"Little sister. I serve the High Council of the Elves of the West. You serve the future king of Odessiya and the Wycaan Master. I agree with Shayth that our futures are intertwined." Her voice went quiet. "You are holding something from me. I know you. Give me a reason to challenge the council."

Pyre winced. "Seanchai and Sellia have three children. The twins are natural-born Wycaans."

"We know this, and, should Sellia bring them here to study, they will be accepted. You have my word."

"Then there is the eldest, Mharina," Pyre continued.

"I hear she is the spitting image of her mother and has the same temperament. It's a shame she hasn't the Wycaan essence inside of her. She would be formidable."

"She *is* formidable, Shathea. More than you can imagine."

Shathea listened to her sister recount Mharina's training under Sa'gola and her Wycaan transformation.

"She has the *Iyzun,* too?" Shathea said, her eyes wide in wonder. "You know what that means?"

Pyre watched her sister pick up a rock heavy enough to require both hands and throw it down the slope. The momentum created a far larger rockslide than before. Peering down at the considerable dust cloud it created, Pyre couldn't help but smile to herself.

"That changes everything," Shathea whispered.

Chapter 23

The officers of Prince Shayth Shindell's bedraggled army entered the command tent at a run. They knew by now when their beloved commander's temper flared. In truth, they also knew the prince's rage had saved many of them in battle.

It was still dark with barely a hint of dawn silhouetting the looming peaks. The prince stood hunched over a map of the Cliftean Pass. Sentries reported that he had prowled around all night, often standing next to the guard in silence as both stared out in to the blackness.

"We must be ready," he growled to his officers, not looking up. "They will attack today."

"How do you know, my prince?" one asked, and then swallowed hard at his audacity.

"Yesterday, I met with council members of the Elves of the West. The Ashen Elves will not know what was said—only that the meeting transpired. They will attack today, fearing that a Markwin army might come out and join forces with us."

"Will they?" asked a broad dwarf with gray streaks running through his chestnut hair and beard.

Shayth shook his head and glared even harder at the map. "No," he said. "Help will not come from the west."

"Cowards," someone muttered.

"I wish it was that simple," Shayth replied. "I could forgive them for being frightened."

"The King in Hothengold has sent troops to bolster our defenses near the capital," the dwarf continued. "Why not call for help there?"

Shayth straightened and sighed. "Our mission is not to win this battle. I fear we cannot. I just want to inflict as heavy a loss as possible. We have not yet seen indicators that they are strong of number. They certainly have not opened up a battle on more than one front, and their supply line must be stretched."

"But why engage them here?" a young officer asked. "Why not where we can use the cavalry?"

"To keep them away from our more populated areas," General Pilau said. She was tall and wiry, her ginger hair cropped. Her demeanor was always taut, and she brooked no nonsense from her soldiers. Her bravery and strategic thinking had earned everyone's respect, and the mostly male command looked up to her. "Let us discuss strategy and not waste time on false hopes of non-existent allies."

She looked at the prince, who nodded for her to continue. The general recounted several potential scenarios. Each one concluded with all but one unit retreating into the Bordan Mountains and the remaining unit accompanying the prince to the capital.

"Each officer has instructions on where to rendezvous, and he will share them only with a single soldier under his command. If one unit is compromised, their officers will not give away the positions of the rest of the army."

She turned to the tallest man in the room, who bore a black strip on his chest. "Crags. Your men have only one mission: to get the prince back to the capital unharmed." She picked up one of many small blocks on the map. "The prince will fight with Trinda's forces here." She placed the block to the north, nearest the route Shayth would take. It was also furthest from the anticipated brunt of the attack.

Trinda spoke up. "My soldiers are honored to fight alongside the prince," she said.

"I would be honored to fight by your side, too, Trinda, but that day will not be today," Shayth said, his voice even. Then he leaned over, took the wooden cube, and put it in front of the vanguard. "I am the crown prince of Odessiya. I do not send my soldiers into battle; I lead them."

He looked up and entered a staring match with General Pilau, a confrontation she knew she could never win.

The battle raged all around him. The Ashen Elves had attacked exactly as General Pilau anticipated, sending volleys of arrows from the slopes that bounced off shields linked to form a steel roof. The sound reminded Shayth of the hail that beat on the inns and stables he frequented all too often during a certain time of his life. He let himself reflect on this dark period; the rage it brought to a boil would serve him well.

The aerial barrage was soon terminated. But keeping the prince's army crouched and barricaded had allowed Ashen Elf warriors with red stones to appear right in front of them, and their engagement was swift and uncompromising.

Shayth's troops were on the back heel right from the start, staggering to retreat in an orderly fashion. The royal guards—Soldiers of the Black Stone, they had dubbed themselves after the meaning of Shayth in the ancient language—fought skillfully around their prince. Crags, even as he fought, marshaled his men fluidly. Shayth began to feel frustrated that Ashen Elves broke through their defense so infrequently. He wanted to fight.

As they backpedaled past a series of gorges, pictorians swarmed out to attack the Ashen Elves from the side. For a short time, the battle turned in their favor, but for every Gray Elf who fell, fresh reinforcements appeared to take their places

Shayth jerked his head when he heard cries to his right. Ashen Elves, red stones gleaming, poured out of multiple small gorges to ambush them. He could tell these elves were a more elite unit, and his troops had no answer.

Shayth cried out to his bodyguards: "To me!" He pointed his sword in the direction he was going and charged in. The battle became brutal, and even his best soldiers were challenged to stand their ground.

He realized the enemy was not engaging with him—just exchanging a few blows and moving on. A thought flickered that maybe they were afraid of his growing reputation, but then he saw the real reason.

A huge elf—his skin more a dirty white than ashen gray—lumbered forward, a broadsword in one hand and a battle sickle in the other. Several other elves sprung forward in a well-coordinated formation, engaging the Soldiers of the Black Stone and pushing them back to peel off a path straight to the prince.

The elf grinned, and Shayth responded with a snarl, his rage rising. He struck at the towering warrior, but the elf was deceptively nimble as he avoided Shayth's attack. They settled into a rhythm, exchanging blows, and the prince felt good that he could match his fearsome adversary.

But then he realized the elf was slowly and subtly directing him away from the main battle. Shayth always feared a knife or arrow would find his back while he was engaging a formidable enemy. But faced with such an adversary, he was forced to narrow his focus.

As the elf pushed harder, his red stone glowed, and Shayth began to realize that, while he exchanged blows with just one elf, others were channeling their energy into him. It dawned on the prince that he was outnumbered even as they fought one-on-one.

"How does it feel, not-King?" the elf rasped. "You rarely meet a warrior who is more than your match."

Shayth didn't have a comeback, and, in truth, it was taking all his concentration to fend off the powerful blows raining down on him. He backed into a rock face, and a protruding edge jarred his head. The Ashen Elf sent him flying, and he banged his head again when he landed.

He rose, nauseated, as the world spun. A cry nearby attracted the elf's attention. Crags had broken through and leapt at the elf, his swordplay almost reckless as he swerved to position himself between the elf and his prince.

Shayth stood, slightly swaying, and watched. The elf had been initially shocked by Crags' technique and unbridled drive to protect Shayth, but he gradually matched the bodyguard and began to beat him back. His speed was uncanny, and his red stone gleamed brightly.

In two blurring moments, he knocked Crags' sword from his hand and landed a crunching blow to the man's ribcage. Crags screamed in pain but still rose to his feet and reached for his sword. The elf watched, and though Shayth looked for some admiration in those cold blue eyes, he found none.

Crags staggered in front of Shayth, arm bent around his ribcage as if holding it together.

"Move aside," Shayth said. "You bought me enough time to recover."

"Never," Crags said, raising his shaking sword with difficulty.

"Do you see this, mage?" Shayth screamed at the stone hanging from the elf's neck. "Here stand the noble men and women you are killing—people who have never wronged you or your people, who offered you a respected place in our society. Witness the bravery and honor you try to crush."

"You are a worthy opponent, a brave adversary," the Ashen Elf rasped to Crags. "Find peace with your ancestors as we seek our own salvation."

Then he slew Crags, the first blow sending the man's sword flying and the return blow cutting his throat. Crags, still fighting to stand, sunk to his knees and crumpled forward.

Shayth's chest heaved. He barely knew this man, but his heart burned for him all the same. With a guttural cry, he sprung at the gray elf, raining blows upon him. The elf retreated momentarily, then, in one deft movement, sent Shayth crashing against the rock wall.

He pressed against Shayth, pinning Shayth's back to the rocks.

"Where are they?" the Ashen Elf hissed, his breath almost overwhelming the prince. "Where are the other elves? Tell me and end these senseless deaths."

Shayth shook his head. "I won't."

"Tell me or die, not-King."

Shayth swallowed. "If I tell you, I betray my people and forever remain a not-King. If I die, it'll be protecting my people—acting as a true king, even if I'm not yet crowned."

The Ashen Elf stared at him, and Shayth wondered if others were deciding his fate. The moments hung; Shayth could not move his arms or legs to fight back. This was it, he thought—a failed end for a failed king.

The Ashen Elf spoke, bringing Shayth back to the moment. "The mage says you live. Go claim your crown and discover the pleasure of power. Give us the elves, and you will go on to reign. Refuse, and you will lose everything. Then you will have wished I had killed you today."

The Ashen Elf moved back, then slammed the hilt of his sword into Shayth's side, cracking at least two ribs. "Dwell on this when you make your painful journey to the capital."

With that, the huge elf vanished.

Chapter 24

Senzia made her way through the dark. She was not afraid of being alone or worried about losing her way. She believed she could fight off anyone or anything that crossed her path. She was very good at walking quietly and hiding her tracks. Pyre had taught her about stealth, and the old Wycaans had taught her to fight and use her magic.

But the best training she had received—that which imbued such self-confidence—was from the Emperor. In the months they had been prisoners at Grogin, he had taken her and Ilan under his tutelage and taught them some of the more obscure arts. He had tried and somewhat succeeded—with her, at least—to woo them to his side. Ilan had been more interested in the science Master Goldspiere taught.

Senzia's main worry was being untested in battle. She had trained with a variety of weapons, including Win Dao swords, but none attracted her. She now carried a bow taken from a wolfheid. It was too big for her, but she enjoyed practicing with it. She had always been attracted to archery because it tested her completely. Any one-on-one combat brought the level of her opponent into the equation.

Now, she carried her small pack, bedroll, and bow and quiver through steep mountain paths. She needed to use trails that were impossible for horses to negotiate so she could prevent her mother from coming after her and avoid army patrols.

She wondered how her mother would react when she found Senzia was gone. Surely, she would be enraged, but her next steps would depend on Ilan. If he could persuade her that he would not follow Sellia if she tried to track Senzia, then maybe their mother would deliver him to the Elves of the West.

But Ilan was changing as he matured. They had never been apart, and he felt they shouldn't be. He also knew he could find her, wherever she went. The Emperor predicted that each of them would become formidable Wycaans, but their twin connection offered far more potential power.

It was getting light now. Senzia was relieved when the dawn confirmed she was heading north. She never expected to keep a straight line in such steep terrain. Her stomach rumbled and, though she had food with her, she was reluctant to stop. When she finally did, it was morning. The light was still subdued, as much from the heavy cloud cover as the early hour.

Crouching to relieve herself, she heard a crunch behind her. Slowly, she tied her breeches and crawled to a nearby rock. She tried to scry to sense what was ahead. There was something near her, something unreadable. She wondered if it was wolfheids, deer, or perhaps the wooly bison she had always dreamed of hunting. She smiled to herself. In such dreams, she had fulfilled this rite of passage with her mother and Pyre watching proudly.

Abruptly, she could no longer sense whatever creature was near her and began to wonder if she had imagined it. She continued along the path she was following. It rose quite steeply and turned a few corners. She hoped it was still heading north. She yawned and, having not slept during the night, tripped on a protruding rock that she really should have seen. She reluctantly conceded that she needed to rest and began seeking a suitably concealed spot.

A little while later, she approached a small cave. She was so tired. She turned at the cave mouth and saw that her tracks were still distinguishable, even if they mixed with those of other animals.

Mafula. Mafula, Mafula.

She made hand gestures to encourage the breeze to blow across the tracks and, once satisfied they were covered, walked into the cave, wiped the blood from her nose, and curled up to sleep out of sight from the mouth of the cave.

Senzia had not meant to sleep for long or so deeply and had no idea how much time had passed. What woke her from her dreamless slumber were growls and pacing footsteps. She first thought that she was trapped by wolfheids, but nothing was attacking her.

She opened her eyes and saw a huge black bear sitting on its haunches, staring at her. Behind it was a mother feeding three cubs. She scolded herself under her breath. A bear's den? There was probably nothing as dangerous—or stupid—as going near bears when they had cubs.

Other bears entered the cave, sniffed in her direction, and then returned outside. She wondered what to do. Any sudden movement interpreted as an attack on the cubs meant she was dead. She could wait and see if these bears would leave but figured the cubs were likely not going anywhere. Still, they were not being openly aggressive toward her. The big one and the mother were definitely wary but not particularly distraught.

Senzia began to slowly sit up. The bear guarding her immediately tensed, and two more entered the cave and took up positions in front of the cubs. When she continued to rise, one of them bared its teeth and growled quietly. She lay back down. Message received.

As slowly as possible, she reached into her pack and took out her water skin. The three bears all tensed and watched her every move. She drank and sat the skin down in front of her.

She closed her eyes and began her Wycaan breathing, relaxing her body and reached out with her mind. She scryed, trying to reach the mind of any of the bears. There was a cacophony of emotions that she could not understand.

I mean you and your cubs no harm, she said wordlessly. *I can stand up and leave. I mean no harm.*

There was silence as the bears stared at her. She sighed. She needed to go. She repeated the message several times and was about to give up and try to leave when a voice came to her.

They know you mean no harm, but they worry for the cubs. They are amused at how silly you are to walk right into a bear's den and go to sleep. I asked them to keep you until I arrive. I am close. Be patient awhile longer.

CHAPTER 25

Senzia tried to reach out again, but her scrying elicited no response. The bears were soon sniffing and glancing out the entrance. Perhaps it was one of the bears who had spoken with her father. She began to get excited at the prospect. Perhaps the bear could help her *ahdahr*.

Moments later, however, a scrawny boy, slightly taller than her and dressed in gray, oversized, ragged clothes, entered. His hair was long, hanging in dreadlocks, and tied back away from his face in the way of elves, though his ears were round.

He went first to the bear guarding Senzia and bowed his head. The bear sniffed him and snorted, pushing the boy's hair up in the air. Then he went to the mother bear and stroked each cub. The cubs seemed particularly pleased to see him. They yipped and snapped at his hands. He feigned hurt and fear. Senzia couldn't help but smile.

Finally, he came back to stand by Senzia's guard bear.

Now I see why they were not afraid of you. He smirked, still speaking in her mind.

"Hey! I might be more than I seem," Senzia retorted.

I hope so. You are in no danger, as long you move slowly and don't go near the cubs. My family is kind but protective.

"Your family?"

Yes., I'm a member of this pack.

"You mean you live here?"

Yes. They found me as a cub and brought me up. I was too young to understand what I was, and they had to force me to walk on two legs. It was just as well. I was pretty awkward on all fours.

"Can you talk out loud?"

Probably. How do you do it?

Senzia frowned. "I've no idea. You simply do."

I will try, but not here. I'm going to ask our pack leader if I can take you out of the cave. Wait a moment.

The boy turned to the big bear and initiated some kind of silent exchange. The bear put its nose to the boy's hair and snorted. The boy's hair again stood up, and Senzia smiled. He was cute.

Come. The boy nodded. *We can leave. Slowly, though.*

Senzia looked at the biggest bear. "Please thank them for allowing me to sleep in their den."

The boy received several grunts when, presumably, he conveyed her message. They rose and walked slowly out, Senzia following the boy. He stopped when the cubs began whimpering, signaled with his hand for her to stay, and ran back inside.

My little brothers are jealous, he said when, he rejoined her outside. He laughed an infectious belly laugh.

They walked over to the side of the cliff. There was a sheltered area, the rock overhanging, and a beautiful view of the mountains and valleys. When they sat down, the rock was warm, and Senzia sighed.

My family comes here to sunbathe and warm their bodies. Even in the winter, this white rock absorbs heat.

"Why is a human boy living with bears?" Senzia asked after a few moments of silence.

He laughed again. *Ooh, never saw that coming. What makes a girl walk into a cave with bear cubs and fall asleep?*

"Ouch! They weren't there when I arrived. I was desperate to sleep somewhere sheltered and hidden."

Who are you hiding from? Are you in danger? His body tensed, and he looked back in the direction of the cave.

"What did you just do?" Senzia asked, as she saw two bears exit in different directions.

The boy's face reddened. *I warned them. We have cubs, and this is my family.*

"I understand; I don't think I'm being followed, but I can't be sure. If I am, it is most likely by my mother and brother. There is a taragusii warrior with them, but he'll follow my mother's commands."

Again, the boy glanced toward the cave, perhaps conveying the information Senzia had just shared. Then he turned back to Senzia. *Why do you run from your family? Are they bad to you?*

"No. I'm not running *from* them. I'm running to help others."

Humans are so complicated.

"You're human…aren't you?"

Sure. I mean, I was born human, but I've only ever known the company of bears. When we discovered I could enter people's minds, I'd sometimes enter a human's mind if they got too close to us and help them decide to leave.

"Really?"

It's nicer than fighting or scaring them, no? Who are you going to save? Do you have a mate?

Senzia thought she might be blushing. "No. I'm too young for that. Look, it's complicated, but I have certain powers. My father and siblings do, too, and we are important to keep the people of this land safe."

Just the two-legged?

"No. My father has a special link with bears, actually. Have you ever heard of a human who turned into a bear?"

The boy's eyes bulged. *Wow! I've dreamed of doing that. Is it possible? I could be just like my pack. Can he teach me?*

"I don't know, but—"

Does it have something to do with your white hair? My father says the white hair means you're special—that you can be very good or very evil. It was your white hair that stopped him and my mother from attacking you.

"He's right. And I am good, as is my family. Our country is being attacked by evil elves who—"

What are elves?

"Um, I'm an elf. We're a race older than humans. You see how my ears are pointed? This is just one such difference between us. We can also see better than humans, but inside we are all the same."

If we are all the same, why do these other elves want to fight you?

"Good question. There is much fighting and evil in this world. Maybe you are better staying here."

The boy's face went sad. *I thought maybe to go with you.*

"It would be wrong to take you with me. Where I go, there is much danger and—"

Then maybe you should stay with me and be my mate.

Now Senzia was sure her cheeks flushed.

Have I upset you? I don't know how to behave around two-leggeds. Even though I'm like you, I'm a bear in so many respects. They found me when I was a mere cub and brought me up. I'm sorry. But you are so beautiful and different from others I have seen.

Senzia smiled. "It's okay. You caught me by surprise; that's all."

A yip made them both turn to the cave.

Men are coming. We must enter the cave. You will be safe.

"They will allow me back inside?"

The boy puffed up his chest. *You are with me. You're my friend.*

Chapter 26

"You can't." The boy was attractive with his hands on his hips and the indignant expression under those thick locks.

Why not?

"It's too dangerous."

Then I'll protect you.

Senzia smiled. "That's very nice, but it might be that I'll need to protect you, and I don't want to see you harmed."

They had stayed in the cave while the travelers passed and then gone to sleep as night closed in. Now, in the fresh morning light, Senzia planned to leave. She had, through the boy, thanked the pack and walked outside. He followed her, a bundle over his shoulder.

There was silence, and the boy bit his lower lip. *I need to come.*

"Why?"

He looked at her, and she noticed his beautiful green eyes were full of despair. *I need to know.*

"Know what?"

Who I am. These bears are my pack—my family—and always will be, but I know I am not a bear. My father has been telling me that I need to return to the world of the two-legged—that, as I grow out of cub form, I will need to find those similar to me. And I like you.

Senzia sighed and thought for a few moments. She didn't like to travel alone. She was used to having Ilan and others around. "I like you, too. How about you join me for a few days while it is just the two of us. But when I near my friends and it gets dangerous, then we discuss it again."

Okay.

"And if I tell you to leave me then?"

He frowned. *I'll do as you say.*

Senzia peeked at the boy as he washed in the lake. She knew she shouldn't but couldn't help it. He was tall and muscular in places that other males weren't. It made him look awkward sometimes, but made sense since he was using muscles similar to the way a bear would. His dreadlocked hair was long and a kind of straw color, perhaps bleached by the sun. It parted in the middle. His face was long and angular, but not sharp, and his smile and laugh were cute.

She instructed him to wash his clothes, as well, and spread them out to dry. She gave him a pair of her breeches, which looked rather absurd on him but hid his nakedness.

They walked in silence for most of the day. Senzia had set a fast pace, though it was she who tired first. He followed, leading on occasions when he knew the terrain better than her.

"What's your name?" she suddenly asked as they sat nibbling carrots.

I don't have one. At least, I don't know it. Choose one.

"I think you should choose it. You'll have to live with it."

He thought for a moment, and then shrugged. *Bear?* He said it almost apologetically.

Senzia laughed. Despite the complex and scary situation she found herself in, this boy made her happy. She realized how important that felt. Though she was not bonded to him like she was to Ilan, she was used to being with someone. It felt natural.

"Artur," she said.

What's that?

"'Bear' in the ancient language. A long time ago, things were different. People lived in a more magical world we call the Age of Mist and Shadow. The land was new, and there was magic everywhere. People spoke a different language, and the magic was imbued in words to give them power and meaning. Artur means bear—at least, I think it does. Could mean warthog!"

He laughed. *Artur is a fine name. Thank you.* He stood up and puffed out his taut chest, which he poked with his thumb. *My name is Artur. What's yours?*

Senzia smiled. "Say it," she said. "Say it out loud."

He opened his mouth, but what came out was a mumbled set of growls. He frowned. *I'm sorry, I don't know how.*

"That's okay." Senzia stroked his forearm. She was surprised how distraught his expression made her feel. "I'll teach you."

The next day, as they walked together, Senzia asked Artur to focus on simple words. She had him repeat the words stone and bear over and over again and reassured him his pronunciation was getting better. She tried to make a joke about it, but Artur was quite anxious about the tools he needed to communicate with humans and elves. Finally, he stopped her.

Let's just talk this way, okay? He said soundlessly. *I want you to get to know me as a normal two-legged, not some idiot.*

"I don't think you're an idiot, Artur, not at all. But okay. Tell me how you got to live with the bear pack."

Unfortunately, there's little to tell. I was a cub. They found me among the ruins of a caravan that had been attacked and gutted with fire. There were dead bodies strewn all around, and the air was thick with smoke and flies. The bears only came so near because they feared a forest fire and hoped to extinguish it before it caught.

A sow, who later died, found me and took me in. Another sow was able to suckle me, and I grew up on their nourishment and love.

"A sow is a female bear?"

Yes. A male is a boar. The sow had two cubs, both male, and we grew up together. Boars are very fierce, but when a sow makes a decision about her cubs, there is no arguing. If they resented me at first, I wouldn't know. They are my family…and they're not.

He went silent, and Senzia glanced over with concern. He was stripping the bark from a twig with his long, untrimmed nails.

"What is it?" she finally asked.

They had reached a river, where the sun broke through the trees hanging back from the banks and flowers grew in scattered clumps. But the improved light did little to impact Artur's mood.

"Why so sad?" she asked again.

Two nights before you appeared, they told me I had to leave; that I'm not meant to live among the four-legged and must find my own people. But they're my family. I don't understand humans—don't like how they smell, or shout, or fight. I've spied on them when they camp nearby, listened as they inhaled burned leaves and drank something that made them even louder.

I'm ashamed, because I'm afraid of your people, whether round eared or pointed. I'm not brave and strong, as a bear should be, and so I belong to no people. I feel so alone. Then you came into my life as though you were meant to lead me out. It feels different with you. You're smart, kind, funny, and I'm not too afraid of you.

At this, the tension that was building up inside of Senzia caused her to explode with laughter. Her eyes watered, and she clutched her stomach as she gasped for air.

Do you mock me? Artur asked, the hurt clear in his voice. *What's so funny about what I said?*

Senzia shook her finger in front of him as she struggled to bring herself under control. She wiped her eyes on her sleeve and, when that failed to work, bent down and washed her face in the cold water. Then she stood and walked to Artur, taking both his hands in hers.

"I don't mock you, Artur. The more time we spend together, the closer I feel to you. I would never intentionally hurt you, you need to know that you are very wrong. Fear the mighty bears, the hotheaded men, and the elusive elf, but know I may be more dangerous than any of them alone—and maybe all of them together."

Chapter 27

"Thank you for helping us back there," Seanchai suddenly called to a clump of bushes.

Mharina stared at him. "What are you doing?"

"He's been tracking us since we left the miner's town," Seanchai said.

She looked toward the bushes. "How do you—"

"You are Wycaan, too, Mharina. You have more than your eyes."

The elfe reached out with her mind and soon located a single human standing perfectly still.

"Why doesn't he reveal himself?"

Her father grinned and replied in a loud voice. "He's an assassin. They prefer to make an entry."

There was a laugh from behind a tree, and a figure swathed in black stepped out, blinking in the sunlight.

"A Master Assassin, if you don't mind. But apparently even a Master Assassin cannot outmaneuver a Wycaan Master."

"Perhaps," Seanchai replied, smiling. "But I'd prefer not to put that to the test. Were you following us since Grogin?"

"Off and on," Ahad replied. "Once the bounty hunter appeared at Grogin, I had to leave quickly. But then I picked up your scent again and had nothing better to do."

"Thanks for helping us out back there," Mharina said. "Will you continue with us?"

"Where are you going?"

"I'm looking for a friend," she replied, feeling her cheeks warm.

"They are few and far between these days," Ahad replied. "And, as your father would recall if he could, I don't excel in choosing them."

Mharina looked at Seanchai, whose face was blank. She sighed. "He doesn't remember much. Please walk with us a while. It'll be nice to have company and an extra sentry for guard duty. If we get into a scrap, we can protect you."

Ahad bristled at this but relaxed when he saw the two elves grinning. They settled into a brisk pace and wound their way up the ascending path. Ahead lay a wall of rocks with a gap that the path passed through.

"Did you walk alone?" Seanchai asked as the rocks loomed up before them.

"Yes," Ahad answered. "Why?"

"There are others," Seanchai answered.

"I can sense three," Mharina agreed. "Not sure we should enter that gorge. We'll be vulnerable."

Ahad peeled off silently and returned alone minutes later. "They're very good. I get near them, and they disappear."

"Disappear?" Mharina's eyes were wide.

"Well, not exactly. It's more that this is their land, and they're very skillful."

"I don't want to hurt anyone," Seanchai said, and turned to his daughter. "Is there another way? Can we avoid this gorge?"

She pointed down along the eastern side of the rocks. "There should be a path further down that we can follow, but it's—"

A spear landed a few paces in front of them, and they turned to see a group of warriors—some bare-chested, but most wearing gray garb. Many grew straggly beards, and they all had long hair that fell in thick, round locks. A second hoisted spear landed very close to the first.

"What are they doing?" Mharina asked, removing her hood and shaking out her hair.

"The first spear was to get our attention. The second was to show their prowess," Ahad answered. "That the spears were not aimed at us indicates a peaceful intent. They might just want to keep us away from their village."

The warriors were chatting to each other now and pointing fingers at Mharina.

"Is this going to spiral down now that they know I'm female?"

"Perhaps," Ahad replied. "But maybe not. Seanchai. Remove your hood, too."

Seanchai did so, and the reaction was the same as it had been for Mharina. A few pointed at him; three others came forward and stopped about halfway between the two groups. They left their spears in the ground but wore knives.

Mharina, Seanchai and Ahad approached slowly, hands held out to their sides, palms facing the natives. It was the sign of peace in Odessiya, but Mharina wondered whether they would know this sign here.

One of the warriors stepped closer to Mharina. He made a clicking sound and, looking her in the eye, reached out slowly to touch her hair. The elfe stiffened but let him. He turned and clicked back to his friends. Another, tall and thin, reached out to Seanchai to touch his hair, too.

Then they began to click to one another in conversation. The eldest picked up his spear and began drawing on the ground as the others joined them, creating a cacophony of discussion. One tried to speak, struggling to enunciate each word.

"Know…white…hair. Story of old one come to us, not us. We Tutan."

Mharina spoke up. "Her name was Mhari. I am named after her."

The one who was drawing the map grunted at the one talking. He nodded and turned to Seanchai. "You need go where?"

Mharina took the spear and added onto the map. She thought they were a day's walk from the forest where Sa'gola lived. She wanted to pick up supplies and a few special items and then seal the house and surroundings so that she could return one day.

Sa'gola's sanctuary was situated in a moist forest near a swamp. Mharina hoped they could pick up the Mushroom Man's trail, as many mushrooms grew in the vicinity and it was an easy terrain to hide in.

On a whim, she drew a mushroom and then a man in the dust. The Tutans started clicking between them. She turned to the one who was able to speak.

"Where is he? Have you seen him?"

"He come and go. We give for special mushroom used in…" he squinted, trying to think of the word.

"Ceremonies?"

He shrugged and nodded. Mharina was unsure he had understood. "I need to find him," she said.

"He come and help sick, too. We guard his secrets. He say not tell where he go, so we not."

"He's my…he's my…" She could not say it.

The Tutan smiled and tapped his heart and then gently touched hers. Mharina nodded. "Yes," she whispered.

Chapter 28

"You really remember nothing?" Ahad asked.

The fire crackled as he peered over at Seanchai, who was sitting on a log to his right. It was just the two of them camping outside the boundary of Sa'gola's home. Mharina had chosen to go in alone. Her teacher had passionately guarded her solitude, and it seemed disrespectful to enter now with strangers.

It was a large fire. As they approached the border into Sa'gola's territory, a dense, cold fog threatened to engulf them. Mharina led them through it, and Ahad was convinced she had used some kind of magic to keep them alive. He still felt cold deep inside his body.

Seanchai was playing with a twig, sticking the tip in the fire and then blowing on it to make it glow. The strange, dense mist that Sa'gola had created to deter people from coming near her land had dampened his spirits. He shook his head. "It returns in fleeting glimpses. The memories hover in the periphery of my mind, and when Mharina and others tell me stories, I experience brief recollections. But it feels like…like all my memories are stored in a trunk, but the lid of the trunk cracks open and a memory almost escapes before it is sucked back in."

Ahad nodded. "So, I would like you to know we were best friends—a perfect combination."

"Really?"

"No," Ahad laughed. "I was driven for years to kill you. I blamed you and Shayth for killing my father. I should probably thank you now, though. I'm so good at everything I do because of my lust for revenge. I knew if I wanted to defeat you I'd have to be the best."

Seanchai stopped playing with the twig. He looked over, and Ahad saw apprehension etched into the Wycaan's face.

"Did I kill him?"

"No. It was Shayth. They had their own history. It's complicated. But it was my father who poisoned your mate."

"Ilana?"

"Yes. You had to walk awa—what is it?"

Seanchai clutched his stomach. "I feel it. I don't remember her. I can't recall her face, but the pain. It was the worst…"

"I'm sorry. I wish I could tell you something comforting about her, but I never knew her."

"Your father killed her because of me?"

"Yes. The Emperor needed you to come to him of your own volition. Your power was already strong enough that no one could force you, though I wonder if you realized that at the time."

Seanchai put the tip of his stick back in the fire. "I'm sorry about your father, Ahad."

"You are? He killed your mate and almost succeeded in executing Shayth, Rhoddan, and Ilana at Galbrieth. He—"

"I'm sorry that we killed your father," Seanchai interrupted, his tone firm. "It seems that this power I have that everyone is so enamored with has denied many children their fathers and mothers."

"They die anyway," Ahad replied harshly.

"What?"

"You aren't the first in this world to fight and kill, Seanchai. Most do it because they are ordered to. I did it for money. But you did it because you believed you were creating a better world, and, frankly, you did. No one can argue about that."

Seanchai opened his mouth to respond, but Ahad raised his hand.

"Hear me out. I'm not one of those who loved or followed you around. Remember, I spent most of my life imagining the sadistic ways I would kill you. Now you intrigue me.

"You're wracked with guilt for what only you seem to think are crimes perpetrated. Perhaps it's easier for me. I have no moral compass. I killed for a living and took pride in it. I developed it into an art. That's what truly annoys me about you." Seanchai frowned as Ahad continued. "I've seen men grapple with their conscience when they look back on their lives and actions, but you don't need to do any such thing."

"I don't remember—"

"Maybe," Ahad replied.

"You doubt me? You think I'm acting?" Seanchai tried to stifle his raised voice.

"Perhaps," Ahad replied, keeping his voice even. "I think there's something happening inside you that even you're not aware of. You're not just a legendary fighter and leader; you have a reputation for fierce friendships. You risked everything for Shayth, Rhoddan, Ilana, and others, disobeying your teachers and probably your own better judgment.

"Here's what I don't understand. You turn your back on your devoted mate, your prince, and your best friend. Everyone else sees a wounded elf, but I only see a dithering coward."

"You don't mince words," Seanchai responded, with what was neither a grimace nor a smile.

"Would you want me to? Would it make life easier for you?"

Seanchai was silent for a moment. He let the stick burn; a flame of bright orange tinged with purple struggled to stay alight as he held it up.

"You don't understand. Who am I to hold the power of life and death over others?"

"Spare me. You aren't the first to kill; nor will you be the last."

Seanchai sighed deeply. "But I am different. I have this power. It's rarely even a fair fight. I can best all but a few—maybe even everyone."

"No one fights to be noble, Wycaan. They fight to win. Those who survive do so because they're ruthless, because they want to die less than their adversary does. You use every weapon at your disposal, every tactic, whatever it takes. Perhaps that's why you're acting so pathetic—because you have the luxury to do so. Hate your power if you want, but hate it for the right reasons."

They went silent again. Ahad added a few more logs to the fire. The damp air made them hiss, spit, and smoke. Moisture sizzled before evaporating. Ahad thought Seanchai would be happy to disappear into the smoke. He was almost surprised when the Wycaan spoke up.

"I don't question what you said, but neither can I embrace it. I witnessed how the Emperor wielded such power, murdered thousands, and took the dignity from tens of thousands of his citizens. I have that power and ability inside of me, but I don't feel I deserve it. I don't want to lead a people just because I'm the one somehow chosen by...by...who knows what."

"Then don't do it for the good of the races. Do it for your friends and family. Do it for Sellia, Shayth, and Rhoddan. Do it for your children. Honor Ilana's memory. The power you possess, the magic, is neither good nor bad. It just is. It's how you wield it that counts. It can be your friend, your ally."

"You don't understand," Seanchai countered.

"No, he doesn't," a male voice said from behind them in the dark. "But I do."

Chapter 29

The man froze as two of the deadliest warriors in Odessiya sprung to their feet and leapt at him. Staying still probably saved his life, but Seanchai was pretty sure the man wasn't happy with the Master Assassin's blade glinting at his exposed neck as he was pinned to a tree.

"Okay," the man said, his voice quivering slightly. "We've established you have the advantage on me. But I have a basket of veiled lady mushrooms back there, and I'm not afraid to cook a mean stew with them."

He slowly raised his right hand, which held a long, white mushroom, the top of which resembled a spearhead. Seanchai grinned. "Let him go, Ahad. I suspect this is the famed Mushroom Man who stole my daughter's heart. He's in far greater trouble for that than from anything you might do."

Ahad released the man and bent to retrieve the straw hat he had knocked off the intruder. "Next time you approach an assassin, ring your mushroom bell," he muttered.

"Well met," Seanchai said, and grasped the man's forearms in friendship.

The Mushroom Man smiled and reciprocated. "My baskets are over there. If you don't mind, I shall join you. Have you eaten?"

"Nothing but cold meat and vegetables for a few days," Ahad admitted.

"Good. Why don't you heat some water and let me do the rest?" He began to turn and then gazed toward the unseen barrier. "How long has she been in there?"

"Not long," Seanchai replied, following the man's gaze. "We arrived around midday. She'll sleep in Sa'gola's house tonight."

A short while later, the three sat around a campfire drinking a thick, earthy mushroom soup. Abel explained the four different kinds of mushrooms in his soup, and Seanchai wondered how he made any money if he ate all he foraged. But he didn't ask. The young man was going out of his way to be nice and Seanchai realized it must be very hard for him.

When they finished eating, Seanchai asked Ahad to take their plates to the stream and then check the perimeter. The assassin looked at him curiously but went. When it was just the two of them, Seanchai stared at Abel without saying a word. The Mushroom Man caught his eyes and then proceeded to look everywhere else. He shuffled on the log and began to remove mushrooms from his wicker basket. With a small cutting knife and a duster brush, he cleaned them, examined each, and then bagged some in burlap. The others, he dropped to his side.

Seanchai continued to stare at him. Abel began to whistle as he focused on his nightly ritual. The pile by his feet grew.

"What's wrong with those mushrooms?" Seanchai asked.

The Mushroom Man did not look up. "If one has small insects on it or is going soft, it must be separated from the others or it'll harm them, as well. They aren't wasted, though. You just ate last night's pile."

"How long do I have to live?"

Abel laughed and then turned serious. "They're a wonderful creation, mushrooms. They are mysterious and powerful, yet so humble. The most powerful ones are often the plainest and hardest to find. The smallest are often the most effective healers. Kind of different from the world we live in."

"Is that why you ran away from Mharina? Because your mushrooms are easier to deal with?"

"I—"

"No. Listen, Abel. I don't know about the Purple Lady, Ithea, or even the Emperor, but I'm told I walk in a long line of Wycaan Masters and teachers who serve the people with their power."

"But you also kill and control with it. I heard your conversation with the assassin."

"Yes. And I grapple with that, myself. I hate the fact that I've killed hundreds, made thousands orphans and widows, but am told that I did everything to serve the greater good. I don't know if that's right. But I believe power and magic can also heal and free. It's not about the essence of magic, but the way we wield it."

Abel shook his head. "If magic was meant to be good, it wouldn't have an evil side."

"You're wrong," Seanchai hesitated, surprised at his newfound perspective. "The presence of good and evil is what makes us free thinkers. Freedom of choice is what moves the world. We can't eradicate evil, but we can ensure the balance always favors the good."

"I prefer my mushrooms," Abel said, shaking his head again and picking up a pointed yellow mushroom to clean. "You are right. They are less complicated."

"You prefer your mushrooms? Tell me, then, Mushroom Man: are all mushrooms good? Are they all meant for cooking or health or spiritual journeys? Are there not mushrooms that can kill you if you ingest them? Are there not mushrooms that, instead of elevating your mind to a higher level, drive you crazy?"

"Of course, but I don't pick them."

Seanchai leaned forward. "So you admit they are both good and bad. Yet you, Mushroom Man, do not reject *all* mushrooms because some are evil. You make the right choices and harvest those that serve good."

Abel nodded, his eyes focused on removing a tiny, nonexistent piece of dirt from the yellow mushroom's underbelly.

"I understand," he said at length, "but I've only ever seen the evil side of magic. My mother created the order that Sa'gola belonged to. She feared the threat of the male half of magic, which had tortured and murdered women to maintain their own power. She hunted down sorceresses who bore male babies and killed their children to prevent women with the power from passing it on to their male offspring. But she could not do the same when her own time came. She hid my brother and I and let us grow up, knowing we might have the power of magic and use it badly. She convinced herself that her mother's love could direct our potential magic, if we possessed any, to good. But she was so wrong and thousands have paid for her mistake."

"What about my daughter?" Seanchai persisted. "Every day you forage, you choose to turn your back on the poisonous mushrooms and harvest the good ones for others to eat and heal with. Perhaps if you truly love Mharina, you can help her make the right choices when she harvests her potential."

They sat in silence for a while, but this time it felt like a more comfortable, contemplative silence. After a while, Abel looked up.

"You hate the magic, maybe as much as I do. What keeps you going?"

"Those I love, I think: my *calhei*, their mother, my friends. It doesn't just keep me going, Mushroom Man; it's all that keeps me sane."

"Then this love, this loyalty, will send you back to help Shayth," Ahad said, standing behind them in the shadows. "I just wonder if it will be enough to save Odessiya."

Chapter 30

Aterrifying, numbing feeling rose slowly inside Mharina's body as she made her way through the swamp, over the bridge, and toward Sa'gola's cottage.

It would always be Sa'gola's cottage, even though Mharina knew her teacher wanted her to take it over. She would use it as a sanctuary, a safe home, but she hoped to share it with her Mushroom Man if Abel took her back. She found it hard to be angry or hurt that he fled Grogin and left her after he had witnessed Ithea's slaying of Sa'gola, and then saw Mharina unleash the fury of her own magic upon the sorcerer.

Ithea. Abel's brother and his exact opposite. Ithea was evil and powerful, egotistical and ambitious. Abel was gentle and soft and… was he unmagical? The thought suddenly occurred to her. Was he without power, or did he just choose not to use it? She knew he hated magic. No surprise, considering how his mother and brother abused it. She assumed he did not possess magic, but she had never asked.

Her staff clicking on the path brought her out of her reverie. She had left the swamp. There were people crossing the bridge, and she stood to one side to let them pass. Before, they had never looked at her, never acknowledged her presence. The Purple Lady was a powerful spirit who protected them and healed their sick but was otherwise not to be bothered.

But a small group of passing farmers all glanced at her furtively, quickly looking away when Mharina caught their eyes. She wondered whether Sa'gola's spells that protected and hid her sanctuary could outlive her. It worried her, but any chance of returning here was a long time off with many obstacles in the way.

She glanced at the lake as she approached the cottage. She had enjoyed swimming and bathing in its cool waters. Looking at the cottage, she sent tendrils of magic around the perimeter and inside. No one had come here since they had left, as far as she could discern.

There was dust on the porch and a spider's web connected to the doorframe. She pulled down the invisible screen Sa'gola had erected around the house and slowly opened the door. There was a gentle whine as the hinges turned. She entered.

She could feel it immediately. She was not alone. Quickly, she sent her magic roaming through the cottage, but nothing was revealed. She put her bags down but not her staff. She would keep it close.

Mharina lit the stove and boiled water as she had always done when Sa'gola returned to the house. She made a mixture of the dried herbs: lavender; melissa; and a subtle mint with long, serrated leaves. The smell was relaxing, and she inhaled deeply. It had been Sa'gola's favorite after a hard day of training.

Then she turned around and screamed.

"You're dead," she gasped. "I saw…"

Mharina pulled her blouse away from her chest. She had spilled tea on herself when she jumped, and it was hot. But she barely noticed. She stared at the figure sitting at the kitchen table.

"Sit down, Mharina."

"Um. Shall I make you tea?"

Sa'gola smiled. "I'm not really here. I created a very complicated spell so I could return from the dead just once, when someone entered the cottage. I cannot drink or even move."

"Err, okay. Well. How are you?" Mharina's mind had frozen.

"Pretty dead, to be honest. How are you, little elfe?"

Mharina shrugged. "I can't believe I lost you." She felt her voice breaking. "I'm so sorry. I promised to protect you. I should have—"

"Should have what? We faced the most powerful sorcerer in Odessiya. I don't even know how you overcame him. What happened?"

Mharina told Sa'gola how Denalion, the Dreamwalker of the West who had lived by hiding inside Ithea's mind after the sorcerer took over his body, had commanded the raging Seanchai to transform into his bear form. Ithea had not anticipated such an attack and had no time to defend himself.

Sa'gola nodded. "I have to confess to disappointment. I thought you had done it. Oh, well. At least you got your father back."

"Not quite." Mharina recounted Seanchai's lost memory and refusal to take up his former role.

"Then it falls on your shoulders, little elfe. What are you going to do? Perhaps you should move into Grogin."

"The place where you died? Never. I'd rather live here, where I have happy memories of you. But right now, the prince fights an invading army of Ashen Elves. He needs me to help turn the tide."

"So, why did you come back here?"

Mharina pursed her lips but didn't answer. Sa'gola laughed. "Your Mushroom Man ran away. Oh, Mharina. We all fall prey to our hearts. Listen. I don't have much more time. What can I help you with?"

Mharina sipped her tea and thought.

"Am I really as powerful as everyone thinks?" she asked.

Sa'gola nodded. "Good question. The truth is, no one alive knows what it is to wield the *Iyzun*. But always remember, Mharina: people will believe what you put forth if you are unwavering."

"That's not enough if I must face powerful adversaries."

"You have a distinct disadvantage in that you're young. Your father or I can insinuate power and experience. But I am dead and he must heal. What happened to him under the sea?"

"We don't know. He doesn't know. But it's the key to everything. What else can you tell me?"

"Well, this cottage is not all it seems. There are various distance tunnels like the one we used to get to the Order or the one that took you to Grogin. There are other invisible caverns folded into time and space." Sa'gola listed many such hiding places, describing a library full of ancient and rare scrolls, another with sacred symbols and weapons, one with dried food and supplies, and a fourth full of artifacts of wealth. "One has many dried herbs and rare mushrooms—gifts from your lover, in fact. And—"

"What's between you and Abel?"

The spirit of Sa'gola winced. "What *was* between us, you mean. I cannot answer that. Tell him he has permission to tell you whatever he sees fit, but I'm sworn to secrecy. Though I release him from his oath, he has not released me from mine."

"Sa'gola. When he ran away, was it from fear of my magic or seeing you die?"

"My guess is both. He loves and fears me."

"Does he possess magic?"

Sa'gola didn't answer. Mharina stared at her and sighed. Then she asked the question she feared most.

"If you considered only what's in my best interest and nothing else, would you advise me to seek him out and make him my mate?"

The spirit of Sa'gola stared at her. Mharina knew her teacher well enough to know she was conflicted. When she finally spoke, the Purple Lady's voice was quiet.

"I love you, Mharina, and I love Abel. I have for a very long time. I so want to see you find happiness together, but…" She stopped and looked to the window, staring out at the reddening sky. Then she turned back to her student. "No, my dear apprentice. If you stay together, it's likely to end in tragedy—for him, you, and maybe all of Odessiya."

"Sa'gola, I…"

But the image of Sa'gola was fading. "I love you," she called from a distance.

"I love you, too," Mharina whispered, and hugged the mug of pungent herbal tea inhaling the memory of her teacher.

Chapter 31

Prince Shayth Shindell almost fell from his horse as pain seared through his ribs, threatening to render him unconscious. Around him rode the surviving Soldiers of the Black Stone. Shayth was never quite sure how many of them there were. Crags seemed to have developed a multi-layer system of defense, but now, the soldiers appeared far fewer and rather stunned, having lost their commanding officer and quite a few men. These were the elite soldiers of Odessiya. They did not expect to face stronger opposition.

Shayth had no energy with which to offer them support or commiserations. He did not have a personal relationship with Crags or any of them. He had only recently accepted their constant presence, and protocol did not allow much interaction.

They rode through narrow, rough mountain passes slowly, in consideration of their wounded prince. The horses had to watch their step, and the mist and fog made the men feel uneasy and claustrophobic. They rode in silence.

There were about thirty other soldiers in the company. The rest of the army was supposed to lead the Ashen Elves into the Cumrian Mountains and try to pick them off or strand them there. But after inflicting the rib-crushing wound on Shayth, the enemy had retreated.

General Pilau had assumed total command of the army, sending multiple units out in wide arcs that all headed back toward Shindellia. Shayth pondered the wisdom of creating a final confrontation scenario. With the additional dwarves and the flat plains around the capital giving an advantage to the cavalry, it might not be such a terrible idea, but only if the Ashen Elves were small in numbers.

It was puzzling that the Ashen Elves had retreated. Why not try and defeat Shayth's army while Shayth was incapacitated? In fact, why not kill him or take him prisoner? The Gray Elf who had fought him revealed just two things: one, that it was possible to transfer power through the red stones, and two, that the mage knew of the Elves of the West. How had she discovered them? Had there been contact between them? He began to wonder if there was a conspiracy to crush all non-elf power.

That sent a shiver of worry through him. Shayth glanced over at Pyre. He did not know the elfe very well, he realized. Seanchai had total faith in her before he lost his memory. But what if Pyre was a spy? She shadowed him and had access to his plans and doubts.

Pyre had stayed with the council members of the Elves of the West after Shayth led his horse away. He had no idea what had transpired then. She was, as far as he knew, exiled for leaving the Forest of Markwin to join Seanchai. He realized he was increasingly relying on her, even though her loyalty was to Seanchai. Yet, she had come to his side instead of going with Seanchai and Mharina. There was, perhaps, a clear, overriding sense of duty. He sighed. Maybe he was just clutching at straws. Would Pyre have been able to fight off the elf who overwhelmed Shayth and Crags?

The party stopped, and one of the men dismounted and came over to Shayth.

"Prince Shayth. The Wycaan elfe requests that I help you dismount. We'll rest a while, and she wants to check the tourniquets wrapped around your ribs."

"I don't need help dismounting, man," Shayth growled. But as he swung his leg around, white-hot pain exploded through his entire body, and he fell, inelegantly, into the man's waiting arms. As the man straightened him on his wobbly feet, Shayth hissed, "Don't tell her."

"She actually anticipated exactly what happened, my prince. I believe she said to prepare to catch the stubborn…" the soldier said, grinning until Shayth's glare wiped it from his face, "the proud price."

Shayth patted his arm. "Just remember where your loyalty lies," he said as congenially as he could manage.

The soldier helped him over to a rock tall enough for him to sit on without lowering himself. He noticed those men not already guarding were bunched together and talking intensely.

"What's going on over there?" Shayth asked.

The man looked over at his friends. "Whenever the unit loses men, we plan between us to take care of their families—to break the news and help with the burial— and we all put a portion of our salaries into a pot to help them. We're more than just a unit, my prince. We're family."

Shayth nodded. "What is your name?"

"Janus, my lord."

"Who has replaced Crags?"

"McCutter, sir. But you can of course appoint—"

"Bring him and come yourself."

The man nodded and jogged off to retrieve a soldier talking to Pyre. They both turned and walked over to Shayth with Janus. Pyre told Shayth to put a hand on each man's shoulder and then pulled up his shirt. She instructed the two men to hold his hands there to prevent any jerking actions in response to the pain. Then she loosened and tightened each tourniquet.

"My lord," McCutter said, standing stiffly. "Do you have new orders?"

"No. Janus told me what the men are discussing. How many did you lose, and did they have children?"

"Three, my lord. Jyles left three children and Crags' wife is expecting their first—might be born already. Young Evans wasn't married."

"Whatever you men have in this pot, I'll double. Janus here will request anything else you need. There's a school in the palace. The children can study there." He turned to Janus. "When we get back to the capital, you will remind me to make sure my scribe puts all this in writing, for now and the future."

"You'll certainly have a lot of time on your hands," Pyre said as she tied the last bandage. "A war, coronation, a wedding…why don't you let Janus go straight to your scribe? You can just add your seal when it is done."

"She fights, heals, and now tells me how to rule," Shayth grunted, mainly from the pain. "Anyway, not sure I can fight or enjoy my wedding much like this."

"We sent a hawk to the capital, asking that the healer Maugwen join us and begin working on you," McCutter said.

"On whose authority?" Shayth snapped, though he thought highly of Maugwen's healing talents.

Neither soldier answered, and Shayth looked at Pyre.

"Guilty as charged" She shrugged. "We need you fit to lead your army. Even though you're only an average soldier, your men seem to get inspired seeing you taken down each time."

Both soldiers had to stifle a laugh. Shayth wasn't as able, and the movement caused him to gasp.

"Arrest her," he said without conviction. "Actually, leave the two of us. Tell the men we leave in a few minutes. Janus. After you check your own horse, please check mine."

Both men nodded and walked away.

"Fine men," Pyre said. "All of them."

"How many more will die?" Shayth asked. "I could stop it, you know."

"By surrendering?"

"No. I could let them pass through and face the Elves of the West. I could persuade the mage that the elves of Odessiya had nothing to do with their sad histories and put all the blame on your people."

Pyre's face was hard, and she stared off into the encroaching fog.

"What are you thinking?" Shayth asked.

"That if you're considering such thoughts, we desperately need Seanchai and Mharina."

Chapter 32

Maugwen met the army when they were about two days away from the capital. She came with a caravan of healers and herbs and immediately created a small healing camp for Shayth and the other wounded soldiers.

"We shouldn't be doing this," Shayth protested. "It's taking too much time."

"It's worth it," Maugwen answered as she removed his bandages. "Rumors are rife, and the people live in fear. They shouldn't see you tottering through the main gates when you arrive."

She helped him lay down on a cot and stuffed some cloths under his knees. "Now, be quiet and let me try to patch this mess up." She moved her hands gently along his rib cage, tutting and shaking her head. "I thought I told you not to play rough with the big boys."

"It was only one," Shayth replied, his eyes closed. "But he was being fueled by others. His stone glowed red. It was eerie."

"But still you bested him, no?"

"What makes you think that?" Shayth asked.

"You're still alive."

"He was ordered not to kill me. I don't know why. It sometimes feels as if the mage actually likes me, as if the warriors I get to know respect me. Maybe they aren't as bad as we think. They're simply incarcerated by their hate and drive for revenge."

"Hate to burst your bubble, Shayth, but all I see are dead and wounded soldiers."

"But if I could somehow bind them to me. If—"

"You're beginning to sound like Seanchai," Maugwen said, smiling.

Shayth regretted the glare he threw at her. She had flinched and the smile vanished from her face. They both went quiet as Maugwen continued to probe his ribcage.

"Any news?" he said at last.

She shook her head.

"I'm sorry," he said, and meant it.

"We're all hurting, Shayth. Rhoddan roams the ramparts, barking orders to improve here, change there. He chastises and compliments the soldiers, but all the time, he looks to the east. When horses approach or when someone enters the eating hall, he immediately looks up. Even his lovely mate, Troja, cannot cure him of the loss he feels."

Shayth didn't respond. He didn't know what to say. He was the prince, the leader. It was for him to reassure his subjects.

"How is Pyre holding up?" Maugwen asked.

"She's fine. Why?"

"She is similar to Rhoddan. She gave up everything to follow Seanchai."

"And if he fails her, where will she turn?"

"What do you mean?" Maugwen stopped her examination and frowned at him. "They'll both support you and do what is right."

"I don't doubt Rhoddan," Shayth said, then stopped and thought for a while. He shared their meeting with the council members of the Elves of the West and that Pyre had stayed behind.

"You think she's a spy? Did you take a blow to the head I'm not aware of?"

"Maybe she didn't start out as one. I believe she followed Seanchai faithfully. But what if he no longer figures in the equation? What if it's a choice between Odessiya and the Elves of the West?"

Maugwen resumed her work. She did not offer a pat answer, and he appreciated that. He felt the warmth of her hands extend into his body. He felt himself begin to sweat. The heat was intense, and he began panting.

"Hang in there," Maugwen whispered.

He let out a groan as he felt his bones extend. It was like stretching without moving, and he was fascinated even as he embraced the pain. With that thought, he felt himself sink into a deep, dreamless sleep.

It was impossible to imagine that the country was at war when walking the beautiful boulevards of Shindellia. Bits of colored glass and crystals hung from every tree. Buildings were draped in purple and gold, the colors Shayth would take when he relinquished the sigil of his uncle. As he led his troops through the streets, people cheered and threw lavender and rosemary onto the road. When the horses trotted over it, a pungent aroma filled the air.

Shayth sat up straight in his saddle. He was feeling sore but much better. Maugwen filled him with a warming energy and had him constantly drinking bitter boneknitting tea. He smiled and tried to wave at the people he passed, but raising an arm and moving it while his body rocked to the horse's momentum was too much, and he soon tired. Still, he forced a smile and bowed to people's greetings and blessings.

Entering the gates of the inner city, the prince allowed himself to relax, and his body slumped forward. He stopped his horse and signaled to McCutter, who jumped from his horse and, with another guard, helped Shayth down. Maugwen was quickly at his side, a frown etched across her face.

He walked stiffly toward the steps that led up to the palace. It looked like the entire staff had been summoned to greet him from the stairs. He frowned. He disliked such pointless pomp, and his councilors knew it. He was sure they did it for their own self-importance, and they bobbed like chickens waiting for feed as he approached.

Looking to the side, the prince saw Rhoddan and Troja. The elfe looked so thin as she leaned into the great warrior. He began to turn back, but then saw a dark elfe with a thick, black curly mane of hair and a young *calhei* next to her.

"Sellia!" he called, and began to walk in her direction.

When the first minister shuffled into his path, Shayth considered drawing his sword. Instead, he turned to McCutter.

"Stay close to me. I'm fading. I must speak with Rhoddan and his party. Everyone else must wait." Then he turned to the minister and spoke, even though his guards stood between them. "Please dismiss the staff. I will dine with my friends in my own quarters and receive my schedule from you in the morning."

He tried to walk past, but the first minister stood his ground. "My prince! Your coronation is in the morning."

"I will put on the clothes you prepared for me, follow everyone else to the ceremony, and repeat whatever the High Priest says."

His soldiers laughed, as did Maugwen, but the minister just slumped, and Shayth finally took pity on him. "Very well. Await my summons after we eat."

As they reached Rhoddan and the others, McCutter called out. "The prince is still wounded. No one is permitted to touch or embrace him."

"On whose orders?" Shayth asked, reaching to embrace Sellia.

McCutter just stared helplessly.

"Maugwen!" Shayth roared, but the healer was gone.

Chapter 33

That night, Shayth stood on the ramparts staring down on his city and kingdom. He rarely felt he, a royal imposter, belonged here, and at this moment in time, he felt especially inadequate. His ribs were mending but still hurt, and this impacted every movement he made. But his unease was something that transcended the physical. Coming back to the capital, spending a depressingly quiet dinner with his closest friends, and seeing the rising expectations for his coronation and impending marriage only served to enhance the enormity of what lay before him.

He slumped onto a wooden bench and absentmindedly scratched his dog's ears. Azura's tail thumped on the stone ground, and she gently pushed against his leg. It would have been so comforting without those sharp blue eyes staring up at him.

Out there somewhere was an enemy more powerful than him with the ability and desire to destroy his kingdom. Also out there was the one person who might hold the key to victory. Seanchai had not been waiting for him in the capital, and Shayth, while he doubted his friend would come, had nonetheless felt a crushing disappointment.

He was further concerned that Sellia was here with Ilan, fraught with worry that his twin, Senzia, had gone missing. Apparently Senzia, angry with Seanchai and Mharina for not coming to answer Shayth's call, had set off by herself to find Pyre and fight alongside her. But Senzia had not arrived, and her trail had gone cold.

Shayth looked out beyond the walls at the faraway lights—mere dots—of fires in his army's camps. Most of the soldiers remained beyond the walls, ready to defend the city. They rotated leave, and those with families inside the walls were given time to visit. Shayth had insisted on this, even though it unfairly left more guard duty for the men conscripted from towns beyond Shindellia. But it was more than a simple gesture of generosity. A soldier who had his back to the city walls and knew he was all that stood between a ruthless enemy and his family would fight beyond personal fear or exhaustion. Shayth wanted to remind these men what was at stake for them all.

"May I join you?" the mage asked, emerging from the shadows. Her black clothes and gray skin had hidden her well in the darkness.

Shayth tried not to look surprised and signaled with his hand for her to sit. "Are you alone?"

"I am," she said, "and I carry no weapon. I have come to talk."

"What about?"

"You. You fascinate me." Her voice was as deep and strong as it was the last time they met, but, underneath, he thought he discerned a certain softness. "The next few days are monumental for you. I won't be able to call you not-King. You'll take a bride and provide an heir. These are important steps of a mature leader."

Shayth laughed but had to grasp his sore ribs. "Why does everyone think I will get my bride pregnant so quickly? Is it that easy?"

"I don't understand the ways of humans," she replied. "If you want advice on such a topic, I suggest you find an older human female."

Again, this elicited a laugh from Shayth, but the pain cut it short. "I find little cause to celebrate, mage. Many good soldiers, both elves and humans, lay dead because of your invasion. Many more women and children have become widows and orphans. I personally know what it means to grow up denied of my parents. I'll do what needs to be done and then focus on repelling your army. You have also suffered losses. Does this not affect you or your people?"

"Not like it does with humans, from what I see. I have a question."

"Ask."

"What are the Elves of the West to you?"

Shayth shrugged. "We have fought together in the past. Some great elves came from there. They trained the Wycaan Master."

"But there is no love lost between you?"

"We're not close. Why do you ask?"

The mage wrapped her black cloak around her but also removed her hood. Her hair seemed to shimmer in the dull light of the city. "I'm trying to understand your honor. You aren't close to them. They do not come to your aid. And yet, you protect them. Why?"

Shayth harrumphed. "I ask myself the same question every time I bury another soldier. I think it's because, even if your narrative is true, the current elves are not to blame for a crime perpetrated centuries ago. I cannot stand aside and let you slaughter innocent elves and *calhei*."

"And so you protect them at such a high cost?"

He nodded. "I do. I must, because if I compromise even once in my responsibility for the safety of my subjects, it would be a slippery slope."

"Then you leave me little choice but to continue this war," the mage said.

"You make your own decisions, and only you can hold yourself responsible for them," Shayth growled. "That is the essence of ruling."

She stared at him. "For one who protests so profusely to being a king, you certainly sound the part. Enjoy your coronation and wedding, *King* Shayth Shindell."

The mage stood and glided back into the shadows. Shayth stared into the blackness. Azura growled and began to look around. There were others on the ramparts—soldiers he did not recognize—and he felt a fleeting panic. He stood, and his hand went to the hilt of his sword.

Two soldiers ran up. "Are you alone, sir? We heard voices."

"I am. I was talking to my dog. Who are you? I don't recognize either of you."

"They are my personal guard, Prince Shayth," a soft, feminine voice said from behind the two guards. "Forgive me. They obeyed my order. I heard you stalk the ramparts at night. I wanted the first meeting with my future husband without tens of thousands of eyes upon us."

The guards walked past Shayth and took up positions to seal a perimeter. In front of him, swathed in a thick, purple cloak, stood a beautiful young woman. Her skin was dark, and he could not see her eyes. Black hair fell out of her hood, and she wrapped her arms around herself.

"My lady," Shayth said, bowing and feeling heat burning his cheeks. "I am Prince Shayth Shindell."

"I know," she said, her voice soft. "Do you even know my name?"

Chapter 34

The crown prince of Odessiya, who led a mighty nation in war and peace, stood before his bride, totally flummoxed.

"I—I've been very busy, my lady," he said as he desperately searched his memory for her name.

"I understand," she said. "You fight a war against a stronger enemy. The protection of your people must always be your highest priority. I have heard that you seek neither the crown, nor a mate. The first I find intriguing. The second, disturbing, given our arranged marriage."

He could discern no emotion in her voice. It was deep and throaty, but, most of all, it was perfectly controlled. Shayth pointed to the bench, and they both sat down. He looked around. Her guards had melted into the darkness.

"They can hear our conversation, my prince, but will share nothing. They're each sworn to my father and bonded to me."

"Please. Call me Shayth," he said. "And put me out of my embarrassment."

She removed her hood, and Shayth gasped as he took in her dark skin, rich brown eyes, and exquisite cheekbones. Her lips were full and her eyebrows thin and arched. He could feel himself flush again and knew from her demure smile that she saw her effect on him, as well.

"My name is Shameka. It means 'made by the gods,' but I have it on good authority that my parents deserve all the credit."

Shayth grinned. "The gods smiled upon your parents, then. You are beautiful. How has your stay been so far?"

"You are kind, my lo—Shayth. I am aware of my beauty, but I hope you will see me in time as more than a placation for your court."

"I don't see you that way. I a—" He stopped as Shameka smiled and rested a delicate hand on his arm.

"Let us not begin our life together by lying to each other," she said, and, behind the smile, he glimpsed a look of earnestness.

"You're right," he said. "You deserve better than that. I have a very dark past, Shameka—one that I've never come to terms with. It seems wrong that I be given this immense privilege to rule, that people look up to me with reverence because I happen to have been born a Shindell. I often believe the gods cursed me by giving me such a name. It's hard for me to think I can ever be worthy of sharing my life completely with a woman."

She squeezed his arm. "You cannot change your past, Shayth, but you can learn from it. When you were most lost, you were alone. When you made friends with the Wycaan and his friends, you found yourself again. Now, as king, you must surround yourself with people you trust, with friends who love you but are empowered enough to offer honest counsel. I have met Rhoddan since coming here, and Maugwen, too. I would like to earn your trust and respect to be, like them, one of your close companions. I seek that more than a crown or the title of queen of Odessiya."

Shayth stared into her eyes, big brown pools that invited him in. He put an arm around her, and she shuffled closer. Her musty fragrance engulfed him.

"That's what I need most of all, Shameka," he whispered into her ear. "Good friends, men and women, elves and elfes, as the Wycaan gathered around him. Those you met are loyal to me, too, yet I feel so alone."

"I will earn myself a place by your side," she replied, and wiggled even closer in his embrace.

They sat together like that in silence, and, for the first time in what seemed like forever, Prince Shayth Shindell felt a glimmer of hope.

The coronation took place not in the Great Hall of Prayers, but on the steps of the palace. Shayth had insisted the ceremony transpire in front of the people. Thousands squeezed into the square to watch the ceremony. Others crowded the walls and ramparts and filled any window or balcony that afforded even a glimpse. The sky was cloudless, and a breeze kept the heat away.

Clad in rich scarlet, three priestesses stood waiting with crown and scepter. One was majestically old, her hair gray and her face deeply lined. A second, with her hair tied back, embraced a swelling stomach, promising an imminent birth. The third was young, her hair golden and her cheeks rosy against pale, alabaster skin.

The huge stone throne could not be brought outside. So a large oak chair, beautifully carved and varnished until it shone in the sunlight, was placed at the top of the stairs. Shayth stood by the chair dressed in what had to be the most uncomfortable garb that could be found. His shirt was beige with lines of gold that made it heavy and stiff. His trousers were likewise thick and uncompromising, with similar threads of gold.

The eldest priestess approached, and a lanky boy walked solemnly behind her, reverently holding the rich red cloak of the king. It was thick and lined at top and bottom with fur. When she spoke, her voice was raspy but strong and carried unnaturally across the great square.

"The gods and goddesses see fit to bless Odessiya with a new king. Will you wrap your people in your care, holding their safety and welfare above all? Do you, of your own free will, take the cloak?"

"I do," Shayth said, and he could almost see his words travel to those furthest away.

"Take the cloak," the old woman said. "You must put it on yourself, showing that you take responsibility for your actions."

The boy stepped in front of her, and Shayth took the heavy cloak and swung it around his shoulders. The pregnant woman approached, holding a tall scepter that towered over her. It was heavy, and Shayth could see her arms trembling, but her expression was set and determined. The staff was wooden, with etched gold bands and inlaid stones that shone as the sun caught them. The tip resembled a phallus.

"The gods and goddesses see fit to bless Odessiya with a new king," the priestess said. "Do you take responsibility for producing an heir so that your people will know stability? Do you swear to provide for your people, to the best of your ability, to give them abundance and harvest and fertility?"

"I do," Shayth called out, and took the scepter from her. It felt heavy but strangely familiar in his grasp.

The young priestess approached. Shayth could see that she was intimidated and working very hard to hold herself together. She held the crown, a surprisingly small and light ring of carved metal. Compared to the heavy cloak and scepter, it seemed almost insignificant, but this was what he would wear more than the other two mostly ceremonial symbols.

Her voice shook when she started to speak but evened out quickly. "The gods and goddesses see fit to bless Odessiya with a new king. The cloak covers the king, providing warmth on cold days. The scepter symbolizes fertility and serves as a weapon with which to protect the people. The crown is a reminder that a king rules with his head, for he assumes great responsibility. Do you swear to rule the people fairly and with as much wisdom as you can learn or gather from your advisors?"

"I do," Shayth replied.

"Bend the knee," she said, her voice growing with the occasion. "Bend before the gods and goddesses of Odessiya. Bend before the people you serve."

He did, and she gently laid the crown upon his head.

"Rise, then, Majesty Shayth Shindell, king of Odessiya."

As Shayth stood, the young woman went to her own knee, and the thousands gathered joined her. He stared out at waves of bent heads, and an unfamiliar feeling of power surged through him. The words flowed unbidden and unrehearsed.

"I am your king!" he cried, "And I am your servant. I will do all I can to protect you, to guide you, to lead you. We will remain a free people, a proud people, and a united people. Race will not tear us apart. Hate will not divide us. Power will not corrupt us. If ever I fail you in my duty, take my crown, cloak, and scepter and pass them to one more deserving. But know this: I will strive to serve you with all my soul. We shall be forever a free and proud people."

King Shayth Shindell looked up to the ramparts where he had stood the night before. Staring back at him, their blue eyes sucking him in, the red stones gleaming, stood the mage and a dozen Ashen Elves.

When the command to rise did not come, the people slowly looked up, first at their king and then at those who were caught in his gaze. No one moved. There were gasps of surprise, but no one cried out or made to attack.

The great square of Shindellia stood frozen, and then the mage put her hand on her red stone and disappeared, followed by her entourage. The people turned their eyes to their new king. Shayth raised the scepter above his head.

"Rise up! Our work begins! A united Odessiya! A free Odessiya!"

A free Odessiya! The cry echoed back ten thousand times stronger.

A free Odessiya!

A free Odessiya!

A free Odessiya!

CHAPTER 35

Senzia continued to coax Artur to speak out loud, and it gradually became more comfortable for him. He still got frustrated and resorted to telepathy when he wanted to make sure she understood him, but his improvement increased his confidence.

They were heading northeast toward Shindellia. Senzia assumed that Prince Shayth and Pyre were fighting in the north. She pondered whether to enter the capital. It was a huge city, and, despite her powers, the idea of entering alone intimidated her. She was still a young elfe unused to being around large concentrations of people. Her white hair would make her stand out and garner attention. She glanced over at Artur, who was muttering to himself, endlessly practicing the sounds of spoken language.

Three nights had passed. Senzia hunted with the bow she took from the dead wolfheid, but it was heavy for her, and she was not well practiced. She also had trouble skinning the rabbits she caught. When she saw a fawn and its mother, she raised her bow, but did not let the arrow fly. She wasn't sure why and felt a mix of embarrassment and relief. Artur's foraging for roots, mushrooms, and berries kept the hunger at bay, but she looked forward to a real meal. Perhaps this was reason enough to enter Shindellia.

When it got dark, they camped, and Senzia told Artur about the history of Odessiya, about Wycaans and Ashen Elves. He asked lots of questions, often interrupting her, which was cute at first but irritating as time passed. She wondered how Ilan was doing, separated from her and needing to placate their mother. Would they continue with their plans to travel to the Elves of the West, or had Sellia's mothering instinct taken over? If it had, Senzia was likely being followed or would receive an anxious reception in the capital.

On the fourth day, they had to hide twice from a two separate bands of ragged soldiers. The first passed by, carrying their wounded. Senzia and Artur crouched in the bushes and watched. There were at least forty men leading horses, a number of which carried wrapped bodies bound to their saddles. Senzia could see the exhaustion etched into their faces as they kept their eyes to the front.

The second regiment was all on foot, except their officer, who was mounted. The men all rested pikes on their shoulders. They, too, wore the dazed expression of men who had not slept for days.

That night, Senzia and Artur did not light a fire and went to sleep without talking. Senzia wondered if they should post guard but realized it would exhaust them. They moved far away from the path before choosing a spot to stop. Artur tried to persuade her to sleep in a tree and showed her how to find the right junction of branches to support her weight. She tried but was too scared she would roll over in her sleep and fall. She also doubted she could actually fall asleep balanced so precariously.

On the ground, you're vulnerable to big cats and other scavengers, Artur said telepathically. *Also, men do not think to look up. Many times, I have hidden from humans right above their heads.*

"Artur. I want you to promise me something. It might be very difficult for you, but it might save my life."

"What?" he asked out loud, a frown on his face.

"Promise me that if I get captured and they don't see you, you won't try to rescue me unless I call for you. Instead, study hard who takes me prisoner—their uniforms and sigils and whether they are humans, elves, dwarves, or especially Gray Elves.

"But—"

"Listen. Then, head south and find bears. Use them to communicate with the new great grizzly what you saw. He's most likely to be found in the dream world. Let him come to rescue me. If you try to do it, we will both die. You'll best help me by finding him."

Artur nodded, but his frown remained. *How do you know he will help you? I don't even know if I can find him or whether he will listen to me.*

She took his hands in hers. "Listen carefully, my good friend. The great grizzly has an elf form. In his elf form, he is a Wycaan Master who is wise and powerful. But more than that, he is my father, and when he knows his daughter is in danger, he will be unstoppable. Promise me."

"I promise," Artur said. *I will find him, even if it takes me forever.*

"Try to do it quicker. I don't think I'll make a very good prisoner."

They both laughed and then, inexplicably, hugged. It was a firm, tight embrace, born of two young people afraid of a cruel world bearing down on them.

Artur's twitching nose should have given it away. But Senzia was so intent on reaching the capital and wondering if her mother and brother were there that she barely took note of what she discounted as another weird bear trait.

So, they walked straight into a unit of seven Ashen Elves camping in a rare open spot in the dense forest they were traveling through. Senzia had chosen this route, rather than the road, to avoid any more military units. This had to be the dumbest luck.

The elves did not move but stared at them with cold, blue eyes. Senzia felt rooted to the spot and had to mentally drag herself back to this reality.

"S—sirs," She faked the stammer and meekness. "Don't want no trouble. We can go around, no problem." She turned her head slightly and whispered to Artur, "Back away."

"Wait." A huge Ashen Elf, taller even than her father and Rhoddan, walked up cautiously. "No need to be afraid, little elfe," he said, taking them both in, his icy eyes moving furtively. "We're elves, as well. What's your name?"

Like the others, he wore tight black armor, but around his neck was a red stone that seemed to be throbbing. Senzia couldn't see that any of the others wore the stone. Perhaps it was a sigil of rank, but then she felt its energy and knew it was something far more.

"Back away," she whispered, but the elf advanced, looking at her with increasing intensity.

"You have beautiful hair," he said. "So white. What's your name?"

"Josie," Senzia replied, taking the name of a doll she had when she was younger. She hated it and Ilan loved it, but she wouldn't let him play with it. It seemed stupid now that she was almost grown up.

"And what's a young *calhei* called Josie doing wandering the forest with a young human, far from any village? Are you running away?"

"Yes," she blurted out, "that's what we're doing. Exactly. They won't let us play together because he's human. It's not fair." She offered her best pout, one she had not needed in many years.

"Hmmm," the elf said, and hesitated. Senzia's eyes returned again to the throbbing red stone. She needed to end this.

"We're going," she announced, and backed away.

"No, you aren't," the elf replied, advancing. "It's too dangerous for a *calhei* to wander around by herself. We will look after you and your friend here. We do not hate humans."

Senzia backed into Artur and realized he had his back to her. She peered around and saw there were two more soldiers blocking the way they had come.

I'm going to clear the two you're facing. Then you run. Remember: Reach the great grizzly, she said silently.

They'll kill you.

No. They'll want me alive. Get ready.

She swung around, drawing a sword that would be more a long knife for anyone else. The elves began to laugh, and the two she faced pretended to be frightened. *Zuzzot*, she whispered, and a branch swung down from the tree next to them, sending them flying. They fell and lay groaning.

As the three elves behind their leader sprung, she held up her other hand, whispered the same word, and watched two branches from adjacent trees arc down and smash right into them. The soldiers staggered back in pain. The officer didn't move and instead watched carefully, arms folded.

"Okay," he said. "You may leave if you wish. Spare my elves. We're no match for you."

Senzia grabbed Artur's arm and backed into the trees. Then she turned and cried, *Run!*

They ran through the forest in a wide arc. After a while, Artur stopped.

That was awesome. You showed them. We can stop now. We're safe.

Senzia turned to him, panting from the exertion. "We aren't safe. He let us go because he was instructed to. I felt it in the red stone he wore. Someone more powerful will come for us now. I must get to Shinde—"

Artur's eyes were wide. *Senzia. You're bleeding. What's happening to you?*

Chapter 36

*Y*ou're bleeding from your mouth and nose and eyes and…Senzia! *Tell me what to do! How can I help?*

Senzia slumped down onto a log. "I'm okay. My head just hurts like a bad headache. This happens whenever I exert myself with magic. I'm not fully trained—nowhere near, to be honest. We were on our way to find teachers for my brother and me before all this happened. Can you find me some leaves of aspen or something else bitter?"

Artur returned moments later with the shiny green leaves, and she chewed on them. He gave her water, and her face crinkled at the bitter taste. But she chewed and swallowed, chewed and swallowed, and the bleeding eventually stopped.

"Come," she said, rising and slightly wobbling. "We must get some distance between us and whoever is coming. We'll walk until dark, and then maybe I'll try to sleep in a tree."

They began to walk, and Artur took her hand in his. *You were still awesome,* he said.

She smiled. "Thank you. But we aren't out of danger by any means. I told you, their officer was receiving instructions. I'm sure of it from the way he hesitated. Now that they've seen what I can do, they'll send someone more powerful to capture me."

Can there be someone more powerful than you?

Now Senzia laughed. "I told you. I've barely begun to learn how to use my magic. This is clearly not the right way, but it's all I know."

She stopped and drank while Artur looked on, an anxious frown on his face. She saw how much he really cared about her. "Remember what you promised me? If they come for me, you must escape and find the great grizzly in the dreamworld. It'll be my only hope."

It will be hard to leave you.

"Thank you. But having them kill you won't serve me—or you, come to think of it. Don't forget you promised me."

I won't forget.

They continued through the day and slept badly that night. Every twig snap, every warning call from an animal, woke them both. Senzia tried to sleep in a tree, but it seemed impossible and she finally returned to the ground. Artur wanted to join her, but she wouldn't let him.

The following day, the sun broke through the clouds, and everything looked so colorful and vibrant that Senzia began to feel happy and almost excited that they would soon be in Shindellia and she would be reunited with her family.

She made Artur speak out loud and, as the sun began its downward descent, he began to express himself more comfortably. She encouraged and complimented him and saw how he basked in her praise. It made her feel good.

They stopped by a stream, and Artur went upstream to catch some fish. Senzia took the opportunity to bathe and wash her clothes. The water was very cold, and she stayed in just long enough to clean herself and wash her hair. Drying herself, she put on fresh clothes and spread the others out to dry.

When Artur returned, he was soaking wet and trying not to shiver. But he proudly held two fish, silver with green and pink fluorescent scales that shimmered in the sun.

Senzia would have been content to camp there, but Artur was anxious to find trees—in the absence of a cave—where he would feel safe. They walked on, Senzia carrying her wet clothes, until they came to a small forest.

Artur placed his bags in the oak where he planned to sleep. Then they set about creating a small fire. However, they soon realized that neither knew how to cook the fish.

"Bears don't cook their catch," Artur explained, feeling each word as he spoke it out loud.

"Well, it can't be that hard," Senzia surmised. "Let's whittle two skewers from twigs and hold them over the flames."

They did this, and the outsides began to char—particularly the tails. Senzia suggested that they let the fire burn down and cook the fish over the embers. She remembered seeing this done before. Artur found a small, flat stone and placed it on the embers with the fish on top.

When they finally ate, Artur gave Senzia the more cooked parts and took the raw pieces for himself. The fish was pretty tasteless and dry, but it filled her up. Senzia chewed on some carrots they had foraged earlier which added some flavor, then yawned.

"I think we'll reach one of the main roads to Shindellia tomorrow or the next day," she said. "Once we're on the road, we should be safe."

"Do you think we've escaped the Gray Elves?" Artur asked, his voice shaking slightly.

"No," she replied. "I don't."

They went to sleep, Artur up in his tree and Senzia near what remained of the fire. She soon fell asleep but woke during the night with a full bladder. When she returned to her bedding, she knew they were not alone.

Standing in front of the smoldering ashes was an old elfe. She was wrapped in a gray cloak that matched her hair. Though her face was wrinkled, her blue eyes were vibrant and bored into the *calhei*.

"Greetings, little one," she said, her voice deep and dry. "I'm glad I caught up with you. Where's your human friend?"

"He ran away when he saw what I did to your friends." Senzia had rehearsed these lines.

"And yet, you continue alone. Where are you going?"

"To Shindellia, the capital."

"Why?"

"My family is there."

"How did you get separated from them?"

Senzia hesitated. "Who are you?" she asked instead of answering.

The old elfe smiled. "A wise tactic. I think you ran away from your family. Maybe you have a boyfriend in the capital—or the army, perhaps. It makes no difference. Your story, that is. What matters is that you're an elfe, and you have magic. So do I."

She brought out the red stone around her neck. It was glowing and pulsating. Then she disappeared and reappeared behind Senzia, making the *calhei* jump.

"Are there others with white hair gifted in magic like you?" she whispered into Senzia's ear.

"If you know I have magic, why aren't you afraid of me?" Senzia asked. Looking around, she added: "Did you come alone?"

"I did," the old elfe replied, her ice-blue eyes glinting. "Because I don't want to fight you. I'm confident I can beat you by myself. I've had decades to refine an art that you barely know. If we become friends, instead, I might be able to teach you some of my art."

Senzia bit her lower lip but didn't say anything.

"I'm going to put my hand on your shoulder and take you to our camp. It won't hurt."

"W-where is this camp?" Senzia asked.

"In the north, beyond the snowline. Come."

Senzia backed away. "Why should I trust you?"

"You shouldn't. Nonetheless, you will come, because I can use force if necessary, and if you wield the magic the way you have, you will eventually die. No one can give blood for the magic and survive long."

Artur watched in terror as the old elfe put a spindly hand on Senzia's shoulder and the two of them disappeared. He stayed in his tree, clinging to the branch and waiting to see if anything would happen. His chest was tight, and he was panting. He could feel beads of sweat trickling down his face.

Four elves appeared and spread out to search the area. They were looking for him, he knew, and he stayed clinging to the tree for the rest of the night.

When the sun began to break through the tree's canopy, Artur slowly slid down from the tree, his nose sniffing for anyone else. He was alone. He turned back the way he had come. He would find his pack. They would know how to contact the great grizzly. He would not fail Senzia.

CHAPTER 37

S enzia woke with a groan. Her head pounded, and, when she took a deep breath, she inhaled frigid air. The chill brought her instantly alert. It was dark, but not the darkness of night—rather, a subdued hue.

She tried to rise, but her head spun and she groaned, carefully resting back on the sack that had been put under her head. She lay on a rough, but not uncomfortable, cot. The young elfe waited a few moments and, when she felt the world stop spinning, opened her eyes again.

Above her was a roughly hewn mass of black and gray stone. She swiveled her eyes to follow the rock. She was in a cave—a really cold one, at that. Footsteps approached, boots clicking on the stone ground. She carefully turned on her side to see who was approaching.

The elfe who loomed over her was huge, bigger than her mother and twice as broad, though there was no sign of anything but wiry muscle. Her shirt clung to a voluptuous body, the sleeves revealing that she trained hard. She wore a huge sword over her back, the hilt wide and double-handed. Her skin was a gray hue, her eyes the same icy blue as the other Gray Elves, and her features chiseled. Her hair hung down, gathered by a leather band in similar fashion to the elves that lived around Wycaan Island. Long, pointed ears protruded out, peeled and scarred.

"Can you rise?" she asked in a raspy voice.

"I'm dizzy," Senzia croaked, then coughed.

The elfe tutted and walked to a nearby table. She returned with a ceramic cup that offered steaming promise. "Drink."

Senzia took the cup and sipped. It was bitter but warming. She drunk some more and felt the dizziness subside. She leaned back on the sacking and sighed. "Thank you," she said, but the elfe was gone.

She dozed for a short while, but the cold and an insistent bladder strengthened her resolve to rise. She walked with tentative steps to a doorway and saw in the second room that the elfe sat with another whose back was to her, but wore a huge battle-axe.

"I need to relieve myself," she said, hearing her own frailty echo off the walls.

The elfe pointed to an alcove, and Senzia went inside. When she returned, she saw the two elfes drinking a hot beverage.

"The tea you gave me helped. Thank you. May I have some more?"

The elfe nodded and pointed to a small fire, where two pots gently simmered. Senzia picked up a cup and went over, distinguishing between the two with ease. Hugging her cup, she turned back.

"Where am I?"

"With us," the Gray Elves' laughter was irritating and sounded like a piece of wood being sanded.

"Very helpful. Am I a prisoner?"

"In a sense," the other replied with a similar rasping voice. "You can walk out into the tundra and die. You have nowhere to go. Does that make you a prisoner?"

Senzia didn't have a comeback. "If I try to walk out that door, will you stop me?"

They both shrugged, and Senzia walked toward the door. She could feel their eyes on her, but neither moved. Through the doorway, she found a completely closed storeroom full of dried herbs, roots, and sacks of dried mushrooms.

She turned back and realized they had taken her long knife.

"Did you get very far?" one elfe asked. The other chortled.

Senzia decided to ignore them. She returned to the room where she had lain and looked for her long knife. It wasn't there. She walked through another doorway into a corridor. Two big Gray Elves, bigger than her father, stood guard. They peered down at her.

She nodded to them and then walked down the corridor. They fell into step and, when Senzia tripped over a protruding rock, one leapt forward and grabbed her arm with amazing speed.

"Thank you," she said, and he nodded. "I'm hungry. May I get some food?"

He signaled with an arm, and she walked forward, soon entering a big hall with rows of benches. There were serving tables, but they were empty. The elf signaled for her to sit, and, while he stood over her, the other went to another room. He returned with a stew, warm and thick, and Senzia's stomach rumbled in anticipation. This elf actually smiled, which she found reassuring.

While she ate, four more heavily armed elves entered and fanned out. The old elfe who had found Senzia in the forest glided in and sat opposite her.

"How is the stew?"

"Delicious, thank you."

"And your head?"

"I'm fine, just a bit queasy. It'll pass."

The mage looked at her for a while, and Senzia focused on her food. When she finished, the guard leaned in and took the bowl.

"You're very composed," the mage said. "How old are you, *calhei*?"

"Fifteen cycles," Senzia answered. "A *calhei* no more."

"Perhaps. Are you scared?"

"Of course. I'd be foolish not to be, no?"

"Correct." The mage looked up to the attending elf, and he walked away, only to return with two cups of a sweeter tea. "Here, this will help you relax."

"What do you want with me?" Senzia asked.

"To understand your power so that we can anticipate what we'll face when we attack the elves of your land."

"Why attack us?"

"Revenge," the mage replied, her tone perfectly frank. "Your people perpetrated terrible crimes against us."

Senzia looked up at her. The mage was old—older even than Denalion, she thought. "If that's true, then I'm sorry. But I assume this happened a long time ago. You thirst to revenge injustices done to your people generations ago?"

"Yes," the mage replied. "It's an integral part of our being. It feeds our desire to survive and prosper."

"That's sad," Senzia said. "Unfortunately, I fear that even when you massacre every innocent elf, you won't be satiated. Fanatics rarely are."

"Fanatics?" The mage arched a thin eyebrow. "Bold words."

Senzia shrugged. "What if Prince Shayth was to offer you a place to live within Odessiya, somewhere with an agreeable climate and fertile lands, where you could become part of a prosperous and free empire? Would you consider it?"

"He already made such an offer."

"You've met the prince? Personally?"

The mage sipped her tea. "He came to parlay with us but would not meet our demands."

"Which were?"

"To kill the elves of Odessiya and beyond."

Senzia laughed. "So the prince left empty-handed, and you resorted to kidnapping innocent *calhei*."

"Not quite empty-handed. We gave him one of our dogs. And you are not as innocent as you want me to think."

Senzia frowned. "Meaning?"

"The power you have, the magic you yield—is it unique, rare, or something all elves possess?"

"You already know not all elves have magical abilities. You've fought elves in Prince Shayth's army."

"Indeed we do," the mage smiled. "You are smart. Actually, it's King Shayth now. He wears a crown. Oh, does that surprise you?"

"I don't know him very well. May I see these dogs?"

The mage frowned. "Why?"

"I have a feeling I'm going to be here a long time and it might get rather boring."

"You're a prisoner of war," the mage snapped. "Boredom is the least of your problems."

Senzia laughed and leaned forward on the table. "I'm a *calhei* who doesn't understand her power. You know that already. I haven't been trained."

"Would your father have trained you if he'd lived? Your father was the Wycaan Master."

Senzia pursed her lips and sighed deeply. She saw now where this was going, but at least they did not know her *ahdahr* was alive. "My *ahdahr* was a great elf—maybe the greatest ever. He was the salvation of the races of Odessiya and could have been your savior, too." She let her voice break as she said this and then paused. "May I see your dogs?"

Chapter 38

Mharina did not run into his arms. Neither did she hug him as she had imagined she would every night since they separated. She was surprised when she saw him, her father, and the Master Assassin drinking a broth to break their morning fast. The Mushroom Man stood at her approach. His skin looked paler than usual and his straw-colored hair more matted. He met her gaze, but she could tell he struggled to maintain it.

"Let's walk," she said, and then turned away from her father and Ahad.

Mharina heard Abel's footsteps as he fell in just behind her, the path between the thick, encroaching brush too narrow for them to walk side-by-side. That was convenient. She needed a moment to compose herself, because, though she had spent many fitful nights playing out various scenarios of what she would say to him, her mind went blank in his presence.

"Turn right," Abel said when they reached a fork in the path.

She did, and it led to a tall rock formation with a small pool at its foot. Mharina saw evidence of a camp, a familiar wicker basket, and a pile of mushroom stems on the ground by a log.

She sat on a rock by the pool, peeled off her boots and stockings, and dangled her feet in the freezing water. The cold helped clear her mind and she sighed. Abel was fussing behind her. The elfe smelled a small fire, and soon she cupped a small mug of herbal tea, the warmth providing a sharp contrast to her numb feet.

The Mushroom Man washed his face in the pool and then sat on a rock facing her from the side. His cheeks were flushed, probably from the cold water, but maybe more. They sat in silence broken only by the singing of birds.

"This is my special place," Abel said at last. "I have dreamed many times of bringing you here." He turned and pointed to a small clearing. "We could build a hut over there and live undisturbed."

"Is that what you want?" she asked.

"More than anything in the world."

She could hear the truth in his earnestness and sighed again. "It is but a dream," she said. "I could never…"

"Because of your precious magic?"

"Maybe. But more because I don't trust you."

"You shouldn't," he replied. "I ran away when you faced great danger. Though I'm not sure I could have afforded you any protection, anyway."

"Why did you run?"

"I'm a coward. I live a solitary life and avoid anyone who isn't young enough to laugh at my stories. This is a world of swords and bows, of conquests and mighty battles. I have nothing to offer and everything to lose."

"I don't believe you."

"Okay. Then what is your guess?"

"You ran from the magic. You disdain it. You told me so. Sa'gola, Ithea, your mother…and now me." The Mushroom Man didn't answer, and Mharina sipped her tea and forged ahead. "But your disputed cowardice is not why I don't trust you. If you want me to stay with you, Abel, then you need to tell me the secrets you hold."

"The secrets?"

"Yes, your relationship with Sa'gola and your own magical path."

"Then we have no future, I'm afraid. I swore an oath of secrecy to Sa'gola, and she to me."

"For her part," Mharina said, "she has released you. It is your choice alone."

Abel jerked his head up. "How do you know?"

"I have spoken to Sa'gola's spirit. I don't understand how. But—"

"You spoke…Can you help me do that?" His eyes were wide, and his expression pleading.

"No. It was a one-time thing. I'm sorry."

Abel sagged, and Mharina stared at him. "What did she mean to you?"

"She was everything to me. My mother rejected me and would have done the same to Ithea if she hadn't…" He shook his head to clear his thoughts. "Sa'gola hid me. I never really knew what compelled her; it certainly wasn't a sense of duty. Perhaps she thought I might grow up to counter Ithea.

"What was she to me? At different times of our lives, she was my savior, teacher, lover, torturer, mother, friend, and enemy. I was infatuated and in love with her. I was hurt and scared by her, angry and despised her. At times, it was one thing or another, but mostly, it was a cacophony of all these emotions simultaneously.

"She did things to me—experimented and probed, using me to see if she could expose a weakness too well hidden in Ithea but easy to find in me. So she abused me and scarred me. But, in her own way, she loved me. The pain and torture was worth it for the brief windows of intimacy and the moments of love.

"Don't be threatened by her. She is dead now, and, even if she wasn't, she sanctioned our relationship."

Mharina looked up. "How do you know that?"

The Mushroom Man laughed. "She would have killed me if she thought I endangered you."

Mharina had to hide a frown. This did not match with what Sa'gola told her last night. Mharina had always thought she was seeing her Mushroom Man against her teacher's better judgment.

Now she began to wonder what opportunity Sa'gola had seen in their coming together. Then it occurred to her.

"Abel. Do you have the magic inside of you as your brother did?"

Now it was the Mushroom Man's turn to frown. He threw a pebble into the pond and watched the ripples ebb out before fading.

"Why does it matter to you?"

"Why?" Mharina was exasperated. "That information means everything. It influences everything. But most of all, it's the very essence of our relationship."

"How so?" Abel snapped.

"Because I can't be in a relationship with someone who keeps secrets."

He sighed. "If I did have magic and you knew about it, it would change the dynamics of what is between us. You would become like Sa'gola and try to dominate and manipulate me, because that is what magic ultimately does. It changes everything."

Mharina pursed her lips. He was closer to the truth than he knew.

"Whatever it would do is irrelevant for now. I can't be with you, knowing you hold a secret like this from me. I'm sorry, Abel. I wish it wasn't so complicated."

They both went silent. Mharina dangled her feet again in the cold water. She welcomed the numbing pain.

"Don't leave me," he said, his voice almost a whisper.

She turned and was swept into the deep sadness in his eyes. Then, a deafening roar from the direction of her father's camp brought Mharina to her feet.

Chapter 39

"What was that?" Mharina looked back at the slouching Mushroom Man.

"What?" he never looked up.

"That roar. It sounded like a bear."

"There are no bears here. I heard nothing."

She stared at him as she heard a second and then a third roar. "I must go."

"STOP," he yelled, his voice rasping, and she froze at the power of such an alien sound. "Don't leave me. You'll regret it. I'll regret it. Don't."

He was looking at her now, and his expression was strange. She felt herself frowning, but then the roar came again and she grabbed her boots and ran, her bare feet pounding the spring moss ground.

She burst, breathless, into her father's camp. Ahad jumped and fell into a defensive crouch, a knife in one hand and a round, jagged disc in the other. He glared at her as he rose.

"What's the rush? Did you spurn the fungus man?"

"Where's my father?" she snapped.

Ahad pointed just beyond the circle where they camped. Among a small cluster of trees, her father stood in one of his meditative stances. She must have imagined the roaring. What would Abel think? She felt so stupid as she approached her father. Then she saw his face.

When he meditated, the Wycaan Master's expression was usually blank and relaxed. But now it was contorted in rage or pain. His mouth moved as though uttering not word, but grunts. What was happening? His body shook and then stilled. She began to move to him but felt repelled. Was he having a nightmare? Bad dreams haunted his nights, but she had never seen this.

She heard a bear grunting, and another. There was a pack nearby, but she saw nothing. She swirled round. "Ahad! Do you hear nothing?"

"What do you want me to hear?" he replied, leaning back against a tree trunk.

"She can hear bears," the Mushroom Man said as he joined them, his face now composed.

"Are there bears here?" Ahad asked.

"No, but she's a Wycaan in a tough space. She can't use her magic on me, so this might be the next best thing. Imagination is the freest form of magic, no?"

He was mocking her, but Mharina nodded.

"Maybe he's in the dream world, but who can I hear?"

"Magic," Abel spat the word. "I was trying to be disdainful. There is no need for excuses to evade our breaking up."

Mharina glanced back at her father then walked up to Ahad and put a hand on his arm. "This isn't the time. Something is happening. Whatever he is discovering, whatever he is dealing with, I need to fulfill my duty as his daughter. Ahad, I am a Wycaan warrior. Even if this is nothing, I must go to the prince and help. If we're successful, once Odessiya is safe, I'll return here. I promise. We'll try again."

The Mushroom Man wore a different composure from any she had ever seen. It was as if she was looking at a stranger in Abel's body, as if… There was something in his expression that alarmed her. Then he looked away, head bowed and shoulders slumped. When he spoke, it was the old Abel.

"Go if you must. I make no promises that I'll be here as you make none that you'll return. I'm sorry, Mharina; I thought you were different." He paused, and then his expression hardened. "If you ever see your teacher again, tell her from me: She taught you well."

He turned and walked slowly away, his head hanging. Mharina had to force herself not to run after him, not to beg his forgiveness. But even as tears fell down his cheeks, she remembered that cold expression that had chilled her so. She had glimpsed another side to Abel. Something about his face at that moment had reminded her of his brother, Ithea.

She shivered and then looked at her father.

She watched him for an hour, but Seanchai never came out of his dream. While his face twisted and twitched, while he growled and yipped, Mharina sat on a log and cried. She cried for the man she might have lost; for her father, who, in many ways, was still lost, though he stood only several paces from her; for her siblings, who she missed so; and for her mother, who she admired even as they grew apart. She cried for Sa'gola, who could have guided her and offered advice. But mostly, she cried for herself.

She was no longer a *calhei,* but she was not ready to be an elfe. She was a Wycaan and a sorceress, and yet she knew her training in both types of magic was far from adequate. She carried the *Iyzun,* which made her so powerful—in potential, at least. But this knowledge only piled a huge weight of expectation and responsibility upon her young shoulders.

A cup of a minty tea found its way to her hands, and she hugged it gratefully. A blanket was laid over her shoulder. She barely glanced at Ahad, the ruthless Master Assassin, but his nod was one of sympathy and softness.

She looked back to the path where her Mushroom Man had gone, and tears consumed her yet again. She had pinned so much on dreams of romance and love. Before meeting Abel, she had not thought much of a mate. Caring for the twins and hunting and archery with her mother were what she enjoyed, along with the rare opportunities she had to sit on her father's lap and hear his outrageous stories.

A while later, Ahad kneeled in front of her. He was blurry, and she wiped her eyes, sniffling pathetically. He offered her bread with a little honey dripping off one side. She took it and chewed, but even the sweetness between the slices could not take away the bitterness she felt.

"Have you ever been in love?" she asked.

Ahad smiled slowly. "Yes," he replied. "I have loved and lost. My destiny was to be an assassin, and it cost me the only woman I've truly loved. I failed her because of what I became, because of the power in my hands to offer life and take death."

She could see pain crease his face, etched with memories and loss.

"Then you know the pain I feel," she mumbled and, rising, fell into his strong embrace.

"Only too well," he whispered, and she heard the breeze rustle through the treetops, disturbed only by the grunts of a bear far away.

Chapter 40

The great grizzly walked awkwardly, his paws sore from lack of use. He looked across the plain, puzzled that he had come into this world, so new yet so familiar. He paced through the short grass, sniffing the fresh, vibrant air. He could pick up the scents of different animals, but none were big cats or two-legged. He had nothing to fear.

He picked up on a pack of bears downwind from him. He stared ahead at the huge mountain that towered over the entire valley, sending half into shade. He had climbed that mountain, he knew. The grizzly stopped and stretched. His muscles were tight, as though he had not walked on all fours for a long time. He tried to think back, but all he could remember were the dreams—dreams of walking on two legs and of being so unhappy.

The scent of the other bears was getting stronger, and now he saw a small river—a snake of teal—slithering across his path and through lush, green grasslands. As he approached, the grass grew taller and sharper in color and flower. He stopped at the river's edge and lapped the invigoratingly cold water.

He heard growls and yips upstream and saw a pack of five—no, six—black bears. Apart from two cubs intent on standing in the river, they all stared at him. He began to walk toward them. Instinct told him to walk slowly and with grace and authority.

He was bigger than the black bears, even the male who came to meet him. The black walked with the same slow gait but lowered his muzzle in clear deference.

"It is good you answered the summons after so long."

"Summons?"

"Yes." The black bear led the great grizzly toward a rock that protruded just above the grass. "The brown said you were wounded, and that is why you neglect your destiny."

"He is right. Who am I?"

"You are one who straddles two worlds. It is told that in the world of the two-legged, you are seen with such respect that they write songs about you. Our stories tell of how you fight for justice and freedom for all two-legged, how you defeated the dragon in both the two-legged and animal worlds.

"In this world, you were chosen by the great grizzly himself to follow in his pawmarks. He was a close friend of the red bear, your teacher. You are like a spiritual leader to us—almost a god, except you cannot catch fish, no matter how often you try."

The black bear laughed to himself, grunting in an infectious manner that had the grizzly smiling and frowning at the same time as he strove to understand.

"In this world, have I killed others? Have others died for me?"

"I don't know what you mean. We rarely fight in this world. There is a…a common understanding. Here, you give advice, dispense wisdom, and solve conflicts if they arise. Come, the others wait for you."

They continued, toward the big rock. The grizzly was shocked when he saw about forty bears gathered. There were snow-white ice bears, black bears, brown, red, and a variety of others. There was even another grizzly.

They all stopped talking when the great grizzly and his escort appeared. The group parted and allowed them to walk to the rock. At its base was a slightly elevated flat rock. The black bear who had brought him nodded for the great grizzly to climb onto the platform and then joined him.

"The rumors are true," the black bear said in a gruff but confidant voice. "He does not remember his past. The great grizzly passed on his mantle to this one, and he battled for us against the violent dragon. We cannot forget. For this reason, we stand by him at this time, as we will in the future."

Snouts nodded, and a few bears grunted in support. The black bear called to a brown, who replaced him on the rock. The brown turned to the grizzly but spoke loudly enough for all to hear.

"Most of you know that my pack did something that is frowned upon. We found a two-legged cub and adopted him. There was much discord with our decision. We taught him to grow as a member of the pack, and he always took care of and protected us.

"The great grizzly, in his wisdom, told us that when the two-legged began to sprout fur on his body, we should send him back to his own kind. Over the past several moons, my mate and I have been preparing him. He resisted, and we agreed that there would be a sign when it was time for him to go.

"Then a young female entered our cave. She is two-legged with pointed ears and white fur on her head."

The great grizzly bared his teeth. "How white?"

"Very. She was on her way to help her friends and the human pack leader. We do not truly understand the ways of the two-legged or how they connect. But our two-legged felt compelled to go with her."

The brown bear took a moment to gather himself for what he wanted to say. The grizzly saw that it was not something easy.

"We do not speak in the other world as we do here. In the other world, our true communication is silent, heard only in each other's heads. It is not something we share with the two-legged, but the cub we took in learned how to do it, and…" He lowered his mighty head in contrition. "And I did not discourage it. On the contrary."

He waited as other bears growled their discontent, then turned to the great grizzly. "Yesterday, my two-legged cub spoke to me from across a great distance.

"Go into the dream world, he said, and summon the great grizzly. Tell him the two-legged of pointed ears and gray skins have captured his white-furred cub, the female. He must be told this. He will know what to do."

All eyes turned to the great grizzly. He raised himself on his hind legs, his head high, and stretched to ten feet of muscle and fury. He roared into the forest, over and over, venting his rage. The energy was contagious, the pain clear, and all the bears rose as one to their hind legs to howl with their leader.

CHAPTER 41

When Seanchai left his dream, he was panting. Mharina saw his chest heaving, and there was a wild look on his face. She shrank back as he screamed into the woods, a long, anguished human howl.

Ahad jumped forward, perhaps to protect her from her father's rage. This was honorable, if not useless, given that both she and Seanchai could kill him with relative ease. Nonetheless, she appreciated the gesture.

But Seanchai did not attack anyone. He just stared around him, his eyes wide and nostrils flared. Finally, his emotions somewhat under control, he moved to the logs around the fire and slumped down. Ahad offered him a water skin, which he took and gulped without remark. Water dribbled down his chin and neck.

Mharina sat next to him and took his hand in hers. He began to jerk it away but stopped and stared at her.

"Whatever happened," she said, her voice soft and steady, "I'm here, and we'll face it together."

Seanchai looked away from her into the ash of the previous night's fire. He still said nothing. Mharina stroked his hand.

"What happened?" she asked, now more insistent. "What did you find out?"

"Senzia," he whispered.

"Is she...is she..." Mharina tightened her grip.

"No," he replied. "The Ashen Elves have her."

"Ilan? Mother?"

"No. She was with a boy who grew up with bears, and he escaped. She sent him to find the great grizzly."

"Who's that?" Ahad asked.

"Me. They came for me in the dream world, but I don't dream as a bear as I apparently did before…so they found me in meditation."

"Where did they take her?"

"Into the north, beyond the pictorian villages. I must go after them."

"Do you know where to go?" Ahad asked, and when the Wycaan shook his head, the Master Assassin sighed. "I never thought I, of all people, would say this, but we must go to Shayth."

"The prince? Why?" Seanchai asked.

"He's the only person I know who's been to their stronghold."

"If I go to him, I face a trial or a fight, neither of which I care about."

"He'll understand," Mharina said.

Ahad laughed. "Yeah. He's a real forgiving son of—"

"He's your prince," Seanchai snapped.

Mharina and Ahad both looked at him with surprise.

"He's yours, too," Ahad replied, "and I imagine he can't wait to remind you."

They all went silent for a few moments, and then Mharina sat up straight.

"He will help," she declared.

"How is that?" Ahad asked.

"I will be the bargaining chip. I'll stay and fight for him, and he'll give *Ahdahr* what he needs."

"I'm going to trade one daughter for another?"

"No," her voice took on a grim but determined tone. "I am a *calhei* no more, *Ahdahr*. I'm a sorceress and a Wycaan. I am possibly the most powerful magical figure still alive. If he can't have you, he needs me."

Seanchai nodded. "Will it work?" he asked Ahad.

The Master Assassin nodded. "It actually makes it easier for Shayth. It gives him a way to forgive your treachery. But more than that, he wants to be good, wants to make the right decision." Ahad rose, sighed, and nodded. "It'll work."

Mharina took them across the barrier onto Sa'gola's land. She did not lead them to the house, but to the cave where she and Sa'gola had passed many pleasant hours wallowing in the hot thermal pool. But this time, Mharina was not interested in bathing, though her muscles ached from her sorrow and emotional turmoil.

She tried not to think of Sa'gola or Abel; it helped that the fear she felt for her little sister now occupied her mind. One of Sa'gola's distance tunnels was from here to the mountain range north of Grogin. Another was located nearby and would take them to Shindellia.

Mharina wondered how Senzia would react to being tortured. She was quick to anger and might quickly provoke them. Being a prisoner and calling for her father surely meant that Senzia was prepared to wait for him, but who could anticipate how they would react to incarceration and torture until it happened.

The young elfe was not sure where the tunnel was. She only saw the scroll Sa'gola drew up once, her teacher forbidding her to ever use it unless it was a dire emergency. Only the two of them knew that a tunnel to and from Sa'gola's land existed, but others had been created and used by the Emperor and Ithea, who also knew the magic. With all the creators dead, it made the tunnels feel dangerous and unpredictable. She thought of Abel and the fire in his eyes when he saw she had chosen the magic over him. Was Abel now her enemy? How much of Ithea and their mother was inside him?

Mharina did not let them dwell in the cave. It felt as if any time spent on Sa'gola's land was an intrusion on her wishes, but they had to get to Shindellia as quickly as possible. Her sister's life might depend upon it, and—she glanced over at her tense *ahdahr*—his sanity might, as well.

They walked deeper into the cave, following a tunnel that twisted down one way and then the other. Mharina, almost without thinking, sent energy through her staff, and the runes lit up their path in an eerie orange hue. She led them with confidence, though she had never walked this path or taken this tunnel before. Finally, they arrived at the spot. She turned to her companions.

"Once we are through, I will change the parameters of this route. If you try to pass through without my consent, you will find yourselves in a different location. Now, this might feel uncomfortable, so stay close."

She led them through a shimmering energy field that tingled and lowered their body temperature considerably. It was similar to the dense, soupy fog they passed through to enter Sa'gola's territory. She felt her body compress and contract. Sometimes she was short of breath and at other times felt stretched in all directions. While she had experienced this before, it still felt strange and somewhat terrifying. She glanced back at the two males following her. Her *ahdahr* was smiling, embracing the situation. She knew he felt the magic around him. Ahad, however, was clearly spooked. She could have prepared him, but… She smiled to herself. Sa'gola would counsel her to instill a little awe or fear when possible. She liked Ahad, despite him being a paid murderer and the once-sworn enemy of her father.

By the time they exited the first tunnel, it was impossible to know how much time had passed; they were all relieved to be in normal time and space. Mharina imagined it being similar to alighting from a boat after a long time and feeling solid ground under your feet.

But she took them on into the second tunnel without stopping to catch their bearings. This one felt different. It had been made by Sa'gola and Ithea and was denser and difficult to negotiate. Her father was now tense, perhaps sensing the man who had worked here. Ahad had a deep frown on his face but refused to stop and rest when she offered.

They would all be so relieved to exit the second tunnel and stretch their legs on solid ground in the capital. But instead, they were greeted by forty archers with bows drawn; a dozen mounted knights with lances ready; numerous foot soldiers; and a scowling king, hands folded over his chest and eyes blazing with rage.

Chapter 42

King Shayth Shindell watched them materialize out of nothing into the square. They blinked, adjusting to the sunlight and stared around at his show of force. The king did not plan to shoot anyone; he just wanted to send a message.

Unfortunately, his message was somewhat undermined when Ilan ran to his sister and jumped into her arms. She staggered backward from the onrush. Ilan had grown and was now as tall as her. Everyone watched as they held each other tight. Shayth noticed that Ilan did not embrace his father.

The young elf turned around. "You see, mother? King Shayth?"

"King?" Ahad said.

Shayth walked around to face him. "Yes—King Shayth, Master Assassin. Tell me: Do your professional colleagues welcome you back?"

Ahad looked around nervously. "There are probably a dozen or so assassins stalking around here right now, waiting to make a reputation for themselves... Your Majesty."

Shayth turned, and his voice boomed out. "This man, despicable as he may be, is under my royal protection. No assassin, or anyone else, shall try to harm or kill him." He turned back to Ahad and grinned. "A benefit that comes with the crown."

Then he turned to Seanchai, and his smile vanished. His voice was ice. "Come to my small council room immediately. We will talk there."

"May I speak to Sellia first?" Seanchai asked. "I have urgent news for her."

Shayth turned to Sellia, and his voice softened. "Bring him to the small council room. I'll come in a short while." He summoned a page. "Please show them the way."

He turned to go but stopped when Mharina called out. "King Shayth. I am a Wycaan and bearer of the *Iyzun*. I wish to join you in the small council room. I am key to this conversation."

"The king decides with whom he meets," said an elderly advisor with a wavy white moustache and a ruffled shirt that burst from his jacket.

Mharina approached slowly. She glared at the advisor as she passed him. When she spoke, it was only for Shayth's ears. "I am a *calhei* no more. If I'm to serve you, you must allow me what I need, which includes being part of any plans."

Shayth looked at her, feeling the power of her presence and seeing the intensity in her eyes. "You are your mother's daughter," he said, and smiled. "I could never refuse her, either. You're welcome to join us, but give your parents some time alone." He turned and watched Seanchai and Sellia walk away, a heavy wall of stony silence between them. "They're going to need it."

"There is water and wine over there, sire. Shall I bring bread and cheese? Some fruit, maybe?"

"No, thank you," Seanchai replied. "We wish to be left alone."

The page bowed his way out and shut the door. The thick iron handles clicked as they fell into place. A stout wooden table was surrounded by a dozen matching chairs. In the corner were several terrain models.

He turned to Sellia. "They have Senzia, these Ashen Elves."

"I know," she replied, hugging herself. "Ilan sensed it."

"Does he know where she is? Can he sense when they are close?"

She glared at him and hissed, "You have already endangered one of our *calhei*, a second is now captive and probably being tortured, and you want the third? What will you leave me with?" Her eyes flared.

"He and Mharina will stay here," Seanchai replied evenly. "I will find Senzia alone. But Mharina has a part to play with Shayth. I cannot vouch for her safety."

Sellia turned to the window, which was little more than an arrow slit, though wide enough to let light in. "We could have been so happy. Ilana told me I would fall in love with you, that she wished us a life of peace and many *calhei*. I laughed at her. I didn't think I could fall in love with you or be a mother."

"You are a wonderful mother," Seanchai said. "I—"

Sellia swung around. "You don't remember me being a mother. Don't patronize me. You don't remember us coming together, our first nights after we bonded. It's as if nothing happened for you. I have to live with what we lost, with this great emptiness inside, but you wander around oblivious."

Seanchai came up behind her and slowly put his hands on her shoulders. She allowed him to pull her back to lean against him. He moved his muscular arms around to hug her. He heard her sigh and felt the pain seep from her eyes as tears ran down her face.

"It's not that things were perfect," she said, her voice barely more than a whisper. "You were always gone, and I'm no natural mother and certainly not a school head, but it made sense. My love for my children and mate made it all worthwhile."

"Give me time," Seanchai whispered into her ear. "Don't give up on me."

"Maybe I should come with you," Sellia said, brightening up. "You can drag me the length and breadth of Odessiya like old times."

"I-I would like that, and maybe we will when all this is over, but Ilan is here and Mharina. They need you."

"Mharina. Did you notice she hugged her brother but not me?"

"You never went to her, either. I think she is very similar to you and loves you. Have no doubt about that. Did you notice that Ilan did not greet me?"

She nodded. "What parents we make. Is she very powerful?"

"Mharina? More than she knows. More than I am, I suspect. She says I have the *Iyzun*, but if I do, it's buried deep. Also, my loss of memory means I don't possess the words to wield the Wycaan magic."

Sellia turned around, forsaking his embrace. She was frowning.

"How will you fight the mage, then?" Sellia asked. "Or her army of red stones?"

"Red stones?"

"Yes. Those with magic wear these stones. Shayth says they can speak with each other and channel energy to one another."

It was Seanchai's turn to frown now. "I must see these stones. What have the dwarves said about them?"

Sellia turned to him. "You have no idea what you face, do you?"

"Of course not. Did I ever?" He offered a brief grin that took her back to their first days together. But it soon vanished. "I will speak with the king about them."

"The king is coming to arrest you," she said.

Seanchai shrugged. "He won't. He has too much to lose."

"Why?"

"Mharina will only serve him on the condition that I go north."

"You use our daughter to bargain with the king?" The look on her face was one of horror. "You really are sick, Seanchai."

She pushed him away and walked to the other side of the room, glaring at him from across the table. This is how Shayth and Mharina found them when they entered the small council chamber.

Chapter 43

" I thought being king meant everyone follows your every whim," Shayth said, ruffling his spiky hair.

"Is that the kind of king you wish to be?" Mharina asked. "This isn't the Shayth my parents spoke of. We are Wycaans. Our loyalty is to Odessiya, and we will support you as long as you remain true to your oath."

"I thought you said she hasn't been trained," Shayth said to Sellia, feigning exasperation. "She sounds pretty Wycaan to me."

"She listened well to our stories, always begging for more. She could probably recount them better than us." Sellia earned only a polite chuckle.

There was an altercation outside the door, raised voices, and the door opened. A guard tried to apologize, but massive Rhoddan and tall, skinny Ilan pushed past.

"Don't blame your guards," Rhoddan said, closing the doors in their face. "They didn't offer me entrance."

"Then how—"

"He never asked," Ilan grinned.

"And who invited you?" Shayth snapped.

"I was told to learn from my elders and need to know when we leave to rescue my sister."

"We?" Seanchai and Sellia spoke together.

"No one has asked you to go," Shayth added.

Ilan shrugged. "No one needs to. I was being polite. Had *Ahdahr* not come, I would have left alone."

"You're not going," Sellia snapped.

"She is my sister, my twin. Do you know where she is, *Ahdahr*? I can find her once I'm near. She and I are linked. And if we need to fight our way out, the two of us together are stronger than either of us is apart."

"Ilan." Seanchai rose and walked over to him. "I appreciate that you want to go, but it presents a practical problem. I plan to run as a bear. I'll have other bears to guide me, and on four legs, I can go faster. If I approach as an elf, the mage will know of our coming. She will try to extract everything she can from Senzia before we arrive."

"Senzia is tough," Ilan said. "We have time."

"She is not that tough. No one is."

"You don't know her like I do. She—"

"I KNOW TORTURE!" Everyone shrank from Seanchai's fury. "THEY CHAINED ME UNDER THE WATER. THEY STRIPPED MY MIND. THEY—" He froze, only his chest rising and falling, his mind taking him far away.

Ilan, the focus of the Wycaan Master's fury, was pinned against the wall, his eyes bulging. Only Sellia moved, taking position in front of their son and facing Seanchai. Shayth saw spittle at his friend's mouth as the huge elf's shoulders heaved with emotion.

Sellia reached out slowly, resting her hand on his heaving chest. "What happened to you?"

"I-I don't know, but I was…" His face creased. "I can't remember. It just comes and then vanishes as quickly. I only know that…"

"And if the Gray Elves capture you, what will happen?"

Seanchai straightened and looked around the room, his expression going from confusion to resolute. "I am better equipped to deal with it than a young, untrained elfe. I have less to lose. Her whole life is before her."

Sellia stared at him and frowned. "You would end your life."

It wasn't posed as a question. Seanchai hesitated. "I don't know. It would depend on where Senzia was."

"And if she was safe?"

"I-I don't know. If I could stop them and if Senzia was safe, yes."

"If it comes to that, know that I do not want you to take your life, not while there is a chance we can still be together—you and me and our *calhei*. Will you remember that?" The elfe raised herself, and, once again, Shayth saw the fierce, proud warrior elfe he had first met at Galbrieth. Her presence held Seanchai and the rest of the room captive. "Swear it to me, and you go north with my blessing."

Seanchai nodded but only after a hesitation.

"Not good enough," his mate said. "Swear it in the ancient language."

"I can't," he whispered. "I want to and I swear not to give my life if I can find another way." Then turned to Ilan. "I'm sorry. I know you want to come, too. But it's our shared love for Senzia that demands I travel fast."

"I'll keep up with you. That won't be a problem."

Seanchai stared at Ilan as a father who really didn't know his son. Ilan was no longer a *calhei*, either. "How?"

"If I fail to keep up with you, I shall return here. Now, excuse me. I must prepare." Ilan turned to go.

"The moment you drop behind, you come back," Sellia called after him. "Not negotiable."

Ilan turned from the door and smiled. "Not a problem," he said, and walked out.

As he left, Queen Shameka entered in a beautiful purple dress. Shayth felt his heart beat faster each time he saw her.

"I brought you food," she said to Shayth. "I hope that's okay."

"Don't we have a reception with the Karlack trade delegation?"

She beamed at him. "They're currently being entertained by those dancers from your coronation. You won't be missed."

"I thought you didn't approve of that troupe—too sensual, if I recall?"

"I don't appreciate *you* watching those beautiful, gyrating bodies," she said, and pecked his cheek. "But they will serve to adequately distract the traders." She turned to Sellia. "Please make sure he eats. Isn't that what a wife is supposed to say?"

CHAPTER 44

S hayth slowly poured himself a goblet of wine. They had been talking for hours, and he was feeling distinctly outnumbered. Seanchai barely spoke, answering questions with short, concise answers, clearly anxious to leave and head north. Sellia sat in stony silence, the fear of a mother lining her face.

Finally, the king turned to Seanchai. "Half my court expect me to arrest you and bring you to trial. The other half think I will cut your head off before the sun sets in a fit of rage. How do I let you go north?"

Seanchai rose and looked at him, his face hard. Then he shrugged. "How do you stop me?"

"That's not what the king asks," Rhoddan said, stepping next to them. "Once you were his closest advisor, his confidant. He asks now for your advice."

Seanchai regarded Rhoddan. They were the same height, and Rhoddan met his gaze without wavering. Seanchai signaled for them to sit, then turned to Rhoddan.

"Pyre told me about you, how you were with me from the very beginning, taking a frightened young wood elf under your wing."

"She is generous," Rhoddan replied. "We were both running scared and making the rules up as we went."

"She said there's no one outside of my family who suffers more from my…my affliction than you. Yet you stand by the king when he considers holding me merely to save face?"

Shayth felt his anger rise and opened his mouth to speak, but Rhoddan put his hand on the king's arm. He leaned forward. The room had fallen silent.

"Pyre and others will tell of your great deeds and wise alliances," Rhoddan said. "Such tales lean towards embellishment, but are more or less true. It was an amazing experience to be in your shadow as you grew into the wise Wycaan Master. But what I loved about you, more than anything else, was your incredible loyalty to your friends. I *knew* you would come to Galbrieth to try and save Ilana, Shayth, and me. Not even Ilana, with her special love for you, was as sure as I was. I *never* doubted you would return from the Elves of the West with an army at your back. I *never* doubted your loyalty.

"And it was more than my sword that you appreciated. You and Ilana used to poke fun that I placed my sense of honor before anything. I turned my back on every opportunity for love, power, and comfort because I was always driven to do the honorable thing. Do you remember any of this?"

Seanchai winced and shook his head. Rhoddan continued.

"Do you doubt anything I say? If so, Sellia or Shayth can vouch for me, right here. Now."

"I do not doubt a word you say," Seanchai said without looking for confirmation.

"Then know that I, as your dearest friend, believe you betrayed your prince and country when Shayth called for help. Know that I left you because I felt honor-bound to come and defend Shindellia and Odessiya from the Ashen Elves. Know that, while I was ready to relinquish our friendship for loyalty to the king, I am most angry that you turned your back on Sellia, who sacrificed everything for you. Know that if you tried to leave for any reason other than to save a member of your family, I would try and prevent you, even knowing that I would probably die in the process.

"But I have never ceased to beg the king to forgive you, to let you back into the fold." Shayth nodded to back him up. Rhoddan continued. "Even now, after everything, I would help you leave and search for Senzia. If the king requested, I would gladly go with you and lay down my life as I always have. But I will not stand here while you disrespect one of your closest friends when he seeks your advice."

The room descended into silence, save for the sound of crackling wood in the fireplace. Then Seanchai turned to Shayth.

"I'm sorry. I will give freely of my advice, and when I return, I'll either stand trial or fight again at your side." He turned to Rhoddan and put a hand on the elf's shoulder. "I'm sorry to cause you so much pain and disappointment. Remember the old Seanchai. I wish I could."

The sun had not yet risen when Shayth, Sellia, Mharina, and Rhoddan met Seanchai outside the northern gate.

"Have you seen Ilan?" Seanchai asked Sellia.

She shook her head, and they exchanged a parental smile. Ilan enjoyed sleeping, and he had no doubt stayed up late preparing. Shayth stepped forward with Azura, her tail wagging at the early morning excitement.

"Take her with you. When you get nearer, she might know her way, though she was only a pup when I took her from the Ashen Elves."

"How will she go with me and leave you?"

"We'll tie her to you once you have transformed."

Then Seanchai walked into the bushes and stripped. The leaves rustled and parted as the great grizzly returned, cold breath rising in clouds from his massive snout. Mharina strapped his weapons and clothes to his back and kissed him. He nuzzled up to her and grunted softly. Then he did the same to Sellia and grunted at Shayth and Rhoddan, who tied the dog's leash to his pack. Shayth bent down.

"Go home, Azura. Find your pack and take my brother to your masters."

Azura's ears went back, and she whimpered as she stared from the bear to her master.

"You'll always be welcome back," Shayth said, "but I need you to do this task for me. Run well."

Shayth turned and walked away without looking back. The grizzly sent a telepathic reassurance to the dog, who looked at him and whimpered. The bear yipped back and then lumbered off into the night.

Once away from the castle, he fell into a steady pace, all the time sending out a message to the nation of bears. The great grizzly was running and needed assistance. Other animals picked up his thoughts and sent them on. He left the plains in the cold, gray light of dawn and watched his breath steam up in heavy clouds in front of him.

They began to climb a path that led through the mountains, and the grizzly thought of his cub. He would be angry when he discovered he had overslept and no doubt vent it on his mother and older sister. The bear wondered whether the boy would try to follow him despite his promise the night before.

A little while later, the bear and dog stopped at a stream and drank. The bear was thankful to soak his paws in the cold water, numbing the soreness. He saw fish flash in the water and attempted to catch one. He had never been good at catching fish, but he managed to flip one out of the water, and Azura pounced on it. But the dog did not eat it. Instead, she stood rooted to the spot, staring across the stream.

The grizzly looked up. A large black cat stood on the opposite bank, rhythmically lapping water. Azura looked over to the grizzly and whimpered again. She slowly moved nearer to the bear, her tail down.

The grizzly stared at the huge cat. Under its shiny black coat was a very thin but muscular body. The grizzly could see the cat's ribs threatening to break through the skin. Its big paws suggested growth yet to come. The bear took all this in, and its deep blue eyes and long, thin tail. But what most caught his eyes was the pack strapped to the black cat's body, a pack that held clothes, food, and swords.

The black cat purred. "*I trust you will be able to keep up, Ahdahr,*" it said telepathically.

Chapter 45

Senzia scratched the dog behind its ear, and it thumped the ground with its tail in appreciation. This one was her favorite. She was a female, maybe a year old, who immediately took to Senzia and began following her around. Senzia didn't ask if this was okay. The dog disappeared to eat and take care of its business, but otherwise came looking for the young elfe. Now it sat on its back haunches, tongue hanging out and piercing blue eyes watching carefully.

"You need a name," Senzia said. "I'll call you Teal, which is a shade of blue. It is also the name of an ancient elven hero. I hope you don't mind having a male name."

The puppy reached up and licked her face, offering a wet approval. Senzia laughed, as did someone else behind her. She turned and saw the mage standing at the door.

"May I come in?" the mage asked.

Senzia smiled. "I've no experience at this, but if I'm your prisoner, then you hardly need my consent."

"True," the mage acknowledged, "but you have behaved well so far, and I see no need to be anything less than polite. We are both elfes, after all."

She was still hovering in the doorway, and Senzia waved her in and pointed to a chair.

"Do you mind me playing with your dog?" Senzia asked.

"The dogs serve us well. We enjoy their intelligence and loyalty. I shall ask the trainer what he thinks. Perhaps you can offer some help caring for the dogs while you're here." Senzia nodded enthusiastically. The mage continued. "I find it fascinating. For us, dogs are workers. We take care of them well because they serve us, but you and your king crave their companionship."

Senzia shrugged. "Like you said, they are loyal and smart."

"Who was Teal?"

"There is a legend of a young elf who tended his family's herds. He enjoyed using the bow and arrows his father gave him to hunt and fight off predators, and he practiced endlessly.

"He found himself in the capital during a big festival and entered the archery tournament. Being poor, he hoped to win the purse and help his family. He reached the final round of twelve archers, and the king came to watch the exciting competition."

The dog settled down and rested its head on Senzia's thigh. She stroked it as she spoke.

"Slowly, the archers were eliminated until it was only Teal and two others. As Teal was about to shoot, he saw an assassin with a blowpipe aimed at the king. He moved quickly and shot the man.

"He was immediately arrested, and the king, furious, declared that he should be executed. When they realized what had really happened, the king felt terrible and immediately pardoned and apologized to Teal. Instead of being angry or hurt, Teal simply said that what was important was that he was able to save his king.

"The king was so impressed that he named Teal his royal archer—a great privilege—which meant he would always be near the king and train the royal family and guards. Teal was incredibly wise, despite growing up a poor shepherd. He taught people about values and life through his lessons with the bow. Though he was uneducated, his lessons were written down as the Scrolls of the Bow, which are highly regarded. I'm afraid I've never read them, but my father did. He is—was—the one who told us the story about Teal."

"I look forward to reading these scrolls one day, when we have conquered your land."

"Perhaps you should read them now. They may change your mind," Senzia shot back.

"How would you know if you haven't read them?"

Senzia smiled. "I'm just guessing. I like you and the other Ashen Elves I've met. I don't want you to be our enemies. Even though the elves are at peace with the humans and dwarves now, we were once an underclass, often mistreated and disrespected. This is what my father worked to overturn. Though our people are free, it would be...nice...to bring strong, proud elves into our society."

The mage nodded. "It's a nice thought, Senzia, and it sadden me that we're on opposite sides. Your king is young, but I admire his courage and principles. Yet our sufferings and injustices are so ingrained in us that we will never be free until we have truly avenged our ancestors.

"We've heard whispers that there are elves more ancient than those of Odessiya who separate themselves from the other races. I told your king that if he let me confront them, we would cease our current battle with him. Certainly, the humans, dwarves, and fierce pictorians would not be hurt."

Senzia knew the mage was trying to probe into her knowledge. She had to be careful and offered her best frown. "Does the king know of these elves?"

She received a frown back for her troubles. "Do you?"

"I've heard stories of them, but they are inconsistent—they live in great forests or in swamps or in deserts. I would love to find out if they really exist and—"

"They exist, Senzia. Your prince all but confirmed it. He doesn't seem to have any affection for them but is still bound by his honor."

Senzia tried not to appear as flustered as she felt. "If they aren't part of Odessiya, why does he protect them? Especially if he doesn't care for them."

"It's this code of honor that I mentioned. It is irresponsible. Many good men, elves, and dwarves have died already, and when we set upon his towns and cities, many more will. You've never seen a city ransacked, Senzia. It's horrific. The females and children are slaughtered. Before that, they are often tortured or abused, sometimes thrown into slavery. There's no glory in such acts. No one wins. Everyone loses."

Senzia nodded but did not say anything.

"Thank you for this little chat. I've enjoyed being with you. I'll ask the trainer to let you care for the one you call Teal, and we'll talk more. There is another coming to speak with you. I advise you to cooperate with her. It seems you have already met and fought each other, and she won't be so forgiving of your lying."

"Lying?" Senzia felt her cheeks flush. "I never met an Ashen Elf before your soldiers found us. She's the one who lies."

"She says that when she fought you," the mage said, her tone stern. "You stood alongside your father, and it was not long ago. He lives, Senzia. We know he does. And this makes your situation far more precarious."

"Precarious? What does that mean?"

The mage smiled. "It means, my dear *calhei*, that you are nowhere near as valuable as I thought you were. Don't play around with us. While you and I have a mutual respect, I'm not your friend. Far from it."

The mage turned and walked to the door. As she left, she snapped her fingers, and Teal rose and trotted out after her.

Chapter 46

Senzia was both scared and angry. The suggestion that she was a liar and the mage's control over the dog was stunning. She sprung up and ran to the doorway.

"I never met an Ashen Elf until your soldiers found me," she yelled down the corridor. "I didn't lie about that."

Her voice echoed back as if the stones were mocking her. She had been caught lying about her *ahdahr*, she admitted. They knew he was alive. But who was this Ashen Elfe the mage mentioned? Senzia had never met one before and wondered if maybe the elfe who claimed to know her had been disguised. But, as she ran through the people she had met in the past year, there was no one she could imagine impersonating a Gray Elf.

She lay down and napped. Teal woke her, licking her face and gently tugging on her sleeve. She rose and washed her face, then followed the dog through the stone corridors to the big eating hall. By now, no one waited on her. She took a plate, filled it with food, and went to sit on a bench with Ashen Elves she did not know. They generally ignored her but were never rude or abusive.

Senzia ate her food without much enthusiasm. The Ashen Elves ate mainly stews of one kind or another. She didn't ask what was inside them, preferring not to know. She must be on her guard when she next met the mage and this mysterious Ashen Elfe.

One of the mage's guards approached and sat opposite her. "When you have finished, I'm to take you to the mage."

"Why?"

He shrugged. "It's not my responsibility to know."

Senzia leaned forward. "Are they going to begin torturing me? Is torturing a young *calhei* part of your responsibility?"

He shrugged again. "I don't know. If you have valuable knowledge, it should be extracted from you."

"You would torture me?"

"If I was so ordered."

"You poor elf. Tell me: Who is the prisoner? You or me?"

"You," he replied without hesitation.

"No. We're both trapped. The only difference between us is that I'm aware of my incarceration."

The Gray Elf just nodded. "Are you finished?"

Senzia looked at her empty plate. She was not sure if he was referring to that or her speech. But she stood, took her plate to the big stone tanks, and washed it leisurely. Outside the eating hall, Teal was waiting and wagged her tail with vigor. "What are you so happy about?" Senzia asked, bending to scratch her ears.

"Why do your kind play with the dogs?" the guard asked.

Senzia straightened. "Why do you not?"

He snorted and led her down a long corridor without speaking anymore. Senzia needed to focus, so the silence suited her. She wondered if she was being taken to a dungeon or cell, but instead they entered a balcony overlooking a huge canyon. She gasped and her eyes grew wide. In front of her was a massive mural from floor to ceiling.

"What do you think?" the mage asked, coming up behind her. The guard had disappeared.

"It's beautiful," Senzia said. "This must have taken ages."

"There is one made in every place where Ashen Elves settle. It is our history. I thought you would appreciate it since you love stories." She began to tell the story of her people as she had to King Shayth.

"The Ashen Elves were the original elves in this land. When those who came from the Western Isles arrived, there was enough room for all. They settled in towns and later cities on the coast and where rivers met. Before they came, we lived in tribes that migrated with the great herds. We would come together at certain seasons to trade, arrange marriages, and share stories. It was not that everything was always peaceful between us. There were feuds that sometimes spiraled out of hand.

"By and large we lived at peace with each other and were proud of small successes. But the Elves of the West wanted more and, as their numbers grew, they thought we competed for their resources. They began to pass strange laws, forbidding us into their compounds unless we served them. We could not marry them, and gradually they began to preach superiority.

"They began to employ us as servants and farmers, workers in their towns. At first we were paid for service, but at some point it stopped and we became slaves. We eventually rose up and fought back. When they tried to push us out of Odessiya, the different tribes joined forces to rebel. We were good warriors, at one with the land and, although we could not destroy their towns, they could not defeat us in the mountains. Finally, they unleashed magic on us, trapping us on a great mountain plateau, and incarcerated us deep underground.

"There we lived, hating the Elves of the West. Over time, the memories passed on and the next generation's thirst for revenge increased, and fueled our survival. We became hardened, fortified by hate when the one you know as the Emperor, the uncle of your present king, found us imprisoned underground. He aided us, gave us medications, expanded the boundaries of our prison so that we could hunt and forage. Most importantly, he gave us the magic and we vowed to avenge ourselves. He taught us that only when these Western Elves are massacred will we ever be truly free once more."

The mage pointed to different scenes on the mural as she spoke. Senzia was mostly quiet but occasionally interrupted to ask questions. She was taking her lesson seriously. When the old elfe finished, Senzia sat down on the edge of the balcony with her legs dangling over the side and followed the story again with her eyes and in her mind.

"I'm sorry," she said at last to the mage. "I'm sorry your people have suffered so. But that cannot serve to justify murdering innocent elves. Those you would put to the sword live peacefully in Odessiya. Not only were they never remotely responsible for what befell your people, but they themselves also suffered from servitude and discrimination."

"I know," said the mage. "This is why I need to know who these other elves are and where they're from. Are you one of them?"

"I told you already. I grew up on Wycaan Island in Odessiya. The only time I left was when the taragusii forcibly took me to Grogin. But I hardly saw any elves there, and those I did see were pretty wretched."

The mage sighed, suggesting she did not believe the *calhei*. "Come," she said. "I need to introduce you to an old acquaintance."

"Can I come back here whenever I want?"

"Yes. But why would you want to?"

"I want to learn your story so I can share it with my people. And, if I one day find these other elves, I want to make sure they know it, too."

The mage stared at her and said, after a moment, "You may return here whenever you want, outside of your interrogation. Come. We should not keep her waiting."

As they left, the mage put her bony hand on Senzia's shoulder. The gesture was not lost on the *calhei*.

Chapter 47

"Who is this Ashen Elfe I have apparently met?" Senzia asked as the mage and several guards led her through endless stone corridors.

Teal padded loyally behind her. The mage did not answer, and Senzia recognized this was deliberate. She sighed. It was working. She rubbed her tight stomach.

"Someone lived in disguise at Wycaan Island or in Grogin?" she continued, receiving no response. "I can think of no other alternative."

But she could not believe it was anyone she was close to. She thought of Rhoddan's mate, Troja, but only because she was the newest to join their company. It made her wonder how Pyre was doing. She had no idea where her friend was and would never find out as long as she was in this endless underground network of caves. She suddenly felt desperate to see the sky and the sun.

"I need to go outside," she said. When the mage didn't answer, she added, "Is that possible?"

"It is," the mage replied. "But everything depends on this meeting."

"What do you mean?"

"Whether you cooperate and tell the truth this time."

They entered another labyrinth of tunnels with small caverns or rooms off the main path. This was where the elves lived, Senzia surmised, but she could not bring herself to ask if she was right. The mage's silent treatment was working. She swallowed as they stopped and entered into a small cavern lit by an orange glow emanating from mushroom-like figures.

This cavern was round with anterooms. They walked into one and stopped. One of the soldiers knocked on a piece of wood with a stick, and a hollow sound filled the corridor. The soldier entered and returned moments later, nodding to the mage.

"Follow me," the elder elfe said, and swept into the room.

This was the first time Senzia had seen one of their living quarters, and she was impressed. In the center of the opposite wall was a fireplace where flames crackled and licked small logs with enthusiasm. But after a closer look, Senzia saw it was not real. She frowned. There was little wood around here to gather, and this looked more like an illusion of a fire. There were woven rugs on the floor; a pallet to sleep on; and five chairs that circled a small, stone table.

A figure faced the fire. She was not as tall as most Ashen Elves, and she held herself differently. She was less stiff, and streaks of purple threaded through her black hair. When she turned, Senzia was sure she had never seen this elfe before. Her skin was not as pale as the others', and her eyes were dark, unlike the ice-blue eyes of the Gray Elves. The elfe frowned and slowly approached Senzia, who took a step back. Teal moved between them and growled. The mage hissed at the dog and pointed toward the table. Ears stiffly erect and twitching, the dog shuffled under, whimpering as she went.

"What is wrong, Seoul?" the mage asked.

"This isn't the one," the elfe replied. "She is much younger." A thin, smooth hand reached out and touched Senzia's hair. The *calhei* had to focus all her control on not moving. "This isn't the one," the elfe repeated, "but…she is one of them."

"Are you sure?" the mage asked.

"Yes. Age apart, the other had dark skin—almost black. Her hair was curly, and I suspect it had not always been white, for her roots were gray. But this one is whiter than snow. Her skin and hair are pure."

"Then there must be more than just one family," the mage said. "We suspected as much."

The elfe moved her hand to Senzia's cheek and grabbed her chin in a manner that clearly brooked no disagreement. She stared into the *calhei*'s eyes and then raised the red stone that hung around her neck.

"There is something familiar about you, though," she said quietly, her voice almost lost to the cracking wood. "Who is your father?"

"My father is dead," Senzia said. "I barely knew him."

The elfe scowled and glanced at the mage.

"Do not lie, Senzia," the mage said. "You will regret it."

"My father traveled continuously. My mother brought me up."

"Where?"

"In a little village on Lake Mhari."

The elfe still stared into her eyes, red stone in hand. She frowned. "Your mother had white hair like you?"

"No. My mother's hair is dark and curly. My—"

"Your father had white hair, then," the elfe said. "How did he die?"

"I'm told the Emperor did it," Senzia said. She was kicking herself for not thinking through a story that she could practice, pick apart, and prepare to defend.

The elfe let go of her chin and moved to the table. She invited the mage to sit, but not Senzia, who remained rooted to the spot.

"The *calhei* I faced had an elder Wycaan with her. I think he was her father. No, I'm sure he was."

"Could he also be this one's father?"

"What are the chances?"

"Our troops have seen very few with white hair. One now fights with the king." She turned to Senzia. "What is the name of the white-haired elfe who fights with the king?"

Senzia hesitated. It was a mistake. The elfe held the red stone in the horizontal palm of one hand and sent a red light from her other palm, which faced Senzia. The *calhei* flew back and fell onto the sleeping pallet. She was not hurt, but the wind was knocked out of her.

"We know when you lie," the elfe said in a tired, uninterested tone. "If the mage requests it, I can extract all the information we need from you very quickly, though what I'll do to get it will haunt you forever."

The mage stood up and faced Senzia. "Stand up. Who is your father?"

"He served the king, advising him, and the king sent him off all over Odessiya and beyond. Far to the east, outside our boundaries, something happened to him. No one knows what. When he returned, he was but a shadow of himself."

"What does your white hair mean?"

Senzia frowned. "I don't understand."

"What powers do those with white hair have?"

When Senzia didn't answer, the elfe stood up and stepped closer, her boots clicking on the stone floor. She raised the red stone and her hand. A blinding light shot out, and Senzia felt herself whirling about and falling back on the mattress. This time, her insides burned and her eyes filled with tears. She lay on the bed, clutching her stomach.

"Get up," the elfe ordered. "You see, Senzia, we don't need to ask nicely. I'm trying to do this gently because the mage has decreed it so.

"However, one will soon be here who doesn't obey the mage, and he won't tolerate the clumsy deceptions of a foolish *calhei*. You aren't stupid enough to think your information is actually valuable, are you? Unless you fear we'll kill you once we have no use for you, and we may. It will depend on what he says, for he decides between life and death. He is the most powerful being in this world."

She turned to the mage. "He will arrive tonight."

CHAPTER 48

I n the ensuing silence, Senzia heard the elfe bringing goblets and smelled an herbal tea.

"Sit up. You told us your mother had dark skin and curly dark hair," the elfe said, looming over her. "The one I faced, though, her hair is white now, had dark skin and curly hair. Is she your sister?"

Senzia bit her lower lip and stared at the red stone. The mage had gone, and it was just her and her interrogator.

"We don't have to use this, little *calhei*," the elfe said, dangling it in front of her. "You can make it easy."

No response.

"What are you thinking? Are you full of fear of the power of the stone? The pain it can inflict? It can do far worse than what you have felt, but it isn't the stone you should fear. Rather, the stone serves as a conduit for our magic, much as the black staff that your sister carries channels her magic."

"What sister? What staff? A clumsy attempt," Senzia replied. "You'll have to do better than that." She stared up at the Ashen Elfe. "You're frustrated, aren't you? The mage won't let you extract the information by torturing me, and now whoever comes is not going to be impressed with you. He'll think that you can't even break down a mere *calhei*."

The elfe bristled. A shot of power left her palm and thundered into Senzia, who was suddenly rigid, her body vibrating from the harsh pulses. She felt her teeth chatter and was almost tempted to fight back, but held herself in check…barely.

When the Ashen Elfe stopped, Senzia collapsed to the ground, gasping for breath. She closed her eyes, but the elfe poked her with her boot.

"Stay awake. Feel the reverberation of pain as it echoes in your body. This is only the beginning, Senzia. It can and will get worse, and for what? Are you hiding something from us? You won't be able to keep it secret for long, not after *he* arrives."

"Who is *he*?" Senzia gasped.

The elfe laughed. "Poor little one. You can't comprehend one with his power or his utter contempt for anyone who tries to oppose him."

"I can," Senzia panted. "I met the Emperor."

"Really? The Master? How impressive. Did you fill his wine cup? Empty his chamber pot?"

Senzia bit her lower lip. She was not good at this, too proud. She wanted to scream at this evil elfe that she had sat at the Emperor's feet and studied with him. Not that she was totally proud of that. She was his prisoner, after all. But at this moment, she sought something to be proud of that her torturer would appreciate. Why? She had understood when she and Ilan had been proud that the Emperor had decided to give them audience and teach them. Mharina had been angry with them for this. But though he was evil, he was a powerful man.

A boot connected with her behind and brought her back to where she was, sprawled on the floor.

"Come, Senzia," the elfe said, her voice pleasant now. "Sit at the table. This tea will help clear the pain."

Senzia's body felt like jelly, and she struggled to rise. She made her wobbly way to the table and collapsed into a chair.

"Sit up," the elfe commanded. "Show pride while you still can."

Nothing else was said until two cups of steaming, aromatic tea sat before them. "I'm drinking the same tea," the elfe said. "I want to show you that you can trust me and that…"

She paused and glanced at the door. They heard movements outside, and the stone door slid open slowly. The mage entered, followed by a tall man with stringy blonde hair and a wide-brimmed straw hat.

"Hello, Senzia," the mage said, her gray hands clasped in front of her. She frowned. "Have you and Seoul become friends?"

Senzia did not respond. She hugged the hot cup and sipped the tea that was relieving her pain.

"Did you find out anything?" the mage asked Seoul.

"No. Only that she knew the Master."

"Really?" the mage said.

"She was his prisoner, too," the man said, his voice deep and mellow. "You don't stay free for very long, do you, Senzia?"

Senzia tried to see him but his hat blocked her view. The mage then sat down, and the man pulled up a chair opposite Senzia. He smelled of pungent earth, and his face was tanned and lined from the elements.

"Don't be deceived," the man said. "I'm not who you think I am. Still, I've heard so much about you."

"From the Emperor?" Senzia was surprised.

The man laughed. "Don't flatter yourself. You may have become important to him at one point, but you were only a pawn used to lure your father, Sa'gola, and your sister to him. No. Your sister talked a lot about you."

"Have you hurt her?" Senzia sprung to her feet and toppled the chair behind her.

"Yes, but not in the way you think." The man thought this very funny, but he was the only one laughing.

"Pick up your chair and sit," the mage said.

Senzia did so. "Who are you?" she asked when the man stopped laughing.

"Your dear father and others know me as the Mushroom Man. Your sister saw me as her future lover, mate, whatever words you elves use."

"You're Abel?" Senzia was confused. "I imagined you to be sensitive and…and nice."

The man laughed again. "That's how your gullible sister described me? Abel *is* like that. But my brother only occupies one part of this fine body. I dominate the rest."

Senzia frowned. "I don't understand."

"What happened when your father and sister bravely charged into Grogin to free you and your brother and the others?"

"Ithea killed Sa'gola. They'd been enemies forever. Then Ithea tried to kill my sister, and my *ahdahr* killed him."

"Kind of. Your father transformed into his bear form, which I did not expect given that he is sick in the head, half-mad, and suffering from deep amnesia. Do you know what prompted him to become a bear?"

"Denalion," Senzia replied.

"Correct. Denalion knew how to transfer his essence into another body whenever his own was failing him. He was smart and patient. He hid in my mind and waited. Then, when he saw a way to defeat me, he sprung out from the shadows.

"I know this magic too, Senzia. In fact, I have done this for hundreds of years—as did Sa'gola, by the way. It can be very complicated to enter the body of a living person, but I know my brother well, and the fool actually loves me. Blood is apparently stronger than common sense. He let me in, and, I must say, I have enjoyed getting to know your sister and father. Now I will enjoy getting to know you."

He offered a smile that was far from comforting. Senzia felt her whole body freeze inside.

"Ithea," was all she could say.

Chapter 49

The great grizzly, the black puma, and the young dog galloped steadily. They passed through the plains that fed Shindellia—great fields of wheat and corn; rows of green-leafed vegetables; and, as the terrain became rougher, homesteads with great herds of cattle. If the two-legged saw them, they did not interfere. All too often, the grizzly felt as though the two-legged almost looked away or saw right through them. There was so much he did not understand.

Where were the great teachers to guide him? Pyre and Sellia had told him about Mhari, his first Wycaan teacher, who sacrificed her life for him at the walls of Galbrieth. They had talked of the dwarf Master Onyxei, who threw his body in front of his ruler to prevent an assassination of the Great King in Hothengold. And there had been others, like the Weapons Master who left the Elves of the West to fight and ultimately die alongside Seanchai. There were his friends, Rhoddan, Shayth, and Ilana, who had traveled with him as an elf. His mind drifted to Sellia, loyal mother of his *calhei*.

Slowly, he realized that, as the great grizzly, he remembered things. It occurred to him that perhaps only in this realm, in this level of consciousness, would he know who he really was and where he belonged.

The puma signaled that it was hungry and nodded to a herd of cows. The grizzly growled his refusal to hunt the livelihood of a farmer.

As the sun began to set to their left, they entered loping foothills. The farms were now sparse, and the bear began to rely on his other senses. He stopped by a small stream and drank. He could hear the elegant lapping of the puma and the more frantic slurping of the panting dog. He moved to Azura and looked at her. She raised her head, and her ears pricked back as she gazed back. Her ice eyes reminded him of the Ashen Elfe who had impersonated Mharina's teacher. He thought of Sa'gola, the sorceress who had almost killed him, who had sent him to...where?

Here, his memory stopped. A thick, impenetrable wall of nothing abruptly confronted him. He needed to know. He had to break down the wall he himself had erected for his own protection and face whatever had been so horrific as to wipe out almost every part of his identity.

The dog whimpered under his gaze, and the bear leaned down and licked him. The dog shook herself and did a small jig of excitement. The bear guffawed but stopped abruptly as he caught a scent that made his stomach rumble. He looked upstream. The puma was also peering in the same direction, his whiskers twitching.

They exchanged a glance and began to prowl in that direction. The bear was careful of his step, fearing his weight would snap every twig in his path. A small herd of wild goats had come to drink. There were twelve of them, including two kids. They all looked plump and healthy.

The grizzly glanced over to the puma. If he could, he would have grinned. *You go*, he said. *I want to see you hunt.*

The puma slunk forward, moving silently. The bear watched in fascination. His son's paws were proportionately larger that the rest of his body, a sign that the *calhei* was still growing. Even as an elf, the bear had not developed a strong impression of his son. The lanky boy had appeared sullen and feeble, following the lead of his dominant twin and the older sister he worshipped. He was closest of the *calhei* to Sellia, though she spoke of past intimacy with their oldest, a relationship supplanted by Sa'gola and the Mushroom Man.

The puma's black fur shimmered under the reddening sun of late afternoon, every muscle tensed and defined. He hung close to the rocks stacked next to the riverbank. The cat curled up, ready to pounce, his hind legs quivering as he coiled up like a spring.

When the puma sprung, the grizzly mentally gasped in admiration as the cat's claws tore into one of the kids. But his pride changed to fear as a volley of arrows fell on the herd and a group of Ashen Elves leapt out with spears and swords ready.

Chapter 50

A mighty roar left the mouth of the great grizzly. Even he froze from its ferocity as he felt the rocks shake. The hunters had clearly not anticipated the puma. A spear had landed in his thigh, and he snarled in pain. Several goats lay bleeding, blood seeping from protruding arrows or quivering spears. A few animals twitched, but most, including all those shot by bows, lay lifeless.

The Ashen Elves had sprung into the clearing, ready to claim their quarry, but now they stood rooted to their spots, watching the black puma roll in pain and gradually transform into a *calhei*, clutching his thigh and gasping.

An order was given, and one soldier approached with caution, his sword drawn and ready. The grizzly remained hidden and watched, fighting every sinew in his body that urged him to attack and protect his cub.

But the Ashen Elves were spreading out now and cautiously looking to see who else might be following. Surely, this young elf was not traveling alone. When it seemed clear that they were not about to harm the elf, the grizzly quietly retreated. He could follow them to their main camp. Their finding a young Wycaan elf would surely ensure that the bear would be led to this mage who held his other *calhei*.

He turned and lumbered away. He was not worried they would see him, a bear also tracking a herd of wild goats. He felt convinced that these soldiers would not dare hurt the *calhei*, preferring instead to deliver him to their leader. And they could treat Ilan's spear wound. Even if he rescued his son, Ilan would be wounded and Seanchai would be torn whether to leave him behind.

Reversing into a small cave—a nook barely large enough to hide his huge body—the bear sighed. He was hungry and would not eat goat tonight. He could wait. This was the least of his problems. He abruptly raised his head and looked around.

Azura was not with him. Had it gone to the Gray Elves? There would be nothing strange in that. She had been born here and grown up with them, but now he could not rely on her to take him to wherever Senzia was being held.

Darkness quickly gathered, and he could hear the Ashen Elves setting up camp nearby. Soon, he smelled the enticing aroma of cooking meat. He strained his ears, picking up snippets of conversations, but there were no screams, no signs of interrogation. He sighed, rested his huge head on his front paws, and closed his eyes. He could use this time more efficiently than fretting.

The Great Grizzly stood on the ridge, the huge, snow-tipped mountain peak behind him. It had been where his predecessor, the original great grizzly, lived in splendid isolation. He closed his eyes and raised his snout, sniffing and twitching, determined to discover the scent, anxious to know that they would come.

They approached, but they were still far off. He counted three of them. He sniffed again. A brown, a black, and a small red one. The great grizzly frowned to himself. They were sending representatives, not a pack ready to fight.

Behind him, he heard grunts. He turned and saw eight ice bears. Of course, they had come from the north, beyond the great mountain that stood as a symbolic boundary between the winter lands and the south. The white bears stopped fifty paces away and sat, all except one, which lumbered slowly toward him.

"Thank you for coming," the great grizzly said.

The ice bear grunted. "It has been a long time, my friend, since you summoned us. Much has happened since you rescued my pack and me from the Emperor's camp. We will be forever in your debt and come when you call. But you cannot expect others to do the same."

"What do you mean?" the great grizzly asked.

"These past cycles have been bad for the bears of the warm lands, yet when we called out for your guidance, you did not answer. You never came to us, never entered our dreams. As the two-legged spread and encroached on our lands, they hunted our prey, decimating herds that we would cull to satisfy our needs. We looked to you. When they developed a taste for the hunt, desired our furs and our heads to mount, we called out for you to represent us. Now it is said that the stone caves they build and live in often have dead bears that have been preserved and stuffed to stand upright. We are being pushed further from our homes. We struggle to find food, and, all the time, you ignore our cries for help." The ice bear nodded toward the approaching bears. "They suffer worse than we do. The two-legged rarely enter the white lands."

The three others—the black, brown, and red bears—had joined them now and were nodding. Each told of the tragedies that had descended upon their packs. They told story after story, and the grizzly listened and offered condolences.

"Even after all this, we came to warn you of your daughter cub's capture," the brown said, his voice even. "We came now out of respect for our long history and to honor the great grizzly who came before you. But do not ask us to risk our packs or expose them to incur the wrath of the two-legged. We are too weak of number."

The Great Grizzly stood and thought hard. "I can't tell you why I didn't hear your pleas. Much of my life faded and is hidden from me. This you know. I've forgotten who I was, what I stood for, and even lost the *memory of myself as a bear. I only discovered this when the Dreamwalker of the West—the one you call small red—evoked it from me in a moment of dire desperation.*

"Even so, this does not justify your losses and sufferings. For these, and for not being there when you needed me, I am truly sorry."

He paused and looked up at the looming mountain where his predecessor had lived. "I wish he was still here to advise us. I'm not as wise as he. I took a family, and my responsibilities went beyond his caring for the natural order of the world. It made me many enemies, and you have paid dearly for what has happened."

Again, the grizzly went silent, many thoughts swirling around his head. "When all of this is over, there will be others to fill my responsibilities in the world of the two-legged. If I live, I will try and put right some of the damage you've suffered. I cannot bring back those who have died, but I can try to stop the pillaging of your packs. I swear that, should I survive, I will try. But I must warn you: My life hangs on a thin thread.

"If something happens to me, then choose a leader of your own from the world of the four-legged, one who can be trusted to stay in this world and fulfill the role that you crave."

He paced around, and the others followed his movements. Staring up at the mountain, his back to them, the great grizzly spoke. "I won't ask for your help this time or again in my lifetime. I release you from your oaths and pray to the mighty spirits that they'll look favorably upon your packs and provide you with a leader better than I can ever be. It was an honor to run with you and to be considered one of you. Live long, and may your packs grow and flourish."

The great grizzly rose on his hind legs, raised his mighty head one last time to the mountain, and howled into the night. The leaders of the ice bears and the brown, black, and red joined him. Others, he hoped, would hear, too. A mighty line, one that had formed even before the Age of Mist and Shadow, was being broken, with no prospect of what would come next. Whatever it was, the great grizzly knew it would be a world of the two-legged, and he feared for those who ran on all fours, for those who swam in the deep depths, and those who flew in the skies above. The world was changing, and he would not be able to forge it the way he had once hoped.

For this too he howled and the mountain bore witness in silence.

CHAPTER 51

Ilan lay on furs and felt burning pain in his thigh. An Ashen Elf, huge and gaunt, crouched and used a sharp, heated knife to scrape away red powder he had previously spread on the wound. It had burned, and once he'd scraped it all away, he spread some on a second time. Ilan was given a piece of leather hide and warned not to scream. He had bitten hard on the leather, and his whole face had screwed up, but he had not screamed. Though he was not sure how they would have reacted to him screaming in pain, he was sure his captors were trying to help him, at least for now.

The pain overtook him, and he felt his head spinning. He was scared to open his eyes, worried he might disgrace himself and vomit. He felt himself spiraling down, as though in free fall, and he thought his arms were flailing, though he knew he lay still on the furs. When the spiraling ceased, it was replaced by a deep, heavy silence. Was he sleeping? No, he felt himself being...guided.

Then a powerful howl sharpened his senses. He felt his eyes bulge, though they stayed closed. It was a bear, a powerful bear—his father as the great grizzly. And then other bears joined, and their cries carried through the world of the two-legged and the dreamworld. Gradually, the howls ceased, and a great silence filled the void.

Ilan waited; there was little else to do. He heard the rhythm of his own breathing, and then another joined it.

Are you okay, my son?

I am, Ilan replied. *They tend my wound and have shared the goat meat with me. I suspect I ate better than you.*

He heard his father laugh, a gruff hawing. *Stay strong, Ilan. They might question you, but they won't torture you until they get to their hideaway.*

And then? Ilan asked. *They know what I can do. They saw me transform, and they have hurt Senzia.*

How do you know that?

I know. In the same way I told you I could find her once we're near. She's tougher than me, Ahdahr, and they've already hurt her.

There was a brief silence before his father spoke. *I was tortured, Ilan, though I remember little of it. My body is scarred, but those superficial wounds hurt less as time passes. The true damage happens in the mind. Defend that as best as you can. But know that I am not far behind, and they will have no defense to match the fury of a Wycaan father.*

His father had always seemed invincible, so Ilan knew that should have helped. But he felt little solace. *You are a wounded Wycaan.*

I am, Seanchai replied. *But even if I am less of a Wycaan, I will not be less of a father.*

I adored you, Ilan said. *Even when I resented you for being away so much, I never stopped loving you. Neither did Senzia. I know that to be true.*

His father didn't answer immediately, but Ilan felt his presence. *I have done many things in my life. Some good, some bad. Some I'm told I should be proud of, others, maybe not. But I'll always regret my absences from you, Senzia, and Mharina.*

And mother? Ilan asked.

He heard his father sigh. *She is perhaps the most tragic character of all. Mharina, Senzia, and you will all have a chance to live your lives, to move on. But your mother sacrificed to be with me, to not be with me, to be a mother, and to run a school. Your mother was a brave, fearsome warrior, a rebel, and I took it all away from her.*

Ilan felt his father's pain, as he had felt his mother's for years. It would be disingenuous to both for him to deny what Seanchai said.

Is there not still time? Can you not give her back what she yearns for?

The bear harrumphed. *No one can reverse time. Not even a Wycaan.*

Ilan nodded, though his father could not see the gesture. *A wise elf once said that you can't change what you've done, but you can strive to learn from it and be the best you can in the future.*

A wise elf, indeed, Seanchai said. *Was that Denalion, your teacher?*

No, Ilan replied. *It was Seanchai, the Wycaan Master of Odessiya, and the elf I'm proud to call my ahdahr.*

Chapter 52

"**D**on't hurt me," he whimpered.

The huge Gray Elf loomed over the prisoner and scowled. "No one has touched you, and yet you cringe like a baby." He spat on the ground.

Ilan curled up into a ball as well as he could with a wounded leg. "I-I just want to go home. I know I should never have left. I just want to find my sister. Don't hurt me."

The guard shook his head. "No one here will hurt you. We're ordered to hold our position. You can't walk. The mage is coming to get you."

"The mage? Will he hurt me?" Ilan whined.

"I hope so," the guard replied. "But the mage is an elfe, and you're a coward. She'll see how worthless you are and leave you to the wolves or that bear that tracks us."

"Bear? Oh, no! There were bears prowling near our village before the snows melted. They ate our sheep. My father made me guard them—the sheep, I mean. I'm sure they want to eat me, too."

"Fool. Bears don't attack elves unless they're trapped or sick or their cubs are near. Sounds like your bear woke too early from its winter sleep and..." The guard trailed off and looked around. "She comes."

Ilan offered another whimper. He seemed to have convinced these soldiers that he was a simple coward who didn't possess any valuable information. It was not a total lie. He was scared; who wouldn't be? But he wondered if this mage would be so easily fooled.

"Stand up," an icy, shrill voice commanded.

Ilan did so, shaking a bit when he accidentally put weight on his wounded leg. He straightened and bit his lower lip as he looked upon an old elfe. He could see very little, as she concealed herself inside her hood. But he felt a powerful presence.

"I could heal your leg, you know," she said, "But your pain makes this less work for me. Now, tell me before we leave: Are you alone?"

Ilan pursed his lips. "I'm looking for my sister," he said, allowing his voice to waver.

"That's obvious. Two white-haired *calhei* wandering around is hardly going to be a coincidence. But you didn't answer my question: Are you alone?"

"Yes," he whispered.

Her foot swung around and kicked him in the thigh. The pain in his wound made him scream, and he crumpled to the ground, clutching his leg and whimpering.

"Just to be clear," the mage said, "I can hurt you without touching you or even being near you. Do not lie to me. That was a test question. Bears do not follow elves. They run away, hide, or attack. And spare me the scared little elf act, too. It won't help you."

"I don't know anything about a bear. There was one nearby with the goats, but—"

He again fell, his leg burning from a kick that never physically happened. The mage, small as she was, loomed over him.

"A bear that tracks elves and was accompanied by one of our own dogs? You're a pathetic liar."

Ilan's head drooped. This time, he was not faking it.

Chapter 53

The great grizzly snarled as he vainly attempted to spike a fish with his sharp claws. He knew this was one aspect glaringly lacking in his bear attributes and was usually happy for it to be a source of amusement among other bears. But they would also feed him.

Now, though, he only felt alone, ensconced in gloom. He could not see the mountain peaks around him; they, too, had withdrawn into thick fog. It was very cold, one reason he had remained in bear form.

He slashed again at a slither of silver and connected with a fish, sending it flying onto the riverbank. It was the only bright thing in this dull world. He ripped the squirming fish with his powerful maw and swallowed it after two bites. He tried to catch a few more times and then gave up.

It was getting dark, and there was a smell of moisture in the air. He lumbered to a cave and curled up inside. He would sleep through the darkness and continue after the Ashen Elves in the morning. He sighed. The great grizzly, who could not even feed himself, would go to sleep hungry.

"When will you come?"

Seanchai opened his eyes. He could tell immediately that he was not awake. The colors were too distinct, the scents too sharp, and the small, gray elfe who stood before him seemed to be shimmer.

Behind the diminutive but powerful figure, the bear saw a world of white. The snow lay thick, and he could make out only gentle contours of buried rocks or bushes. The sky was blue, too bright even in contrast to the snowy ground.

He strained his eyes; they were not as sharp as when he was two-legged, but he thought he spied moving blobs of snow making their way in his direction. Only the ice bears had stood by him at the last gathering. He wondered if they were coming and whether it was to support him.

The elfe continued to stare at him, her piercing blue eyes sending shivers of numbing fear through his great body. What was it about her that suggested such power? She was clothed in a long, nondescript cloak. She held no weapon, yet she exuded a sense of invincibility. The bear reached out with his own energy, sending tentative tendrils towards her. His approach was sucked into the area of her throat. She offered a small smile, acknowledging that she knew he was probing, and revealed a chain with a red stone on it. The great grizzly did not need to ask: This was her source of power.

"I asked you a question," she said, her tone almost bored. "Can you understand me in bear form?"

"Of course," the bear replied, attempting the same level of disdain. "This is not the world of the dead."

"What world is it?" she asked.

"The dreamworld. Few can walk here awake."

"I can," the elfe said.

"I noticed."

"Is this your dream or mine?"

The bear considered this. "We're both dreamwalkers, I think. It's a gift enjoyed only by a few. I don't know whose dream it is. I don't really understand it."

"How can you not understand it? Were you not trained?"

"I was, but I have lost much of my memory."

"Yet you remember how to transform into animal form."

"Apparently."

The mage sighed. *"You seek my people. I have two of your white-haired calhei, who seem untrained but full of potential. How did the male learn to transform? Can the female?"*

The bear shook his heavy maw. *"I don't know; I don't know them well and had no idea until it happened before my eyes that the male could do it."*

The mage frowned. *"They are twins, or at least siblings. You're their father. Do not take me for an idiot. I can make life very painful for all of you."*

"As can I," the bear growled.

"Really? Are you better at it than fishing?"

He felt himself relax and guffaw. Then he became serious. *"The Emperor or Master or whatever you called him—"* She nodded, and the grizzly sniffed. *"I bested him twice."*

"Were you whole then or the shell I see before me?"

The grizzly did not have an answer and looked away. After a few moments, he said, *"But I will be formidable when we meet."*

"Because they're your calhei?"

"Yes. That part of me is intact."

"Very well. I have a proposal," the elfe said. *"Come to me in elf form, and I will let them both go. We do not seek to harm calhei. You have my word. Ashbar."*

"Does the ancient language bind you as it does us?"

"Yes."

"Good. Then maybe you're not as different from us as you think. I will come to your caves in place of my calhei."

Chapter 54

There were two wedding ceremonies. The first was a blur for Shameka, as she was presented to thousands of adoring subjects for the first time. Her king looked royal and handsome. She even fell in love with his rebellious hair that spiked out from within his crown. She found herself smiling at how Shayth subconsciously ran his hands through it, exacerbating its unruliness.

The ceremony was hot and formal, mainly a sea of faces dotted with rituals and speeches. After everyone had eaten, and while the people celebrated with dancing and singing, a second ceremony transpired in a walled garden. Only her family and Shayth's sister and close friends attended.

Shameka's family priestess—a kind, elderly woman with flowing gray hair—facilitated the ceremony. Shayth spoke of his dear friend, Ballendir, a dwarf warrior and close confidant, whose dying wish was for Shayth to become king and marry. The new queen saw many tears shed by his closest friends, and, though she knew she shouldn't, she felt envy at the intimacy her husband shared with them from such a rich history.

She had also initially been envious of the familiarity that he shared with Maugwen the healer, a woman more familiar with his body than she was, having patched Shayth up so many times. Maugwen was free to taunt and berate him when they were not in public. She seemed closer to Shayth than his own sister, who remained reclusive to all outside the healer tents, where she worked incessantly. Shameka might have had an issue with Maugwen, except that the diminutive woman took Shameka's side in everything straight from the start.

Sellia had intimidated her at first. But she and the beautiful, dark-skinned warrior had grown close quickly when Shameka learned of the other's pain and losses. She knew how to be supportive, and Sellia welcomed her empathy.

Rhoddan's mate, Troja, kept to herself and seemed intent only on caring for Rhoddan. He was formal and of single mind, and she suspected she might never get to know him.

"Shameka?"

She stared at the priestess, totally lost on anything that had just happened. "I'm sorry," she said, throwing an apologetic wince at her father and then her husband. She winced again, knowing that, starting today, her husband would take precedence.

"You're nervous, my dear, and that can only be expected. You held yourself beautifully in front of the citizens of Shindellia," the priestess said, and, as everyone nodded in agreement, she added: "And your husband cannot take his eyes off of you."

Everyone laughed, except the groom, who blushed. "I think embarrassing the king might be grounds for treason," Shayth mumbled to more laughter.

Shameka forced a smile. "Please bind us," she blurted. "My words are for my husband's ears alone." They were not, though. She had written and practiced a string of vows that would have made everyone happy, but as she acknowledged the masked strain on the faces of Shayth, Rhoddan, Sellia, and others, she only wanted this to finish.

Too many people were suffering for this ceremony to be anything but an act of duty, and she had no desire to force them to play out a scene she had dreamed of ever since she could remember—a fairytale wedding to a handsome prince and an adoring kingdom. She had her prince, and he seemed a good, if burdened, man. She was a woman now, and the fairy tales would need to wait until she could recount them to her own children.

As the priestess tightened the rope that bound them seven times—Shayth's right hand and her left—Shameka turned to face her family, new and old, and then to Shayth. All of a sudden, her vows tumbled out.

"I am bound to you, my mate and king. I will do my best to serve you and through you, so that our kingdom may vanquish our enemies and our people may live in peace." There were murmurs of appreciation. She entwined her fingers in Shayth's and lowered her voice, "And I hope to be a true mate and support you in every way I can."

He bent forward and kissed her on the lips. When he drew back, she was breathless, and she saw glistening in the dark eyes she was told never wept.

"And I swear before the gods and goddesses to protect, nourish, and love you, too, Shameka," Shayth said. "I only hope I am worthy of being your mate."

It was the way he said that last bit revealing the uncertain boy inside the decisive king. As she fell into his embrace, Shameka knew she needed no fairytale.

The crowd roared as their king and queen—she resplendent in a flowing white dress that ignited her brown skin and wearing a crown for the first time—returned to stand on the balcony. They had accepted the good wishes of the subjects selected to attend the private reception and then quickly made their way to the edge to overlook the square.

The cheers were deafening and the love the people had for their rulers unmistakable. For a few minutes, Shameka stood there and lived her dream, her handsome king's strong arm around her waist. Then she turned to him and cupped his face in her hands, bringing his lips to hers. The people screamed their approval, and Shameka allowed herself to get lost in the exhilaration.

Then she put her mouth to Shayth's ear and whispered, "Let's go. I don't know how long I'll have you, but I want you for as long as I can."

With that, she took his hand and led him away from the thousands below and the family and friends who circled around them and into space that would forever be only theirs.

CHAPTER 55

S hameka expected to wake alone. Shayth had warned her that he needed to ride out with his commanders on a reconnaissance trip, but he would be back when the sun reached its zenith. Their wedding night had been beautiful, and they had finished it by falling asleep in each other's arms. When he left their bed, he kissed her softly and apologized again for leaving her. She purred something and fell back into blissful sleep.

Now, she became aware of people in her room, probably her servants waiting with a hot bath and breakfast. Judging by the light straining through the thick velvet curtains, they were probably concerned about whether or not she was still breathing! She stretched, and a long sigh escaped her.

"Bring me my robe," she said. "Sarita? Are you there, dear?"

Her maidservant did not answer. Still, there was clearly shuffling in the room. A figure approached, holding out a thick leather dress open at the front. It was the one Shameka wore for hunting, totally inappropriate.

"What..."

"If you make a sound, we'll kidnap you naked," a coarse female voice said. "We have been instructed not to harm you more than is necessary to get you out of here unobserved. We aren't allowed to leave any permanent marks on you. Believe me when I say that won't hinder us if you choose not to cooperate. Now, stand up."

Shameka did not doubt these words and slowly rose. She looked and counted five heavily armed, grim-faced elfes near the door and windows. She first picked up her underclothes strewn on the floor and put those on, and then took the dress. She nodded to the bathroom and went in. When she tried to close the door, the Gray Elfe put a huge, scuffed boot in the way and shook her head.

Shameka threw water on her face and considered her options. She had been taught self-defense and enjoyed hunting and archery when her mother had allowed it, but she was no match for even one of these battle-hardened soldiers. She considered screaming, but the doors and walls were thick. Still, she had to try. As she strained and took in a lungful of air, a hand came over her mouth, and she involuntarily inhaled something rancid. All went dark.

Mharina was livid. She had woken early and gone to the eating hall to break her fast. There, she learned that King Shayth and his war council had already eaten and left Shindellia to oversee preparations on the plains.

She felt it unacceptable that she had not been invited. She stormed out, grabbing only an apple on the way, her burnt staff clicking furiously on the stone ground. She considered going to the barracks and grabbing a few soldiers to train with and vent her frustrations, but this would be unfair to the soldiers. Her mother would be no help and probably shared the same frustrations of sitting around while the twins and Seanchai were all gone.

Only duty kept Mharina here to serve the king in her father's place. If he did not want her, she would have preferred to go with her father and rescue her siblings. Perhaps then, her mother might have gone, too, and they could all have reconnected.

A sudden thought occurred to her, and she changed direction, making her way to the royal quarters. Perhaps building an ally with the new bride might help. Surely, the queen was frustrated that Shayth left their wedding bed so abruptly and was probably in need of a friend.

As she approached, Mharina wondered whether the queen's guards would let her through and then realized there were no guards posted. She frowned. The corridor was empty. There wasn't even one outside the room where the king and queen slept. She almost knocked but instead went to the adjacent service room, where there were always servants on call. It would not do to wake the queen.

The place was empty, and a tray of food was getting cold, the eggs turning a sickly yellow. Had the queen gone with Shayth? That made sense and served only to darken her mood. She turned to leave, but a scratching from a storeroom stopped her. Mice? So near the king's chambers? Then she heard a muffled cry and ran to the door, swinging it open. Two bodies tumbled out, the neck of one unnaturally twisted. This woman was certainly dead. Mharina ripped the piece of cloth out of the mouth of the second, and the plump serving girl sputtered for air. Then she grabbed Mharina's arm.

"The queen," the woman wheezed, and Mharina dropped her to the floor. As she turned, she heard boots in the corridor. She rose and faced an Ashen Elfe, who flicked her gloved hand and let loose a metal disc. Mharina spun her staff, felt a thud as the blade embedded itself, and continued the motion to strike at her attacker. The Ashen Elfe raised a heavy broadsword and blocked the strike. There was no attempt to deflect; the grim warrior did not consider Mharina a true adversary.

The block vibrated through the young Wycaan's body. She swung the other way, crouching to hit her adversary's legs. The broadsword lowered and the soldier blocked comfortably, but this time, Mharina was ready. As their weapons connected, she used the break in momentum to swing up with her right leg and strike the Gray Elfe in the cheek, whipping her neck around. The elfe staggered back, but as she raised her broadsword, orange light sizzled from Mharina's staff and sent the elfe crashing into the wall.

Mharina ripped the serrated disc from her staff and was astonished to see the warrior rise. There was blood on the stone wall from the back of her head, but the Ashen Elfe was prepared to fight on. Mharina was about to pass her and head into the corridor.

"Not so fast," the elfe rasped. "We haven't finished."

"'fraid I have," Mharina said, and slashed the elfe's throat with the disc. "This is yours, I believe," she added, dropping the bloody blade by her feet. The disc clinked on the ground, and Mharina sprung out into an empty corridor.

Chapter 56

She ran out onto the balcony and saw four shadows moving down exterior stairs. One had the queen slumped over its shoulder. Mharina moved the other way, jumped over the merlons, and ran silently down the opposite side. She had to reach them without being seen, as they might disappear like the Sa'gola impostor had. Then she would have failed her new queen.

The Ashen Elves made their way past soldiers who seemed not to notice them, running along the edge of a square that Mharina believed led to the royal stables. She ran after them, drawing looks from the same soldiers who had previously been oblivious.

"Close all gates," she screamed to a group of them standing nearby. They just stared back and did not move. Idiots! She didn't have time to stop. She ran to the stables. Two young stable hands slumped in unnatural positions at the doors.

As one mounted horse exited, Mharina pole-vaulted off her staff and kicked an elfe right out of her saddle. The second had the queen lying unconscious across her saddle. Mharina sent orange light from her staff and knocked the horse back into the wooden door, which cracked from the impact. The horse whinnied, and Mharina swung the staff into the horse's front legs, which went down, braying. She whirled her staff the other way and smashed the elfe in the back of the head. She knew her own strength wouldn't be enough to finish this. She summoned power from the ground and struck with ferocity. The elfe fell from her horse, which was trying to rise.

Mharina slapped the horse's hindquarters and sent it stumbling past her with Shameka still tied on. There were soldiers approaching now, and she screamed at them. "The queen! Defend the queen!"

They immediately formed a thick ring around the horse, and Mharina turned her attention back to the two remaining Gray Elfes. They had not remounted and now crept cautiously to either side of her.

She whirled her staff, partly in preparation and partly in trepidation. She could feel their cold blue eyes piercing into her. One nervously played with a chain at her neck. Slowly, she drew the chain from under her shirt. She was not nervous, Mharina realized; she was smiling.

"You know I can beat you," the Wycaan said. "Why not disappear?"

"We're intrigued by you," the one holding the chain said. "You white-haired elves keep turning up at an alarming rate."

"Then stop fighting this war. Make peace. There's a better way. Our king has made a generous offer – fertile lands and freedom top be part of a thriving nation."

The Ashen Elfe paused and glanced up into air. "A fine sentiment," she said, "but no."

"You are tempted. I saw you pause. If I let you go, why not present the offer to your mage?"

The elfe laughed. "I already did. When you saw me hesitate, I was listening to orders." She pulled out the chain from her shirt, revealing a pulsating and glowing red stone. "My mage admires your skill and bravery. She gives you this as a gift."

The elfe tossed the stone and chain to Mharina, who caught it easily. But as her fingers clasped around the pulsing stone, waves of freezing energy flooded her body. She gasped and fell to her knees, sending all her strength into the staff and planting one end into the ground.

The staff's runes ignited and exploded into light, first orange and then a deep red. Sparks shot from along the wood, and then flames of deep heat seemed to envelop her. Mharina's face stretched, and she thought her eyes would pop. Her head fell back, and she stared at the wooden beams supporting the roof.

Before it could consume her, Mharina sent the fire into both Gray Elfes, who staggered from the impact. But redirecting the energy lowered her defenses for a few precious moments.

Gasping, she felt the heat and ice clash, and the fury of the two elements erupted in her body. Still, she clasped the stone in one hand and her staff in the other. She somehow knew her life depended upon not breaking the connection. The stone flared a deeper red, and the staff responded. As one element escalated, the other responded in kind, intensifying the battle inside a convulsing Mharina.

Her eyes clenched shut with pain and then shot open. Before her, a huge mural stretched across an entire stone wall. Ashen Elves marched forth from cave entrances onto snowy tundra in strict battle formation.

Mharina struggled to her feet. She would overcome this. She could feel more energy, more heat, pulsating through her. She had to see this through.

And there was Senzia, sprawled on the stone ground, twitching and whimpering. She saw Ilan limping, a bloody bandage on his thigh. She saw the Ashen Elfe who had pretended to be Sa'gola smirking. She saw an old, wrinkled elfe—surely the mage—watching intently, following every wave of energy, every clash of ice and fire.

And then Mharina screamed. It was not a cry of physical pain, but of sheer, heart-ripping agony. Staring back at her, a smile across his beautiful face, was her Mushroom Man. She helplessly took in his wavy blond hair, his weather-beaten skin...and his hard red eyes. Those eyes burned into her memory.

Abel, she cried out wordlessly. *Ithea! Nooooo!*

Mharina felt her legs buckle as tears poured out. She was vaguely aware of Pyre sweeping past her, Win Dao blades flashing as she charged the two remaining Ashen Elves, who were back on their feet and advancing on Mharina. Mharina dropped the red stone and heard her staff clatter on the ground beside her. Ice and fire drained from her body, and a numbing tidal wave of emptiness filled the void. Exhaustion and despair consumed her, and she curled into a ball. Then she plummeted into darkness.

Through the dense fog of heartache, Mharina heard voices, felt her mother's caresses. Sellia was calling her back. She felt her mother raise her shoulders and pull her daughter to her as she had many times in a long-lost past. It was her mother's unbreakable love that nourished Mharina and helped her find the strength to return.

She found the strength to open her eyes and looked up into the loving face of her mother. Sellia's eyes bulged.

"Oh, my dear daughter. What have they done to you?"

Mharina frowned. "What do you mean?"

"Your eyes. They are ice blue."

Chapter 57

Mharina heard her king yelling while she was still far down the corridor, and she could not help but rub her sore head. She walked, leaning on her staff for support, until she reached a small service room, where three young women jumped to their feet, each staring at her in terror.

"May I have a glass of water?" she asked quietly.

All three sprang into action. One brought a goblet filled with water, a second a bowl of fruit. A third held a damp, warm shawl. She began to wipe Mharina's forehead with it, but the elfe gently took the cloth. The woman stood frozen, staring at Mharina's eyes.

"Am I that scary?" Mharina asked

The woman nodded, and then shook her head vigorously. Confused, she tried to take the cloth back and continue wiping the Wycaan's forehead.

"It's okay," Mharina said, and offered a smile that only made the woman shrink back even more. "I think we're about the same age. My name is Mharina."

When this elicited no response, she rose to leave.

"Do they all have eyes like yours, milady?" one asked.

"I believe so," Mharina replied, startled at being called milady.

"Why do they hate us so?"

"We—our ancestors, that is—treated them very badly centuries ago. Their hearts are full of vengeance."

"Should we hate them back? Seems to me that makes us no better than them."

Mharina looked at her, and the young woman cringed and averted her eyes. "You are very wise," Mharina said, gently putting a finger under the woman's chin and raising her face. "And you're no slave. There's no need to ever avert your eyes."

The woman's face lit up. "Bless you, milady. Thank you for saving our queen."

"Yes," the others agreed. "Thank you."

Mharina smiled. "How long have you served her?"

"Just begun," one answered. "But she's *our* queen."

"She is lucky to have you. Now, I must meet the king."

The women glanced at each other. The older one spoke. "Begging your pardon, milady, but best not when 'e's in a tizzy."

Mharina laughed. "It will be okay. I just saved his bride. Maybe he'll let me do a bit of shouting."

She left the women giggling and smiled to herself. But the smile disappeared at Shayth's rage and the huge, armed sentries outside his room. She really did not know the king, and he only knew her as a *calhei*. This was going to change right now.

The guards did not stop her from entering, but neither did she ask their permission. Shayth stopped berating a group of uniformed men for a moment, stared at her, and frowned. But even her blue eyes could not stop him, and he resumed his tirade. His hair stood up straighter than she had ever seen, and his checks were flushed with rage.

When he finished, Shayth dismissed his men, and they scrambled to get out of the room. As they left through the door Mharina had entered, giving her a wide berth, Shayth came over and looked hard into her eyes. He opened his mouth to speak, but then another door opened behind them and Shameka entered, flanked by two servants. Behind them were Pyre and Sellia.

Mharina watched as her mother broke rank and came to stand with her, looping an arm around her shoulders.

"Have you eaten?" Sellia asked. When Mharina shook her head, Shameka turned and whispered to one of her servants, who disappeared.

"Let's sit," Shayth said, taking his place at the head of a solid, but not ornate, wooden table.

The queen seated herself at the other end, and Mharina went and sat next to her. "How do you feel? I'm sorry for the death of your maid."

Shameka nodded. "She had been with me a long time. It was a horrible way to die. Thank you for all you did."

Mharina nodded and then tuned to Shayth. "What awaits us out there?"

The king was clearly surprised. "I-I wasn't aware that we would be discussing—"

"King Shindell." She made a serious attempt to keep her voice even. "All that has kept me from racing after my siblings and *ahdahr* is my duty to you as a Wycaan and bearer of the *Iyzun*. My sister has been tortured, my brother wounded, and I'm not in a great mood.

"Admittedly, the skirmish earlier helped placate me, but how can I advise you when you go out with your commanders and leave me behind?"

Shayth stared at her, and she thought her point was made. He raised a goblet of wine and sipped. When he spoke, his tone was even. "Thank you, Mharina, for saving my bride. We will definitely talk seriously of your role and how best you can serve me. But I invited you to thank—"

"Very well," Mharina said, and rose. "Your gratitude is appreciated. Please let me know when—"

"Sit down." Shayth's tone hardened. "I haven't given you permission to leave."

Mharina tensed, ready to snap back, but instead sat down. "My apologies, Your Majesty. I have never been around royalty."

"Besides, look at your mother's face," Shayth said more amicably. "You just shared some catastrophic news. Don't leave her now."

Mharina stared at Sellia's pale expression.

"How do you know about Senzia and Ilan?" Sellia asked, her voice hushed.

Mharina sighed and closed her eyes. She had screwed up twice now. "I'm sorry," she said. "I—"

"Please don't apologize," Shameka said. "We can all see you're still not yourself. But do tell how you know about the twins."

Mharina nodded. "When the Gray Elfe threw her red stone at me, it attacked with ice. I'm trained with the elements, so I responded with fire to neutralize it. As I advanced and their defenses fell, I entered one's mind. This has happened before during my training. Unfortunately, there is no one alive who can explain how it works to me, except maybe this mage or Ithea."

"Ithea!" A chorus of voices.

"He's dead, Mharina," Sellia said, her voice shaking with fear. "Your father—"

Mharina grimaced and bit her lip. For a fleeting moment, she yearned to have Sa'gola by her side chiding her for this. "I saw what happened at Grogin, as did all in the room. But I'm afraid much transpired that was not visible to the eye. Do you remember how the Dreamwalker hid in his mind when Ithea took his body? It was Denalion's voice inside Ithea that commanded *Ahdahr* to transform into his bear form."

"Where does he reside?" Shayth understood what she was saying and sprang to his feet.

Mharina's lips quivered, and she struggled to find the words to answer. She didn't need to.

"Oh, my poor *calhei;* I'm so sorry." Sellia pulled her daughter to her and looked across at Shayth. "Her Mushroom Man. He's Ithea's brother. He was there and fled the room."

CHAPTER 58

They descended into despondent silence. Shameka probably understood the least and leaned across to hug Mharina. It was meant as a kind gesture, but it felt awkward.

"You lost your mate?"

Mharina had not had a chance to really process this, so she just nodded. "We were not formally bonded," she said after a while, "but I thought him the one. Elves connect deeply with their mates." She winced, feeling her mother tense, but then another realization hit her. "And I will have to kill him."

The queen also tensed, and it was Mharina who broke away. She turned to her mother and relayed what she had seen of Senzia and Ilan. Then she looked to Shayth. "King Shayth: Were you berating your officers for letting the Gray Elves get through to the queen?"

Shayth nodded. "It was most therapeutic. If you want, I can arrange for you to shout at them, too."

"How many of the queen's bodyguards are female?"

"None," Shameka replied. "What are you suggesting?"

"That we train female soldiers to guard you," Mharina said. "They'll be armed and close, and will know how to fight and raise an immediate alarm."

"Would you like to train them?" Shayth asked.

"No. You need me to be more accessible. You have officers who can do that, and Pyre can supplement. She has experience in, this as does my mother."

Shayth nodded. "What else?"

"Did the Elves of the West send a delegation to either the coronation or the wedding?"

Shayth shook his head. "Our last meeting did not go well."

"Pyre told me. Send an official proclamation that both events have transpired. Offer no admonishment but sign and seal it as the king."

"What's the point?" Shameka asked.

"To establish that their absence was noted," Sellia snapped.

But Shayth was looking at Mharina. "What do you intend to write in the accompanying message?"

Mharina grinned. "You don't yet know me, but do you trust Pyre?"

"I trust Pyre and the daughter of the Wycaan Master," Shayth declared after a brief hesitation.

"Thank you," she replied.

Mharina had not answered the king's question.

"They will attack Shindellia from the south," a general with a large, bushy mustache declared, pointing to nowhere in particular.

There were six of them standing on a hill, a comfortable breeze at their backs. Mharina glanced at Shindellia shimmering behind her and the vast forest before her, the food valley stretching between them. She stood with Shayth, Rhoddan, Sellia, and two officers. They all peered forward, as if expecting the Ashen Elf army to march out in front of them.

"Why do you say that, General?" Rhoddan asked.

"Our forces last encountered them in the great forest and the Cumrian hills, young man."

Rhoddan stiffened at the insult but said nothing. The general, oblivious to his mistake, continued.

"We want them to come through the forest, even though they enter the food bowl. Most of the harvests are in and the land is flat there and presents the best opportunity for us to use the cavalry."

Mharina turned to Shayth. "Have you used your cavalry before against the Ashen Elves?"

Shayth nodded. "In the north, just below the snow line."

"And were they effective?"

"Yes," Shayth frowned.

"Then the Ashen Elves won't make the same mistakes again," she said.

The general harrumphed. "I have served in the army for more than twice your life, young—"

"Elfe!" She snapped without thinking.

The general froze, his mouth open, his cheeks reddening. "I planned to address you as such," he snapped.

"What do you think they plan?" Rhoddan interceded.

Mharina didn't know and just shook her head.

Rhoddan stared at the forest and then back at the walls of the capital. "How can they prevent us from attacking their advance with horsemen?" he wondered out loud.

"They'll have troops stationed at the walls, close enough to strike as we exit," Shayth said, his dark eyes glaring at his capital. "Every red stone will just appear there."

Now they all stared at the walls, daring the Gray Elves to appear.

"Do we bring the cavalry out now? We can set up camp on the plain." It was the other officer, a red-headed man with a permanently sunburned face.

Shayth kicked a stone, and it tumbled down the slope. "Why don't they come? What are they waiting for?"

"Either they don't have enough soldiers assembled, they're worried about our possession of the red stones, or they hope to extract information from Seanchai or my *calhei* first," Sellia said. Everyone turned, surprised that she had spoken. The dark elfe had been silent all day.

"We don't know that they have Seanchai," Shayth said.

"They will if they don't already," Sellia replied. "He'll exchange himself for the twins. Then he'll try to persuade them to join his alliance." There was such certainty in her voice that, at that moment, no one doubted her.

"Why don't we preempt?" the older general asked. "If they aren't yet at full strength, why don't we attack?"

"Because, apart from the pictorians and our very best soldiers, they are bigger, stronger and have magic," Shayth replied. "We defend and run. That is all we have been doing for a long time now. We can chip away at them, but we cannot defeat them in the open. Here, there is nowhere left to run. That is why we must defend our walls."

"Shindellia will stand," the general said, and, to his credit, he did not wither under the glares from his king and Mharina.

"We need to know what they're planning," Shayth muttered. "Those red stones are the key."

"You have a stone?" Mharina asked.

Shayth nodded. "The Elves of the West have another."

"Then I must try to find out what they are." She looked at her mother. "Perhaps I can also see how the twins fare."

After they returned to the capital, Mharina excused herself. She lay in her bed, but sleep eluded her. She worried for the twins, as she always had. Ilan was weak and would not stand up to torture. Their sister was the opposite, aggressive, and that could quickly be her downfall. She wondered what information the mage thought they possessed and how long the torture could go on if they did not.

Mharina rose and dressed. She washed her face and walked down through the castle into the bowels of the keep. Outside a thick wooden door, she paused, hearing muffled voices. She rapped it with her fist, and all went silent. She knocked a second time.

After a few moments, she tried to open the brass handles to no avail. She hesitated, deciding whether or not to summon Shayth. Something was wrong. Surely, the stone must be guarded. But there was no one on watch. She could feel others behind the door.

Mharina turned and retreated, her staff clicking on the stone ground. She turned a bend and stopped. She heard the door creak open and muffled boots on the ground. She swung around, summoning the fire to her staff and sending it into two Ashen Elves. They both screamed and fell. Others retreated quickly, but Mharina felt two appear behind her. She struck fire into one, but the second descended on her with a thick broadsword.

She parried his fast blows, sparks lighting up the dark corridor. It was hard without the space to maneuver her staff in forms she had practiced. In the cramped corridor, Mharina stumbled on a rise in the uneven floor and hit her head on a rock protruding from the wall. She was dazed, but sufficiently conscious to see her adversary spring forward to deliver the final blow. Before he could, he froze, his sword above his head. It left his hands and clattered to the ground. He fell forward, an arrow quivering in his back.

Behind him stood Sellia, bow ready and another arrow nocked, a single bead of sweat dripping down a glistening cheek. At that moment, Mharina saw the legend that her warrior mother had been, and her heart leapt. Sellia wore a grim smile.

"Your father would do the same foolish thing, thinking he could go off by himself and save everyone."

Mharina grinned, and her voice shook with emotion. "You're so beautiful, mother, just as I imagined you in the stories."

Now it was Sellia's turn to smile. "Well, that makes it worthwhile, I guess. Come, we must check the stone or see if there are other Ashen—"

Sellia grunted, her eyes bulging, and Mharina saw the tip of a curved blade protrude through her mother's chest. She screamed and, as her mother toppled forward, she released white-hot fire into the Ashen Elf who stood behind her. His body flew apart.

But Mharina did not care. She ran and knelt by her mother, gathering her to her own chest. Blood dripped from Sellia's mouth.

"Remember me with my bow…in battle one last time," she whispered. "Tell the twins…I love them and…died fighting…by your…side." She coughed, and more blood came out. "Seanchai," she said, struggling for air as blood choked her.

Mharina turned her mother onto her side, and she coughed up blood onto the stone floor. When Mharina felt her mother try to turn her head, she helped.

"What do I tell *Ahdahr*?" she asked as tears blurred her vision.

"I could never…be Ilana…but I tried." She groaned, and tears mingled with the blood. "I tried…so hard. I only wanted to…be loved…back."

"He loves you," Mharina cried. "I know he does. The old *Ahdahr*, he loves you and…"

Her voice trailed off. And what? She didn't know what. Her mother stared through glazed eyes, as if waiting for her answer. But no answer came. Sellia, mate to the Wycaan Master and mother to the twins and Mharina, just stared…lifeless.

Chapter 59

Mharina heard boots and shouting men racing down the stairs. She carefully laid her mother's head on the ground, gathered her staff, and walked to the heavy wooden door.

Numb, and with pain ringing in her ears, she lowered the tip of her staff and fired pure, white fire into the door. The heavy wood flew from its iron hinges and into the room. Mharina stepped inside, and her anger channeled through the staff. She screamed, spraying fire from the staff's tip, an endless stream of pain and rage. The runes on the staff turned orange and then white. Ashen Elves fell before her, one after the other. She did not care how many or who they were. She cared nothing for using the white fire that had almost killed her father. She felt only the rage that consumed her mourning.

"Mage! Where are you?" she screamed. "I'm the only one you don't have. Come and get me. You coward. You worm. Come face me. I'll kill you for what you've done and for whatever you're doing to my brother and sister! Where are you?"

She was alone in the room, its walls covered in shelves groaning from the weight of too many books, scrolls, and other oddments. Mharina panted. Behind her, soldiers had reached the door entrance but feared to step inside.

"Get out of here!" she screamed, reeling on them and pointing her staff, even as it still glowed white. "I'll kill anyone who comes near."

The soldiers shrank back and left. Mharina turned and hissed. "Why do you cower? What honor did you derive in stabbing a noble elfe in the back? Where are you?"

"I am here, little one," a voice said.

"Show yourself."

"No," the mage replied, her voice soft, perhaps sympathetic. "I feel your power and know I am no match for your rage. Feed on it. This is how it happens, little *calhei*. Only the strongest survive. You walk the path you choose and so often walk it alone. All those around you will die, leaving you to wonder whether it was all worth it.

"You wish to stop this? Force your king to reveal where the Elves of the West dwell, and we will turn our attention there. You will have your sister and brother back, maybe even your father, and—"

"Can you return my mother to me?" Mharina snarled.

"Your mother?"

"Can Ithea return to me my lover or my teacher? I will survive, mage, and I'll make you rue the day you attacked my family."

The old elfe spoke slowly and deliberately. "We could not know the elfe warrior was your mother. I am sorry for you and the *calhei*. But—"

"But nothing. I don't want your apologies. I want you and your army. I want your blood. I want vengeance."

The mage laughed, a rasping sound. "You don't want it to stop now, do you? You are so hurt. You crave only revenge. Nothing else matters. It flows through your entire body and soul. It is your lifeblood, your breath. You have the eyes of an Ashen Elf. Now you truly understand us. You have become one of us. Welcome to *our* family."

"Mharina!" Pyre was at the door, and now Mharina became aware of horns blowing in the background. "I'm so sorry, but now is not the time to mourn. Come. The Ashen Elf army attacks. Shayth needs us on the battlements."

Mharina swung around again, but the mage was gone. She turned to Pyre. "My mother," she whispered.

"I know. I'm so sorry, believe me, but you must come. We will mourn her properly after the battle. Come."

Mharina felt her legs move and her body follow Pyre. They passed the corpses of Ashen Elves, but her mother's body had thankfully been removed. Pyre led her through the corridor, and, together, they ascended the steps back into the keep and out onto the ramparts.

Pyre pushed through troops who stood staring out over the walls. "Fetch buckets of arrows, rocks, and pitch," she called out. "Why are you standing here? Go. They won't ask if we're ready before attacking. No one stands still. Move."

The men seemed relieved to be dragged away from whatever they were watching. Shoulders bumped against Mharina. Some men apologized, meeting and then averting their eyes away from her harsh blue ones, but most ignored her, their eyes set on the ground in front of them.

Pyre led her up to one of the ramparts. It was not the one they had used over the past few weeks, which held a tent and food for the king. She glanced across and saw the tent there. She hoped no one was foolish enough to be inside. It would burn in the first attack.

Shayth stood waiting and took her in his arms. "I'm so sorry," he whispered. "Sellia was..." He stopped, his voice breaking. When he continued, she could barely hear his voice. "She was there from the start. I..."

"Not now," Pyre said, and her voice cut like a sword through the air.

Mharina broke from his embrace. She turned so they would not see her tears and gasped.

It had been assumed that the Gray Elves were a thousand strong; that the reason they had not attacked until now in open battle was because they did not possess the sheer numbers required for an assault on the capital.

Now she could see how woefully wrong they had been. On the plains outside Shindellia, rows upon rows of Ashen Elves stood in battalions of four units, each of about a thousand soldiers. Mharina counted eight battalions.

Between each division sat catapults, trebuchets, and ballistae. Huge oxen with shaggy coats and curled horns were harnessed to the machines. Further back, her keen elven eyes made out a sea of tents.

Mharina sighed and turned to Shayth.

"Are they this strong all the way around?"

The king did not look at her. He just shook his head, and, for a moment, she saw the younger Shayth that her parents had spoken of. The mustached general stood beside him and spoke.

"They have a similar force behind us and a weaker one on the flanks, milady."

"What's our plan?"

She was looking at the sullen king, who remained silent. The general twiddled his mustache. "We plan to withstand a siege and an assault. They will lose fifty for every one of ours."

"Let me take the pictorians and attack at night," Mharina said. "A quick raid. Perhaps we can reach their leadership or supplies."

"No," Shayth said abruptly.

"You plan to just wait? The nerves of your soldiers are already frayed. Why not strike some fear into the enemy? Seize a small victory? Why not take the fight to them?"

"I'm sorry, Mharina," Shayth replied, his voice as soft as she had ever heard it. "I want to avenge her death, too; believe me. But to risk the pictorians and to lose you doesn't make sense. You can each take out the fifty gray elves that the general speaks of, but I'm not sure how many others can. We stay within the walls. They will come to us."

Mharina tried to think of a response, but she knew he was right. "You should address your troops. Their fear is pungent."

"There's always fear before engagement. It is natural," the general said, and nodded to the enemy. "Our enemy feels the same pangs as us."

Mharina glared at him. "No. They do not," she replied. "They are excited to finally fulfill their need for revenge."

The general laughed, but it sounded uncertain, and he quickly stopped and cleaned his throat. "You, err, seem to know a lot about them."

"They're making me one of them. My eyes are ice blue and my blood fueled by vengeance."

The general tried a nervous chortle, but Shayth turned to face Mharina. "Be careful, Mharina. The mage is very smart. She may well have done this to make you reckless. You agreed to stay and serve me for the good of our people. I hold you to your oath. But I will address the men as you suggest. I..."

He broke off at a cry of alarm. Ashen Elves bearing the red stone were vaporizing inside the walls.

"Every second archer to face inside," the general roared, and his order was echoed down the line.

A horn blew, and pictorians scrambled from buildings and tents, spreading out to engage the Ashen Elves. Mharina turned to her king, and he offered a grim smile.

"Go," he said. "Quench your thirst. But always remember that you are a Wycaan like your father and an elfe warrior like your mother. Nothing reckless. Now, go."

The carved runes on her staff glowed pure white as Mharina channeled her anger and loss. She leapt from the platform onto the ramparts and skipped down the steps two or three at a time, charging into a dozen Ashen Elves. They never stood a chance.

Chapter 60

The great grizzly's paws compacted the snow and left a distinct trail in his wake. If other animals saw him, they were offering a wide berth, because he saw no one, neither two nor four-legged.

The mage had given him a vision of the route and now, for two days, he headed north, his lumbering pace consistent and determined. He stopped only to drink and rest after dark. On the third day, a snowstorm forced him to seek shelter in an overhanging crag. He did not lay down to sleep as his animal instinct suggested, but prowled the small shelter, anxious to continue.

He thought of his *calhei*. Though he barely knew them, the bond ran deep, and there was nothing he cared for other than to save them. He felt pride in his son, who had mastered his animal transformation with little more than instinct. Senzia was an enigma. He remembered little about her. She seemed so independent, close only to her twin. He wondered if even Sellia knew her.

And then there was Mharina. The elfe had aged beyond her years. Her relationships with Sa'gola and the Mushroom Man had forced her to grow up. The power that flowed through her, the responsibility she had to balance the *Iyzun*, was scary. Mharina was capable of far more than even he could imagine. He searched his mind for knowledge passed down from the Wycaan Masters and swallowed hard. Mharina needed a teacher more than her siblings did. The Wycaan powers the twins possessed were rare, and, even if he was unable to retrieve his memories and his training, they could go to the Elves of the West. But Seanchai knew of no one with the knowledge to train and guide Mharina.

A fleeting fantasy of him guiding her was swiftly dismissed. Even if he could somehow recall his past knowledge or reclaim his memories, Seanchai was convinced he would not leave the north alive.

His mind went to Sellia and the painful and lost expression she wore whenever she sought recognition from him. He felt a cold wave shiver through his body, a feeling of failure and even cruelty from denying her what she so clearly sought.

Mharina told him how Sellia had committed to Seanchai to placate Ilana, his first love, and how, over time, the bond between them flourished without Ilana's shadow. Seanchai did not doubt he had grown to love his mate and that the feeling was reciprocated. He decided that, if he lived, he would take his place again alongside her. If they had learned to fall in love once, he could do it again. He would ask her to retract the oath he had taken and try to recover what they once had.

If he lived.

For the first time since he had dragged himself from the sea, the Wycaan felt a desire to rebuild his life with Sellia. He had no urge to court another elfe, but rather to reclaim the life he lost. He would return to Shindellia and then to Lake Mhari and Wycaan Island. He would peel off the protective layers one at a time until he found his true self. He would face up to what he was and live his life to the values he knew to be true. And he wanted Sellia by his side to help him achieve this.

The storm abated, and the bear left the shelter, sniffing the air before continuing north. He settled into a steady, uncompromising pace as he had before, but this time, there was a spring in his step, a sense of determination moving him forward.

He would save his family and bring them back together as one loving cohort, all five of them. He raised his head and cried up at the vast blue sky and scattered clouds. A roar of excitement and defiance escaped his lips, and a deep sense of purpose settled upon him. The great grizzly and his Wycaan Elf form were ready to rebuild his life.

He saw them as the sun was setting. They were far away on a mountain ridge, mere silhouettes to his bear eyes. He could see they were armed but little beyond that. He wondered whether he would reach them by dark, and then realized that two were gliding down the side of the mountain in long, elegant pendulous movements.

By the time they reached him, Seanchai had transformed back into an elf. He wore the winter clothes that Shayth had given him— dense woolen undergarments and boiled leather trousers and jacket, both lined with fur.

The two Ashen Elves stopped balanced on the long, smooth planks they used to slide down the mountainside.

"Well met, friends. But how will you keep up with me with those strapped to your feet?" Seanchai asked.

They both laughed.

"You're a warmlander. The air is thin here, and you aren't used to running on the white powder," the biggest said, removing the planks from his feet. "Come. We'll let you set the pace."

Seanchai began jogging slowly, which resulted in amused glances between his two guards. He began to speed up, keeping his steps light in the spike-soled boots he received as a gift from Umnesilk the pictorian. As he went faster, the Ashen Elves in turn stretched their gait. Again, they glanced at each other, this time without scorn.

By the time they reached the main party on top of the ridge, both Ashen Elves were panting. Seanchai could feel that he had exerted himself, but he drew energy up from under the snow, and only a thin film of sweat revealed his effort.

He wiped his face on his sleeve, adjusted his weapons, and turned to the biggest Ashen Elf, who stood even taller than him. When he spoke, he felt a familiar but long-lost steel in his voice.

"I am Seanchai, son of Seantai, the Wycaan Master of Odessiya. Take me to your mage and my *calhei*."

Chapter 61

Seanchai marveled at the huge ice cave as he entered, flanked by a half dozen Ashen Elf guards. They followed a snow-packed trail around and through a huge arched ice entrance.

To their immediate right came the sound of dogs yipping and shuffling. Seanchai glanced over, seeing only an assortment of sleighs. He wondered what kind of reception Azura had received. She probably smelled of human, other elves, and bear. He smiled at himself for worrying about Shayth's pet when there was so much more at stake. He turned to one of the guards.

"Could you tell me if the king's dog is being tended to?"

The Ashen Elf frowned at him and did not speak.

"First your king, then your daughter, and now you? What is it with your people and dogs?"

Seanchai turned to the one who spoke. The mage looked small, surrounded by the biggest Ashen Elves the Wycaan had ever seen. There was a bemused expression on her wizened face.

"I have come," Seanchai said, inserting an authoritative tone in his voice.

"You have," she replied. "Let us join your *calhei*. You must be anxious to see them. But be prepared. They have both been through a lot."

"You tortured them?" Seanchai asked, though Ilan had already confirmed this about his sister.

The mage just stared at him.

"They are *calhei*," he said. "Elven youth."

"We understand the old language," the mage replied scornfully. "We are also elves."

"Then act like it," Seanchai snapped back. "I fought and overthrew your oppressor to free *our* people. The elves of Odessiya suffered terrible abuses by humans through acts sanctioned by the Emperor you admired. But, for all our suffering, we protected our young, because they were always the hope for our future—a free future. This is the generation that now takes its place as equal partners in Odessiya."

"These elves you speak of," the mage replied, "are the ones who invaded our lands and massacred our people. They didn't distinguish between elf and elfe, between adult and *calhei*. Do not try to teach me about history, Wycaan."

"What happened to your people was a tragedy, mage. But you and your people remain trapped in the past. You aren't free. You're only frustrated bullies lashing out at a perceived enemy. You kill innocent elves, perpetrating the same crimes that were once visited upon you. You have neither learned nor advanced but instead remain a shell of what you once were. Perhaps you remember the words of the ancient language, but I fear you don't recall their meaning. The ancient language is our history, culture, and, above all, values. Elven values."

"Do the people of Odessiya consider you wise?" the mage asked. "Here, you sound like an idealistic fool."

Seanchai shrugged. "Forget it. Please, take me to my children."

The mage turned and led Seanchai deeper into the tunnel. He had not meant to preach to her, but it had come unbidden, a remnant of his own sad past. It had been foolish, he thought, but not for the reason the mage had suggested.

The truth was, at this moment in time, he had no recollection of the ancient language beyond a few commonly used words, and this was his greatest vulnerability. His Win Dao swords would not get him past more than a few dozen Ashen Elves, if even that. The walls that guarded his memories denied access to the magic that could potentially give him a chance.

They entered a large hall with long tables. The smell of food made his empty stomach rumble. He was no longer a bear with the ability to go long periods of time without sustenance. The mage apparently heard.

"You may get yourself a plate of food."

"Thank you," he replied. "But I wish to see my *calhei*."

"Very well. You'll be taken to them, then, and soon called to eat. Night has fallen. Your *calhei* should leave in the morning." She turned to Seanchai's guard. "See it done." Then the mage turned and walked off to her right, disappearing through an opening.

Seanchai was led down through various tunnels. He tried to remember his way, but it soon became clear that the intention was to disorientate him, and he ceased in his effort.

Senzia was asleep on a cot, her back to the door, when Seanchai arrived at their room. Ilan sat on a straw mattress, eyes open and staring at the opposite wall. When the guards appeared and opened the door for Seanchai to enter, he showed no surprise, but rose and hugged his *ahdahr*.

"How are you?" Seanchai asked. "How is your leg?"

"I'm healed, thank you. Until yesterday, they seemed content to only keep it clean and target it when they wished to make a point. Yesterday, a healer came and worked on me with energy. Feels good. Perhaps it's in your honor."

Seanchai smiled. "Kind of. Tomorrow, you and Senzia will be set free. You'll need your legs to travel. How is your sister?"

Ilan glanced over at her stirring form. For a moment, he didn't speak, and Seanchai thought he was reaching out to his sister to confirm her condition. She turned sluggishly and yawned.

"She's had a harder time," Ilan said. "I told you she wouldn't be a model prisoner." He raised his voice, presumably for her to hear. "She's a pain as a sister. It's only right that she makes her captors suffer, too."

Seanchai laughed. He was happy for the love he heard in his son's voice. "Is she wounded? Will anything stop her from leaving?"

"Not physically," Ilan said, as Senzia slowly brought herself to an upright position, eyes still shut. "But she's stubborn. Though we're estranged from you, I'm not sure she will leave so easily."

"It's part of an agreement," Seanchai said. "She has no choice, and neither do you."

"Telling my sister that she has no choice is often the best way to make her do what you don't want her to."

Seanchai smiled. "I fear she got that from her mother." Senzia had opened her eyes and was looking at him, though it seemed she struggled to focus. "How are you, Senzia?"

"I remember in Grogin seeing some of the fortune swords the morning after they'd had too much to drink. That's how I feel."

"Are you hurt?"

She shook her head. "No. My body aches, but once Ilan came, they left me alone."

"You'll be set free tomorrow," Seanchai said. "This, at least, will soon end for you."

Senzia just laughed and shook her head.

Chapter 62

At dinner, Seanchai requested to see the mural his *calhei* told him about, and six guards escorted them to the great cavern. When they entered, Seanchai asked the Ashen Elves to wait outside. They wouldn't leave, but they hovered around the entrance to give Seanchai and his *calhei* some space. There was nowhere for them to escape, but the idea of not keeping their prisoners in sight seemed too much.

Senzia, the only one of the three who had seen the mural before led them onto the platform that offered the best view. They stood together in silence as Seanchai and Ilan absorbed the story that unfolded across the cave wall.

"There's an identical mural in every place they settle," Senzia told them. "They complete it, conquer those around them, and then move on. Once another base camp is established, they begin the process all over again.

"I was told that everyone has a hand in painting the mural as soon as they are old enough to hold a brush. It's a ritual designed to implant the story in every member of their clan."

"Impressive," her father replied. "Both the mural and the ritual."

He turned and looked over at the guards. They seemed as interested in the mural as he did, as though they were reliving each stage of their history. While he didn't doubt they were keeping an eye on their prisoners, there was no denying the reverence they held for the mural. Nonetheless, when he turned to his *calhei*, he lowered his voice.

"Tomorrow, you will leave here under escort. The mage has agreed to return you to Shindellia in return for me. I don't know if they'll keep their word. If they have decided that a family of Wycaans is a justifiable threat, then it's dangerous for them to allow you back behind the walls of the capital.

"I don't know how much they know about Mharina, but she is their greatest threat. I—"

"They know about her," Ilan replied. "Something happened last night in Shindellia, and Mharina unleashed her power."

"What happened? How do you know? I thought you could only sense Senzia."

Senzia spoke. "Ilan *knew* you were alive when everyone else thought you dead. I felt you, too, but only after he mentioned it. We don't know how, but he can feel other Wycaans. He senses me the strongest, and then you. When Mharina went through her transformation, he knew something had happened. He can sense Pyre, too, though not very well."

"And your mother?" Seanchai asked his son.

"Only Wycaans." Ilan replied.

"Would you know if something happened to Mharina? If she was wounded or…"

"I think so. Look, no one has really trained us in recent years. A lot happens that Senzia and I just muddle through."

Seanchai nodded. "Of course. I am responsible for that. When all this is over, you know where you must go to complete your training."

Both *calhei* nodded.

"But for now, you must return to Shindellia and join your sister. Together with Pyre, you can all help the king repel the Ashen Elves."

"And you?"

"I'll try to do what I'm told I do best."

Both *calhei* stared at him.

"These elves are victims," he continued. "They're not our enemy. I'll try to bring them into the alliance."

"I think their hate has gone beyond that," Senzia replied. "They're truly damaged."

Seanchai nodded and sighed. "Yes. I doubt I've anything to offer that Shayth hasn't already tried."

"Will you try to escape?" Ilan asked.

Seanchai hesitated. "No one can ever know how they'll respond to captivity. I'm not sure why they're so interested in me. Once they realize I'm not the key to their victory, this mage will get pretty bored with me."

"He has faced it before," Ilan said to his sister and Seanchai remembered grabbing his son's collar and screaming at him.

"I'm sorry about that," he said.

"Already forgotten," Ilan smiled, but his hand had gone to his throat.

"Apparently not." Seanchai winced.

Senzia did not ask for details of their interaction. She had not been present at Shindellia and her mind was elsewhere. "We need to know how many are posted here," Senzia said.

"You will return to Shindellia," Seanchai replied, his voice firm. "I am your *ahdahr*. You're young, and your power is untried."

"I'm not going to hide behind castle walls when—"

"That's not what I'm telling you to do. But I want you with Mharina and Pyre. You'll be a greater force together. You can help cover each other's mistakes. Please don't argue. We must do what is best for Odessiya and the king. That is our duty."

"I have not sworn allegiance to—"

"You don't swear allegiance!" Seanchai screamed, towering over his daughter, and, though Ilan stepped back, she stood her ground, her eyes meeting his steadily. He sighed and put a hand on her shoulder. He was panting and bowed his head. "I'm sorry. No one ever asked me if I was interested in the position, if I should run or fight, hide or kill. No one ever asked me whether I was justified to sacrifice all the people who died to help me or fell to my swords or arrows. A Wycaan isn't free, Senzia. Never. I fled the Emperor's forced conscription, but I've been trapped since the day I left my village as a frightened *calhei* no older than you."

He turned from her, walked a few paces, and put his hand on the rock wall. "And that is the sad legacy I leave you. It was necessary to have *calhei*, necessary to produce heirs, because Odessiya demanded it and still needs it. This is your inheritance. I'm sorry. In time, you would have reached this conclusion yourself."

When Seanchai turned back, he saw tears in his daughter's eyes. "Is that what we are to you?" she asked, her voice wavering. "A legacy? A burden? A duty? A chore? Is that what your union with our mother was, a necessity that only Ilana understood?"

"Yes," he rasped. "That was all it was. It had to be, and Ilana recognized it. Your mother never wanted *calhei*. She didn't want to be tied down to a family, though she feels a deep love for you. She certainly didn't want to run the Wycaan Academy. But she understood that that was her role and performed it to the best of her ability. That is all any of us can hope for: to fulfill our duty as best we can. You need to grow up and do your duty."

She turned from him and into her brother's arms. Ilan stared at his *ahdahr*. "Why are you doing this?"

Seanchai's chest was heaving. "Because I need you to understand what role we each play. Because I need you to leave here and not look back—to go forward and fulfill your destinies for the sake of each other, your sister, and mother, and also for Odessiya. We…"

He stopped, his voice cracking. When he spoke again, his voice was little more than a whisper. "We never stop sacrificing, never stop fighting for the races, for freedom. We never stop."

Ilan took a step forward, firmly pulling his sister with him. "I don't believe you. Mother told us that whenever you came home, she never saw you so happy as when you played with us and told us tales as we all vied to sit on your lap. You would tell every story three times so that each of us got to sit on you. You're saying all this now because you want us to leave, to not try and return for you. You are a great Wycaan, *Ahdahr*, but a terrible liar."

Seanchai just stared at his son for a long time. "You must leave here, return to Shindellia, and not look back. Take your places alongside your sister and defend Odessiya. I'm sorry, Ilan; the *ahdahr* you remember is gone. All that stands before you is a shell—an empty shell consumed by guilt."

"I'm sorry, too, *Ahdahr*, if what you say is true," Ilan said, his voice cold but steady. He led his sister forever from the Cave of the Mural.

Chapter 63

Seanchai sat alone in the Great Hall with his guards eating a thick, chewy, broth, but he felt empty inside. The twins had left earlier without saying goodbye. He had remained curled on his cot, facing the wall and feigning sleep. It was easier that way. He could not reveal how he felt about them, how their bond was strong enough to replace his lack of memories. He thought about what Ilan said, how they had made him regale them with stories three times so they could each take a turn to sit on his lap. He had no recollection of this, no memory of his children as little *calhei*.

He did not try and comfort himself with thoughts that they would be better off without him. And he was not oblivious to the fact that he was being denied the same thing he'd taken away from so many others with his Win Dao swords and bloodwood bow. He just sat there, feeling a profound sense of loss.

He looked up with a start. The mage was sitting opposite him suddenly, holding a clay cup full of steaming broth. She sipped it but never took her eyes from him. He glanced at her and then returned to his thoughts, periodically chewing and swallowing a spoonful of broth.

When the bowl was empty, he rose to wash it and then returned to sit opposite the mage. She continued to sip and stare. He sighed and waited, forcing his thoughts to focus on her and his own situation.

"Come," she said, rising as she finished her drink. She slowly took her cup and washed it, though Seanchai was sure a dozen elves would have been proud to have the honor of doing it for her.

She took her time, washing it thoroughly and methodically. He was left hovering, waiting for her, and he tried to strike a pose that would suggest he was at ease waiting. He thrust his hands into his pockets and looked at his guards. But their passive faces offered nothing.

When he looked back at the mage, she was standing before him, smiling. "Ready?" she said.

"For what?"

She turned and walked out of the big cavern. He decided to follow her rather than walk alongside her. He was her prisoner, after all, even if he was not tethered like a dog. They walked into the Cave of the Mural. The mage stopped and stared at it as if this was her first time seeing it. Seanchai did the same, sure it held more interest for him than her.

"What do you see?" she asked finally.

"Tragedy. A people oppressed. My people—"

"*Your* people?" The mage was surprised.

"Elves."

"You're one of them, not one of us."

"We are *all us*," he replied.

He could feel her gaze move to him. He kept looking ahead.

"Explain," she instructed.

"I see pointed ears."

"Is that all?"

"No. I see a mistake in the mural."

"How dare you!" Her glare burned him, but he kept looking forward.

"The Ashen Elves were not always of gray skin. It's a consequence of living underground for generations."

"How do you know that?" she demanded.

"I have seen many records, pictures, and written accounts. There is no mention of Gray Elves. Why?"

"All trace of our past was erased to hide the atrocity from history."

Seanchai turned to face her. He was aware that the ledge where they stood was filling up with curious Gray Elves, and he raised his voice so all could hear.

"Before the Elves of the West battled with you and cast you into exile, you lived in freedom." He pointed to a section of the mural to their right. "Your skin is dark even though you lived in the light. The mural lies, at worst. At best, it misleads you. What else misleads the way your people think? What would bring a once-noble people several generations estranged from tragedy to wage war on innocent people who offer them land and respect?"

A powerful blast, like a punch without any physical contact, sent him flying into the stone wall behind him. The mage stood motionless, though her blue eyes gleamed.

He rose slowly and took his time to dust off. "Do my words frighten you that much? Is the truth so scary?"

"What?"

"You kept the Ashen Elves underground even after they were able to see the light of day. You continued to feed them the same hate that helped your people survive the dark and horrendous years trapped underground, but why do it now?"

He grunted as another invisible blow hit him in the stomach. Seanchai considered defending himself, but there were elves watching who were not as angry as the mage. He saw curiosity on their faces, and, with considerable effort, he stood and straightened again.

"The Emperor, the Master, whatever you called him, exploited you. He fueled your hate and manipulated it to suit his own needs. The terrified nations of the north that fled from your wrath once the Emperor released you from bondage were intended to weaken Odessiya and distract our armies. All he ever planned for your army was to take back what he had lost from Shayth. You were never more than simply pawns to help an evil, deposed despot reclaim his throne."

The mage's laugh echoed around the chamber. "You offer an interesting point of view. I was led to believe that you recall nothing, that you have no memory. Perhaps you are the one fed the lies and deceit. Look at you. Can anyone here believe you bettered the Master?"

She sent another wave of burning energy through him, and he fell to the ground, shaking and convulsing. Already, he could feel another wall erecting in his mind. It was coming automatically, unbidden, but he stopped it with great effort. He could barely hear the mage as she addressed the Ashen Elves around her. Her voice sounded muffled.

"He is weak. They all are. I toyed with the young king, and, in truth, his bravery and duty impressed me. But I could have broken him like I can this one. They have sent their best hope, and he lies at our feet, quivering."

Seanchai rose. His legs felt like jelly, but he pulled himself erect and raised his head high. He summoned strength to carry his voice. "He no longer holds your chains. You are not captives of a greater power. You control your own destiny. You can change history for the better or worse. No one manipulates you and forces you to conspire in the darkness any more."

Don't I? The voice that spoke clearly in his head was mocking in tone…and chillingly familiar.

And then Seanchai crumpled and fell into darkness.

Chapter 64

Cold. Dark. Silence pierced by the echo of a steady drip of water on stone, the sound echoing back off rock walls. Each drop sliced through him. His body ached, and he shuddered with each reverberating ping. He was tied to a hard stone chair deep underground. The air was crisp and dank.

He became aware of others watching him. Slowly, he flexed sore muscles and felt the bonds that restrained him dig into his arms and legs. He opened his eyes, but the darkness continued to engulf him. He felt a wave of panic at having lost his vision, but then realized he wore a hood. He had to concentrate and remember why he was here.

All that was important was to keep the Ashen Elves focused on him so the twins could return safely to Mharina and Sellia. After that, he could lock his mind as he had before. He was hinging a lot on his eldest daughter, but, despite her tender age, she already had a vast amount of knowledge and too much experience. She had wrestled memories from others and now carried the lessons learned by those of her order.

Seanchai, the legendary Wycaan Master of Odessiya on the other hand, instead of carrying the memories and experiences of his teachers, remembered nothing. But he would keep up this façade for as long as his *calhei* needed. It was all he could do.

"It's only going to get worse, fair elf," a female voice said.

Seanchai frowned. The voice was not the mage's, but it was still familiar. He cocked his head to one side but could not place her.

She continued. "We need to know where the Elves of the Western Isles are hiding. The mage doesn't actually want to raze Shindellia to the ground. She takes no pleasure in such wanton massacre. I feel differently, of course, but the mage still adheres to certain ancient values."

"I hadn't noticed," Seanchai sneered.

A jolt of energy pierced his body. He felt his head jerk up and his spine lock straight, and he cried out. When the pain subsided, he was panting and angry with himself for screaming.

"You're being very selfish, very stubborn. Thousands of innocent men, women, and children, elves and dwarves, will die while the real culprits—those who destroyed our people, stole our land, and sent us into exile—live free and unfettered."

"I serve my king." Seanchai heard the absurdity in his own words through the pain and wondered why he had blurted them out.

"Your old friend, Shayth? The one with the temper who is quite the expert at killing anyone in his path, as well? Please. He has more in common with me and Ithea than honorable folk like the mage or yourself."

"That was a long time ago," Seanchai panted, only vaguely aware of Shayth's past she was recounting. "A Wycaan serves his country, his people—*all* his people—through their ruler."

"You really believe that?"

"Yes," Seanchai replied. "Before your people invaded, Shayth was doing a great job bringing the country together and raising all to a level of prosperity. I helped him, went where he requested, and bound the people to him through a common future based upon freedom and civility. Why are those values so easy for you to reject? What's wrong with you people?"

Waves of burning energy sliced through him. This time, he focused all his energy on not crying out, but his body jerked, waves of spasms consumed him, and he felt himself sweat in the cloth hood.

Drool dripped from his mouth, and he could not wipe it away. The sense of helplessness was almost overwhelming but also strangely familiar. He had been through this before. He took a deep breath. He had faced this before and survived. He took another breath and raised his head to show grim determination, an action he was unsure he communicated with the sack over his head.

"Who are you?" he asked, trying to change the subject.

"The one who tried to kill you in that pathetic mining outpost."

"Sa'gola's impersonator?"

"Yes, and much more besides. I call myself the Purple Elfe. I am the mage's enforcer, though, in truth, it felt like such a good fit, playing the Purple Lady. Maybe I will go back to—"

"Sa'gola wasn't an evil woman. She just made some bad decisions. One thing you share is a bad taste in the leaders you follow." He braced himself for another assault, but it didn't come. He had to check her boundaries. "She was very wise and knew when to use her power. I'm not sure you can live up to her standards."

"You know nothing of me. You knew nothing of her."

"She meant a lot to my daughter," Seanchai said, realizing that the more accurate answer was simply no.

"Your daughter? Yes. The oldest. We felt her strength yesterday. Pain is a powerful release."

Seanchai remembered Ilan saying he felt this, as well. "What happened? Did you harm her?"

The elfe laughed. "In a way. It must be devastating to see your mother stabbed through the heart. Scars like that never heal."

"You lie." Seanchai said, his heart sinking at the lack of conviction in his own voice. After a few moments, he whispered, "What happened?"

"I was unfortunately not there. It would have been so fitting for Sa'gola to stab Mharina's own mother in the back."

"You are *not* Sa'gola," Seanchai snapped. "What happened?"

"As I understand it, your daughter was ambushed deep in the catacombs of the palace. We were burrowing our way in underground. We're very much at home underground, you know. Exile does that to you."

"What happened?" he persisted.

"Ashen Elves crept up on your daughter, and her mother stopped one before he loosened an arrow. There were others standing behind her. Would it help if I told you she died quickly? It might be a lie; I wasn't there. Perhaps she died in her daughter's arms. You were certainly not there to protect either of them. *You* failed them.... again." Her voice was close to his head and changed to a hiss. "Are you sad? Did you even love her, or did you just mate with her to breed? Is that how it works for the fair elves?"

Seanchai ignored the insult and everything else the elfe said. Sellia, his mate, the mother of his *calhei*, was dead. He felt an overriding sense of loss, despite his lack of memory and love for her. He knew she had made a great sacrifice to be with him after Ilana made her swear to do so.

Being a mother had not been a natural step, but Sellia had dedicated her life to being the mate of the Wycaan Master and the mother of his *calhei*. She had deserved more. Now, she had made the ultimate sacrifice to save her daughter. It had, at least, been a warrior's end, and he knew she would have wanted to die that way.

He had meant what he said about staying alive and returning to rebuild their life together. The idea had genuinely appealed to him, and he was sure he could rediscover his love for her or learn to love her anew. The news of her death was devastating but he realized it also gave him a reason to let go.

"Maybe we'll soon be reunited, my love," he whispered to himself. "And this time, we'll stay together forever."

But he could almost imagine Sellia chastising him, urging him to live on, accusing him of being selfish. They had *calhei*, and he was still alive. Could he allow himself to die here in this snowy wilderness, even if he destroyed the enemy's leadership? Everyone said he had always put his country first. Was it time now to prioritize his *calhei*? They would be mourning their mother. They needed him. He knew what Sellia would want, what she would demand. He had failed her so much; would he fail again with her final wish?

He sighed and began to silently weep for her, for his *calhei*, for himself. Once he made the decision that trying to live was important, he was truly captive.

A crisp slap on his cheek brought Seanchai back from his reverie.

"Where are the Elves of the West?" It was the purple imposter's voice.

"In the west?" Seanchai suggested sarcastically, and jolts of energy shuddered through his body, which jerked forward, straining against his bonds.

"This isn't a joke. I tire of you. My orders are to keep you alive, no more and no less. There's a lot I can do to you without crossing that line."

"Why am I hooded?" Seanchai asked. "Is this a clumsy attempt to frighten me? Or are you all afraid to look me in the eye while you torture me?"

After a few moments and murmuring consultation, rough hands tugged open the cord around his neck, and the sack was lifted from his head. He blinked, despite the dim lighting from the mushroom stone, and glanced around the small cave. Beyond his seat, there was little of note. Two chairs sat opposite, and he sensed someone sitting behind him. There were two guards in front, one on either side, and, he assumed, more behind him. The Purple Elfe loomed over him, slightly to one side.

Between him and the two chairs was a large, thin, waist-high rock column. It was cupped at its peak, a basin carved by the drops of water that fell from the roof of the cave. The bowl was full of water and the source of the plopping sound.

"Where's the mage?" Seanchai asked.

"She comes and goes," the Purple Elfe said. "She's very busy, and your torture is just one of many of her tasks."

"She's afraid of a little tortu—aaaaaaaagh."

It felt as if the pain would rip his body apart. The intensity even sent the heavy chair he was tied to rocking as his body flailed in all directions. The Purple Elfe stood there, her arms folded. Through the tidal waves of pain, Seanchai realized that the attack had not come from her.

As the pain subsided and he gasped for breath, he heard footsteps behind him.

"Never underestimate me, fool," the mage hissed.

As he struggled to regain his breath, Seanchai forced a smile. "I just didn't want you to miss out on the fun," he replied, and then lost consciousness.

Chapter 65

When he woke, Seanchai's head was pounding. He grimaced as waves of pain engulfed him, and he fought against the urge to vomit. He was still sitting—or rather, was propped up—in the stone chair, and his hands and feet were bound. Slowly, he opened his eyes.

The cavern was illuminated with an orange glow. He blinked, encouraging his eyes to focus, and stared at the source of the light. It was coming from mushrooms. As his pain subsided, he felt his mind momentarily clear. He had been taken through a long underground passage.

He remembered passing through the underground territory of the Aqua'lanis and seeing these same mushrooms. The orange hue emanated from the long stems and the underside of the canopy-shaped heads. Most stood waist-high or less, but they also grew on ridges and from rocks off the ground, and some enough to illuminate even the ceiling of the cave.

The Aqua'lanis? He was remembering.

He swallowed and then grimaced. His throat was dry and sore. Four heavily armed guards were spaced around the room. All scrutinized his every move.

"Water," he croaked.

"We are ordered not to approach you," one guard said.

"Is there a bucket? I might throw up."

"No," the guard replied. "Keep it inside."

Seanchai closed his eyes. It felt easier to control his body that way. He reminded himself that he needed, more than anything, to buy time for the twins to make it back to Shindellia. It was all that mattered. He just needed to hold out for as long as he could.

But he felt different this time than during his previous incarceration. Then, judging by the fleeting shards of recollection, he had closed himself off, sealed his essence and his memory deep inside of himself. In truth, he felt reassured for once that, if he could not unlock it, others probably couldn't, either. It was a grim hope to cling to, but at least it offered something.

His mind went back to the confrontation in front of the mural. He had proved himself too dangerous to be allowed to freely communicate with random Gray Elves. Now he regretted being so bullish.

Then there was that voice in his head. It was so clear and so familiar. His first thought was that the Emperor was somehow alive. But it was not his voice. Then Ithea's image filled his head. But he had killed Ithea. His body had laid on the floor, ripped apart by the powerful claws of the great grizzly, blood seeping everywhere on the marble floor.

He turned at the sound of boots clicking on the rock ground to see another elf walk in.

"He is awake?" the elf asked. "Good." He peered down at Seanchai. His face was as fierce as the others' but somewhat wrinkled, though this was the only sign of age. Otherwise, he exuded authority. "Has he spoken?"

"He asked for water and a bucket."

The elf glanced across to a table with a jug and goblets. "Bring a bucket," he said. "The mage won't want to play with him if he is soiled and stinking."

He walked to the table and slowly poured a goblet of water. He approached Seanchai. "You'll find me to be one of the nicer elves, but do not be deceived. I'm a most experienced warrior and, as my age testifies, I can take care of myself. At the first sign of an attack, I'll strike you down, and please believe me when I say I'm very good. Understand?"

Seanchai nodded. The elf bent over and guided the goblet to the Wycaan's mouth, careful to match the pace of Seanchai's swallowing. A bucket appeared at his feet. The elf took Seanchai's cloak and wiped his mouth with simple efficiency.

"Thank you," Seanchai said.

The elf nodded. "Do you need the bucket?"

"Not for now."

"The mage will be here soon. She's consulting with him. I don't know if he intends to join you."

"Who is he?"

"An old friend of yours. I'm not permitted to share more."

"What's your name?"

"Gunwrath," the elf replied.

"Thank you, then, Gunwrath of the Ashen Elves, for the water and bucket. I'm Seanchai, Wycaan Master of Odessiya."

The elf turned to him. There was no pity or compassion in his voice. "No," he replied. "You are just our prisoner."

The mage did not come, so Seanchai tried to focus on the cavern where he was being held. It appeared to have high walls and two exits. There were a few stone blocks to be used as chairs and a table also made of stone. If there were instruments of torture, he could not see them.

In the absence of anything to look at, all Seanchai could focus on was the water, a single drip that splashed down in front of him. It was strangely hypnotic, and he began to doze.

The bear lumbered through the snow. He was a grizzly, not an ice bear, and he found the ice sheets tiring. He longed for the rock terrain of the southern mountains or the ancient forests that boasted thick mats of pungent bracken and fallen leaves.

"Where are you going?" the ice bear asked.

"To the mountain," he replied.

"Your predecessor isn't there. He died, and you must take his place. You are now the great grizzly."

"I am unworthy. I need guidance."

"It is true that you have not lived up to his legacy. You walked another path that dominated your attention. I'm not sure it serves for you to condemn yourself, or for others to condemn you for that. You are adrift, and this is good for no one—neither those who walk on all fours nor the two-legged. The great grizzly cannot set you back on your chosen path. His time has passed, and he should be left to rest in peace. Delve deep inside and reclaim your own fire."

"How?"

"I don't have such answers," the ice bear said. "But I suspect you know the answer. This is why the great grizzly chose you as his successor. The answer is inside of you. Go deep, and when you feel you have reached your limit, go deeper."

"I don't know how. I have lost it."

"No, you haven't," the ice bear's voice was slow and deliberate, just like his gait. "You locked it away, but you can release it."

"How?"

"The same way you did last time. You told us how once, not so long ago, you faced a similar challenge. You survived torture once before. Only now, it requires more courage. You did what you did instinctually to stay alive and continue your work; you desired to survive above all. Do you not have that similar strength today?"

"I truly don't know. I'm so confused. Maybe not." The answer was soft and unsure.

"Then all is indeed lost. Everything balances precariously on the precipice of…" The ice bear stopped walking and shook its shaggy head. "I am not sure what."

"My sanity?"

The deep blue eyes fell on the younger bear, and there was great sadness there. "No," he said at last. "Your very essence as a Wycaan Master."

The grizzly nodded, and the truth resonated deep within him. He turned and continued walking, plodding steadily through the snow, one mighty paw in front of the other, as he contemplated those words. His companion was right. Everything he needed was there. The question was whether he had the strength to find it. After a long contemplation, he stopped and turned to ask another question, but the ice bear was gone.

Now he walked alone along the ridge of the steep precipice.

CHAPTER 66

Seanchai's world became a constant, unending stream of torture, darkness, and always, the constant drip-dripping of water into the stone basin. The questions he was asked sometimes varied but always returned to the Elves of the West. Whatever knowledge and powers Seanchai possessed seemed unimportant or were deemed insignificant.

His interrogators were relentless. Sometimes it was the Purple Elfe, harsh and cruel, taunting him about his mate, his *calhei*, or his Wycaan principles. She mocked his deeds and his belief in an alliance. She recalled all the people who had died because of their loyalty to him while he lived. She seemed to know more about his past than he did and as she recalled the memories, they filled his mind as truth.

The pain and guilt assailed the mental walls he had erected and he felt the cracks begin. Bereft of choice, in search of his own truth, he focused on what she said—on the thousands of men and elves he had killed or who had died to defend his cause. He thought of the tens of thousands of bereaved sons, daughters, mothers, fathers, and mates. So many faces. So much pain.

Sometimes, Gunwrath ran his interrogation. At first, Seanchai thought that this Ashen Elf was just engaging in conversation, but he soon realized that Gunwrath was a foil for the Purple Elfe, attempting to extract guarded secrets through gentle coaxing rather than pain and denigration.

Occasionally, they left him, but he rarely found relief. His mind could not help but focus on the pinging water drops. Sometimes they fell quicker, and he was jolted from his attempts to sleep. Other times, when the drop gathered more water and seemed to pause, he tensely waited for it to drop.

He tried to ignore it and focus elsewhere. He had to hold on, to allow the twins time to return to Shindellia. Together with Mharina, they represented the future of Odessiya. He just had to hold on, to keep his mind from running wild, to prevent it from going where it had previously sought protection.

As he dozed, Seanchai thought of the ice bear. It would be so easy to just transform and charge out onto the icy tundra and run, his four heavily padded paws pounding on the packed snow. He could run forever, run with the pack of ice bears or alone. He could run until he dropped, and then he would sleep forever, joining his mate and making her happy. It sounded so tempting.

But he had to hold on. There was something the ice bear had said that stuck in his mind. How *had* he survived the last time? He didn't even remember the torture or who had inflicted it upon him. He remembered nothing except allowing himself to get lost somewhere in the abyss of his mind.

What had the ice bear said? The secret lay deep inside him. It was hidden, but he had been there before. How had he survived last time? Was there a clue in that question or the hopeful wishes of a friend who cared and wanted to help?

Seanchai heard the sharp clicking of steel boots on stone. He found he could distinguish between the heavier thuds of the guards or foot soldiers and the lighter, sharper clicks of the elfe. Now there were two sets, and both seemed similar. He frowned to himself. The mage was joining them. Seanchai sighed. The mage was the most unpredictable. The Purple Elfe and Gunwrath interweaved one's cruelty with the other's inviting manipulation, but at least he could predict what they would do.

The mage, however, was quick to switch from a philosophical discussion to the harshest of physical attacks. The heat and intensity of the energy she shot through him was more painful than anyone else's. He must treat her as he had the Emperor or Ithea, never underestimate her or let his guard down.

His thoughts returned to the ice bear. There was a message, a clue, in his wise words. When the bears had convened, the ice bear always stood by the great grizzly's side, offering advice and perspective. He was indebted to the Wycaan for rescuing a pack of ice bears that were tormented and brutalized into allowing the Northern Army's soldiers to ride them. The ice bear always spoke with a sense of purpose, and Seanchai knew he was trying to convey a very important message.

A stabbing pain made him cry out, and he saw flashes of light behind his eyes. He blinked and screwed up his face.

"The mage is speaking to you," the Purple Elfe sneered.

Seanchai tried to turn his head, but the pain had tensed his muscles. "What?"

"I'm sorry to disturb you," the mage said. "Should I have made an appointment?"

"I'm rather tied up right now," Seanchai replied.

The mage laughed. "I thought he had no sense of humor."

"That's what we were told."

"What else have you gotten wrong?" Seanchai asked. "How about...everything?"

Another bolt went through him, and he lost consciousness. Freezing water poured over his head, had him spluttering and gasping and his teeth chattering. A second bucket, equally cold, was poured over him. The same shock, but this time, something else was triggered. *Water. Drowning. Freezing. Depths.* He had faced this kind of torture before and almost died.

"You could k-kill me with such extreme t-temperatures," he wheezed, his teeth chattering uncontrollably.

"Your usefulness, or lack thereof, is coming to a close," the mage said. "We need answers now if you are to live."

He looked up. "Wh-what has ch-changed?"

"The new master has marshaled his troops. He is about to take Shindellia. You will tell us what we need to know. From now on, I will personally oversee the extraction. That is not good news for you."

They've made it, Seanchai thought. The twins are with Mharina and, though it was hardly safe, it was the best he could hope for. He smiled. "So. W-what do you w-want to know?" he said, his tone triumphant and oozing sarcasm.

Chapter 67

What followed was the harshest, most intense torture Seanchai had ever endured, and he discovered new depths of pain. It was incessant, wave after wave of the mage piercing his body with her ice magic, sending numbing cold into every sinew, every bone. She was relentless, pausing only to ask the question that she desperately needed an answer to. Sometimes she whispered the question from the other side of the cavern; other times, she screamed it into his ear.

When she took a moment to rest, the Purple Elfe paced around him, encouraging him to listen to the drops falling from the cavern roof into the stone bowl. He needed no reminder. The dripping, the incessant pinging, followed him in every moment, waking or sleeping. Was it getting louder? More persistent? Was that even possible?

"Where do they cower?" the mage snarled in his ear. "What brazen magic protects and conceals them? Why can I not sense them? I have studied all known elf magic, enough to at least feel its presence. Why can't I feel their barrier?"

Seanchai turned his head. He was gasping from the last assault. Sweat poured down his face in furrowed rivulets, warm against the cold that now exuded from his body. His mind went to the ancient bloodwood forest that protected the Elves of the West. Their High Council had conceded to Seanchai's will only when the forest had taken his side. Seanchai harbored doubts, given the degradation of the elves' moral code and values, that the forest's loyalty to them was unequivocal.

"Where are they? The Elves of the West came to this unspoiled land, this natural haven, and humiliated and exiled my people. Give us the opportunity to exact revenge, to reclaim the dignity wrenched from us. Let me free my people like you freed yours."

"N-not this way," Seanchai wheezed. "The revenge has c-consumed yo—."

More waves of icy attacks, more freezing shards ripped through him. He gasped, and his body shuddered uncontrollably. In between, he heard only the dripping water. Then two buckets of almost-freezing water had him spluttering for breath, spitting out water, inhaling desperately. *The water. Drowning. Cold.* He felt the cracks, the memories straining to be released. This had happened before.

"What can you know of revenge?' the mage screamed. "You took by force when you had to. You laid waste to the armies of the north. You beat back the taragusii, the armies of the Master. You pledged to the Aqua'lanis and then turned your back on them. You chose what best served your people, and so do I."

Another bucket of freezing water. A second. He gasped for air. A third. *He was drowning. They would kill him if the ocean didn't take him first. Threats. Threats to drown him. Must survive. Must return. Sellia, their calhei. He must not drown. The Aqua'lanis must not kill him. The ocean must not claim him. He could taste the metallic salt.*

An icy shiver ran through his body as he fought to fill his lungs with cold, dank air. The Aqua'lanis! Yes. He remembered them, deep in the caves on the way to the dwarves of Hothengold. But it wasn't those Aqua'lanis…

His mind spiraled to the Great Underworld of the Aqua'lanis, to the submerged torture chambers. No man, elf, or dwarf had ever entered this land, not since the Aqua'lanis had fled, their once populous nation decimated by armies of one race or another.

He remembered the hate, the fear, and the rage. Even when he had implored them to believe that their destruction had been by the bloody hands of the Emperor—his enemy, too—it made no difference. He was white-haired and carried powerful magic. The aqua'lanis had seen their cities destroyed by the magic of the white-haired one and his minions. They hated the Wycaans, and he would know the pain they had experienced at the hands of his kind.

As torture within torture played out in his mind and his body, he spiraled to new depths and was assailed now from all directions, without and within. He needed to escape, to free himself. He could not contain it anymore. The cracks appeared and the fissures widened. Then the floodgates broke, and the memories poured out.

He remembered.

He remembered his parents; their razed village; Rhoddan and Ilana leading him, a petrified young wood elf, to Mhari, to his training and transformation. He remembered the Walls of Galbrieth and the sacrifice of his first teacher.

Ping. Ping. The dripping water in the stone bowl called out to him.

He remembered Ballendir and the dwarves he had helped to escape to Hothengold, defying the First Decree; the death of Master Onyxei, who gave his life for his king and race, the destiny of all Wycaans; the great battle in the dwarves' capital; and the death of Ilana. For her, he roared his pain, now transcending the physical, and felt it reverberate deep into the bowels of the caves.

He remembered.

He remembered the deep grief and loss he felt for his mate and the solace he found in the arms of Sellia, Ilana's best friend and a warrior elfe. Together, they traversed the ice plains, brought the pictorians into the alliance, and then travelled to the Elves of the West.

Ping. Ping. Ping.

He remembered the great bloodwood forest, ancient trees still imbued with the magic from the Age of Mist and Shadows. He remembered the Weapons Master who trained him hard and raised him to new heights. He saw the compassionate face of Dyfellion, who guided his animal transformation and his elevation to a Wycaan Master.

He remembered.

He remembered taking a hundred Wycaan warriors across the plains to meet the Emperor for a final confrontation at the Cliftean Pass; how they joined with the dwarves and men that followed Prince Shayth in an historic alliance; how he had confronted the Emperor and, with the help of the bears, defeated him and freed Odessiya.

Ping. Ping.

He remembered how he and Sellia raised their family on Wycaan Island; how he had gathered potential young elves, humans, and dwarves to train as Wycaans and healers. He recalled traveling with Prince Shayth to advise and guide the people of Odessiya. He recalled going to help the pictorians, to discover the northern armies, and to stand and fight against them.

He remembered.

He remembered fleeing the Emperor as a bear, rescuing the ice bears, and the battle between the Emperor and the old great grizzly. He remembered taking his place as the great grizzly, then turning his back on the bear nation.

Ping. Ping. Ping.

He remembered his horror when his *calhei* had been kidnapped, the rage that roared from the mountain and through Odessiya's spine, how the bear nation had taken him to the fishing village where he confronted Sa'gola, and then...

He remembered nothing—only cold, dank water. Darkness.

Not this time, he thought. Dimly, he heard the mage, the Purple Elfe, and Gunwrath. But he would not be denied. Summoning all his strength, Seanchai focused on his own descent.

The Aqua'lanis. He remembered his body sinking into the ocean and followed it into the underground home of the Aqua'lanis. He remembered their rage; their torture; the cold drowning his body, every sinew; and how his mind stayed hidden.

He remembered now how he destroyed the Aqua'lanis as they poured their cold evils into him, how he ignited the fire within him and the fire from below. Now he sought that power again.

He could find it. He could...

Something pulled him back. He heard the shouts of uncertainty and panic.

Seanchai felt his eyes open as the mage screamed in rage. "You won't escape us!"

Chapter 68

Hands grabbed his hair and yanked his head back. Both the mage and the Purple Elfe were glaring down at him, their breath hot on his face.

"What happened?" The Purple Elfe demanded. "What are you doing?"

Seanchai blinked. "Not s-sure."

"Who were you talking to?" the mage demanded. "Your lips moved, and you were oblivious to our torture. Who do you summon?"

"S-summon?"

"A patrol was attacked. Four Ashen Elves are dead. There are no footprints. Twenty of your kind would have been needed to defeat them. Your people are weak. There were covered with pricks and cuts from small blades or darts."

Seanchai tried to shake his head, but it was so stiff from the cold that he was forced to speak instead. He could only think of one assassin who might come after him, but the mage did not know of assassins. "No one has been s-sent. I'm expendable. All efforts are f-focused on the d-defense of the c-capital."

"Then it's the Elves of the West," the Purple Elfe declared. "Yes! Your friends reveal themselves at last to rescue you."

"Sure," Seanchai offered. He had no energy left for games. He wasn't in a better position now than he had been before the memories had awoken, but he had vital pieces of information at his disposal. Perhaps none that could save him, but maybe...

His face was slapped hard, whipping his head to the left.

"Stay with us," the Purple Elfe snarled. "You can't evade us like this."

Seanchai offered a weak smile. He could feel blood trickling from the side of his mouth, but he was so numb from the cold that the pain was negligible.

"I r-really don't know. I don't have many f-friends, but you have many enemies. M-maybe—»

The next slap snapped his head in the opposite direction, but the blow seemed half-hearted, as though she knew it was not having the desired effect.

"Time isn't on our side," the mage said. "The next time I work on you will be the last. Before you hold out on us, consider your children. We killed your mate. Will you condemn them to be orphans? What kind of a father are you? You weren't there to protect your mate—you were rarely there for her, I hear. Will you desert your *calhei,* as well? What kind of an elf are you?"

He didn't answer, though the reference to his family riled him, particularly because it was true. A bucket of ice water was poured over him. Then a second, followed by a third.

"What kind of elf are you?" The Purple Elfe screamed.

"A b-better one t-than you'll e-ever be," Seanchai responded, gasping to get the words out from behind chattering teeth. "I-I have k-killed as many or more than you, th-that is true, but I always s-sought another way. You h-have another p-path. Sh-sh-shayth offered you l-land and a-acceptance. Your p-people could have lived in f-freedom and d-dignity and as t-true elves. B-but your f-fanaticism h-has kept the Ashen E-elves in a w-worse p-prison than they ever e-experienced underground."

"Worse? How do you figure?"

Seanchai could feel himself shaking again, but this time it was from rage, not pain. There was foam frothing from his mouth now as he fought to keep himself under control, to maintain his sanity. His head jerked from one side to the other. The memories had filled many gaps but also showed him what he was sacrificing. His *calhei*. His friends, alive and dead. He was doing it for them. He breathed deeply through sore ribs and a raw throat. He was so cold.

"B-because you have the kn-knowledge and i-insight to know b-better. Because the k-king of O-o-o-dessiya offered you a f-future, and y-you spurned him. Your p-people trust you and b-believe you have their b-best interests at heart, b-but you only serve your own th-thirst for p-power and r-revenge, no m-matter what the c-cost. Is this the l-leadership the E-elves of the W-west encountered w-when first they met your p-people? N-now I know w-why they so r-rejected you."

It was not a slap this time, but a punch, and it was followed by several more. His head whipped from side to side, and he tasted blood. But something stirred in his rage. His body shook and shivered, spasmed and drooled as the punches were replaced with more buckets of icy water. He gasped for air so that he could continue. Despite the pummeling, he was able to take a deep, grounding breath, summoning fire to warm him and control his shivering and stuttering. It came as an old friend. He felt the fire calm and center him. Slowly, he looked up at the mage, his eyes watering and bloodshot. When he spoke, his voice was a dry rasp, but it was steady, and he heard his own power.

"I feel sorry for you, mage. I truly do. But more so for your people. They believe in you, trust you. But they have no idea there's another way. You're worse than the Emperor. He never bothered to hide his evil, but you deceive the people you profess to lead. I leave you now, mage, and we will not meet again." Suddenly, his voice boomed out and around the rock cavern. "Know that the Wycaan Master of Odessiya holds you in the deepest contempt, and, though you imprisoned and tortured me, you never defeated me. You are pathetic. Your desperate torture only made me stronger."

Seanchai closed his eyes and summoned his long-dormant power. *Thank you, noble ice bear. You were right. I know what I must do.*

Ping. Ping. He felt as if the water dripping into the stone bowl was settling into a rhythm, calling him, and now he embraced it. The Wycaan Master's mind submerged into the water of the rock basin in front of him. He felt the drips that had tormented him for so long physically rain down on him, cold and hard. He gasped, but no sound escaped this time. Vaguely, he knew his body was being assaulted, pounded with physical blows and psychic frozen waves, but he had partitioned his mind to protect the magical part of his essence, and with this, he dove into the metallic water, and through the ice, and deeper into the rock.

Far below, he knew what he sought, and he dove deeper down. The dormant fire existed far within the earth's core, encapsulated by sheets of uncompromising ice. But he was the Wycaan Master, and he summoned the fire. As if feeling the potential danger, the ice hardened, reinforced by the defenses of the Ashen Elves. But Seanchai would not be deterred, not this time. He drilled deeper, his razor-sharp instincts forcing their way through plates and fissures a billion years old, formed through struggles that predated even the Age of Mist and Shadows.

As his way became tighter and his progress slowed, Seanchai called out to the fire. *Aieesha*, he cried. *Aieesha! Wake up! Come to me. I am the Wycaan Master. I am the great grizzly. I wield the Iyzun, the great balance of the world, the magic of male and female. I summon you now.*

Answer your ancient vows made to my ancestors, Aieesha. Feel my power and my desperation in these dire times. Give me your strength to save the land and its people.

He felt his Wycaan power pour from his body, a bold, sharp cone of magical intensity. It cut through stone and rock and ice, summoning the fire, the dormant core of this frozen land, calling out to it, urging it to fight for his cause.

Aieesha, awake! Aieesha! Hear the call of the Wycaan Master. Feel the power of my magic, the ancient blend of male and female. Respond to my summons.

Slowly, he began to weaken—a cold and frozen despair—as his body broke and tore under the physical blows and energetic assault of the mage. But it could not reach him here, not this time. Not this one last time.

For Odessiya. For my calhei. For a free future. Come to me, Aieesha. I summon you now.

And *Aieesha,* the ancient fire, the breath of Odessiya and the world, answered the call of the Wycaan Master.

CHAPTER 69

The soldiers on the walls of Shindellia stayed awake at their posts all night. For some, it was due to the constant drumming, vibrating through their minds and bodies, matching the pounding in their hearts. For others, it was the fear. Before the curtain of darkness descended, they watched thousands of huge Ashen Elves slowly approach, taking up positions just out of arrowshot and pounding spear, staff, or bow into the ground, matching the rhythm of their endless drummers.

Now, from the ramparts, the men could see only black masses, and they wondered how many more troops were assembling and what weapons would soon be unleashed to break the walls of Shindellia. Huge fires were lit across the plains. It was unlikely that these most northern elves needed to keep their soldiers warm in this climate, so King Shayth Shindell decided it was to show their force.

He could not sleep, himself, and prowled the ramparts, allowing the hate and adrenaline of war to bubble to the surface and take over. He needed it, craved it, and fed off of it as he had for decades.

But he was different now. He wore the crown. He had a beautiful wife with whom he had spent very little time and who carried his heir inside her. They had told no one. Her chambermaids will have guessed, but it was bad luck where Shameka came from to announce anything before three moons had passed.

Shayth had never feared death—had, in fact, been surprised how death seemed to ignore him while taking so many around him. But now, he wondered if he would live to see his son or daughter. Would the child grow up on the tales of a brave father who gave his life for his country? Such stories, however skillfully woven, would offer no solace. He knew that. He knew that only too well. The heroic tales of his father's bravery and leadership had not prevented the anger and violence that sunk Shayth into such dark depths. If the child created from his seed would be anything like him, stories would provide no solace.

A hand lightly touched his shoulder, and he spun round. He was content to pass the night in his own mood, a place he had once been so comfortable, and it annoyed him that someone would disturb him. He glared up at Rhoddan, one of the few to tower over him, and one of even a smaller number who returned his gaze.

"The sky lightens, and a new day dawns," Rhoddan said. "May I walk with you?"

Shayth nodded. They had so much history between them that there was little he could deny the big elf. "I don't feel much like talking," he added.

"Then listen a while, but know you don't have the luxury of closing yourself off anymore. Your men need to hear you."

"What do you mean?"

"You have stalked the ramparts all night. How many frightened soldiers and boys have you passed? How many furtive glances did you meet with anything more than a distracted scowl?"

"I'm only human, Rhoddan."

"You are their king, my friend."

"*Their* king?" Shayth snapped, regretting his tone. "Are you planning on leaving me after this?"

He felt Rhoddan stiffen. He was not an elf who hid much, Shayth knew.

"This is not the time," Rhoddan muttered. "It's not you."

"Seanchai? How many times can you go looking for him?"

Rhoddan stopped walking, and Shayth saw him stare out into the darkness. "If we all survive, it'll be different. We both have mates, and one day, we will have heirs, if the gods and goddesses allow. Troja has loyally followed me around, not asking anything, but dreaming of a better future."

"You want to settle down; I understand that. But why not here?"

Rhoddan shook his head. "She must face her demons. She remains haunted by her past, by the abuse forced upon her." Rhoddan drew his mighty broadsword, and the rasp of blade leaving sheath cut through the gray light. His voice was as sharp as he stared at the gleaming sword. "And I will give her that justice."

Something stirred inside Shayth, something deep and familiar but long absent. He drew his own sword and lined it next to his friend's.

"Then you will not be leaving me, my friend. This time, it is I who will ride by your side, with and for Troja."

There was a ponderous silence, and then Rhoddan laughed. It seemed strangely alien. "Have we learned nothing these past twenty years? You are the king of Odessiya. Sellia is dead. Ilana, too. Ballendir and probably Seanchai. We are fools, Shayth, clinging to a past whose lessons we fail to learn."

Shayth did not laugh with him. A wave of passion erupted. "It taught us everything, Rhoddan!" he exclaimed rather too loudly. "It taught us that our friends and our loved ones are what enable us to move mountains. Seanchai was close to the truth, but wrong. The alliances that have brought us so far are not those of race, but those of friendship. And if we die here, then let us die beside our friends!"

In the ensuing silence, they both turned. They stood on the rampart above the main gate, their swords still held high together. Below them and across the ramparts, men stared at them in expectation. Shayth took a deep breath.

"Men of Shindellia," he called, but it came out as little more than a croak that disappeared into the graying dawn.

Mharina came up beside him and touched the back of his neck with the tip of her staff. "Again," she whispered.

Shayth felt the power surge into him, filling him with warmth and energy. He took a deep breath. "Brave men and women of Odessiya. Guardians of the Walls of Shindellia. We have known in our lifetime what it means to live under tyranny. We know what it means to be ruled by those who care only for their own power, who live for dominion and suppression of other races."

He pointed his sword to the armies of the Ashen Elves. "They also know of deception and oppression. They, too, were forced to live a life of captivity and humiliation. But they have chosen the wrong way to proceed. They think they can emancipate themselves by killing and controlling others."

Out of the corner of his eye, he sensed the shimmering presence of an Ashen Elf. He glanced at Mharina, who was also looking in that direction. "Continue," she murmured, and he turned back to his men.

"I don't know if we can defeat so many of them. I don't know if we can win against such overwhelming strength. But I will never surrender meekly or live under oppression. I will not see my mate, my children, or my people denied the freedom we so cherish."

There were several Ashen Elves forming in a cluster to his right. Rhoddan had moved to stand alongside Mharina, but she put out her arm to stop him advancing. Shayth glanced beyond at the Ashen Elves standing there. Their weapons were not drawn. They listened, holding their red stones in their hands.

Shayth took another breath. "We face an enemy so corrupted by their anguish and humiliation that they can no longer distinguish between right and wrong. They are so blinded that they do not understand they try to take from others what they themselves tragically lost.

"It's easy to feel sorry for them, easy to pity them. But they have made their choice. I tried to help them see the hypocrisy in their ideology. I offered them land and to join Odessiya as an accepted and integrated part of our society.

"But they remain as consumed by their hate now as they were when imprisoned underground. Now, they threaten our mates and children. They threaten our very way of life. We will show no mercy, give no quarter, offer no compromise. They will not breach the walls of Shindellia. They will not take away our freedom. The time for talking is over." He turned to the Ashen Elves. "Leave now. Return only under a flag of parlay or to meet your death. The king of Odessiya sentences you to die pathetic prisoners of your own incarceration."

The half dozen Ashen Elves smirked; a few drew massive curved swords. One opened his mouth to speak, but Shayth cut him off, his own fury breaking through.

"Go!" he roared.

Mharina stepped forward, and the orange fire ignited through her charred staff. Shayth saw the runes illuminate, heard her murmur, and watched as she calmly walked forward and incinerated those Ashen Elves not quick enough to dissipate.

Then she turned to the stunned soldiers and people of Shindellia.

"Do you value your freedom?" she cried. "Do you stand with the king of Odessiya, the Wycaans, and the Alliance of the races?"

The resulting cheer was halfhearted.

Mharina raised her staff above her head. "Then let us banish the enemy with the darkness!" Bright orange flames ignited into the dawn sky.

Shayth stared at her magnificent presence, a beacon in the pre-dawn light. He saw the hybrid Wycaan-white hair of Seanchai and the warrior daughter of Sellia. The soldiers cheered and Shayth's name echoed against the great stone walls. He turned to Rhoddan.

"We haven't finished here. But when we do, we'll leave this land in good hands and seek justice for Troja. And we will do it together, one last time. I swear it to you, not as your king, but as your friend. *Ashbar!*"

Chapter 70

King Shayth Shindell descended from the ramparts to cries and cheers and shook the forearms offered by his people. To the soldiers who saluted him, he laid a hand on their shoulders and squeezed false reassurance. As he walked, he turned to Rhoddan.

"Gather the officers, Pyre, and Mharina. We meet in the strategy room."

Rhoddan looked at Mharina, who nodded that she had heard, and then he peeled off into the crowd. Shayth walked into the tower where his family lived. Mharina was behind him, and he stopped and turned to her.

"Where is Riona?"

"She has left with Montclair, as per your instructions. I know she felt deep conflict leaving you, but she is not cut for court."

"No. She never was. Where has she gone?"

Mharina stared back at him, meeting his gaze.

Shayth nodded. "You are wise to not tell me. Stay alive, Mharina. I hope after this is over to reunite with my sister. But if not, tell her that she must rule in her own way. I will go now to see my wife. It might be a while until she and I meet again. Does everyone involved in her safety understand what must be done?"

Mharina nodded. "Her guards are devoted and will die before seeing her come to harm."

"I don't want them to die," he snapped, then paused and sighed. "I want them to live and get her out of here. I'm sorry. You did very well out there."

"As did you, my king. I understand your worry for your family. It must be hard to leave her side at such a time."

He nodded, turned, and then turned back. She had not said *mate*, but *family*. "How did you know?"

Mharina forced a smile. "My father left us many times. I saw the pain in his eyes, the pull between family and country."

"To serve me, you mean."

She shrugged and nodded.

"Do you resent me for it?" Shayth asked, looking into her ice-blue eyes.

"Would it bring him or my mother back? Can it give me the childhood I barely tasted?"

"No."

"Then we have more pressing things to worry about."

He nodded, turned again to go to his chambers, and then turned back. She had not answered his question. He cocked his head again to ask. Mharina grinned.

"I'm Wycaan," she said. "But I also channel the feminine magic. Now go to your wife and heir. Time is precious."

Twenty officers waited in a large room with a model of Shindellia and the surrounding countryside. The room was adjacent to a huge hall with about fifty models of different parts of Odessiya. As a child, Shayth had stood on a stool and spent hours peering down and imagining heroically attacking or defending such distant towns.

He walked slowly over to a table and took a hunk of bread, dipping it into the soft cheese nearby. He could feel his men's eyes piercing into his back. He had just left his bride for maybe the last time, touched her stomach to connect with the child he hoped would live. He sighed. *He was the king.* He composed his royal expression and turned to face them. It must have been correct, for they all returned to furiously studying the models.

Rhoddan and Pyre stood whispering in a corner, and Shayth stared. He had questioned Pyre's loyalty when they went to parlay with the Elves of the West. She had stayed behind a while, and he had sensed both familiarity and tension between her and the younger council member, Shathea.

He began to feel his anger rise at the thought of the Elves of the West hiding behind their barrier and the patronage of the great bloodwood forest. At that moment, he was sorely tempted to tell the Ashen Elves where they were hiding, to let them direct their forces at the true perpetrators, yet, even with their racist and elitist philosophies, they did not deserve to be slaughtered.

Mharina entered behind three pictorian officers. Despite their towering over her, all eyes were on the elfe. She wore tight black armor that contrasted with her white hair and ice-blue eyes. The charred staff hung over her back. Pyre went and stood alongside her as she approached Shayth. And suddenly, he got cold feet. Were his principles and sense of honor going to needlessly cost an entire nation, *his* nation, their lives?

Mharina leaned toward him. "Do not question your decision now; it's too late, and your officers watch and see all."

Shayth bristled but straightened up. He gave a curt nod and then turned to his officers.

"General Pilau," he called out, and the room went silent. "Let us begin."

The meeting was short. Plans had already been put in place for just such a situation. Preparations had been going on for five moon cycles, and every man had drilled and practiced his part.

When the general finished speaking, she turned to Shayth, her ungloved hand running through her ginger hair, pushing up the short spikes. She was the perfect choice for his commander. Though younger than other candidates and the only female in the high command, her reputation was flawless. No man questioned her skills as a warrior. Her orders were given with authority, and even those who were older and more experienced soon fell into a comfortable and professional relationship with her.

"Do you have anything to add, King Shayth?"

He began to shake his head, but stopped when he saw Mharina frown at him. "Thank you, General Pilau. I trust your preparations. I trust your bravery and commitment to our people." He took a few strides forward, moving into the midst of his men so he could address them now. "Be ready to change plans, to respond to something unexpected. Know that the general and I have absolute faith in the ability of each and every one of you. So do your men, or you would not hold rank in this fine army.

"There are more of them, true. They are bigger than most of us, true. But we have more to fight for: our families, our freedom, and our dignity. Never lose heart, however intense it becomes. Know that when you show signs of weakness or fear, your men will feel it tenfold. We'll prevail because we have no other choice. Hold every rampart, repel every rope and chain hook. Show no mercy. We will not succumb."

The men seemed to straighten up. They turned to each other and grasped forearms, nodding and offering words of encouragement even though many would not live to look their friends in the eye again.

Shayth grabbed a pewter goblet from the table and raised it.

"For Odessiya," he roared. "For freedom."

Rhoddan and Pyre unsheathed their swords, and the room rang with released metal. Swords were held aloft, and the king received his answer.

Odessiya! Freedom!
Odessiya! Freedom!
The king! The king! The king!

Chapter 71

The king of Odessiya cuffed his squire halfheartedly even though he had done nothing wrong. He had laid out the king's new armor as he had been instructed to. But clearly, a number of people had been involved in its assembly: the blacksmith, armorer, bowyer, and weapons master. Maybe even General Pilau had added her say.

The armor was black, which Shayth admitted to himself he liked, but there were several layers, and it was all buffed up, as if ready for a parade.

"I 'ad to shine it, milord. That's whot we do, like."

The boy received another easy cuff and, out of respect for his liege lord, he staggered rather theatrically across the room. A long, smooth hand steadied him, and he looked up into the beautiful and noble eyes of his queen. He tried a bow and fell for real.

"Is your king giving you a hard time?" she asked, amused.

The squire stammered inaudibly, totally flummoxed about whether to side with his king or queen. Shayth had to suppress a grin, himself.

His beautiful wife continued, "Did you tell your king who required you to prepare this?"

The squire opened his mouth, but apparently decided a shake of the head would suffice.

The queen offered him a beautiful smile. "Then you have served your king well," she said.

"How's that?" Shayth folded his arms. "I think he should be tried for treason."

"Really? Would a king not require those who serve him to obey the word of his wife?"

"I sense a conspiracy," Shayth conceded.

Queen Shameka turned to the squire. "Go attend to your own preparations. I will prepare the king."

The young man flushed and shook his head. "Beggin' yeh pardon, my queen, but I'd be skinned and never forgive meself if something came loose or fell off."

"Your loyalty is admirable, but I have done this too many times, preparing my father and brothers for battle. Where I come from, the women prepare their men, praying to the gods and goddesses as we do, that we may have the opportunity to remove their armor when the battle is won. Now go, or I might side with the king against you."

The squire bowed profusely in all directions as he retreated from the room. Shameka glided to the armor and fingered the chest plate.

"This battle will be fought in your soldiers' minds as much as by their actions. The elves hold an advantage. Men whisper in fear of their magic and superior physical strength. We must do everything we can to inspire their belief and confidence."

"Perhaps I should promote you to general," Shayth quipped.

She cuffed him in the same playful way he had the squire. "I told you there is more to me than my beauty. My father sat me with my brothers as we were tutored and prepared to rule. Please. Treat me as one who can advise you."

"I apologize," Shayth said, and his tone was respectful. "But why kit me out to go on parade?"

"You know what your men want? They wish to follow a fearless and dark demon into battle…and they *will* follow you. Please wear it."

"I will."

"Really?"

"Yes."

"Every part of it?"

"As you desire, my wife."

He felt Shameka's suspicious gaze upon him.

"And you won't take it off?"

"None of it."

She came around in front of him. "Okay," she said, looping her hands around his neck and pressing up against him. She raised an exquisite eyebrow. "What am I missing?"

"I have agreed to your terms," Shayth said, drowning in her eyes.

"What will you do once you're dressed and out of my eyesight?"

"You won't argue?"

"You are my king," she mocked. "Okay, I promise."

"I'll walk straight to the smithy and command him to pound a few dents into it. Then I will grab some dirt and ash and sprinkle it over the shine."

Shameka laughed a beautiful, throaty laugh. "May I make one comment, my king?

"As long as you remember your promise," he commanded with as much regality as he could muster.

"I love you," she said. "I really do. After just a couple of months, I really love you."

"I love you, too," he replied.

"Really?"

"Well, I wasn't sure what love was before, to be honest," Shayth replied. "But I can't imagine being without you. I fear no one on the battlefield, am ready to lose my life or my friends. I will survive and rule. But I can't bear the thought of losing you. It's a strange and daunting feeling. If that is what love is, then I believe I am smitten."

She raised herself on tiptoe, and they kissed. It was a different kiss from any they had exchanged, Shayth thought. It was slow and measured and pure. There was no lust or excitement, just a deep sense of belonging. It carried a maturity that he had never imagined and never wanted to end.

But it did. Shameka pulled herself away from him. "Fear your enemy and guard your friends and yourself. When you're out there, don't think of me. If you love me, win, survive, any way you can and return to me."

Her voice quivered, and she turned, tucking a long, curly strand of hair behind her ear. She picked up his hauberk—a dark gray mail shirt made of small, intricate metal rings—and lifted it over his head. Shayth was surprised at how light it felt and said so.

"My father commissioned it for you. He had a host of dwarf craftsmen and women make this even before we were to wed. It was meant as his present to you as his king. Wearing dwarf craft might help you feel your friend Ballendir fights by your side."

Shayth sighed. "I need all the friends I can find."

Over this, she placed his pixane, which hung from his neck and was made of similar light material. Then she went to her knees and helped him pull on first mail hosen and then armored cuisses and greaves. Shayth bent his knees and stretched in various postures. The armor did not restrict him. Someone had studied his stances and fighting style, and he felt a wave of admiration for the thoughtfulness and art of the craftsmen. To his boots, she snapped on sharp sabatons, edged armor that protected and deflected blows to his feet. Their pointed tips were clearly meant as additional weapons, and he turned from Shameka to try a few kicks. When he turned back, he could not suppress a grin.

She stood up and smiled when he said he must thank her father. "You can thank him by winning and staying alive. He doesn't like you, but he wants his daughter happy."

She was joking, and he reveled in her laughter. Shameka then attached two levels of breastplates. "It's better to have two thinner layers than one heavy," she explained. "Also, if the top splits, there is another underneath that remains intact."

At least, we will hope so, Shayth thought, thinking of pictorians swinging axes. When she began to add his upper and lower vambraces and the gauntlets to his lower arms, Shayth glanced at the different parts and sighed.

"I usually have just two or three vambraces and gauntlets," he said.

"And you can't use your bow then. My father knows you wouldn't be happy if you can't empty a few quivers over the wall."

"I won't be able to use a bow with armor," Shayth said. "That's why—"

"You will shoot your bow," his wife replied, "and if you miss, you'll only have yourself to blame."

"I won't miss," he growled back playfully as she added pauldrons and couters, each made in separate parts to free the shoulder and elbow while not exposing either joint to attack.

Everything clicked into place, and Shayth moved around the room, testing for any restrictions he might need to compensate for. There were none, and he again felt a sense of awe. He stopped in front of a mirror. Shameka came up behind him and put a mail coif over his head. He barely felt it. Then she lowered his helmet, a black burgonet with a Y-shaped opening for his eyes, nose, and mouth. She had known he would not closet his face. The top of the helmet had a ridge shaped like a sleek dragon, the face baring its teeth at his adversary. For a moment, he imagined breathing fire and then laughed to himself.

"My husband," Shameka said, staring into the mirror. "My king."

CHAPTER 72

Shayth had to admit that, when he left their chambers, he felt good in his new armor. He was used to being stared at – he was the king, after all – but this was different. He had to refrain from drawing his sword and swirling it around as he had to impress young women in his youth.

He led his guards out of the tower and into the main square. As he turned a corner, he stopped. A boy, no more than twelve cycles, stood in front of a doorway. He held a rusty sword too long for him. He was staring at it in terror, and his cheeks were flushed. The raised voices of a man and woman spilled out from the adjacent building.

"When I was his age, I had already fought in battles for the Emperor," a male voice growled.

"But you were trained," a woman pleaded. "We chose for him to study. He has the opportunity, and he's smart. He'll join the military later. We decided all this already."

"I stood to defend my country. So will he."

"And he'll die."

"I faced down dozens of barbarians."

"And he'll face one huge, well-trained Ashen Elf. No more. He'll never get the chance."

"I'm his father. I won't be disgraced."

"And I bore him. I don't want to bury him."

Shayth took the boy's forearm. "Come with me," he said quietly.

Around another corner, he stopped. "They both love you," he said. The boy nodded. Shayth tapped the boy's sword. "Do you know how to use it?"

"Not really," the boy whispered. "My mother's right. I'll be killed by the first Ashen Elf I fight."

Shayth nodded. It felt disingenuous to lie. "Do you know who I am?"

Again, the boy nodded. "I-I should bow or something, I know. It just all seems..." His voice trailed off.

"Don't worry about that for now. If we both live through this, you can owe me a few bows." The boy looked up at his king and smiled. "Listen," Shayth continued. "I have a job for you—one that will ensure more Ashen Elves meet their deaths—and it's something you can do well. Will you help me?"

The boy stood a bit straighter. "You're my king," he said, his voice still quiet but now also steady and formal. "I serve at the pleasure of the King of Odessiya."

The boy glanced behind Shayth, and Shayth guessed the boy's parents were nervously peering at them. He turned back to the boy and spoke loudly, his voice traveling along the stone walls.

"Then I command you as your king," he said, loud enough for the boy's parents to hear. "You are appointed the king's personal archery squire. In the future, you will care for my bows and arrows. For now, go to my steward and tell him to bring my bow to the ramparts. Then run to the fletcher. Tell him to put all the arrows he has into buckets so you, personally, can bring them to my position on the ramparts. Do you understand?"

The boy puffed out his chest and sheathed his own sword after two attempts. "I won't fail you, my king. How many buckets of arrows should I bring?"

Shayth mussed the boy's hair. "All of them."

Shayth strode to the outer walls and up the steps to the rampart. Here and there, he exchanged words of encouragement with soldiers as he passed them. Men moved out of his way, and he took the steps two at a time.

Once on the rampart, he paused to look out at the gathered Ashen Elf army. He realized they were not thumping the ground with their weapons. But then he saw that his own men were all staring up to the raised ramparts above the main gates. He walked over slower now. No one was fighting, but he felt a growing sense of tension.

As he neared, he needed to push men out of his way; such was the focus on whatever was happening. He thought that he might see the mage, but a man stood there, at ease judging by his stance. His periphery shimmered, and Shayth wondered if this man was even physically present.

The man faced Mharina, who had her back to Shayth. She held her staff diagonally across her body, ready for action. Her right leg was forward, and her weight was distributed evenly as she crouched.

Her coiled stance and his relaxed air was a dichotomy. He had curly blond hair and a goatee. His eyes were a rich blue—not icy like the Gray Elves—and his face looked sunburned and wrinkled by the elements.

"Who are you?" Shayth demanded as he moved nearer Mharina.

Mharina had put a hand out and answered for the man. "This is Ithea, King Shayth. He was your uncle's lackey."

Shayth felt a wave of cold go through him. He straightened and took a moment to consider what this meant. "What do you want? Seems rather late to parley, no?"

"Probably," Ithea said. "I understand you're as stubborn as your uncle was strategic. Unfortunately for you, that will be your downfall.

But I did not come to talk. The mage already gave you the opportunity to let her army pass through to the Elves of the West. And since you do not possess magic, you hold little of relevance to me."

"What do you want with Mharina, then?" Shayth asked.

"Well, it might be hard for you to comprehend. I'm not only Ithea. I'm also Abel, the Mushroom Man, who won Mharina's heart. I stopped in to share these morels I had. They're her favorite, I recall. Fry them lightly with ginger and tur root. Delicious."

"You came to deliver mushrooms? Nice. I'm sure we'll have plenty of time to cook before they spoil."

"Oh, my boy. Why do you, the wild prince—as you were known for so many years—who fought and defeated great warriors with only a sword and bow, get all dressed up in that shiny armor for us? I'll hazard a guess that your beautiful bride arranged for it." Shayth squirmed, and Ithea grinned. "Bet you prefer we discussed mushrooms?"

Mharina took a step forward. "Is Abel alive?"

"Oh, yes, very much so. But he's sort of like…a prisoner. Still, he can see you and feel for you, though I'm somewhat curious why he would." He winced ever so slightly and smiled.

"And when I kill you, will he die, too?"

"Most likely. With the correct knowledge, it's possible he could transfer to another body. But he spurns the magic that might have helped him, so… Anyway, you are not going to kill me."

Ithea looked around. "Where are your siblings?"

"Where is my father?" Mharina countered.

"Your father, if he still lives, is the plaything of the mage and her inquisitor. The latter now calls herself the Purple Elfe. I believe you've met. She was most infatuated with your dear teacher. I just hope that, when she finishes playing with your father, she kills him more effectively than her pathetic namesake did."

"Her pathetic namesake seemed to get the better of you," Mharina said.

Shayth realized she was speaking faster than normal. She was afraid and had not responded about where the twins were. Maybe she didn't know.

"Not in the end, my dear."

"So, have you come to kill me?" Mharina asked.

"I just wanted you to see me in your beloved's body and know that to kill me, you'll have to kill him. That must be a very difficult prospect for you, like losing Sa'gola, except you'll have to do it with your own hands. I wonder if you're up to it."

Mharina slowly raised the burlap sack Ithea had brought her and pulled out a tall morel mushroom. She fingered its indentations. "I have always loved your knowledge of the mushroom world, my love—your stories and your desire to heal with them. Thank you for giving that to me. It's how I'll remember you."

Then she opened her palm, and the mushroom slowly spiraled up, the sun catching its scaly head.

Still staring at Ithea, she spoke in a soft voice, "I know you will understand, my love." And, from the tip of her staff, a short burst of orange fire burned the mushroom in the air.

Chapter 73

Despite tens of thousands of bloodthirsty Gray Elves marching toward him intent on destroying his capital, murdering his people, and usurping his rule, King Shayth Shindell felt a moment of completeness. The tension as he pulled back his bowstring was both familiar and reassuring.

No one fired. The archers all stood with bowstrings similarly taut, straining to release their nocked arrows. All others watched their king, holding their breath, saying their prayers, filling their minds with images of their mates and offspring.

"Steady," General Pilau cried, her voice booming, yet calm. "On my command."

The general was watching Shayth. He could not see her, but her eyes bore into his back. He would fire the first shot, a signal for her to give the command. He waited. Faced with such large numbers, there was no luxury of sending warning shots or wasting arrows. He looked down the shaft of his arrow, its black feathers tickling his cheek in the slight breeze. He was focused upon a large Ashen Elfe urging her troops forward. Her helm was split like his, with a Y shape in the front. She was within range, but still, he waited. She was shouting orders, cracking a whip. But she was not facing him.

"Turn, damn you," Shayth murmured.

Mharina, who was standing next to him, flicked her staff, and a bright reflection danced up the blade of the Ashen Elfe's sword. She stopped shouting, stared at it, and then looked up to the walls.

Shayth loosed his arrow and watched it twirl in a narrow arc before thudding into its target. The elfe screamed in pain, grasping for the black-feathered arrow that protruded from her helm.

"Fire!" General Pilau cried, and a volley of arrows arched from above the ramparts.

The archers were lined in two rows. The front line would shoot and then kneel to nock a fresh arrow while the second line aimed and shot. When an archer fell, the man behind him took his place.

Shayth needed no second. He reached into the bucket the boy held for him and grasped arrow after arrow: reach, nock, fire, repeat. He knew he was being watched, but he no longer cared. It was only him and his bow and the enemy below.

He fired arrow after arrow. Most found their mark, and elves fell beneath volley after volley. He was vaguely aware of the boy switching buckets, and then of his steward holding the full ones.

"Where's the boy?" Shayth cried.

"Gone for more arrows, milord."

Shayth turned back. The first wave of elves had halted and were joined by a second wave that held shields above their heads, each interlinked with others in an impenetrable web. They would reach the wall, Shayth realized. It was happening so quickly, so easily.

"Fire arrows!" General Pilau shouted. "Pitch!"

Shayth's arrows were replaced with ones with heavier tips covered in a foul-smelling black substance. Small fires were lit in heavy metal buckets in front of each archer. As the elves swung long ladders against the walls, Shayth saw that smaller buckets of burning pitch were being poured down the wall and lit.

"Wait for my orders," the general cried. "I want them already climbing when we burn the ladders. Be patient. Archers, focus on the towers."

Shayth looked up and saw ten, then twelve, huge wooden towers being pulled along on logs. It was an awkward but effective exercise, as two huge, hairy, tusked beasts pulled each tower.

The fire arrows bounced off the towers. The elves had used some kind of fire-resistant material. Arrows that made it inside the towers caused damage, but the elves were prepared for this.

He stared down at the animals pulling the towers. The huge beasts were armored over the backs of their heads and down the sides of their bodies. They wore huge helmets that covered their eyes to blind them from the melee and also protect them. Shayth swore as he considered how to inflict pain upon these noble beasts.

He grabbed one of his black-feathered arrows and drew the bowstring to its limit. Then he aimed at one of the beast's trunks, specifically at its horned protrusions. The arrow shot straight in through one protrusion and out the other. The pachyderm bellowed and twisted its trunk, trying to shake it off, but this only seemed to increase its pain.

Upon the walls, the solders cheered and watched the animal wrench its trunk into the air, dragging the elves who held its chains, and crash into its partner. The tower they pulled trembled and then, when both beasts headed in the same direction, toppled over.

The archers followed their king's lead. Four more of the great beasts were felled. Ashen Elves with huge shields jumped in front of the unhurt pachyderms to protect the creatures. While Shayth's bowmen could not hit another creature, they at least stopped the advance of the towers.

But their respite was short-lived, as more elves came and locked shields to create a wall with narrow gaps. Through the gaps, they threw hundreds of spears and shot heavier ones from machines like giant crossbows on carts.

General Pilau called for the archers to crouch behind the merlons, but this only gave the elves the opportunity to again approach the walls. Before the men on the ramparts realized it, hundreds of ladders were thrown against the walls, and the sound of boots scrambling up could be clearly heard.

Men reached to drop pitch and oil down onto the ladders, but elven spears and javelins immediately cut them down.

Shayth drew his broadsword and picked up his huge shield. The next few moments would be crucial. He heard his general order pitch and oil. A young man rose next to Shayth and poured oil down the nearest ladder. The king rose and protected the soldier with his shield. Others followed his example, but huge javelins pounded the shields and sent the men flailing. The first Ashen Elves came over the walls.

Shayth exchanged a brisk nod with Pilau. They had not wanted to use this measure so soon, but there was no choice. Using a small mirror, the general signaled to the bell tower, which responded in kind with a larger mirror.

Shayth leapt into the fray, calling for his guard and the pictorians. The elves could hold their own against any pictorian or human, but their numbers, for now, were on the king's side. He saw Umnesilk lead his boars into the thickest frays. As Shayth tore into three Ashen Elves, Narasilk, the first boar's nephew, joined him, springing through Shayth's own guard. They stood back to back, and Shayth felt the battle rage take over.

It was so familiar, so powerful, and so angry. He welcomed it back like an old friend, and, together, they swung his mighty broadsword with strength. Shayth was so caught up that he barely registered the pounding hooves and the clash of his cavalry into the main force of the Elven army that was scaling the wall.

Chapter 74

The deep, ancient fire rose slowly to meet him. His cone of Wycaan power—thin, sharp, and insistent—reached out to embrace the fire through the ice. He heard cracks through the mist. It could be the sound of great ice plates melting in slow submission - or that of his own bones being broken by a desperate mage who was beginning to comprehend that she faced defeat.

He pushed the cracking from his mind. Only the fire was important. He had to destroy their caverns, their supplies, their leadership—but most of all, he had to destroy their mural. A tragic story had been manipulated to fuel the hate and violence of an entire people; a story of liberation had been terribly twisted.

The fire met him, and he realized that the icy numbness had partially insulated him from his pain. He gasped at both the enormity of such an ancient force and the destruction of his body.

As he bonded the fire to his will—not subjugating but gently manipulating—he felt water, released from its own frozen incarceration, rush by and through him. He shivered from the chill and sweated from the heat, but still he felt the power course though him. He had experienced such brazen power only at his Wycaan transformation under the cave lake and in the bloodwood forest when the trees had accepted his transition into his bear spirit.

Now, he felt walls of ice crumble, revealing stone walls that twinkled with embedded crystals. He directed the fire toward the great mural, and there he met the mage, her eyes wide open in shock.

Next to her stood the Purple Elfe, her teeth bared in a snarl. They stared at the mural as fissures slowly appeared. Fire and ice. Seanchai had harnessed two diametrically opposed elements in a sacred Wycaan alliance.

He felt his body being dragged onto the rock wedge where he had previously been brought to view the mural. His eyes opened, and his blurred vision distinguished the form of a man dressed in black.

"Your king sends but one puny human to rescue you?" the Purple Elfe shrieked. "Does he think so little of you?"

"Puny human," Ahad muttered, spitting blood, "who slew forty-six of your heralded warriors."

"By creeping up on them and blowing darts into the backs of their necks. A coward, not a warrior."

"But effective." Ahad choked out a laugh. "An assassin deals death efficiently, not through some ineffective honor code."

"Let him go," Seanchai whispered. "He's an assassin. It's all he knows, and—"

"No!" the Purple Elfe screamed. "He has been kept alive so that you can see another die for you, Wycaan. Another one in a long line of thousands."

With great effort, Seanchai raised his bruised and battered head. He glared at the elfe. "Tens of thousands," he hissed. "And they died for something they believed in."

"But your assassin dies with only the knowledge that he failed," the mage sneered. "How tragic. How pointless."

She nodded, and two elves dragged Ahad to the edge of the balcony.

"I came because I wanted to, Seanchai," the assassin shouted, struggling to look back at him. "No one sent me. I die aiding one I want to help, not one I must in exchange for someone's gold. I won't be one of your victims. You hear? I die the way I want."

"Then die well, my friend," Seanchai whispered as the elves threw Ahad over the edge.

Seanchai closed his eyes. Their past had been one of hate and confrontation, but they had grown older and wiser, and now he mourned the death of a friend. He waited to hear the thud of Ahad's body, but it never came.

Instead, the cavern echoed with the sound of pounding air. A shadow rose from its depths—a pounding flapping of wings and a rush of power. From the dragon's great white back, a black panther sprung at the Gray Elf guards, savaging them with its fury. When the Purple Elfe moved to attack, the pale white dragon sent a volley of fire to stop her. Seanchai saw Ahad clutching the dragon's haunches.

He watched in awe as the Wycaan dragon turned to face him. He felt the guards release him as they sprang to defend themselves. Other hands grabbed him—young, male human hands—and he felt a scrawny boy drag him to the wall and lean him against the cold stone.

"You all must die," the dragon cried to the mage, but then turned to the Purple Elfe. "And you who sully the memory of my sister's teacher will die first. But before that…"

The dragon flapped her wings in the other direction, struggling to harness the sheer size and power of her animal form. She turned to the mural and filled her lungs.

Flames licked the rock walls, melting the paint. Seanchai squinted in the bright light. They all did, except the panther, who simply looked on with pride. When the flames were extinguished, all that was left was the beginning and the end of the mural.

"Behold," Senzia roared. "Your exile—a historical travesty— remains so all may bear witness to the terrible injustice your people endured."

Then she spoke of the last scene, the Ashen Elves settled and living in grassy orchards heavy with multicolored fruit.

"This, too, will remain—a constant reminder of what your hatred and vengeance cost your people: peace."

The Purple Elfe leapt forward as if to attack the hovering dragon. Ilan sprung from his heavily muscled haunches, and the panther's jaws clamped around the elfe's throat. The ominous crack reverberated off the cavern's walls.

The mage stepped forward, her mouth open, tears rolling down her cheeks. Staring at what was left of the mural, she moved to the edge.

"It's not too late," Seanchai wheezed. The pain in his crushed body was excruciating. "Your people stand before the walls of Shindellia. You can stop them. Shayth will understand."

She turned to him slowly. "I wish you were right, Wycaan. But I have failed my people and do not deserve a second chance."

"Maybe," Seanchai gasped as a sharp, cutting wave of pain almost made him faint. "But it's our job as leaders to make decisions. Some will be good, others bad. The measure of a good leader is their drive to lead their people. It's not too late."

"It is," she said. "You've forgotten that I'm not the leader. I allowed myself to become one of the Master's pawns."

"The Emperor is dead!" Seanchai tried to shout, but his hoarse voice barely squeaked. "It's over. It can be over. Together…"

"Not together," the mage said. "I know what I just did to you, and you forget a greater force."

"What?"

"Ithea."

The mage took three graceful steps and fell from the precipice. This time, Seanchai heard the dull thud as her body smashed against the bottom of the cavern.

Chapter 75

The ancient fire, the core of the earth, continued to rise, reducing great ice walls to soft slush and then water. Ilan, back in his elf form, helped Artur half carry, half drag Ahad up toward the higher caverns. Senzia, remaining in her dragon form, took her father.

She walked awkwardly through the tunnel she had used to get into the cavern and then sprung out into the cold air. Seanchai gasped from the shocking change of temperature, but he soon welcomed the numbing cold. His body was battered and broken, but he clung to his daughter's scaly body as her powerful wings lifted him high in a graceful turn. Through the pain, he felt the thrill of flying and his daughter's pride as she carried him.

After a short while, they landed at the mouth of the cave. Great puddles of water steamed around them The others joined them, and Seanchai was carefully laid next to Ahad. Both leaned against the rock walls. When Senzia, back in elfe form, joined them, Seanchai noticed stains of blood around her mouth and nose. They were smeared, as if she had wiped them away.

"You look terrible," Ahad said to Seanchai, offering a grimace that was meant to be a smile.

"You've seen better days, yourself," Seanchai replied. "Did they teach you at assassin school how to get captured and flung off cliffs?"

They both laughed and winced together. Then Seanchai turned to his *calhei*.

"You disobeyed me," he said. "You were supposed to go to your sister's aid."

"We will," Senzia said, "but Ilan could feel your pain. It was too much. Who turns their back on their *ahdahr*?"

"One who serves a greater good. You must go now with all haste. Wait. Do you always bleed when you use magic?"

"Only when I exert myself, and less each time. There'll be time enough to deal with this. But now, we must go to Mharina." She pointed to her left at the boy from the mural room. "This is Artur. He's my friend and will stay to take care of you. He has no place in battle."

Seanchai turned slowly to look at the scrawny boy. "Thank you," he said.

It is my honor, great grizzly.

Seanchai frowned, confused.

"I was brought up by bears," Artur said aloud.

"He was able to track you and bring me to rescue you," Ahad said, grabbing his side. "Kind of regret he was so good."

There was a scuffle nearby, and Seanchai realized Ilan was not with them. Just then, he appeared with several Gray Elves, holding a sword to the one Seanchai recognized as Gunwrath.

"*Ahdahr.* This one says he tortured you."

"I deserve no mercy," Gunwrath said, his voice deep and calm, "and ask for none. But behind me are elves who serve as healers, make food, or tend the community in other ways. I ask that you spare them."

Seanchai stared at him, trying to decide what to do. He felt no anger toward the Gray Elf, but feared his prowess. Gunwrath perhaps recognized this.

"Kill me," he said flatly.

"Bind him, Senzia," Seanchai said, and a cord left her belt and wound its way around the Ashen Elf's hands and feet. "Listen to me, both of you."

He winced, and Senzia and Ilan came closer and knelt down. "Change into your animal forms and return to Shindellia. You are very good, but still young. You cannot face Ithea. Do you understand? Your responsibility must be to defend the king and support Mharina. She must be the one to face Ithea. She's our only chance, but she must be focused and know that you protect her. She will need everything she has learned to face and defeat him. Tell her to dig into her memories.

"And tell her I love her. Tell her…I remembered in the end. I couldn't heal what happened between your mother and me, but what I found in my mind included my love for all of you."

"Mother," Ilan said, and his upper lip quivered.

Senzia moved next to her brother and put her arm around his waist. "She would tell us that now's not the time to mourn her. Let us return and take revenge in her honor."

Ilan nodded, and Seanchai knew his *calhei* would be all right.

"Then go," he said. "Travel fast and keep Odessiya free. Let that be your mother's legacy…and mine too."

Senzia glided on freezing currents. It was night, but a fat moon illuminated the way. Below her, she saw only the dark, sleek form of her brother pounding along on his powerful paws.

They would rest after dawn and then fall upon the enemy at night, when her fire would not only burn, but blind. She ached to unleash her power on the Ashen Elves. She felt no sympathy. They had killed her mother, almost killed her *ahdahr*, and broken her family forever.

She could feel the anger boiling inside of her—the anguish and the desire for revenge. It fueled her. She was Wycaan and bound by a sense of duty, but she was also an elfe and her mother's daughter, and she would ride all these powerful emotions.

Ilan called to her telepathically as the sky grayed to their left. He had reached a river and was stopping. She glided down and changed as she landed. It was a neat trick, but her brother was lapping water with a long, red tongue and didn't notice. She realized that, had she stayed a dragon a few minutes more, she could have drunk her full and replenished her energy.

She drank a bit and then sat on a rock. Nearby, she saw a small cave and realized Ilan had deliberately chosen this place to stop.

"This is where *Ahdahr* and I hunted."

"Where you were hunted, you mean," she grinned.

"I had no idea a party of Ashen Elves was intent on eating at the same banquet. There's a cave there. I want to rest and see if I can connect to Mharina. She is in great pain."

"Do you think she saw…was she there?"

"Yes. I know she was with mother."

"How?"

"Her pain was so…so intense, so raw. The power it took to do whatever she did afterwards was… Do you remember her talking about the white fire, the killing fire?"

Senzia nodded.

"She unleashed it. I think you need uncontrolled rage to generate such magic. She was there, Senzia, and she is all alone, without *Ahdahr*, you, or me." He paused for a moment and chewed his lower lip. "I…I can't believe mother is really dead."

"Don't go there, Ilan; not yet. Think of the battle; focus your pain and rage on what awaits us at Shindellia."

Ilan stared at his sister. "How can you be so in control?"

"You can feel me. You know the answer. My control is fragile, but it stands. I crave only to reach the plains of Shindellia. Then I will wreak my mourning on the Gray Elves. I will light them up."

"I believe you will, sis, but there are thousands—maybe tens of thousands—of them, and I'm not sure how effective I'll be as a panther on the battlefield. I have no armor and only teeth and claws for weapons. It won't be difficult to take me down with an arrow or spear."

"True," Senzia snickered. "You discovered that already."

They laughed for a moment, each reveling in the closeness they had always shared. But the darkness crept in, and Senzia could sense her brother brooding.

"Will he live?" Ilan asked.

"I think so," Senzia answered, "but he suffered serious damage back there. I wonder if retrieving his memories was a blessing or a curse."

"I'm not ready to take over." Ilan's voice sounded small.

Senzia moved closer and put an arm around her taller brother. "What made it so hard for *Ahdahr* was that he did it alone. He had wonderful friends, but they weren't Wycaan. But we have each other: you, Mharina, and me. It'll be different."

"If we all survive the next few days."

"We will, little brother. Don't worry."

But she knew Ilan could read everything about her. He would sense her doubt and fear.

Chapter 76

The onslaught of the cavalry had, for the moment, at least, stunned the Ashen Elves into retreat. *We have earned some more time,* Mharina thought, *but to do what?* The horsemen rode to a secret rendezvous so they and their steeds could recover. But next time, there would be no surprising the Ashen Elves. They were harsh and closed-minded, but they were not stupid. In fact, Mharina conceded that, tactically, they were quite astute. She was not convinced the cavalry would be so effective next time.

She walked slowly along the ramparts, ignoring the uneasy stares of the soldiers and enjoying how each click of her staff on the smooth stones elicited cringes from the superstitious. Occasionally, she let it drag so sparks would trail behind her. Fire would always be her preferred element. Her thoughts went to her training with Sa'gola in the caves, when she had lit up the caverns with her fire, exuding extraordinary strength that left her sore and bathed in sweat. But always, her teacher guided her to the hot mineral ponds where they shared profound intimacy.

She had just shown her mother some of her mastery the night before Sellia died. It had been mere morsels, but Sellia had praised her growing skills and, for a few moments, Mharina was allowed to be a young *calhei* basking in the unequivocal love of her mother.

Tears welled in her eyes. She and her mother had been so close once. With the twins clearly natural-born Wycaans, Sellia had tried to give her eldest other strengths, teaching Mharina to use the bow and hunt and passing on her own considerable skill in stealth. Such times had been precious, just the two of them hunting beyond the walls of the Wycaan Academy before lying together, stomachs full from their quarry, and staring up at the star-filled sky.

Those moments had been precious beyond worth, a feminine intimacy similar to but different from those she shared with Sa'gola. Lying with her head on her mother's firm stomach, they had shared secrets and dreams. Sellia had promised she would always do her best to protect her daughter and had proved her loyalty, relentlessly chasing the taragusii who had kidnapped Mharina and the twins. Now, her mother lay buried in the dirt because she had protected her daughter with her life.

Mharina had not really grieved her mother—had not had the opportunity either alone or with her siblings. All she could do was erect a shield of numbness. These were dangerous times, her role critical. There would be time to mourn, and right now, such emotions needed to be kept tightly in check. But the time between battles was cracking the shield she had so carefully erected.

It would be different if Senzia and Ilan were here. They would mourn together; Senzia would close herself up, and Mharina, as the elder sister, would comfort the sensitive Ilan. He would take it hard, much as he had when they thought their father was dead. It would add considerable work for her and take a lot of emotional energy, but there would be a certain comfort, and, despite the danger, she wished they were here, instead of…

She wondered where they were. Had Senzia really been held prisoner by the Ashen Elves? Had Ilan been correct, and had he reached his twin sister? She knew the answer to both. Ilan had never been wrong when it came to Senzia. Mharina had always been jealous of the bond the two had, even though she knew they both loved her dearly. But now she found comfort in the twins' connection. They would support each other.

Still, she could not imagine either sibling being tortured. Senzia would fight back, and that might prove more disastrous than Ilan capitulating. Would he? He had not waffled about whether or not he should go rescue his sister. Perhaps Ilan had not reached the ice caves to begin with. Their *ahdahr* had been adamant that he would not wait for Ilan, and there was surely no way her brother could keep up with Seanchai in his bear form.

Raised voices from the tower ahead wrenched the elfe from her thoughts. Her keen elven hearing registered swords being drawn, but she did not hear the clash of steel. There was a stand-off. She quickened her pace, feeling both a rising sense of trepidation and an overriding wave of excitement and anger. It was, as Sa'gola had warned, an awesome combination. She knew it to be empowering and seductive, positive and negative, the same fuel that would help her win or make her fall in defeat.

At the steps leading up to the tallest tower, she met a soldier running down. She grabbed his arm as he slipped, and he gasped as he looked up at her.

"Sorry, milady. 'e's calling for you. 'e says 'e can kill us all. There be twelve soldiers up there, but I still fink 'e can. Know what I mean?"

"Yes," Mharina answered, knowing now whom she would face.

"I'll get the king and—"

"No, you won't." She stared hard into his eyes. "Clear?"

He nodded and sidled off. She wasn't sure what he would do. The soldier's allegiance to his king was probably stronger than his fear of her. But she had more immediate problems. She skipped up the stairs and pushed between the soldiers cowering there.

The top of this tower was an open, square-shaped rampart with merlons and crenels around its perimeter. It afforded a magnificent view of the surrounding kingdom. Nothing obscured its panorama except the remnant of one cube, an extension that had once taken the ancient tower even higher. Behind it was a crumbling staircase that hugged the outer wall. With a dozen or so soldiers present, it was crowded, though there was room between the men and Ithea, who stood with a congenial smile across his Mushroom Man face and his sizzling whip in hand, its tail twitching on the ground like an agitated snake.

"What do you want?" Mharina snarled. She hated seeing the man she had fallen in love with possessed by this evil creature.

"You," Ithea replied, his smug tone revealing that he knew of her turmoil. "These pathetic souls will leave us, one way or another."

A slight flick of his wrist, and the whip hissed its readiness to comply. Mharina turned to the soldiers.

"Leave us," she commanded.

The men shuffled but did not move.

"You cannot help me and are more likely to hinder if we fight. None of you can face him. It will be a futile death. Now, please, give me the space I need." When there was still no response other than each soldier's intense scrutiny of his own boots, she invoked her power. "GET OUT!"

The response was instant, and when Mharina turned to face Ithea, they were alone.

CHAPTER 77

"You look quite striking, Mharina."

"Really? That's what you came here to—"

"We share all of each other's memories, my brother and I. I can *remember* every intimate moment"—Ithea's face twitched—"between the two of you." Another twitch, and he seemed to have difficulty with his next sentence. "I feel a part of it."

"It was never *us*, Ithea," she snapped. "It was Abel and me. Just the two of us. I see him fighting your obscenity."

"Obscenity?"

"Yes, it's obscene that you try to desecrate such personal moments. He's your brother, and—"

"I know he's my brother! I lived with him for most of his life. He, too, was hidden away in shame and from pathetic fear of a so-called fearless order. He, too, was made to hide his identity, his power, and—"

"What power?" Mharina asked. She might finally have the answer she was looking for.

"He has the same potential you and I have. He could wield the I*yzun*. Imagine an offspring from the two of you. What potential might that child hold? Perhaps you and I should mate and see."

"Yuck! You disgust me."

Ithea laughed. "Funny. I made a similar offer to your mother, you know. Not to mate, but to possess her body in exchange for your life. But, alas, she did not love you enough, and now she rots, food for the worms."

"The world revolves around you?" Mharina sneered, trying to regain her composure. It was so hard to look at Abel's beautiful, weather-browned face; his straw-colored hair that parted in the middle and fell down to his shoulders; and the goatee she had stroked in better times.

"No," Ithea said. "The world does not revolve around me. I make the world revolve."

He laughed loudly. Mharina turned to see the Ashen Elf army again approaching. She looked to the flanks and saw no reinforcement.

"Surprised? Nowhere near as much as your young king's cavalry will be when they hit a magical barrier."

She turned back sharply, feeling the frown upon her face. Sa'gola had once created such a barrier powerful enough to keep Ithea, her order, and even the Emperor out.

Mharina sighed. "So I must kill you to allow reinforcements through?"

"Even that won't be enough. I have helped, but the magic of the Ashen Elves should keep it intact. How fitting that the people who were incarcerated for so long are now the incarcerators. It's quite poetic."

"Then I guess I need another reason to slay you," she deadpanned. "Shame. I was about to let you surrender and leave peacefully."

"Oh, really?"

"No," Mharina said, her voice sharpening. "You killed my teacher. She was my mentor, my…"

"Lover?" Ithea asked. "She might have been fond of you, but she used others before you. I doubt it was quite like you thought. She took what she needed from you and everyone who came into contact with her."

"She told me what you did to her," Mharina replied. "How you tortured her and scarred her lovely body, how you paraded her in front of the Order. Was that because she would not give herself to you?"

"Give herself?" He laughed, and it was rasping, lecherous sound. "I take what I want. Maybe I will take you…for my brother's pleasure, of course."

"Never," the elfe responded. "And you couldn't defeat Sa'gola, even after everything you did to her, you couldn't break her. And I am Mharina, Wycaan Master and bearer of the *Iyzun*. You will not break me, either."

Ithea laughed again. It was sickening, bitter laughter that floated around the battlements.

"Here I am trying to belittle your Purple Lady, and you insult her with your arrogance. Hilarious. So you have all these titles. Surely you don't think for one minute that they replace the decades of study, practice, and experience that Sa'gola had. You foolish, impotent pup! She was formidable, brave, unique, the most strategic min…"

His tirade trailed off as he saw Mharina grinning.

"What?" His surprised expression suggested he already knew.

"So we do have something in common, Ithea. We both loved Sa'gola. So did Abel, you know. Of course you do. He is inside your head, screaming it in your brain. Were you jealous of his special relationship with her? She rejected you and you hurt her. She loved your own brother and me, but scorned you."

Mharina let out a cruel laugh. "Was it such a hard lesson for the all-powerful sorcerer to discover? You learn and master the deepest magical secrets of the female and male magic, only to discover there is one element that magic cannot control or subjugate. What a painful lesson after a lifetime driven to become the most powerful yielder of the *Iyzun*: to learn that your magic is powerless in the face of love.

"You killed Sa'gola, destroyed Abel, and butchered your own mother. You had my mother killed, and yet I stand here feeling sorry for you. You are pathetic, Ithea. Dear Gods. I can't believe I actually feel sorry for you. I *pity* you."

His cry was ear-splitting, a bitter screech that burned ears and made eyes water. His whip snaked up and flew in a wide arch. It was easy to avoid, but Ithea was not interested in her. His anger sent the whip, glowing orange with his rage, into the stone tower to his left. It stood four men tall and two wide, molded from heavy rocks and cemented together with mortar and time. The tower had defied the elements for centuries, but now the fury of the sorcerer's whip cut through it.

Bits of rock—grains, almost—splintered and fell. Ithea howled, and his strokes became harder and faster, the whip glowing from his raw pain. The tower slowly screeched, gave way and crumbled. Then there was a deep, painful creak from the bowels of the castle, and the ancient stone toppled in front of them.

Ithea stood there, breathless. Mharina watched him with dread and wonder. Slowly, he turned back to her. His voice was a harsh whisper, a hiss to match his whip.

"Yes: my brother, mother, Sa'gola. I loved them and then destroyed them. Now, it's your turn."

Chapter 78

It seemed as though the world stopped for a fleeting moment as Mharina and Ithea eyed each other. If there were sounds from below—and surely there were after the destruction that Ithea had just wrought—Mharina never heard it.

She began to summon her powers. His whip was still glowing and twitching. Ithea commanded it using the fire element, she realized, making her strongest element less effective against him. She wished now they had met on earth or near water.

"What are you thinking, little pup? Do you feel the fear rising? Be careful; it will paralyze you." He had recovered his composure. "Are you scared to face your death? You will join worthy company: your mother, lover, teacher, and all those you killed along the way."

His face began twitching furiously. Mharina just focused on summoning her energy. *Aieesha*, she whispered, and the runes on her staff began to glimmer and throb. The fire ignited and rose through her.

"Let's end this, Ithea. I—"

"I'm here, Mharina." It was Abel's voice coming from the contorted face. "Show no mercy. I'll…I'll wait for…you on…the other…side."

Ithea's—or rather, Abel's—face twitched as the brothers each struggled to gain control. When the struggle subsided, it was Ithea who spoke. "Yes, you'll have to kill him, too: your other lover; your brave, sullen Mushroom Man. Are you ready to do that, Mharina?"

"I'll do my duty," she replied, trying to exude more confidence than she felt. "I'm sorry, Abel. It could have worked, I'm sure. But I must fulfill my destiny."

Ithea's face twitched once but stayed silent.

"I love you, too, Abel. Goodbye."

Mharina began to whirl her staff, feeling the balance, the energy, and the power. Moving faster, her staff and arm became as one and then fused with her mind. She attacked. Though Ithea's whip was scary and effective, the elfe only needed to get inside of it, and the man would be powerless to her staff.

Ithea grinned as if reading her mind and unsheathed a huge broadsword from deep within his cloak. He twirled it in a disparaging rhythm that mimicked the way Mharina did with her staff.

Then the big man sprung forward, his whip sizzling as it cut through the air. Mharina deflected it with her staff. Despite her perfect timing, she still felt a shuddering impact from the power emanating from the whip.

She staggered back but quickly adapted her stance. She deflected the next blow in a similar manner, and this time stepped forward to strike with the other tip of her staff. Ithea brought up his sword and blocked. There was something arrogantly dismissive in the fact that he never tried to parry or deflect, knowing he was far stronger than her.

He stepped forward, and the movement sent her crashing into a stone wall and landing on her knee. She grunted and, though slightly winded, rose quickly. Ithea laughed.

"You're going to have to try harder, pup," he taunted. "You've never faced anyone like me."

"Even your mother?"

Ithea frowned. "When did you…" Then he glanced at the staff. "You fight me with the staff you stole from my mother's grave? How dare you."

"Oh, please," Mharina shot back. "She fought you, her own son, with this staff, no? Don't try the sentimental bluff. You sound ridiculous. And I didn't steal it. I took it from her."

Ithea jumped forward, simultaneously attacking with whip and sword. Mharina ducked and twisted away from the wall. She skipped up onto the crenels, tempting Ithea. But he just stood and forced her to skip from one crenel to the next with his whip.

Realizing she wasn't getting anywhere, she dug her staff into the stone and launched herself over Ithea and down onto her feet behind him. As she landed in a crouch, she realized jumping had been a foolish thing to do. His whip had shot up after her and could have pulled her apart.

Ithea turned, no sign of fatigue on Abel's beautiful face. She, on the other hand, was panting and sweating. Behind Ithea, a crowd, including Shayth, watched from a nearby tower. She was relieved they were leaving her alone as she had requested, though they might intervene soon if she didn't make some headway.

"We have quite a crowd," Ithea said. "The Ashen Elves approach from below, as well. Your prince is most courteous to not attack them. We would find that distracting. Shall we put on a show?"

Now, he stepped forward, his whip snapping and hissing through the air and his sword slashing in kind. Mharina, after skipping backward a few times, began to feel she could not wait for anything to change and instead pushed forward.

As their sparring settled into a rhythm, the taunts ceased. For a moment, Mharina had Ithea on the back foot, but he slid away and attacked again. The momentum swung from one to the other. The sun lowered and set, and now the bright orange staff and whip illuminated the platform.

Their lights blinded their own night vision, and Mharina, retreating and parrying, slipped on a piece of rubble. As she stumbled, Ithea threw his sword above him, freeing his hand, and extended his palm to send a bolt of energy that slammed her into the wall. A protruding stone jarred her back, and she crumpled, winded. She cried out in pain.

"Now," Ithea roared, "feel the cut of my whip as your teacher did." The whip rained down on her, ripping her clothes and armor. "Whimper as she did! Beg for me to cease. Beg and know my power over you."

Mharina began to curl into a defensive ball as Sa'gola had but stopped herself. Gritting her teeth, she reached for a rock but found only mud. Then she remembered: there was water in the tower. Summoning her draining strength, she gathered the water and sent up a thick wave. The fire in the whip hissed, and Ithea gasped as the shock reverberating through the whip sent him crashing against the wall. For a moment, he disappeared from sight, enveloped in thick steam.

Gathering her strength and leaning on the staff, Mharina rose and staggered over. The steam dissipated in the evening breeze. Ithea was lying on the ground. She raised her staff, calling up all her remaining power.

"Stop!" It was Abel's voice, and the expression on the fallen man's face undeniably his. She had seen this face full of fear and panic before, when her magic flared as Ithea killed Sa'gola.

Mharina froze long enough for his expression to turn malicious and his sword to stab her in the gut. She staggered back, gasping for breath. Her hand went to her stomach and felt the soaking warmth of her own blood.

She felt oddly at peace. She would see her mother and Sa'gola, but she had failed everyone else. Odessiya would fall. Shayth would be executed. Her sister and brother would be devastated—first their mother, perhaps their father, and now her.

She tried to stand straight but couldn't. Ithea rose shakily to his feet.

"Nice try," he whispered, "but you never had a chance."

He raised the whip, which ignited brightly in the dark. *Fire*, Mharina thought. *My element.* Then, as the whip swung round, a dark figure leapt from the rubble and grabbed Ithea in a tight bear hug. The figure was as big as the sorcerer and evidently strong, as Ithea struggled to free himself. The whip curled around the two tightly, its sizzling intensifying. Both men screamed in pain, as the whip exploded in energy, lighting up the sky with a massive assault of pure white fire that engulfed them both. The attacker held his grip and dragged Ithea over the castle walls. They both continued screaming. Then there was a hard thud and silence.

Shayth! You idiot, Mharina thought, her eyes welling up in tears from pain and sorrow. But when she looked to the other tower, the king was still there. Then she gasped from the pain and closed her eyes as everything slid away.

Chapter 79

*I*t was so peaceful…so safe. She felt herself glide along a path, flanked by tall, reedy grasses. Muted but growingly urgent voices floated toward her from each side. Mharina felt the presence of familiar people.

She stood at a junction and hesitated. She was unsure what lay in either direction and felt the correct decision was critical. Something was wrong. Where was she? The colors were too vivid, too bright…almost unreal.

From the path to her right, three figures approached. Mharina felt her heart beat faster as she recognized the silhouettes of her mother, Sa'gola, and Mhari. Her mother looked awkward, clearly not yet acclimatized to her new state. Sa'gola was as beautiful as ever, the purple streaks in her black hair shiny and glistening. Mhari stood old, wrinkled, and yet still erect, and her eyes watched Mharina with clear apprehension.

Sellia opened her mouth and tried to speak, but no sound could be heard. She became frustrated and turned to her companions. Mhari just shook her head and continued to look at Mharina. Sa'gola frowned, trying to circumvent whatever was preventing them from speaking.

Sellia shook her head and wordlessly shouted at the others. Sa'gola shrugged, and Mhari continued to stare. Mharina could do nothing but watch.

"They cannot talk to you. The veil is shut because you have come to the Valley of the Dead once before. But we can hear them."

Mharina turned her head slowly and saw her brother and sister standing on the path to the left. They both looked tattered, their clothes soiled and their faces smeared with dirt. But they both smiled. Mharina felt a wave of panic.

"Tell me you aren't dead, too," she heard herself whisper.

"No," Senzia said. "Ilan can dreamwalk. Someone summoned us here."

"Mother is there. Do you see her? Do you understand what this means?"

Neither twin spoke. Ilan gulped and clasped Senzia's hand. Then he nodded. "We already knew," he said simply.

"How?"

He shrugged. "Our powers develop fast. Whatever training we received from the Emperor seems to speed our advancement with every level we reach. I could sense Senzia and Ahdahr, now you..."-

His voice trailed off, and he stared at his mother, lost in thought.

"Don't leave us, Mharina," Senzia said. "We need you. Odessiya needs you."

Mharina followed Ilan's gaze, wondering if the dead were talking to him.

"The living are allowed only once to hear the voices of the dead," Ilan said, interpreting a message from the women on the right. He was still looking at them. "And you spoke with the dead once already."

"I also spoke with Sa'gola in her cottage."

Ilan looked at Sa'gola and replied. "That was a spell she created. She seems pretty proud of it. Mother and the others urge you to stay in the land of the living, but how effective you'll be there is unclear."

"What? That's ridiculous," Mharina snapped at him.

"I'm only passing on the message," Ilan replied, his tone more mature and assured than Mharina could ever recall. He frowned. "You are badly wounded. If you go back, a life must be sacrificed in your place."

"What? Who? No." Mharina said. "If I return, it will be by my own volition."

The three women shook their heads. Ilan spoke for them. "You should already be dead. Maugwen has used more than her healing powers on you. It's wrong to cheat death. Another must sacrifice."

"I will not let anyone take my pl—"

"You will," a voice said from behind her. "You already have. I have made the choice."

Mharina swung around. Maugwen stood before her, her hair as spiky and rebellious as ever, but her face a deathly pallor.

"What have you done?" Mharina asked.

"What should not have been but needed to be." Maugwen turned to the three women. "You tried so hard to help me unlock the key, Sa'gola, and I thank you for that. It's odd that Mharina was the one I needed." She paused as Sa'gola mouthed something. "No, I have no magic. I'm a pure healer, one who can use their ethereal form to heal.

"Still, there are lines that cannot be crossed, and I have crossed them. I am a healer. I should not choose who lives and who dies. But you have a destiny, Mharina. Odessiya needs you. I take your place with full knowledge and acceptance. Come, little one; there isn't time, and I must escort you back."

Mharina turned to her mother. "I love you," she said, and Sellia nodded. Then she turned to Sa'gola. "I didn't kill him. I'm sorry. Someone else did. I saw the fire. It was pure white. He died from his own rage and unbridled magic."

Sa'gola nodded and blew her a kiss. Mharina felt it softly alight on her cheek and moved her hand there. Her own skin felt clammy and cold.

"Come," Maugwen said. "Please don't make my sacrifice a waste."

Mharina turned to the twins, but they were gone. When she turned to the three women, they were fading. She felt Maugwen take her hand and lead her out.

A scream woke Mharina, but she did not emerge to full consciousness. She heard cries for help, others enter, a body being lifted, and then a flurry of activity as others tended the person on an adjacent bed. Then she fell asleep to the sound of soft sobbing.

It was the same muted crying that woke her again. This time, everything seemed clearer. Someone whispered that she was stirring, and footsteps approached. Gentle hands helped her rise, while others held her torso in place. Pillows were stuffed under her head and shoulders.

"Do not move your stomach yet, my dear," an elderly female voice said. "The stitches are fresh."

A goblet was brought to Mharina's mouth, and she sipped a strong and sweet elixir. It gave her a burst of energy, and she opened her eyes. Shayth was standing over her, his eyes red and swollen. The muted sobbing continued in the corner.

"Maugwen?" Mharina whispered.

Shayth nodded to the cot next to hers. It was empty. Then he turned back and took a deep breath. "We lost her," he whispered, his voice cracking.

"For me." Mharina said. "I never would have asked her. She gave her life for me. I never asked, Shayth."

"You didn't have to," he replied, his voice soft and raw. "Maugwen was a healer—an extraordinary one—and a close, close friend. She was tough and bull-headed. I know she made her choice freely."

"She really did," Mharina answered. "I spoke with her."

The king frowned, but Mharina felt her strength sapping.

"Shayth. Is Ithea dead?"

Shayth nodded. "Their bodies were burned to a crisp."

"Who was it?" she whispered.

He ruffled his spiky hair furiously and half turned. Mharina saw Troja sitting in a ball on the floor in the corner, her shoulders shaking. She knew her answer. The tall, skinny elfe rose and slowly walked to the door. Shameka appeared beside the grieving elfe and draped an arm around her.

"Wait," Mharina said. "Please come here." The queen led the elfe over, and Mharina offered a hand that Troja took. "You're not alone, Troja. I can't replace Rhoddan, but if I survive, we'll be close forever, and I offer you my protection. He saved both of our lives. We are bonded. *Ashbar.*"

Troja said nothing, just squeezed her hand and left the room. Shayth returned to sit on the bed.

"What have I taken from her?" Mharina said.

"You did nothing," Shayth answered.

"I did. He swore to my *ahdahr* that he would protect us *calhei* with his life. It was my failure to finish Ithea that killed him. I hesitated, and Rhoddan paid the price."

Shayth shook his head and ordered the healers to leave. Even though the room was empty, he bent over and whispered in her ear. "I swore to Rhoddan never to reveal this, but I break my oath so that you will not be burdened with what happened."

He again looked around the empty room and brushed his hand through his hair. "Before he met Troja, Rhoddan confided in me his love for your mother. It ran very deep and conflicted greatly with his loyalty to Seanchai. He disobeyed my order when he came to protect you. But he needed to avenge Sellia's death. What he did was fueled by his own need to kill Ithea for his own closure."

He smiled. "I think it was the only time Rhoddan ever disobeyed a direct order. I think I'm quite proud of him."

He laughed, but it sounded out of place. "I'm sorry, Mharina. Too many people have died: your mother, your Mushroom Man, Rhoddan, Maugwen. So many good friends, so many legends. I don't know if I can defeat the Ashen Elves. Even with Ithea off the battlefield, they severely outnumber us. I don't know if I can prevent others from dying, too."

"You can," Mharina said. "You are the rightful king. My father believed deeply in you, as did my mother." She held out her hand, and he took it. "As do I."

She felt her eyes close and her thoughts drift. She thought she said something else but was not sure.

Help will come.

CHAPTER 80

Shayth once again brooded on the ramparts. He was surrounded by his officers, guard, and aides, but he felt so alone. No Seanchai or Sellia. No Rhoddan or Maugwen. No Ballendir and, for now, no Mharina. The healers had warned that she might not rise to fight in this battle.

He needed Mharina. What had she meant by "help will come"? She was mumbling as the elixir numbed her to sleep. It would not be his cavalry. Ithea's barrier had prevented them from entering the fray again. Only the heroic pictorians, their own numbers tragically dwindling, had kept the Gray Elves at bay. His army could not hold out much longer.

A young woman approached—a healer, Shayth thought. She curtsied, though fatigue made it clumsy and stiff.

"Get up," he said. "We can dispel with that nonsense for now."

"My lord. The Master Healer gives the Wycaan herbs to keep her asleep and ease the pain, but she just woke up and began crying out: *Shayth! It's not Ithea's.* When I went to her she grabbed me and kept repeating: *The barrier. The Ashen Elves.* I calmed her only by promising to bring you the news, milord. Does it make sense?"

Shayth's hands returned to his spiky hair but encountered the crown obstructing his usual mannerism. It was so light, it would take some getting used to. "It does," he said, though he felt his frown probably revealed the lie. "If she wakes, tell her her message is received. Thank you. You may go."

The healer began to curtsy again, then stopped, apologized, and scurried away. General Pilau overheard the conversation and asked, "What does it mean, milord?"

"I don't know, but it must be important." He turned to his squire. "Find Pyre. We must talk."

He had not seen her in a while and was shocked when the elfe approached. Her armor was battered. Scars and scratches covered every inch of exposed skin. Her light gray hair was knotted and barely held back by the plain elven band she wore. The band was speckled with blood.

She offered an exhausted nod to Pilau and then turned to him. "Milord? I was sleeping. I'm sorry to keep you waiting."

"I'm sorry I woke you. I need your advice." He recounted what Mharina had said about the barrier and how she told him help was on the way. "If Seanchai and the twins come, how can we get them through?"

Pyre looked away for the moment and pursed her lips. "The old Seanchai might have found a way. I'm not a full-fledged Wycaan, as you well know. I have little knowledge of the secrets Seanchai has learned that come naturally to Senzia and Ilan." She turned to General Pilau. "I must be called when the mage arrives. It is critical."

Pilau nodded. Though she had been constantly in the thick of the fighting, the general held herself erect and turned crisply to give orders. She was the epitome of a military officer, Shayth thought, all bound up in discipline. She would not stand here like he was, feeling sorry for himself.

When she had imparted her orders, Pilau turned to Pyre. "Begging your pardon, but why is that so important?"

"I'm assuming we won't have Mharina," Pyre said. "If she appears on the battlefield, I must face her."

"Can you defeat her?" Shayth asked.

"I doubt it." Pyre said. "If she's here—and we should assume she'll come to take command once word reaches her that Ithea has fallen—we'll know that Seanchai and Ilan failed to free Senzia. Perhaps if I kill her, we can stop this senseless desire for revenge."

"We must assume that the battle will continue. But at least we'll know that we stand and fall alone," Shayth said. "What is it, Pyre?"

She turned from him, her expression a flash of anger or frustration or…

"What?" he demanded.

"Just a worthless fantasy," she spat, and stalked off.

The next attack came before dawn. The sky filled with balls of fire, and smoldering rocks catapulted beyond the walls. Screams spread through the city as people were startled out of their sleep and fled their burning homes. As buildings burned and collapsed, soldiers guided the people to the great stone halls of the keep.

The solid buildings would not catch fire, and, while they might not withstand the boulders being catapulted, for now they stood untested and out of range of the huge siege machines. When the assault finished, elven foot soldiers already stood at the walls and ladders were already being erected. They must have advanced under cover of darkness.

Ashen Elves, their red stones glowing, appeared on the ramparts, and Shayth sprung down to face them, his guard following closely. He felt the battle rage surge through his body, and he welcomed it with a cry. The waiting was over. Now a red veil descended, a bloody mist of war, and he reveled in it. His fury made him more than a match for his larger adversaries, and the pictorians also seemed to have the upper hand. He heard General Pilau cry out.

"Archers! Shoot them as they appear…it's taking time for them to recover. Shoot!"

Her order echoed around the walls. It was true. There was something almost sluggish in their appearance this time. Pilau had seen it first. Could there be a limit to the amount of magic the Ashen Elves possessed? Was it being directed to the wall? He wondered whether such constant use of power was even sustainable, but dismissed any hope he had of it being true. They had run out of time to find out.

Ashen Elves were now swarming over the walls. Shayth did not have enough soldiers to repel them. This would be it, then. The walls were breached, the enemy inside. General Pilau would order a retreat to the keep, but Shayth knew that was the beginning of the end. The keep was fortified to seal off the ruling family from a force far smaller and less sophisticated than this. The Ashen Elves would probably be able to enter using their red stones. He glanced around for his general but could not find her.

"Fight! Fight for your lives! Fight for your families. Fight for your freedom!" His voice seemed to carry, but his throat burned. Still, his mouth spoke the words as instinctually as his arms swung his broadsword. He was their king. He knew what he had to do. "Fight! Fight for me! Fight for glory and honor! Fight for your wives and children. We will not be defeated. Shindellia will greet the dawn with the proud blood of our ancestors!"

As the words left his mouth, a mighty wall of red cut across the exterior of the castle walls.

CHAPTER 81

Shayth stopped, frozen by the fire's intensity. All eyes went to the walls, and men and elves forgot they were fighting. Ashen Elves on the ladders screamed as they burst into flame.

Then the aerial barrage of fire rocks ceased as, one by one, the great catapults burst into flame. A dark form flew above, wreaking destruction and roaring as it splayed fire.

"By the ancient gods!" Shayth exclaimed. "What is that?"

"That would be my sister," a voice said from his side. "She's rather proud of herself right now."

Shayth turned. Ilan—tall, skinny, and almost naked—stood before him. "Where are your clothes?" he heard himself ask.

"Really? That's your first question?" Ilan twirled an Ashen Elf's curved sword. When he saw Shayth frown at it, he said, "Yeah, sorry. I lost my own, and this was the first one I could borrow."

"Get this man clothed," Shayth cried and turned to the sound of a great horn. The Ashen Elves outside were retreating. Those still within the walls grasped their stones and vanished.

Shayth turned to his general. "Mount a guard, ensure the wounded are tended to, and meet me in the strategy room with whatever officers are still standing."

He turned to Pyre. "Get the twins clothed and armed. Then bring them to me." When he made to leave, Ilan stood in his path.

"What is it?" he snapped, the battle adrenaline still coursing through him. "Do you want a thank you?"

"No," Ilan said, his voice abruptly cold. "I wanted you to ask me if my *ahdahr* still lives." The boy turned and followed Pyre down the stone stairs. Shayth just stared after him.

They met in the great hall, where models of cities, valleys, and strategic passes were scattered around most of the room. Shayth loved coming to play with them as a child. Now, he barely noticed them. In one corner sat a long wooden table and chairs. There was food and flagons of ale and wine in the corner.

The king could not remember when last he had eaten and folded some meat and vegetables inside thin dough. He barely registered what he had taken and ignored the servants who offered to prepare it for him.

He felt both annoyed and admonished by Ilan. It was an important lesson from a young Wycaan not yet bound to him. He thought of the scrawny boy who had left the castle not so long ago. He had returned very different. Something had happened.

The room was already filling with officers when the twins entered with Pyre. He signaled for them to follow him to a corner.

"I'm sorry," he said to Ilan. "These are difficult times for all. Mharina is badly wounded and lies with the healers."

"We'll go to her as soon as this meeting is over," Ilan said. "We'll do what we can."

"There's more. Your mother. She…" Shayth trailed off.

"We know."

Shayth stared at him. The *calhei* had rarely spoken before, but now he carried himself with such authority. He nodded and didn't ask how they found out. "I'm sorry. We'll all miss her. Now, tell me of your father."

They paused as a servant brought over a plate of rolls. The elves all took some and thanked him. The twins shoved whole rolls in their mouths and chewed. They must have been really hungry, Shayth thought. Young, growing elves forced to grow up too fast.

"Tortured and badly wounded," Senzia replied, her mouth full with food. "He lives, though, and is being tended by a friend. Ahad is there, too, also wounded."

Shayth nodded, not showing his surprise that Ahad had gone after Seanchai.

"The mage is dead," Senzia added.

"I wonder if those Ashen Elves who fight us know that. Ithea too is dead. They have no leader. Perhaps–"

"The hate is deep inside each of them," Ilan replied. "Since birth, each one has breathed on revenge, dined on it. It is too engrained." There was a silence before he continued. "While they tortured him, our *ahdahr* got his memories back. We came here on his insistence."

"Thank you. Your intervention was crucial. I think we would have been overrun otherwise."

"Unfortunately, that might yet be the case," Senzia said. "Ilan cannot battle fight in his panther form. He has no armor and will be picked off. I cannot sustain what I just did for long. If I needed to turn now, I don't even know if I could produce such a volume of fire."

"There is more," Ilan added. "Before they closed the barrier again, the Ashen Elves brought more soldiers through. Though you killed many, their numbers have been replenished."

"General Pilau thinks their numbers have doubled," Pyre said. "I was just speaking to—"

"How did you get through the barrier?" Shayth interrupted. "Can I get my cavalry through?"

"Only if their horses sprout wings," Senzia said.

"We flew over," Ilan added. "I got to ride on my sister's back. It made up for years of bullying."

They all forced weary smiles and turned back to meet with Shayth's command. His officers were standing around, eating quickly. In such times, they could never know when their next meal would be.

General Pilau called them to gather around the table, and they came instantly. Shayth was again admiring how she held command without shouting or using force. The men wanted to follow her, craved to fulfill her commands. He had chosen well.

Pilau introduced the twins and then quickly ticked off who had been killed. The officers were recalled by name and replacements solemnly acknowledged. Each officer provided casualty totals. They had all been hit hard, and Shayth was shocked when he realized how few of his army remained alive and unwounded.

"The good news," Pilau said, "is that, while their numbers have been reinforced, they have lost their ladders and siege machines. Thank you for that." She nodded to Senzia, who raised her goblet and nodded back.

"First Boar Umnesilk," Pilau continued. "Your boars will no longer participate in guard duties. They are ordered to rest between fighting."

Umnesilk, battered and bloody with one eye almost swollen shut, frowned, but Pilau cut him short. "That's an order, First Boar. We both know the reason. I offer you no favors."

Umnesilk glared over at Shayth, who nodded as if he had been part of the decision. The pictorians were the only ones who could match an Ashen Elf in terms of strength and size, and they had constantly been in the thick of battle. Their numbers were seriously depleted. The implications for their race beyond the battle would be devastating, but, for now, all that seemed important was to stay alive another night.

"We cannot know from where the next attack will come. We continue to scour the underbelly to ensure no hidden tunnels are being used. We must be ready for anything."

Chapter 82

The battle raged through the next day. The Ashen Elves produced more ladders. It was strange, their desire to use this more traditional siege method, rather than utilizing those with red stones, transporting inside the walls. At all times, arrows and thick spears filled the air above the walls.

The archers of Shindellia also fired arrows continually from their posts high on the towers, and Shayth spent hours with them, falling into a rhythm that allowed him to focus on nothing else. Those who approached the main gate with a huge battering ram were met with oil and burning stones.

There was a moment in the early afternoon when the Ashen Elves withdrew, but almost immediately, a fresh army attacked. It was a debilitating sight for the defenders of Shindellia, who were exhausted and had no opportunity to rest.

Shayth realized they were being worn down. The Ashen Elves could substitute soldiers in and out, allowing their own troops to rest and return refreshed. He looked across the long line of exhausted men, soldiers living on adrenaline and fear. How long could they keep it up?

When the fighting ceased at dusk, Shayth sent a runner to find General Pilau and the twins. General Pilau brought three other officers with her. They met in a small armory near the walls. Shayth's aides brought them food and drink, but no one but Ilan seemed to have the energy needed to eat.

Shayth liked the young elf. He reminded the king of a younger Seanchai, always slightly out of place and awkward. Like his father, Ilan wore his emotions on his sleeve and was loyal to his friends and family.

"I wish we could find out how your father is doing," Shayth said.

Ilan finished chewing and swallowed. "He is alive. I would know if he wasn't."

"How?"

Ilan shrugged. "Don't expect me to explain. I'm discovering something new every day."

"Have you been to see Mharina?"

"We have. We worked on her while she slept."

"Worked on her?" Shayth looked at the young elf. "Let me guess: You don't know how that works, either."

Ilan just grinned, and Shayth felt a smile escape his own lips, as an image of Seanchai at this age filled his head. He reached out and grasped the elf's bony arm. "Thank you," he said, "for all both of you do, intentionally and intuitively."

"King Shayth," General Pilau said. "We're all here."

Shayth surveyed his battered officers. "I'm worried that we're going to lose because of exhaustion," he said simply. "I'm considering an offensive."

They all seemed startled by this and shook their heads.

"It would be a slaughter," Pyre said quietly, reflecting what Shayth knew they were all thinking. "We don't even have cavalry."

"Well, I'm open to ideas," Shayth snapped. "We're all dead on our feet."

"Let's just try and survive another night," Pyre replied.

"If anyone has any other ideas," General Pilau said, "let's hear them now."

No one else spoke.

Wave after wave of Ashen Elves attacked after dusk. Huge shield walls protected them. Thick, twisted ropes with heavy iron hooks flew up and lodged into the crenels and merlons. Ashen Elves ran up them, demonstrating perfect balance. On the ground, another shield-protected group battered the gate, and the walls began, ever so slightly, to shake.

Umnesilk led the pictorians to deal with those who had made it over the top, while Shayth fired arrows as fast as his stock could be replenished. His arm was numb, but he did not care. He encouraged his archers to bring down every elf they could. Still, he felt the incessant pounding of iron against the gate and was convinced the breach was near.

A deafening roar rose from the far corner of the castle, and a great white dragon rose again, burning rope and runners alike with waves of flame. This time, Ashen Elf archers fired arrows into the sky, and Senzia banked sharply up and out of range.

She swept around and this time attacked the archers, leaving nothing but burning skin and haunting screams. Ilan was standing next to Shayth and gasped, clutching his shoulder. Shayth turned sharply but saw no wound.

"An arrow," Ilan hissed. "I can feel it. Get out of there, Senzia."

"Is she wounded?" Shayth asked, and the young elf just nodded. His face was creased in fear and pain.

"Yes, but she won't come back," Ilan suddenly said. "The gate. She wants to attack…"

There was no need for commentary. The dragon flew low, along the foot of the walls, and her fire burned the elves assaulting the main gate. At first, the flames seemed to reflect off their shields, but on her second swoop, she broke their lines.

"Archers!" Shayth screamed. "Bring them down! Bring them all down!"

"Oil!" he heard General Pilau cry from above the gate. "Firestone, now!"

"We have them Senzia," Ilan murmured. "Return."

"Tell her I command her to come back," Shayth shouted.

"Not if that's what you really want," Ilan said, a wry smile appearing on his tired, pinched face.

The line was finally broken, and any Ashen Elves still alive retreated, holding their shields aloft for protection from the archers. A cheer went up from the men on the wall.

"We live a few more hours," Shayth muttered.

"I'm not so sure," Pyre said.

Shayth craned his head and saw two long lines of Gray Elves forming carefully beyond their arrow range. He could just make them out as the sun dropped behind the mountains to the west. He looked in that direction wondering if he would live to see the sun rise again over the mountain ridges.

From behind the two lines, drums thumped dully. The elves in the front banged their sword hilts against their shields in turn.

"Ilan," Shayth called. "Where is Senzia?"

"She's back in elf form and exhausted. Healers are tending that arrow wound."

"When will she be ready to fly again?"

"Hard to tell. That took a lot of energy. Maybe not 'til morning."

Shayth pursed his lips. He ruffled his hair and felt ready to tear it out. "What are they doing?" he muttered.

As darkness descended, he got his answer. One by one, the first row lit their red stones, followed by the second row and the third, fourth, and fifth. Maybe five hundred magical elf warriors, Shayth thought.

He felt bile in his mouth. This was the end.

CHAPTER 83

Shayth knew the attack was imminent. He ran to the ramparts over the main gate. Mharina could have projected his voice, but he would receive no help from her this time.

"They're about to use their magic to enter beyond the gates," he cried. "When you see a red light forming, strike. Do not hesitate. They need a few moments to recover. We will not give them that luxury.

"This is it. They think this is the final encounter, but we will show them it is not. We will repel them. We will see out the night and live to greet another dawn. We will see our wives and children again on the morrow. We will not give an inch, not yield a stone of Shindellia. We are the free races of Odessiya, and we will stay free!"

Free!

Free!

Free!

But that was it. The men retreated into exhausted silence. They had no more breath to waste.

The Ashen Elves began to appear. They arrived in a coordinated fashion, the first line sacrificed so others could recover and begin fighting.

The battle was hand-to-hand, and the Gray Elves fought with refreshed ferocity. In almost every point of battle, the men of Odessiya were on the retreat. Only the strength and tenacity of the pictorians prevented a quick massacre, but men were falling at an alarming rate. Shayth saw a bolt of fire shoot from the roof of a nearby building.

Mharina, supported by two healers, raised her staff, and her orange bolts saved several groups of men. But she wobbled where she stood.

Pyre stood in front of another group of soldiers, her Win Dao swords a blur as she cut through even the strongest of the Gray Elves, but she was one buoy in a sea of death. To Shayth's right, Umnesilk and twenty boars were actually winning and pushing forward, but an endless stream of Ashen Elves were running to engage them.

Still, despite these pockets of resistance, it was clear they could not hold. More Ashen Elves landed, their red stones illuminating the ground. But then there was an abrupt lull in fighting. Everyone stared up at a large, elevated stone platform away from the fight. Shayth screwed up his eyes and watched. There were green lights assembling there.

"Do they have other battalions, other magic?" Shayth wondered out loud. If so, this would surely be the end.

"The Ashen Elves are as surprised as we are," Ilan said, still by the king's side, his elven eyes more able to see. "But those appearing are elves."

Shayth could not see more than silhouettes of figures forming. "Their swords," he cried suddenly. "What swords!"

"Win Dao!" Ilan screamed and his voice squeaked. "Like *ahdahr*. Win Dao swords!"

Moments before, Shayth had looked to the sun setting in the west and prayed for a miracle, and it had come. The Elves of the West moved into arrow formation and advanced.

Though outnumbered, they tore into the Ashen Elves. In the fading light, the streets of Shindellia became a mass of red and green lights as the two elven armies clashed.

"To me," Shayth cried, and the remains of his army fell in beside him. To his left stood a beaming Pyre, her own Win Dao swords vibrating with anticipation. On his right walked Umnesilk, First Boar of the Pictorians, blood oozing from a dozen wounds, proudly leading his boars once more into the fray without a moment's hesitation.

The battle became brutal. The Ashen Elves, though numerically superior, were being attacked on two sides. They were not trained to fight wielders of Win Dao swords and fell in droves before the white-haired Elves of the West.

Fighting scattered into the side streets as the Ashen Elves sought to break the dual attack, but they were pursued in every direction. Shayth wondered briefly why they did not dissipate and retreat. Perhaps the Elves of the West were preventing them from doing so.

He realized he had followed Pyre away from the main battle. She was chasing after a group fighting in a smaller square. There were more Western Elves here—maybe twenty or more—and they faced twice as many Ashen Elves. As Pyre and Shayth charged from behind the Ashen Elves, he spied Shathea, the young council member of the Elves of the West.

Pyre hacked her way through to the tall elfe, and Shayth realized that the Ashen Elves, their numbers swelling, were also trying to reach her. Something instinctual struck Shayth. This elfe must not die. He doubled his efforts, realizing the Gray Elves were more interested in slaying her than they were the King of Odessiya.

And then one blade broke through, and Shathea stumbled backwards. As a huge Ashen Elf raised his sword, Pyre leapt in front of the elfe leader and met his thick blade with her Win Dao swords crossed. But in his other hand was a huge serrated knife, and he plunged it into her body. Shayth felt a cold, paralyzing shiver run through him, but when he was able to look again, Shathea was on her feet, and and slew the Ashen Elf. She cried for her warriors to fight harder and they responded. Pyre, however, lay on the ground in a pool of blood.

When they had slain the last Ashen Elf, Shayth ran and knelt by Pyre. Shathea was on her other side.

"You shouldn't have sacrificed yourself," Shathea said, her voice breaking.

Pyre smiled, blood dripping from the corner of her mouth. "You came," she whispered, and both Shayth and Shathea leaned forward while other elves stood guard. "I knew you would. I knew you would convince the council."

"I didn't really convince them. I threatened them. I told them I was going to stand beside my precocious little sister and honor her values. I told them her courage filled me with shame at our complacency."

"Sister?" Shayth exclaimed.

"Yes," Pyre said, grasping Shathea's arm with shaking fingers. "M-my dear sister, leader of the High Council after this. I'm willing to d-die for you, Shathea. It's worth...ugh."

"You committed the ultimate act of sacrifice—one of pure love," Shathea said as tears rolled down her cheeks. When Pyre frowned, she said, "This is how I know," she whispered, and raised a handful of Pyre's hair, now snow-white. "My Wycaan sister, at last you found your rightful place."

"Shayth," Pyre said, turning to him. "Tell Seanchai. In the end, it happened. Love was the catalyst, nothing else. Just love."

"Tell him yourself," a voice said from behind Shayth, and a firm hand moved the king aside.

Shayth thought for a moment it was Seanchai, and his heart leapt, but it was Ilan who knelt beside her. "You're not done yet, Pyre. You taught Senzia and me so much; we aren't letting you go. Besides, Senzia will kill me if I lose you."

He closed his eyes and laid his hands on her wound. Senzia came running up and, pushing Shathea aside, laid her hands, too.

"Our father is a great warrior," Ilan said, his voice strong and steady, "but he always desired to first be a healer. Shayth, Shathea: Go finish the battle, both of you. We're here. We'll save her if we can. There is great symbolism in the two of you leading the final assault side-by-side."

When Shayth stood, his muscles cramped, but he ignored their cries. "Shathea. Together. This is what Seanchai and Pyre would want of us. An alliance."

And the High Council leader from the Elves of the West and the King of Odessiya charged side-by-side into the thick of the fray. Elves, both dark and pale of skin, humans, dwarves, and pictorians swarmed to their ranks.

The alliance of Odessiya, the vision of a bewildered *calhei* from Morthian Wood, stood strong once again, and the tide of battle firmly turned.

Epilogue

They stood around the graves in the newly named Garden of Heroes. King Shayth had said all the right words, and his beautiful wife, her belly slightly swelling, gave him support when his royal façade slipped.

Mharina stood with her siblings, finally able to let the tears fall and mourn the death of their mother, laid to rest under what would one day become a beautiful apple tree.

Shayth knelt beside Maugwen's grave and made his peace with the death of the girl he had been so mean to in the dungeons at Galbrieth, but who had become his closest friend.

Then he went to an adjacent grave, where a shattered Troja lay hugging the mound of earth. He knelt beside her, and Shameka crouched on the other side, pulling the lost elfe into her arms.

"It was Rhoddan who bound us all together," Shayth said to Troja. "He did it quietly and unassumingly and, with duty and principle, brought us to a single vision and into a single family. You are part of that family, Troja. You will never again be alone."

There were others who had fallen, too many. One section was dedicated to the hundreds of pictorian boars who had fallen. The Elves of the West formed an honor guard, and Shathea walked through to stand first with the king and then with the Wycaan Elves, the *calhei* of Seanchai and Sellia.

Behind her, Pyre was brought on a litter proudly borne by soldiers of Shindellia who had almost come to blows for the honor of carrying a corner. She was pale, but her hair was a shiny Wycaan white as she took her place by Shathea's side, their hands entwined.

When the ceremony was over, everyone moved solemnly back inside the great walls to celebrate the lives of those who had made the ultimate sacrifice. The music was slow and respectful, the atmosphere heavy. Soon, there would be speeches and tributes.

Ilan touched his sisters' arms, and they withdrew from their table. They walked together, Mharina leaning heavily on her staff, to the ramparts overlooking the plains and the Garden of Heroes.

They watched without surprise as two bears approached the grave of Sellia. The ice bear sat on its haunches a little way off, but the grizzly stood on all fours, its huge muzzle close to the freshly turned earth.

Ilan put his arms around his sisters and sighed. They knew he would come, and they knew he would go. His time had passed, and the responsibility lay with them now. Their father would be happier in the world of the bears. They would know where to find him, for Denalion, Dreamwalker of the West, had told them of the great mountain with the waterfall and the sun-warmed rock.

Maybe one day they would visit him, but right now, the great grizzly needed his own time, his own space. His wounds were many and complex, but his dream of a free Odessiya, of an alliance of races, was still intact.

The great grizzly raised its head and looked up at them. *You will succeed,* they heard in their heads. *Your mother and I are proud of you, our calhei, so very proud. Odessiya needs you. The king needs you. And you are calhei no more. We love you.*

Slowly, the great grizzly turned and began to head north. The ice bear walked alongside him, and Ilan thought he saw others waiting. He strained his eyes and then closed them, reaching out with his mind. He saw a dozen white bears and more browns and blacks all form a large ring around the grizzly, escorting him to the great mountain and hopefully to a life of peace.

"We will try to guard your legacy, *Ahdahr*," Ilan mumbled, and the three of them whispered together.

"*Ashbar.*"

THE END

Author's Note:

Dear Reader,

It feels surreal to write this note. Six years ago, on a whim, I began to write At *The Walls Of Galbrieth* as a shared adventure with my young sons while on our summer vacation. I never dreamed then that *Galbrieth* would win a national award, or that every year since; we would sit in the shade of the ancient redwoods, around the campfire or snuggled in my tent and read the next manuscript in the series.

My sons are growing up fast and will soon forge their own adventures. I hope you got a sense of that as you saw the characters of the Wycaan Master series mature. I am aware that closure was not complete for all my characters but I did not want to force the plot. Sometimes you have to let the story tell itself.

A couple of beta readers interpreted this to mean the story will continue. At the time of writing I do not know if there will be another Wycaan Master series. What I can assure you is that I have not lost my love of writing or my enthusiasm to tell a story.

The world of epic fantasy continues to thrive, and there are many great authors producing fine novels to choose from. I am honored you took the time to read *Calhei No More* and the Wycaan Master series. Thank you for staying with me all these years.

Once more, if we meet upon the road or at a tavern, let us meet as companions and tell tales of old times: of battles won, love lost, and alliances formed. Let us speak with pride of those who died along the way and weep with bitter joy that we had a chance to share their path.

If we do not meet on the open road, feel free to contact me at anelfwriter@gmail.com or sign up for my blog post at http://www.elfwriter.com. I also tweet at @elfwriter. Please consider leaving a brief review of this book online wherever you bought it and on Goodreads –it really helps the book garner attention!

Thank you again for being such a great companion,

Alon

http://www.alonshalev.com

Non-Fantasy Novels by Alon Shalev:

Unwanted Heroes (Three Clover Press, 2012)
A Gardener's Tale (Three Clover Press, 2011)
The Accidental Activist (Three Clover Press, 2010)

www.ingramcontent.com/pod-product-compliance
Lightning Source LLC
Chambersburg PA
CBHW031132260626

47153CB00021B/5